"A wickedly clever tale."
—*The Miami Herald*

"Ruiz Zafón's narrative twists and soars, part dream and part slippery reality brought to life in vivid detail. . . . A book for story lovers: expansive, rich and slow to digest."—*Denver Post*

"A dream from which it would be imprudent to awake. . . . Ruiz Zafón can write up a storm."
—*The Washington Post*

"Absorbing. . . . A literary centaur in which a meditation on the craft of writing is combined with a thriller."
—*Los Angeles Times*

"A thriller laden with Gothic elements. . . . A pleasure to read."
—*The Christian Science Monitor*

"Ruiz Zafón, a master of mood and emotional manipulation, guides us through Barcelona's backstreets. . . . Readers will find themselves spellbound."
—*San Antonio Express-News*

More praise for Carlos Ruiz Zafón's

The Angel's Game

"Zafón is a superb and often witty weaver of suspense." —*The Plain Dealer*

"A love letter to all things literary, and a paean to the power of the written word. . . . Zafón is a storyteller with vast gifts." —*The Onion*

"Zafón takes us into sinful corners, indulging fantasies that are erotic, magical or violent. In the end Zafón is the tempter. Many will fall for his vigorous and exhaustingly relentless storytelling." —*The Guardian* (London)

"Gothic, fantastical and lushly atmospheric." —*The Wall Street Journal*

"Irresistible. . . . Writhes and twists. . . . We can compare Zafón to Dickens or Poe, but his brilliant writing puts him in a league of his own. . . . Exquisite." —*Bookreporter*

"Endearing and addictive." —*Financial Times*

Carlos Ruiz Zafón

The Angel's Game

Carlos Ruiz Zafón, author of *The Shadow of the Wind* and other novels, is one of the world's most read and best-loved writers. His work has been translated into more than forty languages and published around the world, garnering numerous international prizes and reaching millions of readers. He divides his time between Barcelona and Los Angeles.

ALSO BY CARLOS RUIZ ZAFÓN

The Shadow of the Wind

The
Angel's
Game

Anchor Books
A Division of Random House, Inc.
New York

The
Angel's
Game

Carlos
Ruiz
Zafón

Translated into English by Lucia Graves

FIRST ANCHOR BOOKS EDITION, MAY 2010

Translation copyright © 2009 by Lucia Graves

All rights reserved. Published in the United States by Anchor Books, a division of Random House, Inc., New York. Originally published in Spain as *El Juego del Ángel* by Planeta, Barcelona, in 2008. Copyright © 2008 by Dragonworks, S. L. Copyright © 2008 by Editorial Planeta, S. A. This translation originally published in hardcover in the United States by Doubleday, a division of Random House, Inc., New York, in 2009.

Anchor Books and colophon are registered trademarks of Random House, Inc.

The Library of Congress has cataloged the Doubleday edition as follows:
Ruiz Zafón, Carlos, 1964–
[Juego del ángel. English]
The angel's game / by Carlos Ruiz Zafón ; translated by Lucia Graves. —
1st U.S. ed.
p. cm.
1. Journalists—Spain—Barcelona—Fiction. 2. Authors—Spain—Barcelona—
Fiction. 3. Antiquarian booksellers—Spain—Barcelona—Fiction. 4. Barcelona
(Spain)—Fiction. I. Title.
PQ6668.U49J8413 2008
863'.64—dc22   2008053650

Anchor ISBN: 978-0-7679-3111-3

Book design by Maria Carella
Photographs on title page and part openers are copyright © Veer Incorporated

www.anchorbooks.com

Printed in the United States of America
10 9 8 7 6 5 4 3 2 1

For MariCarmen

"a nation of two"

The
Angel's
Game

City of the
Damned

I

A writer never forgets the first time he accepted a few coins or a word of praise in exchange for a story. He will never forget the sweet poison of vanity in his blood and the belief that, if he succeeds in not letting anyone discover his lack of talent, the dream of literature will provide him with a roof over his head, a hot meal at the end of the day, and what he covets the most: his name printed on a miserable piece of paper that surely will outlive him. A writer is condemned to remember that moment, because from then on he is doomed and his soul has a price.

My first time came one faraway day in December 1917. I was seventeen and worked at *The Voice of Industry,* a newspaper that had seen better days and now languished in a barn of a building that had once housed a sulfuric acid factory. The walls still oozed the corrosive vapor that ate away at furniture and clothes, sapping the spirits, consuming even the soles of shoes. The newspaper's headquarters rose behind the forest of angels and crosses of the Pueblo Nuevo cemetery; from afar, its outline merged with the mausoleums silhouetted against the horizon—a skyline stabbed by hundreds of chimneys and factories that wove a perpetual twilight of scarlet and black above Barcelona.

On the night that was about to change the course of my life, the newspaper's deputy editor, Don Basilio Moragas, saw fit to summon me, just before closing time, to the dark cubicle at the far end of the editorial staff room that doubled as his office and cigar den. Don Basilio was a forbidding-looking man with a bushy moustache who did not suffer fools and who subscribed to the theory that the liberal use of adverbs and adjectives was the mark of a pervert or someone with a vitamin deficiency. Any journalist prone to florid prose would be sent off to write funeral notices for three weeks. If, after this penance, the culprit relapsed, Don Basilio would ship him off permanently to the "House and Home" pages. We were all terrified of him, and he knew it.

"Did you call me, Don Basilio?" I ventured timidly.

The deputy editor looked at me askance. I entered the office, which smelled of sweat and tobacco in that order. Ignoring my presence, Don Basilio continued to read through one of the articles lying on his table, a red pencil in hand. For a couple of minutes, he machine-gunned the text with corrections and amputations, muttering sharp comments as if I weren't there. Not knowing what to do, and noticing a chair placed against the wall, I slid toward it.

"Who said you could sit down?" muttered Don Basilio without raising his eyes from the text.

I quickly stood up and held my breath. The deputy editor sighed, let his red pencil fall, and leaned back in his armchair, eyeing me as if I were some useless piece of junk.

"I've been told that you write, Martín."

I gulped. When I opened my mouth only a ridiculous, reedy voice emerged.

"A little, well, I don't know, I mean, yes, I do write . . ."

"I hope you write better than you speak. And what do you write—if that's not too much to ask?"

"Crime stories. I mean . . ."

"I get the idea."

The look Don Basilio gave me was priceless. If I'd said I devoted my time to sculpting figures for Nativity scenes out of fresh dung I would have drawn three times as much enthusiasm from him. He sighed again and shrugged his shoulders.

"Vidal says you're not altogether bad. He says you stand out. Of course, with the sort of competition in this neck of the woods, one doesn't have to run very fast. Still, if Vidal says so."

Pedro Vidal was the star writer at *The Voice of Industry.* He penned a weekly column on crime and lurid events—the only thing worth reading in the whole paper. He was also the author of a dozen modestly successful thrillers about gangsters in the Raval quarter carrying out bedroom intrigues with ladies of high society. Invariably dressed in impeccable silk suits and shiny Italian moccasins, Vidal had the looks and the manner of a matinee idol: fair hair always well combed, a pencil moustache, and the easy, generous smile of someone who feels comfortable in his own skin and at ease with the world. He belonged to a family whose forebears had made their pile in the Americas in the sugar business and, on their return to Barcelona, had bitten off a large chunk of the city's electricity grid. His father, the patriarch of the clan, was one of the newspaper's main shareholders, and Don Pedro used its offices as a playground to kill the tedium of never having worked out of necessity a single day in his life. It mattered little to him that the newspaper was losing money as quickly as the new automobiles that were beginning to circulate around Barcelona leaked oil: with its abundance of nobility, the Vidal dynasty was now busy collecting banks and plots of land the size of small principalities in the new part of town known as the Ensanche.

Pedro Vidal was the first person to whom I had dared show rough drafts of my writing when, barely a child, I carried coffee and cigarettes round the staff room. He always had time for me: he read what I had written and gave me good advice. Eventually, he made me his assistant and would allow me to type out his drafts. It was he who told me that if I wanted to bet on the Russian roulette of literature, he was willing to help me and set me on the right path. True to his word, he had now thrown me into the clutches of Don Basilio, the newspaper's Cerberus.

"Vidal is a sentimentalist who still believes in those profoundly un-Spanish myths such as meritocracy or giving opportunities to those who deserve them rather than to the current favorite. Loaded as he is, he can allow himself to go around being a free spirit. If I had one hundredth of the cash he doesn't even need I would have devoted my life to honing sonnets and little twittering nightingales would come to eat from my hand, captivated by my kindness and charm."

"Señor Vidal is a great man!" I protested.

"He's more than that. He's a saint, because although you may look scruffy he's been banging on at me for weeks about how talented and hardworking the office boy is. He knows that deep down I'm a softy and, besides, he's assured me that if I give you this break he'll present me with a box of Cuban cigars. And if Vidal says so, it's as good as Moses coming down from the mountain with the lump of stone in his hand and the revealed truth shining from his forehead. So, to get to the point, because it's Christmas and because I want your friend to shut up once and for all, I'm offering you a head start, against wind and tide."

"Thank you so much, Don Basilio. I promise you won't regret it."

"Don't get too carried away, boy. Let's see, what do you think of the indiscriminate use of adjectives and adverbs?"

"I think it's a disgrace and should be set down in the penal code," I replied with the conviction of a zealot.

Don Basilio nodded in approval.

"You're on the right track, Martín. Your priorities are clear. Those who make it in this business have priorities, not principles. This is the plan. Sit down and concentrate, because I'm not going to tell you twice."

The plan was as follows. For reasons that Don Basilio thought best not to set out in detail, the back page of the Sunday edition, which was traditionally reserved for a short story or a travel feature, had fallen through at the last minute. The content was to have been a fiery narrative in a patriotic vein about the exploits of Catalan medieval knights who saved Christianity and all that was decent under the sun, starting with the Holy Land and ending with the banks of our Llobregat delta. Unfortunately, the text had not arrived in time or, I suspected, Don Basilio simply didn't want to publish it. This left us, only six hours before deadline, with no other substitute for the story than a full-page advertisement for whalebone corsets that guaranteed perfect hips and full immunity from the effects of buttery by-products. The editorial board had opted to take the bull by the horns and make the most of the literary excellence that permeated every corner of the newspaper. The problem would be overcome by publishing a four-column human interest piece for the entertainment and edification of our loyal family-oriented readership. The list of proven talent included ten names, none of which, needless to say, was mine.

"Martín, my friend, circumstances have conspired so that not one of the champions on our payroll is on the premises or can be contacted in time. With disaster imminent, I have decided to give you your first crack at glory."

"You can count on me."

"I'm counting on five double-spaced pages in six hours, Don Edgar Allan Poe. Bring me a story, not a speech. If I want a sermon, I'll go to Midnight Mass. Bring me a story I have not read before and, if I have read it, bring it to me so well written and narrated that I won't even notice."

I was about to leave the room when Don Basilio got up, walked round his desk, and rested a hand, heavy and large as an anvil, on my shoulder. Only then, when I saw him close up, did I notice a twinkle in his eyes.

"If the story is decent I'll pay you ten pesetas. And if it's better than decent and our readers like it, I'll publish more."

"Any specific instructions, Don Basilio?" I asked.

"Yes. Don't let me down."

. . .

I spent the next six hours in a trance. I installed myself at a table that stood in the middle of the editorial room and was reserved for Vidal, on the days when he felt like dropping by. The room was deserted, submerged in a gloom thick with the smoke of a thousand cigarettes. Closing my eyes for a moment, I conjured up an image, a cloak of dark clouds spilling down over the city in the rain, a man walking under cover of shadows with blood on his hands and a secret in his eyes. I didn't know who he was or what he was fleeing from, but during the next six hours he was going to become my best friend. I slid a page into the typewriter and without pausing, I proceeded to squeeze out everything I had inside me. I quarreled with every word, every phrase and expression, every image and letter as if they were the last I was ever going to write. I wrote and rewrote every line as if my life depended on it, and then rewrote it again. My only company was the incessant clacking of the typewriter echoing in the darkened hall and the large clock on the wall exhausting the minutes left until dawn.

. . .

Shortly before six o'clock in the morning I pulled the last sheet out of the typewriter and sighed, utterly drained. My brain felt like a wasp's nest. I heard the heavy footsteps of Don Basilio, who had emerged from one of his brief naps and was approaching unhurriedly. I gathered up the pages and handed them to him, not daring to meet his gaze. Don Basilio sat down at the next table and turned on the lamp. His eyes skimmed the text, betraying no emotion. Then he rested his cigar on the end of the table for a moment, glared at me, and read out the first line:

Night falls on the city and the streets carry the scent of gunpowder like the breath of a curse.

Don Basilio looked at me out of the corner of his eye and I hid behind a smile that didn't leave a single tooth uncovered. Without saying another word, he got up and left with my story in his hands. I saw him walking toward his office and closing the door behind him. I stood there, petrified, not knowing whether to run away or await the death sentence. Ten minutes later—it felt more like ten years to me—the door of the deputy editor's office opened and the voice of Don Basilio thundered right across the department.

"Martín. In here. Now."

I dragged myself along as slowly as I could, shrinking a centimeter or two with every step, until I had no alternative but to show my face and look up. Don Basilio, the fearful red pencil in hand, was staring at me icily. I tried to swallow, but my mouth was dry. He picked up the pages and gave them back to me. I took them and turned to go as quickly as I could, telling myself that there would always be room for another shoeshine boy in the lobby of Hotel Colón.

"Take this down to the composing room and have them set it," said the voice behind me.

I turned round, thinking I was the object of some cruel joke. Don Basilio pulled open the drawer of his desk, counted out ten pesetas, and put them on the table.

"This belongs to you. I suggest you buy yourself a better suit with it—I've seen you wearing the same one for four years and it's still about six sizes too big. Why don't you pay a visit to Señor Pantaleoni at his shop in Calle Escudellers? Tell him I sent you. He'll look after you."

"Thank you so much, Don Basilio. That's what I'll do."

"And start thinking about another of these stories for me. I'll give you a week for the next one. But don't fall asleep. And let's see if we can have a lower body count this time—today's readers like a slushy ending in which the greatness of the human spirit triumphs over adversity, that sort of rubbish."

"Yes, Don Basilio."

The deputy editor nodded and held out his hand to me. I shook it.

"Good work, Martín. On Monday I want to see you at the desk that belonged to Junceda. It's yours now. I'm putting put you on the crime beat."

"I won't fail you, Don Basilio."

"No, you won't fail me. You'll just cast me aside sooner or later. And you'll be right to do so, because you're not a journalist and you never will be. But you're not a crime novelist yet, even if you think you are. Stick around for a while and we'll teach you a thing or two that will always come in handy."

At that moment, my guard down, I was so overwhelmed by gratitude that I wanted to hug that great bulk of a man. Don Basilio, his fierce mask back in place, gave me a steely look and pointed toward the door.

"No scenes, please. Close the door. And happy Christmas."

"Happy Christmas."

. . .

The following Monday, when I arrived at the editorial room ready to sit at my own desk for the very first time, I found a coarse gray envelope with a ribbon and my name on it in the same recognizable type that I had been typing out for years. I opened it. Inside was a framed copy of my story from the back page of the Sunday edition, with a note saying:

"This is just the beginning. In ten years I'll be the apprentice and you'll be the teacher. Your friend and colleague, Pedro Vidal."

2

My literary debut survived its baptism of fire and Don Basilio offered me the opportunity to publish a few more stories in a similar style. Soon the management decided that my meteoric career would have a weekly outlet as long as I continued to do my job in the editorial room for the same salary. Driven by vanity and exhaustion, I spent the days going over my colleagues' stories and churning out countless reports about local news and lurid horrors, so that later I could spend my nights alone in the office writing a serialized work that I had been toying with in my imagination for a long time. Entitled *The Mysteries of Barcelona,* this byzantine melodrama was a farrago shamelessly indebted to Dumas and Stoker and borrowing from Sue and Féval along the way. I slept about three hours a night and looked like I'd spent those inside a coffin. Vidal, who had never known the kind of hunger that has nothing to do with the stomach though it gnaws at one's insides, was of the opinion that I was burning up my brain and that, at the rate I was going, I would be celebrating my own funeral before I reached twenty. Don Basilio, who was unmoved by my diligence, had other reservations. He published each of my chapters reluctantly, annoyed by what he considered to be an excess of morbidity and an unfortunate waste of my talent at the service of plots and stories of dubious taste.

The Mysteries of Barcelona gave birth to a fictional starlet in install-ments, a heroine I had imagined as one can only imagine a femme fatale at the ripe age of seventeen. Chloé Permanyer was the dark princess of all vamps. Beyond intelligent, and even more devious, always clad in fine lingerie, she was the lover and evil accomplice of the mysterious Baltasar Morel, king of the underworld, who lived in a subterranean mansion, staffed by automatons and full of macabre relics, reached through secret tunnels buried under the catacombs of the Gothic quarter. Chloé's favorite way of finishing off her victims was to seduce them with a hypnotic striptease, then kiss them with a poisoned lipstick that entirely paralyzed them so that they died from silent suffocation as she looked into their eyes, having herself drunk an antidote mixed in vintage Dom Pérignon. Chloé and Baltasar had their own code of honor: they killed only the dregs of society, cleansing the world of bullies, swines, fanatics, and morons who, in the name of flags, gods, tongues, races, and other such rubbish, made life unnecessarily miserable for the rest of mankind in order to serve their own greed and meanness. For me, Chloé and Baltasar were rebellious heroes, like all true heroes. For Don Basilio, whose literary tastes were grounded in the Spanish verse of the Golden Age, it was all a monstrous lunacy, but in view of the favorable reception my stories enjoyed and the affection that, despite himself, he felt toward me, he tolerated my extravagances and attributed them to an excess of youthful ardor.

"You have more zeal than good taste, Martín. The disease afflicting you has a name, and that is Grand Guignol: it does to drama what syphilis does to your privates. Getting it might be pleasurable, but from then on it's all downhill. You should read the classics, or at least Don Benito Pérez Galdós, to elevate your literary aspirations."

"But the readers like my stories," I argued.

"You don't deserve the credit. That belongs to your rivals: they are so bad and pedantic that they could render a donkey catatonic in less than a paragraph. When are you going to mature and stop munching the forbidden fruit once and for all?"

I would nod, full of contrition, but secretly I caressed those forbidden words *Grand Guignol,* and I told myself that every cause, however frivolous, needed a champion to defend its honor.

. . .

I was beginning to feel like the most fortunate of creatures when I discovered that some of my colleagues at the paper were annoyed that the junior and official mascot of the editorial room had taken his first steps in the world of letters while their own literary ambitions had languished for years in a gray limbo of misery. The fact that readers were lapping up these modest stories more eagerly than anything else the newspaper had published in the last twenty years only made matters worse. In just a few weeks I saw how the wounded pride of those whom until recently I had considered to be my only family now transformed them into a hostile jury. They stopped greeting me and ignored me, sharpening their malice by aiming phrases full of sarcasm and spite at me behind my back. My inexplicable good fortune was attributed to Pedro Vidal, to the ignorance and stupidity of our readers, and to the widely held national belief that achieving any measure of success in any profession was irrefutable proof of one's lack of skill or merit.

In light of this unexpected and ominous turn of events, Vidal tried to encourage me, but I was beginning to suspect that my days at the newspaper were numbered.

"Envy is the religion of the mediocre. It comforts them, it soothes their worries, and finally it rots their souls, allowing them to justify their meanness and their greed until they believe these to be virtues. Such people are convinced that the doors of heaven will be opened only to poor wretches like themselves who go through life without leaving any trace but their threadbare attempts to belittle others and to exclude—and destroy if possible—those who, by the simple fact of their existence, show up their own poorness of spirit, mind, and guts. Blessed be the one at whom the fools bark, because his soul will never belong to them."

"Amen," Don Basilio would agree. "Had you not been born so rich you could have become a priest. Or a revolutionary. With sermons like that even a bishop would fall on his knees and repent."

"You two can laugh," I protested. "But the one they can't stand the sight of is me."

. . .

Despite the wide range of enmity and distrust that my efforts were generating, the sad truth was that, even though I gave myself the airs of a popular writer, my salary allowed me only to subsist, to buy more books than I had time to read, and to rent a dingy room in a pension buried in a narrow street near Calle Princesa. The pension was run by a devout Galician woman who answered to the name of Doña Carmen. Doña Carmen demanded discretion and changed the sheets once a month: residents were advised to abstain from succumbing to onanism or getting into bed with dirty clothes. There was no need to forbid the presence of the fair sex in the rooms because there wasn't a single woman in all Barcelona who would have agreed to enter that miserable hole, even under pain of death. There I learned that one can forget almost everything in life, beginning with bad smells, and that if there was one thing I aspired to, it was not to die in a place like that. In the low hours—which were most hours—I told myself that if anything was going to get me out of there before an outbreak of tuberculosis did the job, it was literature, and if that pricked anyone's soul, or their balls, they could scratch them with a brick.

On Sundays, when it was time for Mass and Doña Carmen went out for her weekly meeting with the Almighty, the residents took advantage of her absence to gather in the room of the oldest person among us, a poor devil called Heliodoro whose ambition as a young man had been to become a matador but who had ended up as a self-appointed expert and commentator on bullfighting, in charge of the urinals on the sunny side of the Monumental bullring.

"The art of bullfighting is dead," he would proclaim. "Now it's just a business for greedy stockbreeders and bullfighters with no soul. The public cannot distinguish between bullfighting for the ignorant masses and an authentic faena only connoisseurs can appreciate."

"If only you'd been allowed to show your skills as a bullfighter, Don Heliodoro, things would be very different."

"Truth is, only the useless get to the top in this country."

"Never better said."

After Don Heliodoro's weekly sermon came the fun. Piled together like a load of sausages by the small window of his room, we residents could see and hear, across the interior shaftway, the exertions of Marujita, a neighbor who lived in the next building and was nicknamed Hot Pepper because of her spicy language and the shape of her generous anatomy. Marujita earned her bread scrubbing floors in second-rate establishments, but she devoted her Sundays and feast days to a seminarist boyfriend who took the train down from Manresa and applied himself, body and soul, to the carnal knowledge of sin.

One Sunday, my fellow pension inhabitants were crammed against the window hoping to catch a fleeting sight of Marujita's titanic buttocks in one of those undulations that pressed them like dough against the tiny windowpane, when the doorbell rang. Since nobody volunteered to go open the door, thereby losing his spot and a good view of the show, I gave up my attempts at joining the audience and went to see who had come. When I opened the door I was confronted with a most unlikely sight inside that miserable frame: Don Pedro Vidal, cloaked in his panache and his Italian silk suit, stood smiling on the landing.

"And there was light," he said, coming in without waiting for an invitation.

Vidal stopped to look at the sitting room that doubled as dining room and meeting place and gave a sigh of disgust.

"It might be better to go to my room," I suggested.

I led the way. The jubilant shouts and cheers of my fellow residents in honor of Marujita and her venereal acrobatics bored through the walls.

"What a lively place," Vidal commented.

"Please come into the presidential suite, Don Pedro," I invited him.

We went in and I closed the door. After a very brief glance around my room he sat on the only chair and looked at me with little enthusiasm. It wasn't hard to imagine the impression my modest home had made on him.

"What do you think?"

"Charming. I'm thinking of moving here myself."

Pedro Vidal lived in Villa Helius, a huge Modernist mansion with three floors and a large tower perched on the slopes that rose up to Pedralbes, at the intersection of Calle Abadesa Olzet and Calle Panamá. The house had been given to him by his father ten years earlier in hope of his settling down and starting a family, an undertaking that Vidal had somewhat delayed. Life had blessed Don Pedro Vidal with many talents, chief among them that of disappointing and offending his father with every gesture he made and every step he took. To see him fraternizing with undesirables like me did not help. I remember that once, when visiting my mentor to deliver some papers from the office, I bumped into the patriarch of the Vidal clan in one of the hallways of Villa Helius. When he saw me, Vidal's father told me to go and fetch him a glass of soda water and a cloth to clean a stain off his lapel.

"I think you're confused, sir. I'm not a servant . . ."

He gave me a smile that clarified the order of things in the world without any need for words.

"You're the one who is confused, young lad. You're a servant, whether you know it or not. What's your name?"

"David Martín, sir."

The patriarch considered my name.

"Take my advice, David Martín. Leave this house and go back to where you belong. You'll save yourself a lot of trouble, and you'll save me the trouble too."

I never confessed this to Vidal, but I immediately went off to the kitchen in search of soda water and a rag and spent a quarter of an hour cleaning the great man's jacket. The shadow of the clan was a long one, and however much Don Pedro liked to affect a bohemian air, his whole life was an extension of his family network. Villa Helius was conveniently situated five minutes from the great paternal mansion that dominated the upper stretch of Avenida Pearson, a cathedral-like jumble of balustrades, staircases, and dormer windows that looked out over the whole of Barcelona from a distance, like a child gazing at the toys he has thrown away. Every day, an expedition of two servants and a cook left the big house, as the paternal home was known among the Vidal entourage, and went to Villa Helius to clean, shine, iron, cook, and cosset my wealthy protector in a nest that comforted him and shielded him from the inconveniences of everyday life. Pedro Vidal got around the city in a resplendent Hispano-Suiza piloted by the family chauffeur, Manuel Sagnier, and he had probably never set foot in a tram in his life. A creature of the palace and good breeding, Vidal could not comprehend the dismal, faded charm of the cheap Barcelona pensions of the time.

"Don't hold back, Don Pedro."

"This place looks like a dungeon," he finally proclaimed. "I don't know how you can live here."

"With my salary, only just."

"If necessary, I could pay you whatever you need to live somewhere that doesn't smell of sulfur and urine."

"I wouldn't dream of it."

Vidal sighed.

" 'He died of suffocation and pride.' There you are, a free epitaph."

For a few moments Vidal wandered around the room without saying a word, stopping to inspect my meager wardrobe, stare out of the window with a look of revulsion, touch the greenish paint that covered the walls, and gently tap with his index finger the naked bulb that hung from the ceiling, as if he wanted to verify the wretched quality of each thing.

"What brings you here, Don Pedro? Too much fresh air in Pedralbes?"

"I haven't come from home. I've come from the newspaper."

"Why?"

"I was curious to see where you lived and, besides, I've brought something for you."

He pulled a white parchment envelope from his jacket and handed it to me.

"This arrived at the office today."

I took the envelope and examined it. It was closed with a wax seal on which I could make out a winged silhouette. An angel. Apart from that, the only other thing visible was my name, neatly written in scarlet ink in a fine hand.

"Who sent this?" I asked, intrigued.

Vidal shrugged.

"An admirer. Or admiress. I don't know. Open it."

I opened the envelope with care and pulled out a folded sheet of paper on which, in the same writing, was the following:

> *Dear friend:*
>
> *I'm taking the liberty of writing to you to express my admiration and to congratulate you on the success you have obtained this season with* The Mysteries of Barcelona *in the pages of* The Voice of Industry. *As a reader and lover of good literature, I have had great pleasure in discovering a new voice brimming with talent, youth, and promise. Allow me, then, as proof of my gratitude for the hours of pleasure provided by your stories, to invite you to a little surprise that I trust you will enjoy tonight at midnight at El Ensueño del Raval. You are expected.*
>
> *Affectionately,*
>
> *A.C.*

"Interesting," mumbled Vidal, who had been reading over my shoulder.

"What do you mean, interesting?" I asked. "What sort of a place is this El Ensueño?"

Vidal pulled a cigarette out of his platinum case.

"Doña Carmen doesn't allow smoking in the pension," I warned him.

"Why? Does it ruin the perfume from the sewers?"

Vidal lit the cigarette with twice the enjoyment, as one relishes all forbidden things.

"Have you ever known a woman, David?"

"Of course I have. Dozens of them."

"I mean in the biblical sense."

"As in Mass?"

"No, as in bed."

"Ah."

"And?"

The truth is that I had nothing much to tell that would impress someone like Vidal. My adventures and romances had been characterized until then by their modesty and a consistent lack of originality. Nothing in my brief catalog of pinches, cuddles, and kisses stolen in doorways or the back row of the picture house could aspire to deserve the consideration of Pedro Vidal—Barcelona's acclaimed master of the art and science of bedroom games.

"What does this have to do with anything?" I protested.

Vidal adopted a patronizing air and launched into one of his speeches.

"In my younger days the normal thing, at least among my sort, was to be initiated in these matters with the help of a professional. When I was your age my father, who was and still is a regular of the most refined establishments in town, took me to a place called El Ensueño, just a few meters away from that macabre palace that our dear Count Güell insisted Gaudí should build for him near the Ramblas. Don't tell me you've never heard the name."

"The name of the count or the brothel?"

"Very funny. El Ensueño used to be an elegant establishment for a select and discerning clientele. In fact, I thought it had closed down years ago, but I must be wrong. Unlike literature, some businesses are always on an upward trend."

"I see. Is this your idea? Some sort of joke?"

Vidal shook his head.

"One of the idiots at the newspaper, then?"

"I detect a certain hostility in your words, but I doubt that anyone who devotes his life to the noble profession of the press, especially those at the bottom of the ranks, could afford a place like El Ensueño, if it's the same place I remember."

I snorted.

"It doesn't really matter, because I'm not planning to go."

Vidal raised his eyebrows.

"Don't tell me you're not a skeptic like I am and that you want to reach the marriage bed pure of heart and loins. That you're an immaculate soul eagerly awaiting that magic moment when true love will lead you to the discovery of a joint ecstasy of flesh and inner being, blessed by the Holy Spirit, thus enabling you to populate the world with creatures who bear your family name and their mother's eyes—that saintly woman, a paragon of virtue and modesty in whose company you will enter the doors of heaven under the benevolent gaze of the Baby Jesus."

"I was not going to say that."

"I'm glad, because it's possible, and I stress possible, that such a moment may never come: you may not fall in love, you may not be able to or you may not wish to give your whole life to anyone, and, like me, you may turn forty-five one day and realize that you're no longer young and you have never found a choir of cupids with lyres or a bed of white roses leading to the altar. The only revenge left for you then will be to steal from life the pleasure of firm and passionate flesh—a pleasure that evaporates faster than good intentions and is the nearest thing to heaven you will find in this stinking world where everything decays, beginning with beauty and ending with memory."

I allowed a solemn pause by way of silent ovation. Vidal was a keen operagoer and had picked up the tempo and style of the great arias. He never missed his appointment with Puccini in the Liceo family box. He was one of the few—not counting the poor souls crammed together in the gods—who went there to listen to the music he loved so much, music that tended to inspire the grandiloquent speeches with which at times he regaled me, as he did that day.

"What?" asked Vidal defiantly.

"That last paragraph rings a bell."

I had caught him red-handed. He sighed and nodded.

"It's from *Murder in the Liceo*," admitted Vidal. "The final scene where Miranda LaFleur shoots the wicked marquis who has broken her heart by betraying her during one night of passion in the nuptial suite of Hotel Colón, in the arms of the tsar's spy Svetlana Ivanova."

"That's what I thought. You couldn't have made a better choice. It's your most outstanding novel, Don Pedro."

Vidal smiled at the compliment and considered whether or not to light another cigarette.

"Which doesn't mean there isn't some truth in what I say," he concluded.

Vidal sat on the windowsill, but not without first placing a handkerchief on it so as to avoid soiling his classy trousers. I saw that his Hispano-Suiza was parked below, on the corner of Calle Princesa. The chauffeur, Manuel, was polishing the chrome with a rag as if it were a sculpture by Rodin. Manuel had always reminded me of my father; they were men of the same generation who had suffered too much misfortune and whose memories were written on their faces. I had heard some of the servants at Villa Helius say that Manuel Sagnier had done a long stretch in prison and that when he'd come out he had endured hardship for years because nobody would offer him a job except as a stevedore, unloading sacks and crates on the docks, a job for which by then he no longer had the requisite youth or health. Rumor had it that one day Manuel, risking his life, had saved Vidal from being run over by a tram. In gratitude, Pedro Vidal, having heard of the poor man's dire situation, offered him a job and the possibility of moving, with his wife and daughter, into a small apartment above the Villa Helius coach house. He assured him that little Cristina would study with the same tutors who came every day to his father's house on Avenida Pearson to teach the cubs of the Vidal dynasty, and Manuel's wife could work as seamstress to the family. He had been thinking of buying one of the first automobiles that were soon to appear for sale in Barcelona and if Manuel would agree to take instructions in the art of driving and forget the trap and the wagon, Vidal would be needing a chauffeur, because in those days gentlemen didn't lay their hands on combustion machines or any other device with gaseous exhaust. Manuel, naturally, accepted. Following his rescue from penury, the official version assured us all, Manuel Sagnier and his family felt blind devotion for Vidal, eternal champion of the dispossessed. I didn't know whether to believe this story or to attribute it to the long string of legends woven around the image of the benevolent aristocrat that Vidal cultivated. Sometimes it seemed as if all that remained for him to do was to appear wrapped in a halo before some orphaned shepherdess.

"You've got that rascally look about you, the one you get when you're harboring wicked thoughts," Vidal remarked. "What are you scheming?"

"Nothing. I was thinking about how kind you are, Don Pedro."

"At your age and in your position, cynicism opens no doors."

"That explains everything."

"Go on, say hello to good old Manuel. He's always asking after you."

I looked out the window, and when he saw me the driver, who always treated me like a gentleman and not like the bumpkin I was, waved up at me. I returned the greeting. Sitting on the passenger seat was his daughter, Cristina, a creature of pale skin and well-defined lips who was a couple of years older than me and had taken my breath away ever since I saw her the first time Vidal invited me to visit Villa Helius.

"Don't stare at her so much, you'll break her," mumbled Vidal behind my back.

I turned round and met with the Machiavellian face that Vidal reserved for matters of the heart and other noble parts of the body.

"I don't know what you're talking about."

"Never a truer word spoken," replied Vidal. "So, what are you going to do about tonight?"

I read the note once again and hesitated.

"Do you frequent this type of venue, Don Pedro?"

"I haven't paid for a woman since I was fifteen years old and then, technically, it was my father who paid," replied Vidal without bragging. "But don't look a gift horse in the mouth . . ."

"I don't know, Don Pedro . . ."

"Of course you know."

Vidal patted me on the back as he walked toward the door.

"There are seven hours left to midnight," he said. "You might like to have a nap and gather your strength."

I looked out the window and saw him approach the car. Manuel opened the door and Vidal flopped onto the backseat. I heard the engine of the Hispano-Suiza deploy its symphony of pistons. At that moment Cristina looked up toward my window. I smiled at her but realized that she didn't remember who I was. A moment later she looked away and Vidal's grand carriage sped off toward its own world.

3

In those days, the streetlamps and illuminated signs of Calle Nou de la Rambla projected a corridor of light through the shadows of the Raval quarter. On either pavement, cabarets, dance halls, and other ill-defined venues jostled cheek by jowl with all-night establishments that specialized in arcane remedies for venereal diseases, condoms, and douches, while a motley crew, from gentlemen of some cachet to sailors from ships docked in the port, mixed with all sorts of extravagant characters who lived only for the night. On both sides of the street narrow, misty alleyways housed a string of brothels of ever-decreasing quality.

El Ensueño occupied the top story of a building. On the ground floor was a music hall with large posters depicting a dancer clad in a diaphanous toga that did nothing to hide her charms, holding in her arms a black snake whose forked tongue seemed to be kissing her lips.

"Eva Montenegro and the Tango of Death," the poster announced in bold letters. "The Queen of the Night, for six evenings only—no further performances. With the guest appearance of Mesmero, the mind reader who will reveal your most intimate secrets."

Next to the main entrance was a narrow door behind which rose a long staircase with walls painted red. I went up the stairs and stood in front of a large carved oak door adorned with a brass knocker in the shape of a nymph wearing a modest clover leaf over her pubis. I knocked a couple of times and waited, shying away from my reflection in the tinted mirror that covered most of the adjoining wall. I was debating the possibility of hotfooting it out of the place when the door opened and a middle-aged woman, her hair completely white and tied neatly in a bun, smiled at me calmly.

"You must be Señor David Martín."

Nobody had ever called me "señor" in all my life, and the formality caught me by surprise.

"That's me."

"Please be kind enough to follow me."

I followed her down a short corridor that led into a spacious round room, the walls of which were covered in red velvet dimly lit by lamps. The ceiling was formed of an enameled crystal dome from which hung a glass chandelier. Under the chandelier stood a mahogany table holding an enormous gramophone that whispered an operatic aria.

"Would you like anything to drink, sir?"

"A glass of water would be very nice, thank you."

The lady with the white hair smiled without blinking, her kindly countenance unperturbed.

"Perhaps the gentleman would rather a glass of champagne? Or a fine sherry?"

My palate did not go beyond the subtleties of the different vintages of tap water, so I shrugged my shoulders.

"You choose."

The lady nodded without losing her smile and pointed to one of the sumptuous armchairs that were dotted round the room.

"If you'd care to sit down, sir. Chloé will be with you presently."

I thought I was going to choke.

"Chloé?"

Ignoring my perplexity, the lady with the white hair disappeared behind a door that I could just make out through a black bead curtain, leaving me alone with my nerves and unmentionable desires. I wandered around the room to cast out the trembling that had taken hold of me. Apart from the faint music and the heartbeat throbbing in my temples, the place was silent. Six corridors led out of the sitting room, each one

flanked by openings that were covered with blue curtains and each corridor leading to a closed white double door. I fell into one of the armchairs, one of those pieces of furniture designed to cradle the backsides of
princes and generalissimos with a predilection for coups d'état. Soon the
lady with the white hair returned carrying a glass of champagne on a silver tray. I accepted it and saw her disappear once again through the same
door. I gulped down the champagne and loosened my shirt collar. I was
starting to suspect that perhaps all this was just a joke devised by Vidal
to make fun of me. At that moment I noticed a figure advancing toward
me down one of the corridors. It looked like a little girl. She was walking with her head down, so that I couldn't see her eyes. I stood up.

. . .

The girl made a respectful curtsy and beckoned me to follow her.
Only then did I realize that one of her hands was fake, like the hand of a
mannequin. The girl led me to the end of the corridor, opened the door
with a key that hung round her neck, and showed me in. The room was
in almost complete darkness. I took a few steps, straining my eyes. Then
I heard the door closing behind me and when I turned round, the girl
had vanished. Hearing the key turn, I knew I had been locked in. For almost a minute I stood there without moving. My eyes slowly grew used
to the darkness and the outline of the room materialized around me. It
was lined from floor to ceiling with black cloth. On one side I could just
about make out a number of strange contraptions—I couldn't decide
whether they looked sinister or tempting. A large round bed rested beneath a headboard that looked to me like a huge spider's web from which
hung two candleholders with two black candles burning, giving off that
waxy perfume that nests in chapels and at wakes. On one side of the bed
stood a latticework screen with a sinuous design. I shuddered. The place
was identical to the fictional bedroom I had created for my heroine,
Chloé, in her adventures in *The Mysteries of Barcelona*. I was about to try
to force the door open when I saw that I was not alone. I froze. I could see
a silhouette through the screen. Two shining eyes were watching me and

long white fingers with nails painted black peeped through the holes in the latticework.

"Chloé?" I whispered.

It was her. *My Chloé.* The incomparable operatic femme fatale of my stories made flesh—and lingerie. She had the palest skin I had ever seen and her short hair was sharply angled, framing her face. Her lips were the color of fresh blood and her green eyes were surrounded by a halo of dark shadow. She moved like a cat, as if her body, hugged by a corset that shone like scales, were made of water and had learned to defy gravity. Her slender, endless neck was circled by a scarlet velvet ribbon from which hung an upside-down crucifix. I watched, unable to breathe, as she slowly approached, my eyes glued to those lusciously shaped legs in silk stockings that probably cost more than I earned in a year and shoes, pointed like daggers, that tied round her ankles with silk ribbons. I had never seen anything as beautiful—or as frightening.

I let that creature lead me to the bed, where I fell for her, literally, on my backside. The candlelight hugged the outline of her body. My face and my lips were level with her naked belly and without even realizing what I was doing I kissed her under her navel and stroked her skin with my cheek. By then I had forgotten who I was or where I was. She knelt down in front of me and took my right hand. Languorously, like a cat, she licked my fingers one by one and then fixed her eyes on mine and began to remove my clothes. When I tried to help her she smiled and moved my hands away.

"Shhh."

When she had finished, she leaned toward me and licked my lips.

"Now you do it. Undress me. Slowly. Very slowly."

I understood then that I had survived my sickly, unfortunate childhood just to experience that instant. I undressed her slowly, as if I were pulling petals off her skin, until all that was left on her body was the velvet ribbon round her throat and those black stockings—the memory of which could keep a poor wretch like me going for a hundred years.

"Touch me," she whispered in my ear. "Play with me."

I caressed and kissed every bit of her skin as if I wanted to memorize it forever. Chloé was in no hurry and responded to the touch of my hands and my lips with gentle moans that guided me. Then she made me lie on the bed and covered my body with hers until I felt as if every pore was on fire. I placed my hands on her back and followed the exquisite line of her spine. Her impenetrable eyes were just a few centimeters from my face, watching me. I felt as if I had to say something.

"My name is—"

"Shhhhh."

Before I could make any other foolish comment, Chloé placed her lips on mine and, for the space of an hour, spirited me away from the world. Aware of my clumsiness but making me believe that she hadn't noticed, she anticipated each movement and directed my hands over her body without haste, and with no modesty either. I saw no boredom or absence in her eyes. She let herself be touched and enjoyed the sensations with infinite patience and a tenderness that made me forget how I had come to be there. That night, for that brief hour, I learned every line of her skin as others learn their prayers or their fate. Later, when I had barely any breath left in me, Chloé let me rest my head on her breast, stroking my hair for a long time, in silence, until I fell asleep in her arms with my hand between her thighs.

. . .

When I awoke, the room was still in darkness and Chloé had left. I could no longer feel the touch of her skin on my hands. Instead I was holding a business card printed on the same white parchment as the envelope in which my invitation had arrived. Under the emblem of the angel, it read:

ANDREAS CORELLI
Éditeur
Éditions de la Lumière
Boulevard St.-Germain, 69. Paris

On the back was a handwritten note:

Dear David, life is filled with great expectations. When you are ready to make yours come true, get in touch with me. I'll be waiting. Your friend and reader,

A.C.

I gathered my clothes from the floor and got dressed. The door was not locked now. I walked down the corridor to the sitting room, where the gramophone had gone silent. No trace of the girl or the woman with white hair who had greeted me. Complete silence. As I made my way toward the exit I had the feeling that the lights behind me were going out, the corridors and rooms slowly growing dark. I stepped out onto the landing and went down the stairs, returning, unwillingly, to the world. Back on the street, I made my way toward the Ramblas, leaving behind me all the hubbub and the nocturnal crowds. A warm, thin mist floated up from the port and the glow from the large windows of Hotel Oriente tinged it with a dirty, dusty yellow in which passersby disappeared like wisps of smoke. I set off as Chloé's perfume began to fade from my mind and I wondered whether the lips of Cristina Sagnier, the daughter of Vidal's chauffeur, might taste the same.

4

You don't know what thirst is until you drink for the first time. Three days after my visit to El Ensueño, the memory of Chloé's skin still burned my very thoughts. Without a word to anyone—especially not to Vidal—I decided to gather up what little savings I had and go back, hoping the money would be enough to buy even just one moment in her arms. It was past midnight when I reached the stairs with the red walls that led up to El Ensueño. The light was out in the stairway and I climbed cautiously, leaving behind the noisy citadel of cabarets, bars, music halls, and random establishments that the years of the Great War had strewn along Calle Nou de la Rambla. Only the flickering light from the main door below outlined the stairs as I ascended. When I reached the landing I stopped and groped about for the door knocker. My fingers touched the heavy metal ring and, when I lifted it, the door gave way slightly and I realized that it was open. I pushed it gently. A deathly silence caressed my face and a bluish darkness stretched before me. Disconcerted, I advanced a few steps. The echo of the streetlights fluttered in the air, revealing fleeting visions of bare walls and broken wooden flooring. I came to the room that I remembered, decorated with velvet and lavish furniture. It was empty. The blanket of dust covering the floor shone like sand in the glimmer from the illuminated signs in the street. I walked on, leaving a trail of footsteps in the dust. No sign of the gramophone, of the armchairs or the pictures. The ceiling had burst open, revealing blackened beams. The paint hung from the walls in strips. I walked over to the corridor that led to the room where I had met Chloé, crossing through a tunnel of darkness until I reached the double door, which was no longer white. There was no handle on it, only a hole in the wood, as if the mechanism had been yanked out. I pushed open the door and went in.

Chloé's bedroom was a shadowy cell. The walls were charred and most of the ceiling had collapsed. I could see a canvas of black clouds crossing the sky and the moon projected a silver halo over the metal skeleton of what had once been a bed. It was then that I heard the floor creak behind me and turned round quickly, aware that I was not alone. The dark, defined figure of a man was outlined against the entrance to the corridor. I couldn't distinguish his face, but I was sure he was watching me. He stood there silently for a few seconds, time enough for me to react and take a step toward him. In an instant the figure withdrew into the shadows, and by the time I reached the sitting room there was nobody there. A breath of light from a sign on the other side of the street flooded the room for a second, revealing a small pile of rubble heaped against the wall. I went over and knelt down by the remnants that had been devoured by fire. Something protruded from the pile. Fingers. I brushed away the ashes that covered them and slowly the shape of a hand emerged. I grasped it and when I tried to pull it out, I realized that it had been severed at the wrist. I recognized it instantly and saw that the girl's hand, which I had thought was wooden, was in fact made of porcelain. I let it fall back on the pile of debris and left.

I wondered whether I had imagined that stranger, because there were no other footprints in the dust. I went downstairs and stood at the foot of the building, inspecting the first-floor windows from the pavement, utterly confused. People passed by laughing, unaware of my presence. I tried to spot the outline of the stranger among the crowd. I knew he was there, maybe a few meters away, watching me. After a while I crossed the street and went into a narrow café packed with people. I managed to elbow out a space at the bar and signaled to the waiter.

"What would you like?"

My mouth was as dry as sandpaper.

"A beer," I said, improvising.

While the waiter poured me my drink, I leaned forward.

"Excuse me, do you know whether the place opposite, El Ensueño, has closed down?"

The waiter left the glass on the bar and looked at me as if I were stupid.

"It closed fifteen years ago," he said.

"Are you sure?"

"Of course I'm sure. After the fire it never reopened. Anything else?"

I shook my head.

"That will be four céntimos."

I paid for my drink and left without touching the glass.

The following day I arrived at the newspaper offices before my usual time and went straight to the archives in the basement. With the help of Matías, the person in charge, and going on what the waiter had told me, I began to check through the front pages of *The Voice of Industry* from fifteen years back. It took me about forty minutes to find the story, just a short item. The fire had started in the early hours of Corpus Christi Day 1903. Six people had died, trapped in the flames: a client, four of the girls on the payroll, and a small child who worked there. The police and firemen believed that the cause of the tragedy was a faulty oil lamp, although the council of a nearby church alluded to divine retribution and the intervention of the Holy Spirit.

When I returned to the pension I lay on my bed and tried in vain to fall asleep. I put my hand in my pocket and pulled out the business card from my strange benefactor—the card I was holding when I awoke in Chloé's bed—and in the dark I reread the words written on the back. *"Great expectations."*

5

In my world, expectations—great or small—were rarely fulfilled. Until a few months previously, the only thing I longed for when I went to bed every night was to be able to muster enough courage to speak to Cristina, the daughter of my mentor's chauffeur, and for the hours that separated me from dawn to pass so that I could return to the newspaper offices. Now, even that refuge had begun to slip away from me. Perhaps if one of my literary efforts was a resounding failure I might be able to recover my colleagues' affection, I told myself. Perhaps if I wrote something so mediocre and despicable that no reader could get beyond the first paragraph, my youthful sins would be forgiven. Perhaps that was not too high a price to pay to feel at home again. Perhaps.

. . .

I had arrived at *The Voice of Industry* many years before, with my father, a tormented, penniless man who, on his return from the war in the Philippines, had found a city that preferred not to recognize him and a wife who had already forgotten him. Two years later she decided to abandon him altogether, leaving him with a broken heart and a son he had never wanted. He did not know what to do with a child. Barely able to read or to write his own name, he had no fixed job. All he had learned during the war was how to kill other men before they killed him—in the name of great and empty-sounding causes that seemed more absurd and repellent the closer he came to the fighting.

When he returned from the war, my father—who looked twenty years older than the man who had left—searched for work in various factories in the Pueblo Nuevo and Sant Martí neighborhoods. The jobs lasted only a few days, and sooner or later I would see him return home, his eyes blazing with resentment. As time went by, for want of anything better, he accepted a post as night watchman at *The Voice of Industry.* The pay was modest, but the months passed by and for the first time since he came back from the war it seemed he was not getting into trouble. But the peace was short-lived. Soon some of his old comrades in arms, living corpses who had come home maimed in body and soul only to discover that those who had sent them off to die in the name of God and the Fatherland were now spitting in their faces, got him involved in shady affairs that were too much for him and that he never really understood.

My father would often disappear for a couple of days, and when he returned his hands and clothes smelled of gunpowder and his pockets of money. He would retreat to his room and, although he thought I didn't notice, he would inject himself with whatever he had been able to get. At first he never closed his door, but one day he caught me spying on him and slapped me so hard that he split my lip. He then hugged me until there was no strength left in his arms and lay down, stretched out on the floor with the hypodermic needle still stuck in his skin. I pulled out the needle and covered him with a blanket. After that, he began to lock himself in.

We lived in a small attic suspended over the building site of the new auditorium, the Palau de la Música. It was a cold, narrow place in which wind and humidity seemed to mock the walls. I used to sit on the tiny balcony with my legs dangling out, watching people pass by and gazing at the battlement of weird sculptures and columns that was growing on the other side of the street. Sometimes I felt I could almost touch the building with my fingertips, at other times—most of the time—it seemed as far away as the moon. I was a weak and sickly child, prone to fevers and infections that dragged me to the edge of the grave although, at the last minute, death always relented and went off in search of larger prey. When I fell ill, my father would end up losing his patience and after the second sleepless night would leave me in the care of one of the neighbors and disappear. As time went by I began to suspect that he hoped to find me dead on his return and so free himself of the burden of a child with brittle health who was no use for anything.

More than once I, too, hoped that would happen, but my father always came back and found me alive and kicking, and a bit taller. Mother Nature didn't hold back: she punished me with her extensive range of germs and miseries but never found a way of successfully finishing the job. Against all prognoses, I survived those first years on the tightrope of a childhood before penicillin. In those days death was not yet anonymous and one could see and smell it everywhere, devouring souls that had not even had time enough to sin.

Even then my only friends were made of paper and ink. At school I had learned to read and write long before the other children. Where my school friends saw notches of ink on incomprehensible pages, I saw light, streets, and people. Words and the mystery of their hidden science fascinated me, and I saw in them a key with which I could unlock a boundless world, a safe haven from that home, those streets, and those troubled days in which even I could sense that only a limited fortune awaited me. My father didn't like to see books in the house. There was something about them—apart from the letters he could not decipher—that offended him. He used to tell me that as soon as I was ten he would send me off to work and that I'd better get rid of all my scatterbrained ideas if I didn't want to end up a loser, a nobody. I used to hide my books under the mattress and wait for him to go out or fall asleep so that I could read. Once he caught me reading at night and flew into a rage. He tore the book from my hands and flung it out of the window.

"If I catch you wasting electricity again, reading all this nonsense, you'll be sorry."

My father was not a miser and, despite the hardships we suffered, whenever he could he gave me a few coins so that I could buy myself some treats like the other children. He was convinced that I spent them on licorice sticks, sunflower seeds, or sweets, but I would keep them in a coffee tin under the bed, and when I'd collected four or five reales I'd secretly rush out to buy myself a book.

My favorite place in the whole city was the Sempere & Sons bookshop on Calle Santa Ana. It smelled of old paper and dust and it was my sanctuary, my refuge. The bookseller would let me sit on a chair in a corner and read any book I liked to my heart's content. He hardly ever allowed me to pay for the books he placed in my hands, but when he wasn't looking I'd leave the coins I'd managed to collect on the counter before I left. It was only small change—if I'd had to buy a book with that pittance, I would probably have been able to afford only a booklet of cigarette papers. When it was time for me to leave, I would do so dragging my feet, a weight on my soul. If it had been up to me, I would have stayed there forever.

One Christmas Sempere gave me the best gift I have ever received. It was an old volume, read and experienced to the full.

"Great Expectations, by Charles Dickens," I read on the cover.

I was aware that Sempere knew a few authors who frequented his establishment and, judging by the care with which he handled the volume, I thought that perhaps this Mr. Dickens was one of them.

"A friend of yours?"

"A lifelong friend. And from now on, he's your friend too."

That afternoon I took my new friend home, hidden under my clothes so that my father wouldn't see it. It was a rainy winter, with days as gray as lead, and I read *Great Expectations* about nine times, partly because I had no other book at hand, partly because I did not think there could be a better one in the whole world and I was beginning to suspect that Mr. Dickens had written it just for me. Soon I was convinced that I didn't want to do anything else in life but learn to do what Mr. Dickens had done.

One day I was awoken at dawn by my father shaking me. He had come back from work early. His eyes were bloodshot and his breath smelled of spirits. I looked at him in terror as he touched the naked bulb that hung from the ceiling.

"It's warm."

He fixed his eyes on mine and threw the bulb angrily against the wall. It burst into a thousand pieces that fell on my face, but I didn't dare brush them away.

"Where is it?" asked my father, his voice cold and calm.

I shook my head, trembling.

"Where is that fucking book?"

I shook my head once more. In the half-light I hardly saw the blow coming. My sight blurred and I felt myself falling out of bed, blood in my mouth and a sharp pain like white fire burning behind my lips. When I tilted my head I saw what I imagined to be pieces of a couple of broken teeth on the floor. My father's hand grabbed me by the neck and lifted me up.

"Where is it?"

"Please, Father . . ."

He threw me face-first against the wall with all his might and the bang on my head made me lose my balance and crash down like a bag of bones. I crawled into a corner and stayed there, curled up in a ball, watching as my father opened my wardrobe, pulled out the few clothes I possessed and hurled them on the floor. He looked in drawers and trunks without finding the book until, exhausted, he came back for me. I closed my eyes and pressed myself up against the wall, waiting for another blow that never came. I opened my eyes again and saw my father sitting on the bed, crying with shame and hardly able to breathe. When he saw me looking at him, he rushed off down the stairs. His footsteps echoed as he walked off into the silence of dawn, and only when I was sure he was a good distance away did I drag myself as far as the bed and pull my book out of its hiding place under the mattress. I got dressed and went out, clutching the book under my arm.

A sheet of sea mist was descending over Calle Santa Ana as I reached the door of the bookshop. The bookseller and his son lived on the first floor of the building. I knew that six o'clock in the morning was not a good time to call on anyone, but my only thought at that moment was to save the book, for I was sure that if my father found it when he returned home he would destroy it with all the anger that boiled inside him. I rang the bell and waited. I had to ring two or three times before I heard the balcony door open and saw old Sempere, in his dressing gown and slippers, looking at me in astonishment. Half a minute later he came down to open the front door, and when he saw my face all trace of anger disappeared. He knelt in front of me and held me by my arms.

"God Almighty! Are you all right? Who did this to you?"

"Nobody. I fell."

I held out the book.

"I came to return it, because I don't want anything to happen to it . . ."

Sempere looked at me but didn't say a word—he simply took me in his arms and carried me up to the apartment. His son, a twelve-year-old boy who was so shy I didn't remember ever having heard his voice, had woken at the sound of his father going out and was waiting on the landing. When he saw the blood on my face he looked at his father with fear in his eyes.

"Call Dr. Campos."

The boy nodded and ran to the telephone. I heard him speak, realizing that he was not dumb after all. Between the two of them they settled me into an armchair in the dining room and cleaned the blood off my wounds while we waited for the doctor to arrive.

"Aren't you going to tell me who did this to you?"

I didn't utter a sound. Sempere didn't know where I lived, and I was not going to give him any ideas.

"Was it your father?"

I looked away.

"No. I fell."

Dr. Campos, who lived four or five doors away, arrived five minutes later. He examined me from head to toe, feeling my bruises and dressing my cuts as delicately as possible. You could see his eyes burning with indignation, but he made no comment.

"There's nothing broken, but the bruises will last awhile and they'll hurt for a few days. Those two teeth will have to come out. They're no good anymore and there's a risk of infection."

When the doctor had left, Sempere made me a cup of hot cocoa and smiled as he watched me drink it.

"All this just to save *Great Expectations,* eh?"

I shrugged. Father and son looked at each other with conspiratorial smiles.

"Next time you want to save a book, save it properly. Don't risk your life. Just let me know and I'll take you to a secret place where books never die and nobody can destroy them."

I looked at both of them, intrigued.

"What place is that?"

Sempere gave me a wink and smiled at me in that mysterious manner that seemed to be borrowed from an Alexandre Dumas romance and that people said was a family trait.

"Everything in due course, my friend. Everything in due course."

. . .

My father spent that whole week with his eyes glued to the floor, consumed with remorse. He bought a new lightbulb and even told me that I could turn it on, but not for long, because electricity was very expensive. I preferred not to play with fire. That Saturday he tried to buy me a book and went to a bookshop on Calle de la Palla, opposite the old Roman walls—the first and last bookshop he ever entered—but as he couldn't read the titles on the spines of the hundreds of tomes that were displayed, he came out empty-handed. He gave me some money then, more than usual, and told me to buy whatever I wanted with it. It seemed the perfect moment to bring up something that I'd wanted to say to him for a long time but never found the opportunity.

"Doña Mariana, my teacher, has asked me whether you could go by the school one day and talk to her," I said, trying to sound casual.

"Talk about what? What have you done?"

"Nothing, Father. Doña Mariana wanted to talk to you about my future education. She says I have possibilities and thinks she could help me win a scholarship for a place at the Escolapios—"

"Who does that woman think she is, filling your head with nonsense and telling you she's going to get you into a school for rich kids? Have you any idea what that pack is like? Do you know how they're going to look at you and treat you when they find out where you come from?"

I looked down.

"Doña Mariana only wants to help, Father. That's all. Please don't get angry. I'll tell her it's not possible, and that's it."

My father looked at me angrily, but controlled himself and took a few deep breaths with his eyes shut before speaking again.

"We'll manage, do you understand? You and me. Without the charity of those sons of bitches. And with our heads held high."

"Yes, Father."

He put a hand on my shoulder and looked at me as if, for a split second that was never to repeat, he was proud of me, even though we were so different, even though I liked books that he could not read, even if Mother had left us both to face each other. At that moment I thought my father was the kindest man in the world and that everyone would realize this if only, just for once, life saw fit to deal him a good hand of cards.

"All the bad things you do in life come back to you, David. And I've done a lot of bad things. A lot. But I've paid the price. And our luck is going to change. You'll see."

. . .

Doña Mariana was razor sharp and could figure out what was going on, but despite her insistence I didn't mention the subject of my education to my father again. When my teacher realized there was no hope she told me that every day, when lessons were over, she would devote an hour just to me, to talk to me about books, history, and all the things that scared my father so much.

"It will be our secret," said the teacher.

I had begun to understand that my father was ashamed that others might think him ignorant, a residue from a war which, like all wars, was fought in the name of God and country to make a few men who were already far too powerful when they started it even more powerful. Around that time I started occasionally to accompany my father on his night shift. We'd take a tram in Calle Trafalgar that left us by the entrance to the Pueblo Nuevo cemetery. I would stay in his cubicle reading old copies of the newspaper and now and then trying to chat with him, a difficult task. By then, my father hardly ever spoke at all, either about the war in the colonies or about the woman who had abandoned him. Once I asked him why my mother left us. I suspected it had been my fault, something I'd done, perhaps just being born.

"Your mother had already left me before I was sent to the front. I was the idiot, I didn't realize until I returned. Life's like that, David. Sooner or later, everything and everybody abandons you."

"I'm never going to abandon you, Father."

I thought he was about to cry and I hugged him so as not to see his face.

The following day, unannounced, my father took me to El Indio, a large store that sold fabrics on Calle del Carmen. We didn't actually go in, but from the windows at the shop entrance my father pointed at a smiling young woman who was serving some customers, showing them expensive flannels and other textiles. "That's your mother," he said. "One of these days I'll come back here and kill her."

"Don't say that, Father."

He looked at me with reddened eyes, and I knew then that he still loved her and that I would never forgive her for it. I remember that I watched her secretly, without her knowing we were there, and that I recognized her only because of a photograph my father kept in a drawer, next to his army pistol. Every night, when he thought I was asleep, he would take it out and look at it as if it held all the answers, or at least enough of them.

For years I would return to the doors of that store to spy on her. I never had the courage to go in or to approach her when I saw her coming out and walking away down the Ramblas, toward a life that I had imagined for her, with a family that made her happy and a son who deserved her affection and the touch of her skin more than I did. My father never knew that sometimes I would sneak round there to see her or that some days I even followed close behind, always ready to take her hand and walk by her side, always fleeing at the last moment. In my world, great expectations existed only in the pages of a book.

. . .

The good luck my father yearned for never arrived. The only courtesy life showed him was not to make him wait too long. One night when we reached the doors of the newspaper building to start the shift, three men came out of the shadows and gunned him down before my eyes. I remember the smell of sulfur and the halo of smoke that rose from the holes the bullets burned through his coat. One of the gunmen was about to finish him off with a shot to the head when I threw myself on top of my father and another of the murderers stopped him. I remember the eyes of the gunman fixing on mine as he debated whether to kill me too. Then, all of a sudden, the men hurried off and disappeared into the narrow streets between the factories of Pueblo Nuevo.

That night my father's murderers left him bleeding to death in my arms and me alone in the world. I spent almost two weeks sleeping in the workshops of the newspaper press, hidden among Linotype machines that looked like giant steel spiders, trying to silence the excruciating whistling sound that perforated my eardrums when night fell. When I was discovered, my hands and clothes were still stained with dry blood. At first nobody knew who I was, because I didn't speak for about a week and when I did it was only to yell my father's name until I was hoarse. When they asked me about my mother I told them she had died and I had nobody else in the world. My story reached the ears of Pedro Vidal, the star writer at the paper and a close friend of the editor, who, at his request, arranged for me to be given a runner's job and to live in the caretaker's modest rooms in the basement until further notice.

Those were years in which bloodshed and violence were beginning to be everyday occurrences in Barcelona. Days of pamphlets and bombs that left strewn bodies shaking and smoking in the streets of the Raval quarter, of gangs of black figures who prowled about at night maiming and killing, of processions and parades of saints and generals who reeked of death and deceit, of inflammatory speeches in which everyone lied and everyone was right. The anger and hatred that years later would lead such people to murder one another in the name of grandiose slogans and colored rags could already be smelled in the poisoned air. The continual haze from the factories slithered over the city and masked its cobbled avenues, furrowed by trams and carriages. The night belonged to gaslight, to the shadows of narrow side streets shattered by the flash of gunshots and the blue trace of burned gunpowder. Those were years when one grew up fast, and with childhood slipping out of their hands, many children already had the look of old men.

With no other family to my name but the dark city of Barcelona, the newspaper became my shelter and my universe until, when I was fourteen, my salary permitted me to rent that room in Doña Carmen's pension. I had lived there barely a week when the landlady came to my room and told me that a gentleman was asking for me. On the landing stood a man dressed in gray, with a gray expression and a gray voice, who asked me whether I was David Martín. When I nodded, he handed me a parcel wrapped in coarse brown paper, then vanished down the stairs, the trace of his gray absence contaminating my world of poverty. I took the parcel to my room and closed the door. Nobody, except two or three people at the newspaper, knew that I lived there. Intrigued, I removed the wrapping. It was the first package I had ever received. Inside was a wooden case that looked vaguely familiar. I placed it on the narrow bed and opened it. It contained my father's old pistol, given to him by the army, which he had brought with him when he returned from the Philippines to earn himself an early and miserable death. Next to the pistol was a small cardboard box with bullets. I held the gun and felt its weight. It smelled of gunpowder and oil. I wondered how many men my father had killed with that weapon with which he had probably hoped to end his own life, until someone got there first. I put it back and closed the case. My first impulse was to throw it in the rubbish bin, but then I realized that it was all I had left of my father. I imagined it had come from the moneylender who, when my father died, had tried to recoup his debts by confiscating what little we had in the old apartment overlooking the Palau de la Música: he had now decided to send me this gruesome souvenir to welcome me to adulthood. I hid the case on top of my cupboard, against the wall, where filth accumulated and where Doña Carmen would not be able to reach it, even with stilts, and I didn't touch it again for years.

That afternoon I went back to Sempere & Sons and, feeling I was now a man of the world as well as a man of means, I made it known to the bookseller that I intended to buy that old copy of *Great Expectations* I had been forced to return to him years before.

"Name your price," I said. "Charge me for all the books I haven't paid you for all these years."

Sempere, I remember, gave me a wistful smile and put a hand on my shoulder.

"I sold it this morning," he confessed.

6

Three hundred and sixty-five days after I had written my first story for *The Voice of Industry* I arrived as usual at the newspaper offices but found the place almost deserted. There were just a handful of journalists, colleagues who, months ago, had given me affectionate nicknames and even words of encouragement but who now ignored my greeting and gathered in a circle to whisper among themselves. In less than a minute they had picked up their coats and disappeared as if they feared they would catch something from me. I sat alone in that cavernous room staring at the strange sight of dozens of empty desks. Slow, heavy footsteps behind me announced the approach of Don Basilio.

"Good evening, Don Basilio. What's going on here today? Why has everyone left?"

Don Basilio looked at me sadly and sat at the desk next to mine.

"There's a Christmas dinner for the staff. At the Set Portes restaurant," he said quietly. "I don't suppose they mentioned anything to you."

I feigned a carefree smile and shook my head.

"Aren't you going?" I asked.

Don Basilio shook his head.

"I'm no longer in the mood."

We looked at each other in silence.

"What if I take you somewhere?" I suggested. "Wherever you

fancy. Can Solé, if you like. Just you and me, to celebrate the success of *The Mysteries of Barcelona*."

Don Basilio smiled, slowly nodding.

"Martín," he said at last. "I don't know how to say this to you."

"Say what to me?"

Don Basilio cleared his throat.

"I'm not going to be able to publish any more installments of *The Mysteries of Barcelona*."

I gave him a puzzled look. Don Basilio looked away.

"Would you like me to write something else? Something more like Galdós?"

"Martín, you know what people are like. There have been complaints. I've tried to put a stop to this, but the editor is a weak man and doesn't like unnecessary conflicts."

"I don't understand, Don Basilio."

"Martín, I've been asked to be the one to tell you."

Finally, he shrugged his shoulders.

"I'm fired," I mumbled.

Don Basilio nodded.

Despite myself, I felt my eyes filling with tears.

"It might feel like the end of the world to you now, but believe me when I say that it's the best thing that could have happened to you. This place isn't for you."

"And what place is for me?" I asked.

"I'm sorry, Martín. Believe me, I'm very sorry."

Don Basilio stood up and put a hand affectionately on my shoulder.

"Happy Christmas, Martín."

. . .

That same evening I emptied my desk and left for good the place that had been my home, disappearing into the dark, lonely streets of the city. On my way to the pension I stopped by the Set Portes restaurant under the arches of Casa Xifré. I stayed outside watching my colleagues laughing and raising their glasses through the windowpane. I hoped my absence made them happy or at least made them forget that they weren't happy and never would be.

I spent the rest of that week pacing the streets, taking shelter every day in the Ateneo library and imagining that when I returned to the pension I would discover a note from the newspaper editor asking me to rejoin the team. Hiding in one of the reading rooms, I would pull out the business card I had found in my hand when I woke up in El Ensueño and start to compose a letter to my unknown benefactor, Andreas Corelli, but I always tore it up and tried rewriting it the following day. On the seventh day, tired of feeling sorry for myself, I decided to make the inevitable pilgrimage to my maker's house.

I took the train to Sarriá in Calle Pelayo—in those days it still operated aboveground—and sat at the front of the carriage to gaze at the city and watch the streets become wider and grander the farther we drew away from the center. I got off at the Sarriá stop and from there took a tram that dropped me by the entrance to the monastery of Pedralbes. It was an unusually hot day for the time of year and I could smell the scent of the pines and broom that peppered the hillside. I set off up Avenida Pearson, which at that time was already being developed. Soon I glimpsed the unmistakable profile of Villa Helius. As I climbed the hill and got nearer, I could see Vidal sitting in the window of his tower in his shirtsleeves, enjoying a cigarette. Music floated on the air and I remembered that Vidal was one of the privileged few who owned a radio receiver. How good life must have looked from up there, and how insignificant I must have seemed.

I waved at him and he returned my greeting. When I reached the villa I met the driver, Manuel, who was on his way to the coach house carrying a handful of rags and a bucket of steaming hot water.

"Good to see you here, David," he said. "How's life? Keeping up the good work?"

"We do our best," I replied.

"Don't be modest. Even my daughter reads those adventures you publish in the newspaper."

I was amazed that the chauffeur's daughter not only knew of my existence but had even read some of the nonsense I wrote.

"Cristina?"

"I have no other," replied Don Manuel. "Don Pedro is upstairs in his study, in case you want to go up."

I nodded gratefully, slipped into the mansion, and went up to the third floor, where the tower rose above the undulating rooftop of polychrome tiles. There I found Vidal installed in his study with its view of the city and the sea in the distance. He turned off the radio, a contraption the size of a small meteorite that he'd bought a few months earlier when the first Radio Barcelona broadcast had been announced from the studios concealed under the dome of Hotel Colón.

"It cost me almost two hundred pesetas, and it broadcasts a load of rubbish."

We sat facing each other, with all the windows wide open and a breeze that to me, an inhabitant of the dark old town, smelled of a different world. The silence was exquisite, like a miracle. You could hear insects fluttering in the garden and the leaves on the trees rustling in the wind.

"It feels like summer," I ventured.

"Don't pretend everything is OK by talking about the weather. I've already been told what happened," Vidal said.

I shrugged my shoulders and glanced over at his writing desk. I was aware that my mentor had spent months, or even years, trying to write what he called a "serious" novel, entirely unlike his crime fiction, so that his name would be inscribed in the more distinguished sections of libraries. I didn't see many sheets of paper.

"How's the masterpiece going?"

Vidal threw his cigarette butt out the window and stared into the distance.

"I don't have anything left to say, David."

"Nonsense."

"Everything in life is nonsense. It's just a question of perspective."

"You should put that in your book. *The Nihilist on the Hill.* Bound to be a success."

"You're the one who is going to need success. Correct me if I'm wrong, but you'll soon be short of cash."

"I could always accept your charity."

"It might feel like the end of the world to you now, but—"

"I'll soon realize that this is the best thing that could have happened to me," I said, completing the sentence. "Don't tell me Don Basilio is writing your speeches now. Or is it the other way round?"

Vidal laughed.

"What are you going to do?"

"Don't you need a secretary?"

"I've already got the best secretary I could have. She's more intelligent than me, infinitely more hardworking, and when she smiles I even feel that this lousy world still has some future."

"And who is this marvel?"

"Manuel's daughter."

"Cristina."

"At last I hear you utter her name."

"You've chosen a bad week to make fun of me, Don Pedro."

"Don't look at me all doe-eyed. Did you think Pedro Vidal was going to allow that mediocre, constipated, envious bunch to sack you without doing anything about it?"

"A word from you to the editor could have changed things."

"I know. That's why I was the one who suggested he fire you," said Vidal.

I felt as if he'd just slapped me in the face.

"Thanks for the push," I improvised.

"I told him to fire you because I have something much better for you."

"Begging?"

"Have you no faith? Only yesterday I was talking about you to a couple of partners who have just opened a publishing house and are looking for fresh blood to exploit. You can't trust them, of course."

"Sounds marvelous."

"They know all about *The Mysteries of Barcelona* and are prepared to tender an offer that will make your name."

"Are you serious?"

"Of course I'm serious. They want you to write a series in installments in the most baroque, bloody, and delirious Grand Guignol tradition—a series that will tear *The Mysteries of Barcelona* to shreds. I think that this is the opportunity you've been waiting for. I told them you'd go talk to them and that you'd be able to start work immediately."

I heaved a deep sigh. Vidal winked and then embraced me.

7

That was how, only a few months after my twentieth birthday, I received and accepted an offer to write penny dreadfuls under the name of Ignatius B. Samson. My contract committed me to hand in two hundred pages of typed manuscript a month packed with intrigue, high society murders, countless underworld horrors, illicit love affairs featuring cruel, lantern-jawed landowners and damsels with unmentionable desires, and all sorts of twisted family sagas with plots as thick and murky as the water in the port. The series, which I decided to call *City of the Damned,* was to appear in monthly hardback installments with a full-color illustrated cover. In exchange I would be paid more money than I had ever imagined could be made doing something that I cared about, and the only censorship imposed on me would be dictated by the loyalty of my readers. The terms of the offer obliged me to write anonymously under an extravagant pseudonym, but it seemed a small price to pay for being able to make a living from the profession I had always dreamed of practicing. I would put aside any vanity about seeing my name on my work, while remaining true to myself, to what I was.

My publishers were a pair of colorful characters called Barrido and Escobillas. Barrido, who was small and squat and always affected an oily, sibylline smile, was the brains of the operation. He sprang from the sausage industry and although he hadn't read more than three books in his life—and those included the catechism and the telephone directory—

he was possessed of a proverbial audacity for cooking the books, which he falsified for his investors, displaying a talent for fiction that any of his authors might have envied. These, as Vidal had predicted, the firm swindled, exploited, and, in the end, kicked into the gutter when the winds were unfavorable—something that always happened sooner or later.

Escobillas played a complementary role. Tall, gaunt, with a vaguely threatening appearance, he had gained his experience in the undertaker business and beneath the pungent eau de cologne with which he bathed his private parts there always seemed to be a faint, disturbing whiff of formaldehyde. His role was essentially that of the sinister foreman, whip in hand, always ready to do the dirty work that Barrido, with his more cheerful nature and less athletic disposition, wasn't naturally inclined to. The ménage à trois was completed by their secretary, Herminia, who followed them around like a loyal dog wherever they went and whom we all nicknamed Lady Venom because, although she looked as if butter wouldn't melt in her mouth, she was as trustworthy as a rattlesnake in heat.

Social niceties aside, I tried to see them as little as possible. Ours was a strictly commercial relationship and none of the parties felt any great desire to alter the established protocol. I had resolved to make the most of the opportunity and work hard: I wanted to prove to Vidal, and to myself, that I was worthy of his help and his trust. With fresh money in my hands, I decided to abandon Doña Carmen's pension for more comfortable quarters. For some time now I'd had my eye on a huge pile of a house at 30 Calle Flassaders, a stone's throw from Paseo del Borne, which for years I had passed as I went between the newspaper and the pension. Topped by a tower that rose from a façade carved with reliefs and gargoyles, the building had been closed for years, its front door sealed with chains and rusty padlocks. Despite its gloomy and somewhat melodramatic appearance, or perhaps for that very reason, the idea of inhabiting it awoke in me that desire that comes only with ill-advised ideas. In other circumstances I would have accepted that such a place was far beyond my meager budget, but the long years of abandonment and oblivion to which the dwelling seemed condemned made me hope that, if nobody else wanted it, perhaps its owners might accept my offer.

Asking around in the area, I discovered that the house had been empty for years and was handled by a property manager called Vicenç Clavé, who had an office in Calle Comercio, opposite the market. Clavé was a gentleman of the old school who liked to dress in a fashion similar to that of the statues of mayors or national heroes that greeted you at the various entrances of Ciudadela Park, and if you weren't careful he would take off on rhetorical flights that encompassed every subject under the sun.

"So you're a writer. Well, I could tell you stories that would make good books."

"I don't doubt it. Why don't you begin by telling me the story of the house in Flassaders, number 30?"

Clavé adopted the look of a Greek mask.

"The tower house?"

"That's the one."

"Believe me, young man, you don't want to live there."

"Why not?"

Clavé lowered his voice. Whispering as if he feared the walls might hear us, he delivered his verdict in a funereal tone.

"That house is jinxed. I visited the place when I went along with the notary to seal it up and I can assure you that the oldest part of Montjuïc cemetery is more cheerful. It's been empty since then. That place has bad memories. Nobody wants it."

"Its memories can't be any worse than mine. Anyhow, I'm sure they'll help bring down the asking price."

"Some prices cannot be paid with money."

"Can I see it?"

. . .

My first visit to the tower house was one morning in March, in the company of the property manager, his secretary, and an auditor from the bank who held the title deeds. Apparently, the building had been trapped for years in a labyrinth of legal disputes until it finally reverted to the lending institution that had guaranteed its last owner. If Clavé was telling the truth, nobody had set foot in it for at least twenty years.

8

Years later, when I read an account about British explorers penetrating the dark passages of an ancient Egyptian burial place—mazes and curses included—I would recall that first visit to the tower house in Calle Flassaders. The secretary came equipped with an oil lamp because the building had never had electricity installed. The auditor turned up with a set of fifteen keys with which to liberate the countless padlocks that fastened the chains. When the front door was opened, the house exhaled a putrid smell, like a damp tomb. The auditor started to cough and the manager, who was making an effort not to look too skeptical or disapproving, covered his mouth with a handkerchief.

"You first," he offered.

The entrance resembled one of those interior courtyards in the old palaces of the area, with flagstone paving and a stone staircase that led to the front door of the living quarters. Daylight filtered in through a glass skylight, completely covered in pigeon and seagull excrement, that was set on high.

"There aren't any rats," I announced once I was inside the building.

"A sign of good taste and common sense," said the property manager, behind me.

We proceeded up the stairs until we reached the landing on the main floor, where the auditor spent ten minutes trying to find the right key for the lock. The mechanism yielded with an unwelcoming groan and the heavy door opened, revealing an endless corridor strewn with cobwebs that undulated in the gloom.

"Holy Mother of God," mumbled the manager.

No one else dared take the first step, so once more I had to lead the expedition. The secretary held the lamp up high, looking at everything with a baleful air.

The manager and the auditor exchanged a knowing look. When they noticed that I was observing them, the auditor smiled calmly.

"A good bit of dusting and some patching up and the place will look like a palace," he said.

"Bluebeard's palace," the manager added.

"Let's be positive," the auditor corrected him. "The house has been empty for some time: there's bound to be some minor damage."

I was barely paying attention to them. I had dreamed about that place so often as I walked past its front door that now I hardly noticed the dark, gloomy aura that possessed it. I walked up the main corridor, exploring rooms of all shapes and sizes in which old furniture lay abandoned under a thick layer of dust and shadow. One table was still covered with a frayed tablecloth on which sat a dinner service and a tray of petrified fruit and flowers. The glasses and cutlery were still there, as if the inhabitants of the house had fled in the middle of dinner.

The wardrobes were crammed with threadbare, faded clothes and shoes. There were whole drawers filled with photographs, spectacles, fountain pens, and watches. Dust-covered portraits observed us from every surface. The beds were made and covered with a white veil that shone in the half-light. A gramophone rested on a mahogany table. It had a record on it and the needle had slid to the end. I blew on the film of dust that covered it and the title of the recording came into view: Mozart's *Lacrimosa*.

"The symphony orchestra performing in your own home," said the auditor. "What more could one ask for? You'll live like a lord here."

The manager shot him a murderous look, clearly in disagreement.

We went through the apartment until we reached the gallery at the back where a coffee service lay on a table and an open book on an armchair was still waiting for someone to turn the page.

"It looks like whoever lived here left suddenly, with no time to take anything with them," I said.

The auditor cleared his throat.

"Perhaps the gentleman would like to see the study?"

The study was at the top of a tall tower, a peculiar structure at the heart of which was a spiral staircase that led off the main corridor, while its outside walls bore the traces of as many generations as the city could remember. There it stood, like a watchtower suspended over the roofs of the Ribera quarter, crowned by a narrow dome of metal and tinted glass that served as a lantern and topped by a weather vane in the shape of a dragon. We climbed the stairs and when we reached the room at the top, the auditor quickly opened the windows to let in air and light. It was a rectangular room with high ceilings and dark wooden flooring. Its four large arched windows looked out on all four sides, giving me a view of the cathedral of Santa María del Mar to the south, the large Borne Market to the north, the railway station to the east, and to the west the endless maze of streets and avenues tumbling over one another toward Mount Tibidabo.

"What do you say? Marvelous!" proposed the auditor enthusiastically.

The property manager examined everything with a certain reserve and displeasure. His secretary held the lamp up high, even though it was no longer needed. I went over to one of the windows and leaned out, spellbound.

The whole of Barcelona stretched out at my feet and I wanted to believe that when I opened those windows—my new windows—each evening its streets would whisper stories to me, secrets in my ear, that I could catch on paper and narrate to whomever cared to listen. Vidal had his exuberant and stately ivory tower in the most elegant and elevated part of Pedralbes, surrounded by hills, trees, and fairy-tale skies. I would have my sinister tower rising above the oldest, darkest streets of the city, surrounded by the miasmas and shadows of that necropolis which poets and murderers had once called the "Rose of Fire."

What finally decided the matter was the desk that dominated the center of the study. On it, like a great sculpture of metal and light, stood an impressive Underwood typewriter for which, alone, I would have paid the price of the rent. I sat in the plush armchair facing the desk, stroked the typewriter keys, and smiled.

"I'll take it," I said.

The auditor sighed with relief and the manager rolled his eyes and crossed himself. That same afternoon I signed a ten-year rental agreement. While the workmen were busy wiring the house for electricity, I devoted my time to cleaning, tidying, and straightening the place up with the help of three servants whom Vidal sent trooping down without first asking me whether or not I wanted any help. I soon discovered that the modus operandi of that commando of electrical experts consisted in first drilling holes right, left, and center and then asking. Three days after their deployment, the house did not have a single lightbulb that worked, but one would have thought that the place had been infested by a plague of woodworm that devoured plaster and the noblest of minerals.

"Are you sure there isn't a better way of fixing this?" I would ask the head of the battalion, who resolved everything with blows of the hammer.

Otilio, as this talented man was called, would show me the building plans supplied by the property manager when I was handed the keys and argue that the problem lay with the house, which was badly built.

"Look at this," he would say. "I mean, when something is badly made, it's badly made and there are no two ways about it. Here, for example. Here it says that you have a water tank on the terrace. Well, no, sir, you have a water tank in the backyard."

"What does it matter? The water tank has nothing to do with you, Otilio. Concentrate on the electrics. Light. Not taps, not water pipes. Light. I need light."

"But everything is connected. What do you think about the gallery?"

"I think it has no light."

"According to the plans, this should be a supporting wall. Well, my mate Remigio here tapped it ever so slightly and half the wall came crashing down. And you should see the bedrooms. According to this plan, the size of the room at the end of the corridor should be almost forty square meters. Not in a million years! I'd be surprised if it measured twenty. There's a wall where there shouldn't be a wall. And as for the waste pipes, well, best not talk about them. Not one of them is where it's supposed to be."

"Are you sure you know how to read the plans?"

"Listen, I'm a professional. Mark my words: this house is a jigsaw puzzle. Everybody's grandmother has poked their nose into this place."

"I'm afraid you're going to have to make do with what there is. Perform a few miracles or do whatever you want, but by Friday I want to see all the walls plastered and painted and the lights working."

"Don't rush me, this is precision work. One has to act strategically."

"So what is your plan?"

"For a start we're off to have our breakfast."

"You got here only half an hour ago!"

"Señor Martín, we're not going to get anywhere with that attitude."

The ordeal of building work and botched jobs went on a week longer than expected, but even with the presence of Otilio and his squadron of geniuses making holes where they shouldn't and enjoying two-and-a-half-hour breakfasts, the thrill of being able to live in that old rambling house, which I had dreamed about for so long, would have kept me going for years with candles and oil lamps if need be. I was lucky that the Ribera quarter was a spiritual home for all kinds of craftsmen: near my new home I found someone who could put in new locks that didn't look as if they'd been stolen from the Bastille, as well as twentieth-century wall lights and taps. The idea of having a telephone line installed did not appeal to me and, judging by what I'd heard on Vidal's wireless, these "intercommunicating systems," as the press called them, were not aimed at people such as myself. I decided that my existence would be one of books and silence. All I took from the pension was a change of clothes and the case containing my father's gun, his only memento. I distributed the rest of my clothes and personal belongings among the pension residents. Had I also been able to leave behind my memories, even my skin, I would have done so.

. . .

The day the first installment of *City of the Damned* was published, I spent my first official and electrified night in the tower house. The novel was an imaginary intrigue I had woven round the story of the fire in El Ensueño in 1903, about a ghostly creature who had bewitched the streets of the Raval quarter ever since. Before the ink had dried on that first edition I had already started work on the second novel of the series. By my reckoning, based on thirty uninterrupted days' work a month, Ignatius B. Samson had to produce an average of 6.66 pages a day to comply with the terms of the agreement, which was crazy but had the advantage of not giving me much time to think about it.

I hardly noticed that, as the days went by, I was beginning to consume more coffee and cigarettes than oxygen. As I gradually poisoned my brain, I had the feeling that it was turning into a steam engine that never cooled down. But Ignatius B. Samson was young and resilient. He worked all night and collapsed from exhaustion at dawn, possessed by strange dreams in which the letters on the page trapped in the typewriter would come unstuck and, like spiders made of ink, would crawl up his hands and face, working their way through his skin and nesting in his veins until his heart was covered in black and his pupils were clouded in pools of darkness. I would barely leave the old, rambling house for weeks on end and would forget what day of the week it was or what month of the year. I paid no attention to the recurring headaches that would sometimes plague me, arriving all of a sudden, as if a metal awl were boring a hole through my skull, burning my eyes with a flash of white light. I had grown accustomed to living with a constant ringing in my ears that only the murmur of wind or rain could mask. Sometimes, when a cold sweat covered my face and I felt my hands shaking on the Underwood keyboard, I told myself that the following day I would go to the doctor. But then there was always another scene, and another story to tell.

To celebrate the first year of Ignatius B. Samson's life, though, I decided to take the day off and reacquaint myself with the sun, the breeze, and the streets of a city I had stopped walking through and now only imagined. I shaved, tidied myself up, and dressed in my best suit. I left the windows open in the study and in the gallery to air the house and let the thick fog that had become its scent be scattered to the four winds. When I went out into the street, I found a large envelope at the bottom of the letter box. Inside was a sheet of parchment, sealed with the angel motif and written on in that exquisite writing. It said:

> *Dear David:*
> *I wanted to be the first to congratulate you on this new stage of your career. I have thoroughly enjoyed reading the first installments of* City of the Damned. *I hope you will like this small gift.*
> *I would like to reiterate my admiration for you and my hope that one day our paths may cross. Trusting that this will come about, please accept the most affectionate greetings from your friend and reader,*
>
> ANDREAS CORELLI

The gift was the copy of *Great Expectations* that Señor Sempere had given me when I was a child, the same copy I had returned to him before my father could find it and the same copy that, years later, when I had wanted to recover it at any price, had disappeared only hours before in the hands of a stranger. I stared at the bundle of paper that to me, in a not so distant past, had seemed to contain all the magic and light of the world. The cover still bore my bloodstained fingerprints.

"Thank you," I whispered.

9

Señor Sempere put on his reading spectacles to examine the book closely. He placed it on a cloth he had spread out on his desk in the back room and pulled down the reading lamp so that its beam focused on the volume. His examination lasted a few minutes, during which I maintained a reverential silence. I watched him turn the pages, smell them, stroke the paper and the spine, weigh the book with one hand and then the other, and finally close the cover and examine with a magnifying glass the bloodstained fingerprints left by me many years earlier.

"Incredible," he mused, removing his spectacles. "It's the same book. How did you say you recovered it?"

"I really couldn't tell you, Señor Sempere. Do you know anything about a French publisher called Andreas Corelli?"

"For a start he sounds more Italian than French, although the name Andreas could be Greek . . ."

"The publishing house is in Paris. Éditions de la Lumière."

Sempere looked doubtful.

"I'm afraid it doesn't ring a bell. I'll ask Barceló. He knows everything. Let's see what he says."

Gustavo Barceló was one of the senior members of the secondhand booksellers' guild in Barcelona and his vast expertise was as legendary as his somewhat abrasive and pedantic manner. There was a saying in the trade: when in doubt, ask Barceló. At that very moment Sempere's son put his head round the door and signaled to his father. Although he was two or three years older than me he was so shy that he could make himself invisible.

"Father, someone's come to collect an order that I think you took."

The bookseller nodded and handed me a thick, worn volume.

"This is the latest catalog of European publishers. Why don't you have a look at it and see if you can find anything while I attend to the customer?" he suggested.

I was left alone in the back room, searching in vain for Éditions de la Lumière, while Sempere returned to the counter. As I leafed through the volume, I could hear him talking to a woman whose voice sounded familiar. I heard them mention Pedro Vidal. Intrigued, I peeked through the door to find out more.

Cristina Sagnier, the chauffeur's daughter and my mentor's secretary, was going through a pile of books that Sempere was noting down in his ledger. When she saw me she smiled politely, but I was sure she did not recognize me. Sempere looked up and, noticing the silly expression on my face, took a quick X-ray of the situation.

"You do know each other, don't you?" he said.

Cristina raised her eyebrows in surprise and looked at me again, unable to place me.

"David Martín. A friend of Don Pedro's," I said.

"Oh, of course," she replied. "Good morning."

"How is your father?" I asked.

"Fine, fine. He's waiting for me on the corner with the car."

Sempere, who never missed a trick, quickly interjected.

"Señorita Sagnier has come to collect some books Vidal ordered. As they are so heavy, perhaps you could help her take them to the car."

"Please don't worry—" protested Cristina.

"But of course," I blurted out, ready to lift the pile of books that turned out to weigh as much as the luxury edition of the *Encyclopaedia Britannica,* appendices included.

I felt something go crunch in my back and Cristina gave me an embarrassed look.

"Are you all right?"

"Don't worry, miss. My friend Martín here might be a man of letters, but he's as strong as a bull," said Sempere. "Isn't that right, Martín?"

Cristina was looking at me unconvinced. I offered her my "strong man" smile.

"Pure muscle," I said. "I'm just warming up."

Sempere's son was about to offer to carry half the books, but his father, in a display of great diplomacy, stopped him. Cristina held the door open for me and I set off to cover the fifteen or twenty meters that separated me from the Hispano-Suiza parked on the corner of Puerta del Ángel. I only just managed to get there, my arms almost on fire. Manuel, the chauffeur, helped me unload the books and greeted me warmly.

"What a coincidence, meeting you here, Señor Martín."

"Small world."

Cristina gave me a grateful smile and got into the car.

"I'm sorry about the books."

"It was nothing. A bit of exercise lifts the spirit," I volunteered, ignoring the tangle of knots I could feel in my back. "My regards to Don Pedro."

I watched them drive off toward Plaza de Cataluña and when I turned I noticed Sempere at the door of the bookshop, looking at me with a catlike smile and gesturing to me to wipe the drool off my chin. I went over to him and couldn't help laughing at myself.

"I know your secret now, Martín. I thought you had a steadier nerve in these matters."

"Everything gets a bit rusty."

"I should know! Can I keep the book for a few days?"

I nodded.

"Take good care of it."

IO

A few months later I saw her again, in the company of Pedro Vidal, at the table that was always reserved for him at La Maison Dorée. Vidal invited me to join them, but a quick look from her was enough to tell me that I should refuse the offer.

"How is the novel going, Don Pedro?"

"Swimmingly."

"I'm pleased to hear it. *Bon appétit.*"

My meetings with Cristina were always by chance. Sometimes I would bump into her in the Sempere & Sons bookshop, where she often went to collect books for Vidal. If the opportunity arose, Sempere would leave me alone with her, but soon Cristina grew wise to the trick and would send one of the young boys from Villa Helius to pick up the orders.

"I know it's none of my business," Sempere would say. "But perhaps you should stop thinking about her."

"I don't know what you're talking about, Señor Sempere."

"Come on, Martín, we've known each other for a long time . . ."

The months seemed to slip by in a blur. I lived at night, writing from evening to dawn and sleeping all day. Barrido and Escobillas couldn't stop congratulating themselves on the success of *City of the Damned* and when they saw me on the verge of collapse they assured me that after a couple more novels they would grant me a sabbatical so that

I could rest or devote my time to writing a personal work that they would publish with much fanfare and with my real name printed in large letters on the cover. It was always just a couple of novels away. The sharp pains, the headaches, and the dizzy spells became more frequent and intense, but I attributed them to exhaustion and treated them with more injections of caffeine, cigarettes, and some tablets tasting of gunpowder that contained codeine and God knows what else, supplied on the quiet by a chemist in Calle Argenteria. Don Basilio, with whom I had lunch on alternate Thursdays in an outdoor café in La Barceloneta, urged me to go to the doctor. I always said yes, I had an appointment that very week.

Apart from my old boss and the Semperes, I didn't have much time to see anybody else except Vidal, and when I did see him it was more because he came to see me than through any effort on my part. He didn't like my tower house and always insisted that we go out for a stroll, to the Bar Almirall on Calle Joaquín Costa, where he had an account and held literary gatherings on Friday evenings. I was never invited to them because he knew that those who attended, frustrated poetasters and ass kissers who laughed at his jokes in the hope of some charity—a recommendation to a publisher or a compliment to soothe their wounded pride—hated me with unswerving vigor and determination that were quite absent from their more artistic endeavors, which were persistently ignored by the fickle public. At the Bar Almirall, knocking back absinthe and puffing on Caribbean cigars, he spoke to me about his novel, which was never finished, about his plans for retiring from his life of retirement, and about his romances; the older he got, the younger and more nubile his conquests became.

"You don't ask after Cristina," he would sometimes say, maliciously.

"What do you want me to ask?"

"Whether she asks after you."

"Does she ask after me, Don Pedro?"

"No."

"Well, there you are."

"The fact is, she did mention you the other day."

"And what did she say?"

"You're not going to like it."

"Go on."

"She didn't say it in so many words, but she seemed to imply that she couldn't understand how you could prostitute yourself by writing second-rate serials for that pair of thieves, that you were throwing away your talent and your youth."

I felt as if Vidal had just plunged a frozen dagger into my stomach.

"Is that what she thinks?"

Vidal shrugged his shoulders.

"Well, as far as I'm concerned she can go to hell."

. . .

I worked every day except Sundays, which I spent wandering the streets, always ending up in some bar on the Paralelo where it wasn't hard to find company and passing affection in the arms of another solitary soul like myself. It wasn't until the following morning, when I woke up lying next to a stranger, that I realized they all looked like her: the color of their hair, the way they walked, a gesture or a glance. Sooner or later, to fill the painful silence of farewells, those one-night stands would ask me how I earned my living, and when, surrendering to my vanity, I explained that I was a writer, they would take me for a liar, because nobody had ever heard of David Martín, although some of them did know of Ignatius B. Samson and had heard people talk about *City of the Damned*. After a while I began to say that I worked at the Customs Offices in the port or that I was a clerk in a solicitors' office called Sayrach, Muntaner, and Cruells.

One afternoon I was sitting in the Café de la Ópera with a music teacher called Alicia, helping her get over—or so I imagined—someone who was hard to forget. I was about to kiss her when I saw Cristina's face on the other side of the glass pane. When I reached the street, she had already vanished among the crowds in the Ramblas. Two weeks later Vidal insisted on inviting me to the premiere of *Madama Butterfly* at the Liceo.

The Vidal family owned a box in the dress circle and Vidal liked to attend once a week during the opera season. When I met him in the foyer I discovered that he had also brought Cristina. She greeted me with an icy smile and didn't speak to me again, or even glance at me until, halfway through the second act, Vidal decided to go down to the adjoining Círculo club to say hello to one of his cousins. We were left alone together in the box, with no other shield than Puccini and the hundreds of faces in the semidarkness of the theater. I held back for about ten minutes before turning to look her in the eye.

"Have I done something to offend you?" I asked.

"No."

"Can we pretend to be friends then, at least on occasions like this?"

"I don't want to be your friend, David."

"Why not?"

"Because you don't want to be my friend either."

She was right, I didn't want to be her friend.

"Is it true that you think I prostitute myself?"

"Whatever I think doesn't matter. What matters is what you think."

I sat there for another five minutes, then left. By the time I reached the wide Liceo staircase I'd already promised myself that I would never give her a second thought or look or a kind word.

The following afternoon I saw her in front of the cathedral and when I tried to avoid her she waved at me and smiled. I stood there, glued to the spot, watching her approach.

"Aren't you going to invite me for a snack?"

"I'm a streetwalker and I'm not free for another two hours."

"Well then, let me invite you. How much do you charge for accompanying a lady for an hour?"

I followed her reluctantly to a chocolate shop on Calle Petritxol. We ordered two cups of hot chocolate and sat facing each other, seeing who would break the silence first. For once, I won.

"I didn't mean to offend you yesterday, David, I don't know what Don Pedro told you, but I've never said such a thing."

"Maybe you only thought it, which is why he would have told me."

"You have no idea what I think," she replied harshly. "Nor does Don Pedro."

I shrugged.

"Fine."

"What I said was very different. I said that I didn't think you were doing what you felt inside."

I smiled and nodded. The only thing I felt at that moment was the need to kiss her. Cristina held my gaze defiantly. She didn't turn her face when I stretched out my hand and touched her lips, sliding my fingers down her chin and neck.

"Not like this," she said at last.

By the time the waiter brought the steaming cups of cocoa she had left. Months went by before I even heard her name again.

. . .

One day toward the end of September when I had just finished a new installment of *City of the Damned,* I decided to take a night off. I could feel the approach of one of those storms of nausea and burning stabs in my brain. I gulped down a handful of codeine pills and lay on my bed in the darkness waiting for the cold sweat and the trembling of my hands to stop. I was on the point of falling asleep when I heard the doorbell. I dragged myself to the hall and opened the door. Vidal, in one of his impeccable Italian silk suits, was lighting a cigarette under a beam of light that seemed painted for him by Vermeer himself.

"Are you alive, or am I speaking to an apparition?" he asked.

"Don't tell me you've come all the way from Villa Helius just to throw that at me."

"No. I've come because I haven't heard from you in two months and I'm worried about you. Why don't you get a telephone installed in this mausoleum, like normal people would?"

"I don't like telephones. I like to see people's faces when they speak and for them to see mine."

"In your case I'm not sure that's a good idea. Have you looked at yourself in the mirror recently?"

"That's your department."

"There are bodies in the mortuary at the Clínico hospital with a rosier face than yours. Go on, get dressed."

"Why?"

"Because I say so. We're going out for a stroll."

Vidal would not take no for an answer. He dragged me to the car that was waiting in Paseo del Borne and told Manuel to start the engine.

"Where are we going?" I asked.

"Surprise."

We crossed the whole of Barcelona until we reached Avenida Pedralbes and started to climb up the hillside. A few minutes later we glimpsed Villa Helius, with all its windows lit up, projecting a bubble of bright gold across the twilight. Giving nothing away, Vidal smiled mysteriously at me. When we reached the mansion he told me to follow him and led me to the large sitting room. A group of people were waiting for me there and as soon as they saw me, they started to clap. I recognized Don Basilio, Cristina, Sempere—both father and son—my old schoolteacher Doña Mariana, some of the authors who, like me, published their work with Barrido & Escobillas and with whom I had established a friendship, Manuel, who had joined the group, and a few of Vidal's conquests. Vidal offered me a glass of champagne and smiled.

"Happy twenty-eighth birthday, David."

I'd forgotten.

After the meal I excused myself for a moment and went out into the garden for some fresh air. A starry night cast a silver veil over the trees. I'd been there for only a minute or so when I heard footsteps approaching and turned to find the last person I was expecting to see: Cristina Sagnier. She smiled at me, as if apologizing for the intrusion.

"Pedro doesn't know I've come out to speak to you," she said.

She had dropped the "Don," but I pretended not to notice.

"I'd like to talk to you, David," she said, "but not here, not now."

Even in the shadows of the garden I was unable to hide my bewilderment.

"Can we meet tomorrow somewhere?" she asked. "I promise I won't take up much of your time."

"On one condition," I said. "That you stop addressing me with the formal *usted*. Birthdays are quite enough to make one feel older."

Cristina smiled.

"All right. I'll use the *tu* form if you do the same with me."

"The *tu* form is one of my specialities. Where shall we meet?"

"Could it be at your house? I don't want anyone to see us, and I don't want Pedro to know I've spoken with you."

"As you wish . . ."

Cristina smiled with relief.

"Thanks. Will tomorrow be all right? In the afternoon?"

"Whenever you like. Do you know where I live?"

"My father knows."

She leaned over a little and kissed me on the cheek.

"Happy birthday, David."

Before I could say anything, she had vanished across the garden. When I went back to the sitting room she had already left. Vidal glanced at me coldly from one end of the room and smiled only when he realized that I'd seen him.

An hour later Manuel, with Vidal's approval, insisted on driving me home in the Hispano-Suiza. I sat next to him, as I did whenever we were alone in the car: the chauffeur would take the opportunity to give me driving tips, and, unbeknownst to Vidal, would even let me sit at the steering wheel for a while. That night Manuel was quieter than usual and did not say a word until we reached the town center. He looked thinner than the last time I'd seen him and I had the feeling that age was beginning to take its toll.

"Is anything wrong, Manuel?" I asked.

"Nothing important, Señor Martín."

"If there's anything worrying you . . ."

"Just a few health problems. When you get to my age, everything is a worry, as you know. But I don't matter anymore. The one who matters is my daughter."

I wasn't sure how to reply, so I simply nodded.

"I'm aware that you have a certain affection for her, Señor Martín. For my Cristina. A father can see these things."

Again I just nodded. We didn't exchange any more words until Manuel stopped the car at the entrance to Calle Flassaders, held out his hand to me, and once more wished me a happy birthday.

"If anything should happen to me," he said then, "you would help her, wouldn't you, Señor Martín? You would do that for me?"

"Of course, Manuel. But nothing is going to happen to you!"

The chauffeur bade me farewell. I saw him get into the car and drive away slowly. I wasn't absolutely sure, but I could have sworn that, after a journey in which he had hardly opened his mouth, he was now talking to himself.

11

I spent the whole morning running about the house, straightening things and tidying up, airing the rooms, cleaning objects and corners I didn't even know existed. I rushed down to a florist in the market and when I returned, laden with bunches of flowers, I realized I had forgotten where I'd hidden the vases in which to put them. I dressed as if I were going out to look for work. I practiced words and greetings that sounded ridiculous. I glanced at myself in the mirror and saw that Vidal was right; I looked like a vampire. Finally I sat down in an armchair in the gallery to wait, with a book in my hands. In two hours I hadn't turned the first page. At last, at exactly four o'clock in the afternoon, I heard Cristina's footsteps on the stairs and jumped up. By the time she rang the front doorbell I'd been at the door for an eternity.

"Hello, David. Is this a bad moment?"

"No, no, on the contrary. Please come in."

Cristina smiled politely and stepped into the corridor. I led her to the reading room in the gallery and offered her a seat. She was examining everything carefully.

"It's a very special place," she said. "Pedro did tell me you had an elegant home."

"He prefers the term *gloomy,* but I suppose it's just a question of degree."

"May I ask why you came to live here? It's a rather large house for someone who lives alone."

Someone who lives alone, I thought. You end up becoming what you see in the eyes of those you love.

"The truth?" I asked. "The truth is that I came to live here because for years I had seen this house almost every day on my way to and from the newspaper. It was always closed up, and I began to think it was waiting for me. In the end I dreamed, literally, that one day I would live in it. And that's what happened."

"Do all your dreams come true, David?"

The ironic tone reminded me too much of Vidal.

"No," I replied. "This is the only one. But you wanted to talk to me about something and I'm distracting you with stories that probably don't interest you."

I sounded more defensive than I would have wished. The same thing that had happened with the flowers was happening with my longing: once I held it in my hands, I didn't know where to put it.

"I wanted to talk to you about Pedro," Cristina began.

"Ah."

"You're his best friend. You know him. He talks about you as if you were his son. He loves you more than anyone. You know that."

"Don Pedro has been like a father to me," I said. "If it hadn't been for him and for Señor Sempere, I don't know what would have become of me."

"The reason I wanted to talk to you is that I'm very worried about him."

"Why are you worried?"

"You know that some years ago I started work as his secretary. The truth is that Pedro is a very generous man and we've ended up being good friends. He has behaved very well toward my father, and toward me. That's why it hurts me to see him like this."

"Like what?"

"It's that wretched book, the novel he wants to write."

"He's been at it for years."

"He's been destroying it for years. I correct and type all his pages. Over the years I've been working as his secretary he's destroyed at least two thousand pages. He says he has no talent. He says he's a fraud. He's constantly at the bottle. Sometimes I find him upstairs in his study, drunk, crying like a child."

I swallowed hard.

"He says he envies you, he wants to be like you, he says people lie and praise him because they want something from him—money, help— but he knows that his book is worthless. He keeps up appearances with everyone else, his smart suits and all that, but I see him every day and I know he's losing hope. Sometimes I'm afraid he'll do something stupid. It's been going on for some time now. I haven't said anything because I didn't know who to speak to. If he knew I'd come to see you he'd be furious. He always says: Don't bother David with my worries. He's got his whole life ahead of him and I'm nothing now. He's always saying things like that. Forgive me for telling you all this, but I didn't know who to turn to."

I felt an intense cold invading me: the knowledge that while the man to whom I owed my life had plunged into despair, I had been locked in my own world and hadn't paused for one second to notice.

"Perhaps I shouldn't have come . . ."

"No," I said. "You've done the right thing."

Cristina looked at me with a hint of a smile and for the first time I felt that I was not a stranger to her.

"What can we do?" she asked.

"We're going to help him," I said.

"What if he doesn't let us?"

"Then we'll do it without his noticing."

12

I will never know whether I did it to help Vidal, as I kept telling myself, or simply as an excuse to spend more time with Cristina. We met almost every afternoon in my tower house. Cristina would bring the pages Vidal had written in longhand the day before, always full of deletions, with whole paragraphs crossed out, notes all over the page, and a thousand and one attempts to save what was beyond repair. We would go up to the study and sit on the floor. Cristina would read the pages out loud and then we would discuss them at length. My mentor was attempting to write an epic saga covering three generations of a Barcelona family that was not very different from his own. The action began a few years before the Industrial Revolution with the arrival in the city of two orphaned brothers and developed into a sort of biblical parable in the Cain and Abel mode. One of the brothers ended up becoming the richest and most powerful magnate of his time, while the other devoted himself to the Church and helping the needy, only to end his days tragically during an episode that was quite evidently borrowed from the misfortunes of the priest and poet Jacint Verdaguer. Throughout their lives the two brothers were at loggerheads, and an endless list of characters filed past in torrid melodramas, scandals, murders, tragedies, and other requirements of the genre, all set against the background of the birth of modern Barcelona and its world of industry and finance. The narrator was a grandchild of one of the two brothers, who reconstructed the story as he watched the city burn from a palatial mansion in Pedralbes, during the riots of the Tragic Week of 1909.

The first thing that surprised me was that the story was one that I had suggested to him some years earlier, as a means of getting him started on his most significant work, the novel he always said he would write one day. The second thing was that, not for any lack of opportunity, he had never told me he'd decided to use the idea or that he'd already spent years on it. The third thing was that the novel, as it stood, was a complete and utter flop: not one of the elements of the book worked, starting with the characters and the structure, continuing with the atmosphere and the plot, and ending with a language and a style that suggested the efforts of a pretentious amateur with too much time on his hands.

"What do you think of it?" Cristina asked. "Can it be saved?"

I preferred not to tell her that Vidal had borrowed the premise from me, not wishing her to be more worried than she already was, so I smiled and nodded.

"It needs some work, that's all."

As the day grew dark, Cristina would sit at the typewriter and between us we rewrote Vidal's book, letter by letter, line by line, scene by scene.

The storyline put together by Vidal was so vague and insipid that I decided to recover the one I had invented when I originally suggested it to him. Slowly we brought the characters back to life, rebuilding them from head to toe. Not a single scene, moment, line, or word survived the process and yet, as we advanced, I had the impression that we were doing justice to the novel that Vidal carried in his heart and had decided to write without knowing how.

Cristina told me that sometimes, weeks after he remembered writing a scene, Vidal would reread it in its final typewritten version and be surprised at his craftsmanship and the fullness of a talent in which he had ceased to believe. She feared he might discover what we were doing and told me we should be more faithful to his original work.

"Never underestimate a writer's vanity, especially that of a mediocre writer," I would reply.

"I don't like to hear you talking like that about Pedro."

"I'm sorry. Neither do I."

"Perhaps you should slow down a bit. You don't look well. I'm not worried about Pedro anymore—I'm concerned about you."

"Something good had to come of all this."

. . .

In time I grew accustomed to savoring the moments I shared with her. It wasn't long before my own work suffered the consequences. I found the time to work on *City of the Damned* where there was none, sleeping barely three hours a day and pushing myself to the limit to meet the deadlines in my contract. Both Barrido and Escobillas made it a rule not to read any book—neither the ones they published nor the ones published by the competition—but Lady Venom did read them and soon began to suspect that something strange was happening to me.

"This isn't you," she would say every now and then.

"Of course it's not me, dear Herminia. It's Ignatius B. Samson."

I was aware of the risks I was taking, but I didn't care. I didn't care if I woke up every day covered in sweat and with my heart beating so hard I felt as if it were going to crack my ribs. I would have paid that price and much more to retain the slow, secret contact that unwittingly turned us into accomplices. I knew perfectly well that Cristina could read this in my eyes every time she came, and I knew perfectly well that she would never respond to my advances. There was no future, there were no great expectations, in that race to nowhere, and we both knew it.

Sometimes, when we grew tired of attempting to refloat the leaking ship, we would abandon Vidal's manuscript and try to talk about something other than the intimacy that, from being so hidden, was beginning to weigh on our consciences. Now and then I would muster enough courage to take her hand. She let me, but I knew it made her feel uncomfortable. She felt that it was not right, that our debt of gratitude to Vidal united and separated us at the same time. One night, shortly before she left, I held her face in my hands and tried to kiss her. She remained motionless and when I saw myself in the mirror of her eyes I didn't dare speak. She stood up and left without saying a word. After that, I didn't see her for two weeks and when she returned she made me promise nothing like that would ever happen again.

"David, I want you to understand that when we finish working on Pedro's book we won't be seeing each other as we do now."

"Why not?"

"You know why."

My advances were not the only thing Cristina didn't approve of. I began to suspect that Vidal had been right when he said she disliked the books I was writing for Barrido & Escobillas, even if she kept quiet about it. It wasn't hard to imagine her thinking that my efforts were strictly mercenary and soulless, that I was selling my integrity for a pittance and lining the pockets of a couple of sewer rats because I didn't have the courage to write from my heart, under my own name and with my own feelings. What hurt me most was that, deep down, she was probably right. I fantasized about backing out of my contract and writing a book just for her, a book with which I could earn her respect. If the only thing I knew how to do wasn't good enough for Cristina, perhaps I should return to the gray, miserable days of the newspaper. I could always live off Vidal's charity and favors.

. . .

I had gone out for a walk after a long night's work, unable to sleep. Wandering about aimlessly, my feet led me uphill until I reached the building site of the Sagrada Familia. When I was small, my father had sometimes taken me there to gaze up at the babel of sculptures and porticoes that never seemed to take flight, as if the building were cursed. I liked going back to visit the place and discovering that it had not changed, that although the city was endlessly growing around it, the Sagrada Familia remained forever in a state of ruin.

Dawn was breaking when I arrived: the towers of the Nativity façade stood in silhouette against a blue sky, scythed by red light. An eastern wind carried the dust from the unpaved streets and the acrid smell from the factories shoring up the edges of the Sant Martí quarter. I was crossing Calle Mallorca when I saw the lights of a tram approaching through the early morning mist. I heard the clatter of the metal wheels on the rails and the sound of the bell the driver was ringing to warn people of the tram's advance. I wanted to run, but I couldn't. I stood there, glued to the ground between the rails, watching the lights of the tram leaping toward me. I heard the driver's shouts and saw the plume of sparks that shot out from the wheels as he slammed on the brakes. Even then, with death only a few meters away, I couldn't move a muscle. The smell of electricity invaded the white light that blazed in my eyes, and then the tram's headlights went out. I fell over like a puppet, conscious for only a few more seconds, time enough to see the tram's smoking wheel stop just centimeters from my face. Then all was darkness.

13

I opened my eyes. Thick columns of stone rose in the shadows toward a naked vault. Needles of dusty light fell diagonally, revealing endless rows of ramshackle beds. Small drops of water fell from the heights like black tears, exploding with an echo as they touched the ground. The darkness smelled of mildew and damp.

"Welcome to Purgatory."

I sat up and turned to find a man dressed in rags who was reading a newspaper by the light of a lantern. He brandished a smile that showed half of his teeth were missing. The front page of the newspaper he was holding announced that General Primo de Rivera was taking over all the powers of the state and installing a gentlemanly dictatorship to save the country from imminent disaster. That newspaper was at least five years old.

"Where am I?"

The man peered over his paper and looked at me curiously.

"At the Ritz. Can't you smell it?"

"How did I get here?"

"Half dead. They brought you in this morning on a stretcher and you've been sleeping it off ever since."

I felt my jacket and realized that all the money I'd had on me had vanished.

"What a mess the world is in," cried the man, reading the news in his paper. "It seems that in the advanced stages of stupidity, a lack of ideas is compensated for by an excess of ideologies."

"How do I get out of here?"

"If you're in such a hurry . . . There are two ways, the permanent and the temporary. The permanent way is via the roof: one good leap and you can rid yourself of all this rubbish forever. The temporary way is somewhere over there, at the end, where that idiot is holding his fist in the air with his trousers falling off him, making the revolutionary salute to everyone who passes. But if you go out that way you'll come back sooner or later."

The first man was watching me with amusement and the kind of lucidity that shines occasionally only in madmen.

"Are you the one who stole my money?"

"Your suspicion offends me. When they brought you here you were already as clean as a whistle, and I only accept bonds that can be cashed at a bank."

I left the lunatic sitting on his bed with his out-of-date newspaper and his up-to-date speeches. My head was still spinning and I was barely able to walk more than four steps in a straight line, but I managed to reach a door that led to a staircase on one of the sides of the huge vault. A faint light seemed to filter down from the top of the stairwell. I went up four or five floors until I felt a gust of fresh air that was coming through a large doorway at the top. I walked outside and at last understood where I was.

Spread out before me was a lake, suspended above the treetops of Ciudadela Park. The sun was beginning to set over Barcelona and the weed-covered water rippled like spilled wine. The water reservoir building looked like a crude castle or a prison. It had been built to supply water to the pavilions of the 1888 Universal Exhibition, but in time its vast, cathedral-like interior had become a shelter for the destitute and the dying who had no other refuge from the night or the cold. The huge water basin on the flat rooftop was now a murky stretch of water that slowly bled away through the cracks in the building.

Then I noticed a figure posted on one of the corners of the roof. As if the mere touch of my gaze had alerted him, he turned round sharply and looked at me. I still felt a bit dazed and my vision was blurred, but I thought the figure seemed to be getting closer. He was approaching too fast, as if his feet weren't touching the ground when he walked, and he moved in sudden, agile bursts, too quick for the eye to catch. I could barely see his face against the light, but I was able to tell that he was a gentleman with black, shining eyes that seemed too big for his face. The closer he got to me the more his shape seemed to lengthen and the taller he seemed to grow. I felt a shiver as he advanced, and I took a few steps back without realizing that I was moving toward the water's edge. I felt my feet treading air and began to fall backwards into the pond when the stranger suddenly caught me by the arm. He pulled me up gently and led me back to solid ground. I sat on one of the benches that surrounded the water basin, then looked up and saw him clearly for the first time. His eyes were normal size, his height similar to mine, and his walk and gestures were like those of any other gentleman. He had a kind and reassuring expression.

"Thank you," I said.

"Are you all right?"

"Yes. Just a bit dizzy."

The stranger sat down next to me. He wore a dark, exquisitely tailored three-piece suit with a small silver brooch on his lapel, an angel with outspread wings that I readily recognized. It occurred to me that the presence of an impeccably dressed gentleman here on the roof terrace was rather unusual. As if he could read my thoughts, the stranger smiled at me.

"I hope I didn't alarm you," he ventured. "I suppose you weren't expecting to meet anyone up here."

I looked at him in confusion and saw my face reflected in his black pupils as they dilated like an ink stain on paper.

"May I ask what brings you here?"

"The same thing as you: great expectations."

"Andreas Corelli," I mumbled.

His face lit up.

"What a great pleasure it is to meet you in person at last, my friend."

He spoke with a light accent that I was unable to identify. My instinct told me to get up and leave as fast as possible, before the stranger could utter another word, but there was something in his voice, in his eyes, that transmitted calm and trust. I decided not to ask myself how he could have known he would find me there, when even I had not known where I was. He held out his hand and I shook it. His smile seemed to promise redemption.

"I suppose I should thank you for all the kindness you have shown me over the years, Señor Corelli. I'm afraid I'm indebted to you."

"Not at all. I'm the one who is indebted to you, my friend, and I should excuse myself for approaching you in this way, at so inconvenient a place and time, but I confess that I've been wanting to speak to you for a while and have never found the opportunity."

"Go ahead then. What can I do for you?" I asked.

"I want you to work for me."

"I'm sorry?"

"I want you to write for me."

"Of course. I'd forgotten you're a publisher."

The stranger laughed. He had a sweet laugh, the laugh of a child who has never misbehaved.

"The best of them all. The publisher you have been waiting for all your life. The publisher who will make you immortal."

The stranger offered me one of his business cards, which was identical to the one I still had, the one I was holding when I awoke from my dream of Chloé.

ANDREAS CORELLI
Éditeur
Éditions de la Lumière
Boulevard St.-Germain, 69. Paris

"I'm flattered, Señor Corelli, but I'm afraid it's not possible for me to accept your invitation. I have a contract with—"

"Barrido & Escobillas. I know. Riffraff with whom, without wishing to offend you, you should have no dealings whatsoever."

"It's an opinion shared by others."

"Señorita Sagnier, perhaps?"

"You know her?"

"I've heard of her. She seems to be the sort of woman whose respect and admiration one would give anything to win, don't you agree? Doesn't she encourage you to abandon those parasites and be true to yourself?"

"It's not that simple. I have an exclusive contract that ties me to them for six more years."

"I know, but that needn't worry you. My lawyers are studying the matter and I can assure you there are a number of ways in which legal ties can be rendered null and void, should you wish to accept my proposal."

"And your proposal is?"

Corelli gave me a mischievous smile, like a schoolboy sharing a secret.

"That you devote a year exclusively to working on a book I would commission, a book whose subject matter you and I would discuss when we signed the contract and for which I would pay you, in advance, the sum of one hundred thousand francs."

I looked at him in astonishment.

"If that sum does not seem adequate I'm open to considering any other sum you might think more appropriate. I'll be frank, Señor Martín, I'm not going to quarrel with you about money. And between you and me, I don't think you'll want to either, because I know that when I tell you the sort of book I want you to write for me, the price will be the least of it."

I sighed, laughing quietly.

"I see you don't believe me."

"Señor Corelli, I'm an author of penny dreadfuls that don't even bear my name. My publishers, whom you seem to know, are a couple of second-rate crooks who are not worth their weight in manure, and my readers don't even know I exist. I've spent years earning my living in this trade and I have yet to write a single page that satisfies me. The woman I love thinks I'm wasting my life and she's right. She also thinks I have no right to desire her because we're a pair of insignificant souls whose only reason for existence is the debt of gratitude we owe to a man who pulled us both out of poverty, and perhaps she's right about that too. It doesn't matter. Before I know it, I'll be thirty and I'll realize that every day I look less like the person I wanted to be when I was fifteen. If I reach thirty, that is, because recently my health has been about as consistent as my work. Right now I'm satisfied if I manage one or two decent sentences in an hour. That's the sort of author and the sort of man I am. Not the sort who receives visits from Parisian publishers with blank checks for writing a book that will change his life and make all his dreams come true."

Corelli observed me with a serious expression, carefully weighing every word.

"I think you judge yourself too severely, a quality that always distinguishes people of true worth. Believe me when I say that throughout my professional life I've come across hundreds of characters for whom you wouldn't have given a damn but who had an extremely high opinion of themselves. But I want you to know that, even if you don't believe me, I know exactly what sort of author and what sort of man you are. I've been watching you for years, as you are well aware. I've read all your work, from the very first story you wrote for *The Voice of Industry* to *The Mysteries of Barcelona,* and now each of the installments of the Ignatius B. Samson series. I dare say I know you better than you know yourself. Which is why I'm sure that in the end you will accept my offer."

"What else do you know?"

"I know we have something, or a great deal, in common. I know you lost your father, and so did I. I know what it is like to lose one's father when you still need him. Yours was snatched from you in tragic circumstances. Mine, for reasons that are neither here nor there, rejected me and threw me out of his house—perhaps that was even more painful. I know that you feel lonely, and believe me when I tell you that this is a feeling I have also experienced. I know that in your heart you harbor great expectations, none of which have come true, and that, although you're not aware of it, this is slowly killing you with every passing day."

His words brought about a long silence.

"You know a lot of things, Señor Corelli."

"Enough to think that I would like to be better acquainted with you and become your friend. I don't suppose you have many friends. Neither do I. I don't trust people who say they have a lot of friends. It's a sure sign that they don't really know anyone."

"But you're not looking for a friend. You're looking for an employee."

"I'm looking for a temporary partner. I'm looking for you."

"You seem very sure of yourself."

"It's a fault I was born with," Corelli replied, standing up. "Another is my gift for seeing into the future. That's why I realize that perhaps it's still too soon: hearing the truth from my lips is not enough for you yet. You need to see it with your own eyes. Feel it in your flesh. And believe me, you'll feel it."

He held out his hand and waited until I took it.

"Can I at least be reassured that you will think about what I've told you and that we'll speak again?" he asked.

"I don't know what to say, Señor Corelli."

"Don't say anything right now. I promise that next time we meet you'll see things more clearly."

With those words he gave me a friendly smile and walked off toward the stairs.

"Will there be a next time?" I asked.

Corelli stopped and turned.

"There always is."

"Where?"

In the last rays of daylight falling on the city his eyes glowed like embers.

I saw him disappear through the door to the staircase. Only then did I realize that during the entire conversation I had not once seen him blink.

14

The doctor's surgery was on a top floor with a view of the sea gleaming in the distance and the slope of Calle Muntaner dotted with trams that slid down to the Ensanche between grand houses and imposing edifices. The place smelled clean. The waiting rooms were tastefully decorated. The paintings were calming, with landscapes full of hope and peace. The shelves displayed books that exuded authority. Nurses moved about like ballet dancers and smiled as they went by. It was a purgatory for people with well-lined pockets.

"The doctor will see you now, Señor Martín."

Dr. Trías was a man with a patrician air and an impeccable appearance who radiated serenity and confidence with every gesture. Gray, penetrating eyes behind rimless glasses. A kind, friendly smile, never frivolous. Dr. Trías was accustomed to jousting with death and the more he smiled the more frightening he became. Judging by the way he escorted me to his room and asked me to sit down, I got the feeling that although some days before, when I had begun to undergo medical tests, he had spoken about recent medical breakthroughs in the fight against the symptoms I had described to him, as far as he was concerned there was no doubt.

"How are you?" he asked, his eyes darting hesitantly between me and the folder on his desk.

"You tell me."

He smiled faintly, like a good player.

"The nurse tells me you're a writer, although here, on the form you filled in when you arrived, I see you put down that you are a mercenary."

"In my case there's no difference at all."

"I believe some of my patients have read your books."

"I hope it has not caused permanent neurological damage."

The doctor smiled as if he'd found my comment amusing and then adopted a more serious expression, implying that the banal and kind preambles to our conversation had come to an end.

"Señor Martín, I notice that you have come here on your own. Don't you have any close family? A wife? Siblings? Parents still alive?"

"That sounds a little ominous," I ventured.

"Señor Martín, I'm not going to lie to you. The results of the first tests are not as encouraging as we'd hoped."

I looked at him. I didn't feel fear or unease. I didn't feel anything.

"Everything points to the fact that you have a growth lodged in the left lobe of your brain. The results confirm what I feared from the symptoms you described to me and there is every indication that it might be a carcinoma."

For a few seconds I was unable to say anything at all. I couldn't even pretend to be surprised.

"How long have I had it?"

"It's impossible to say for sure, but I assume the tumor has been growing there for some time, which would explain the symptoms you told me about and the difficulties you have recently experienced with your work."

I took a deep breath and nodded. The doctor observed me patiently, with a kindly mien, letting me take my time. I tried to start various sentences that never reached my lips. Finally our eyes met.

"I suppose I'm in your hands, doctor. You'll have to tell me which treatment to follow."

I saw his despairing look as he realized I had not wanted to understand what he was telling me. I nodded once more, fighting the tide of nausea that was beginning to rise up my throat. The doctor poured me a glass of water from a jug and handed it to me. I drank it in one gulp.

"There is no treatment," I said.

"There is. There are a lot of things we can do to relieve the pain and ensure maximum comfort and peace—"

"But I'm going to die."

"Yes."

"Soon."

"Possibly."

I smiled to myself. Even the worst news is a relief when all it does is confirm what you already knew without wanting to know.

"I'm twenty-eight," I said, without quite knowing why.

"I'm sorry, Señor Martín. I'd like to have given you better news."

I felt as if I had finally confessed to a lie or a minor sin and the large slab of remorse that had been pressing down on me was instantly removed.

"How much longer do I have?"

"It is difficult to determine exactly. I'd say a year, a year and a half at most."

His tone clearly implied that this was a more than optimistic prognosis.

"And of that year, or whatever it is, how long do you think I'll still be able to work and cope on my own?"

"You're a writer and you work with your brain. Unfortunately that is where the problem is located and where we will first meet limitations."

"*Limitations* is not a medical term, doctor."

"The most likely outcome is that as the disease progresses the symptoms you've been experiencing will become more intense and more frequent and after a time you'll have to be admitted to hospital so that we can take care of you."

"I won't be able to write."

"You won't even be able to think about writing."

"How long?"

"I don't know. Nine or ten months. Perhaps more, perhaps less. I'm very sorry, Señor Martín."

I nodded and stood up. My hands were shaking and I needed some air.

"Señor Martín, I realize you need time to think about all the things I've told you, but it is important that we start your treatment as soon as possible—"

"I can't die yet, doctor. Not yet. I have things to do. Afterwards I'll have a whole lifetime in which to die."

15

That night I went up to the study in the tower and sat at my typewriter, even though I knew that my brain was a blank. The windows were wide open, but Barcelona no longer wanted to tell me anything; I was unable to finish a single page. Anything I did manage to conjure up seemed banal and empty. It was enough to reread my words to understand that they were barely worth the ink with which they'd been typed. I was no longer able to hear the music that issues from a decent piece of prose. Bit by bit, like slow, pleasant poison, the words of Andreas Corelli began to drip into my thoughts.

I still had at least a hundred pages to go for my umpteenth delivery of those comic book adventures that had provided both Barrido and Escobillas with such bulging pockets, but in that moment I knew I was never going to finish it. Ignatius B. Samson had been left lying on the rails in front of that tram, exhausted, his soul bled dry, poured into too many pages that should never have seen the light of day. But before departing he had conveyed to me his last wishes: that I should bury him without any fuss and that, for once in my life, I should have the courage to use my own voice. His legacy to me was his considerable repertoire of smoke and mirrors. And he asked me to let him go, because he had been born to be forgotten.

I took the finished pages of his last novel and set fire to them, sensing that a tombstone was being lifted off me with every page I threw into the flames. A moist, warm breeze blew that night over the rooftops and as it came in through my windows it took with it the ashes of Ignatius B. Samson, scattering them through the streets of the old city, where they would always remain—even if his words were lost forever and his name slipped from the memory of even his most devoted readers.

The following day I turned up at the offices of Barrido & Escobillas. The receptionist was new, almost a child, and didn't recognize me.

"Your name?"

"Hugo, Victor."

The receptionist smiled and connected to the switchboard to let Herminia know.

"Doña Herminia, Señor Hugo Victor is here to see Señor Barrido."

I saw her nod and disconnect the switchboard.

"She says she'll be right out."

"Have you been working here long?"

"A week," the girl replied earnestly.

Unless I was mistaken, she was the eighth receptionist Barrido & Escobillas had employed since the start of the year. The firm's employees who reported directly to the artful Herminia didn't last long because as soon as Lady Venom discovered that they had one ounce of common sense more than she had—which happened nine times out of ten—fearing she might be overshadowed, she would accuse them of theft or some other absurd transgression and make a scene until Escobillas kicked them out, threatening them with a hired assassin if they let the cat out of the bag.

"How good to see you, David," said Lady Venom. "You're looking very handsome. You seem well."

"That's because I was run over by a tram. Is Barrido in?"

"The things you come out with! He's always in for you. He's going to be very pleased when I tell him you've come to pay us a visit."

"You can't imagine how pleased."

Lady Venom took me to Barrido's office, which was decorated like a chancellor's palatial rooms in a comic opera, with a profusion of carpets, busts of emperors, still lifes, and leather-bound volumes bought in bulk that I imagined were probably blank inside. Barrido gave me the oiliest of smiles and shook my hand.

"We're all waiting impatiently for the next installment. I must tell you, we've been reprinting the last two and they're flying out the window. Another five thousand copies, how about that?"

I thought it was more likely at least fifty thousand, but I just nodded enthusiastically. Barrido & Escobillas had perfected what was known among Barcelona publishers as the double print run, and theirs was as neatly arranged as a bunch of flowers. Every title had an official print run of a few thousand copies that was declared and on which a ridiculously small margin was paid to the author. Then, if the book took off, they would print a covert edition—or several—of tens of thousands of copies that were never declared and for which the author never saw a penny. This edition could be distinguished from the official one because Barrido had the books printed on the sly in an old sausage plant in Santa Perpètua de Mogoda and if you leafed through the pages they gave off the unmistakable smell of vintage pork.

"I'm afraid I have bad news."

Barrido and Lady Venom exchanged looks but kept on grinning. Just then, Escobillas materialized through the door and looked at me with that dry, disdainful air he had, as if he were measuring you for a coffin.

"Look who has come to see us. Isn't this a nice surprise?" Barrido asked his partner, who replied with a nod.

"What bad news?" asked Escobillas.

"Is there a bit of a delay, Martín, my friend?" Barrido added in a friendly tone. "I'm sure we can accommodate—"

"No. There's no delay. Quite simply, there's not going to be another book."

Escobillas took a step forward and raised his eyebrows. Barrido giggled.

"What do you mean, there's not going to be another book?" asked Escobillas.

"I mean that yesterday I burned it and there's not a single page of the manuscript left."

A heavy silence fell. Barrido made a conciliatory gesture and pointed to what was known as the visitors' armchair, a black, sunken throne in which authors and suppliers were cornered so that they could meet Barrido's eyes from the appropriate height.

"Martín, sit down and tell me what this is about. There's something worrying you, I can see. You can be open with us, we're like family."

Lady Venom and Escobillas nodded with conviction, showing the measure of their esteem in a look of spellbound devotion. I decided to remain standing. They all did the same, staring at me as if I were a pillar of salt that was about to start talking. Barrido's face hurt from so much smiling.

"And?"

"Ignatius B. Samson has committed suicide. He left a twenty-page unpublished story in which he dies together with Chloé Permanyer, locked in an embrace after swallowing poison."

"The author dies in one of his own novels?" asked Herminia, confused.

"It's his avant-garde farewell to the world of writing installments. A detail I was sure you would love."

"And could there not be an antidote, or . . ." Lady Venom asked.

"Martín, I don't need to remind you that it is you, and not the allegedly deceased Ignatius, who has a contract," said Escobillas.

Barrido raised his hands to silence his colleague.

"I think I know what's wrong, Martín. You're exhausted. You've been overloading your brain for years without a break—something this house values and is grateful for—you just need a breather. I can understand. We do understand, don't we?"

Barrido glanced at Escobillas and at Lady Venom, who nodded and tried to look serious.

"You're an artist and you want to make art, high literature, something that springs from your heart and will engrave your name in golden letters on the steps of history."

"The way you put it makes it sound ridiculous," I said.

"Because it is," said Escobillas.

"No, it isn't," Barrido cut in. "It's human. And we're human. I, my partner, and Herminia, who, being a woman and a creature of delicate sensitivity, is the humanest of all, isn't that right, Herminia?"

"Indeed," Lady Venom agreed.

"And as we're human, we understand you and want to support you. Because we're proud of you and convinced that your success will be our success and because in this firm, when all's said and done, what matters is the people, not the numbers."

At the end of his speech, Barrido paused theatrically. Perhaps he expected me to break into applause, but when he saw that I wasn't moved he charged on, unimpeded, with his exposition.

"That is why I'm going to propose the following. Take six months, nine if need be, because, after all, this is like a birth. Lock yourself up in your study to write the great novel of your life. When you've finished it, bring it to us and we'll publish it under your name, putting all our irons in the fire and all our resources behind you. Because we're on your side."

I looked at Barrido and then at Escobillas. Lady Venom was about to burst into tears from the emotion.

"With no advance, needless to say."

Barrido clapped his hands euphorically in the air.

"What do you say?"

. . .

I began work that very day. My plan was as simple as it was crazy. During the day I would rewrite Vidal's book and at night I'd work on mine. I would polish all the dark arts Ignatius B. Samson had taught me and place them at the service of what little decency and dignity were left in my heart. I would write out of gratitude, despair, and vanity. I would write especially for Cristina, to prove to her that I too was able to pay the debt I had with Vidal and that, even if he was about to drop dead, David Martín had earned himself the right to look her in the eye without feeling ashamed of his ridiculous hopes.

. . .

I didn't return to Dr. Trías's surgery. I didn't see the point. The day I could no longer write another word, or imagine one, I would be the first to know. My trustworthy and unscrupulous chemist supplied me with as many codeine treats as I requested, without asking any questions, as well as the occasional delicacy that set my veins alight, obliterating both pain and consciousness. I didn't tell anyone about my visit to the doctor or about the test results.

My basic needs were covered by a weekly delivery that I ordered from Can Gispert, a wonderful grocer's emporium on Calle Mirallers, behind the cathedral of Santa María del Mar. The order was always the same. It was usually brought to me by the owner's daughter, a girl who stared at me like a frightened fawn when I told her to wait in the entrance hall while I fetched the money to pay her.

"This is for your father, and this is for you."

I always gave her a ten céntimos tip, which she accepted without saying a word. Every week the girl rang my doorbell with the delivery, and every week I paid her and gave her a ten céntimos tip. For nine months and a day, the time it took me to write the only book that would bear my name, that young girl whose name I didn't know and whose face I forgot every week until I saw her standing in the doorway again was the person I saw the most.

Without warning, Cristina had stopped coming to our afternoon meetings. I was beginning to fear that Vidal might have got wind of our ploy. Then one afternoon when I was waiting for her after about a week's absence, I opened the door thinking it was her, and instead there was Pep, one of the servants at Villa Helius. He brought me a parcel sent by Cristina. It was carefully sealed and contained the whole of Vidal's manuscript. Pep explained that Cristina's father had suffered an aneurysm that had left him practically disabled and she'd taken him to a sanatorium in Puigcerdà, in the Pyrenees, where apparently there was a young doctor who was an expert in the treatment of such ailments.

"Señor Vidal has taken care of everything," Pep explained. "No expense spared."

Vidal never forgot his servants, I thought, not without some bitterness.

"She asked me to deliver this to you by hand. And not to tell anyone about it."

The young man handed me the parcel, relieved to be free of the mysterious item.

"Did she leave an address where I could find her if I needed to?"

"No, Señor Martín. All I know is that Señorita Cristina's father has been admitted to a place called Villa San Antonio."

A few days later, Vidal paid me one of his surprise visits and spent the whole afternoon in my house, drinking my anisette, smoking my cigarettes, and talking to me about his chauffeur's misfortune.

"It's hard to believe. A man who was as strong as an ox, and suddenly he's struck down, just like that. He doesn't even know who he is anymore."

"How is Cristina?"

"You can imagine. Her mother died years ago and Manuel is the only family she has left. She took a family album with her and shows him photographs every day to see whether the poor fellow can remember anything."

While Vidal spoke, his novel—or should I say my novel—rested facedown on the table in the gallery, a pile of papers only half a meter from his hands. He told me that in Manuel's absence he had urged Pep—apparently a good horseman—to take up the art of driving, but so far the young man was proving hopeless.

"Give him time. A motorcar isn't a horse. The secret is practice."

"Now that you mention it, Manuel taught you how to drive, didn't he?"

"A little," I admitted. "And it's not as easy as it seems."

"If the novel you're writing doesn't sell, you can always become my chauffeur."

"Let's not bury poor Manuel yet, Don Pedro."

"That comment was in bad taste," Vidal admitted. "I'm sorry."

"How's your novel going, Don Pedro?"

"It's going well. Cristina has taken the final manuscript with her to Puigcerdà so that she can type up a clean copy and get it all shipshape while she's there with her father."

"I'm glad to see you looking happy."

Vidal gave me a triumphant smile.

"I think it's going to be something big," he said. "After all those months I thought I'd wasted, I reread the first fifty pages Cristina typed out for me and I was quite surprised at myself. I think it will surprise you too. I may still have some tricks to teach you."

"I've never doubted that, Don Pedro."

That afternoon Vidal was drinking more than usual. Over the years I'd got to know the full range of his anxieties and reservations, and I guessed that this visit was not a simple courtesy call. When he had polished off my supply of anisette, I served him a generous glass of brandy and waited.

"David, there are things about which you and I have never spoken . . ."

"About football, for example."

"I'm serious."

"I'm listening, Don Pedro."

He looked at me for a while, hesitating.

"I've always tried to be a good friend to you, David. You know that, don't you?"

"You've been much more than that, Don Pedro. I know and you know."

"Sometimes I ask myself whether I shouldn't have been more honest with you."

"About what?"

Vidal stared into his glass of brandy.

"There are some things I've never told you, David. Things that perhaps I should have told you years ago . . ."

I let a moment or two go by. It seemed an eternity. Whatever Vidal wanted to tell me, it was clear that all the brandy in the world wasn't going to get it out of him.

"Don't worry, Don Pedro. If these things have waited for years, I'm sure they can wait until tomorrow."

"Tomorrow I may not have the courage to tell you."

I had never seen him look so frightened. Something had got stuck in his heart and I was beginning to feel uncomfortable.

"Here's what we'll do, Don Pedro. When your book and mine are published we'll get together to celebrate and you can tell me whatever it is you need to tell me. Invite me to one of those expensive places I'm not allowed into unless I'm with you, and then you can confide in me as much as you like. Does that sound all right?"

When it started to get dark I went with him as far as Paseo del Borne, where Pep was waiting by the Hispano-Suiza, wearing Manuel's uniform—which was far too big for him, as was the motorcar. The bodywork was peppered with unsightly new scratches and bumps.

"Keep at a relaxed trot, eh, Pep?" I advised him. "No galloping. Slowly but surely, as if it were a draft horse."

"Yes, Señor Martín. Slowly but surely."

When he left, Vidal hugged me tight, and as he got into the car it seemed to me that he was carrying the whole world on his shoulders.

16

A few days after I had put the finishing touches to both novels, Vidal's and my own, Pep turned up at my house unannounced. He was wearing the uniform inherited from Manuel that made him look like a boy dressed up as a field marshal. At first I thought he was bringing me some message from Vidal, or perhaps from Cristina, but his somber expression spoke of an anxiety that made me rule out that possibility as soon as our eyes met.

"Bad news, Señor Martín."

"What has happened?"

"It's Señor Manuel."

While he was explaining what had happened his voice faltered and when I asked him whether he wanted a glass of water he almost burst into tears. Manuel Sagnier had died three days earlier at the sanatorium in Puigcerdà after prolonged suffering. At his daughter's request he had been buried the day before in a small cemetery at the foot of the Pyrenees.

"Dear God," I murmured.

Instead of water I handed Pep a large glass of brandy and parked him in an armchair in the gallery. When he was calmer, Pep explained that Vidal had sent him to meet Cristina, who was returning that afternoon on a train due to arrive at five o'clock.

"Imagine how Señorita Cristina must be feeling," he mumbled, distressed at the thought of having to be the one to meet her and comfort her on the journey back to the small apartment above the coach house of Villa Helius, the home she had shared with her father since she was a little girl.

"Pep, I don't think it's a good idea for you to go meet Señorita Sagnier."

"Orders from Don Pedro."

"Tell Don Pedro that I'll do it."

By dint of alcohol and persuasion I convinced him that he should go home and leave the matter in my hands. I would meet her and take her to Villa Helius in a taxi.

"I'm very grateful, Señor Martín. You're a man of letters so you'll have a better idea of what to say to the poor thing."

At a quarter to five I made my way toward the recently opened Estación de Francia railway station. That year's International Exhibition had left the city strewn with wonders, but my favorite was that temple-like vault of glass and steel, even if only because it was so close and I could see it from the study in the tower house. That afternoon the sky was scattered with black clouds galloping in from the sea and clustering over the city. Flashes of lightning echoed on the horizon and a charged warm wind smelling of dust announced a powerful summer storm. When I reached the station I noticed the first few drops, shiny and heavy, like coins falling from heaven. By the time I walked down to the platform where the train was due to arrive, the rain was already pounding the station's vault. Night seemed to fall suddenly, interrupted only by the lightning now bursting over the city, leaving a trail of noise and fury.

The train came in almost an hour late, a serpent of steam slithering beneath the storm. I stood by the engine waiting for Cristina to appear among the passengers emerging from the carriages. Ten minutes later everybody had descended and there was still no trace of her. I was about to go back home, thinking that perhaps Cristina hadn't taken that train after all, when I decided to have a last look and walked all the way down to the end of the platform, peering carefully into all the compartment windows. I found her in the carriage before the last, sitting with her head against the window, staring into the distance. I climbed into the carriage and walked up to the door of her compartment. When she heard my steps she turned and looked at me without surprise, smiling faintly. She stood up and hugged me silently.

"Welcome back," I said.

Cristina's only baggage was a small suitcase. I gave her my hand and we went down to the platform, which by now was deserted. We walked all the way to the main foyer without exchanging a word. When we reached the exit we stopped. It was raining hard and the line of taxis that had been there when I arrived had vanished.

"I don't want to return to Villa Helius tonight, David. Not yet."

"You can stay at my house if you like, or we can find you a room in a hotel."

"I don't want to be alone."

"Let's go home. If there's one thing I have it's too many bedrooms."

I sighted a porter who had put his head out to look at the storm and was holding an impressive-looking umbrella. I went up to him and offered to buy it for five times its worth. He gave it to me wreathed in an obliging smile.

Protected by the umbrella we ventured out into the deluge and headed toward the tower house, where we arrived ten minutes later, completely drenched, thanks to the gusts of wind and the puddles. The storm had caused the power to go out; the streets were buried in a liquid darkness speckled here and there with the light cast by oil lamps or candles from balconies and doors. I had no doubt that the marvelous electrical system in my house must have been one of the first to succumb. We had to fumble our way up the stairs, and when we opened the front door of the apartment a flash of lightning emphasized its gloomiest and most inhospitable aspect.

"If you've changed your mind and you'd rather we looked for a hotel . . ."

"No, it's fine. Don't worry."

I left Cristina's suitcase in the hall and went to the kitchen in search of a box of assorted candles I kept in the larder. I started to light them, one by one, fixing them on plates and in tumblers and glasses. Cristina watched me from the door.

"It will take only a minute," I assured her. "I have a lot of practice."

I began to distribute the candles around the rooms, along the corridor, and in various corners, until the whole house was enveloped in a flickering twilight of pale gold.

"It looks like a cathedral," Cristina said.

I took her to one of the rooms that I didn't use but kept clean and tidy because of the few times Vidal, too drunk to return to his mansion, had stayed the night.

"I'll bring you some clean towels. If you don't have anything to change into I can offer you a wide selection of dreadful Belle Epoque clothes the former owners left in the wardrobes."

My clumsy attempt at humor barely drew a smile from her and she simply nodded. I left her sitting on the bed while I rushed off to fetch the towels. When I returned she was still sitting there, motionless. I left the towels next to her on the bed and brought over a couple of candles that I'd placed by the door, to give her a bit more light.

"Thanks," she murmured.

"While you change, I'll go prepare some hot soup for you."

"I'm not hungry."

"It will do you good, all the same. If you need anything, let me know."

I left her alone and went off to my room to remove my sodden shoes. I put water on to boil and sat waiting in the gallery. The rain was still crashing down, angrily machine-gunning the large windows; it poured through the gutters up in the tower and funneled along the flat roof, sounding like footsteps on the ceiling. Farther out, the Ribera quarter was plunged into almost total darkness.

After a while the door of Cristina's room opened and I heard her approaching. She was wearing a white dressing gown and had thrown an ugly woolen shawl over her shoulders.

"I've borrowed this from one of the wardrobes," she said. "I hope you don't mind."

"You can keep it if you like."

She sat in one of the armchairs and glanced round the room, stopping to look at a pile of paper on the table. She looked at me and I nodded.

"I finished it a few days ago," I said.

"And yours?"

I thought of both manuscripts as mine, but I just nodded again.

"May I?" she asked, taking a page and bringing it nearer the candlelight.

"Of course."

I watched her read, a thin smile on her lips.

"Pedro will never believe he's written this," she said.

"Trust me," I replied.

Cristina put the sheet back on the pile and looked at me for a long time.

"I've missed you," she said. "I didn't want to, but I have."

"Me too."

"Some days, before going to the sanatorium, I'd walk to the station and sit on the platform to wait for the train coming from Barcelona, hoping you might be on it."

I swallowed hard.

"I thought you didn't want to see me," I said.

"That's what I thought, too. My father often asked after you, you know? He asked me to look after you."

"Your father was a good man," I said. "A good friend."

Cristina nodded and smiled, but I could see that her eyes were filling with tears.

"In the end he couldn't remember anything. There were days when he confused me with my mother and would ask me to forgive him for the years he spent in prison. Then weeks would go by when he hardly seemed to notice I was there. Over time, loneliness gets inside you and doesn't go away."

"I'm sorry, Cristina."

"In the last few days I thought he was better. He was beginning to remember things. I had brought with me one of his albums and I started to show him the photographs again, pointing out who was who. There is one very old picture, taken at Villa Helius, in which you and he are both sitting in the motorcar. You're at the steering wheel and my father is teaching you how to drive. You're both laughing. Do you want to see it?"

I hesitated but didn't dare break that moment.

"Of course."

Cristina went to look for the album in her suitcase and returned with a small book bound in leather. She sat next to me and started turning pages that were filled with old snapshots, cuttings, and postcards. Manuel, like my father, had barely learned to read and write and his memories were made up mostly of images.

"Look, here you are."

I looked at the photograph and vividly recalled the summer day when Manuel had let me climb into the first car Vidal ever bought and had taught me the basics of driving. Then we had taken the car out along Calle Panamá and, doing about five kilometers per hour—a dizzying speed to me at the time—had driven as far as Avenida Pearson, returning with me at the wheel.

"You're an ace driver!" Manuel had concluded. "If you're ever stuck with your stories, you could consider a future in racing."

I smiled, remembering that moment which I thought I had lost. Cristina handed me the album.

"Keep it. My father would have liked you to have it."

"It's yours, Cristina. I can't accept it."

"I would rather you kept it."

"It's in storage then, until you want to come and collect it."

I turned the pages, revisiting faces I remembered and gazing at others I had never seen. There was the wedding photograph of Manuel Sagnier and his wife, Marta, whom Cristina resembled a great deal, studio portraits of her uncles and grandparents, a picture of a street in the Raval quarter with a procession going by, another of the San Sebastián bathing area on La Barceloneta beach. Manuel had collected old postcards of Barcelona and newspaper cuttings with photos of a very young Vidal—one of him posing by the doors of the Hotel Florida at the top of Mount Tibidabo and another where he stood arm in arm with a staggering beauty in the halls of La Rabasada casino.

"Your father worshipped Don Pedro."

"He always said we owed everything to him," Cristina answered.

I continued to travel through poor Manuel's memories until I came to a page with a photograph that didn't seem to fit in with the rest. It was a picture of a girl of about eight or nine, walking along a small wooden jetty that stretched out into a sheet of luminous sea. She was holding the hand of an adult, a man dressed in a white suit who was partly cut off by the frame. At the end of the jetty you could make out a small sailboat and an endless horizon on which the sun was setting. The girl, who was standing with her back to the camera, was Cristina.

"This is my favorite," said Cristina.

"Where was it taken?"

"I don't know. I don't remember that place or that day. I'm not even sure whether that man is my father. It's as if the moment never existed. I found the picture years ago in my father's album and I've never known what it means. It seems to be trying to say something to me."

I went on turning the pages while Cristina told me who each person was.

"Look, this is me when I was fourteen."

"I know."

Cristina looked at me sadly.

"I didn't realize, did I?"

I shrugged my shoulders.

"You'll never be able to forgive me."

I preferred to go on turning the pages rather than look into her eyes.

"There's nothing to forgive."

"Look at me, David."

I closed the album and did as she asked.

"It's a lie," she said. "I did realize. I realized every day, but I thought I had no right."

"Why?"

"Because our lives don't belong to us. Not mine, not my father's, not yours . . ."

"Everything belongs to Vidal," I said bitterly.

Slowly, she took my hand and brought it to her lips.

"Not today," she murmured.

I knew I was going to lose her as soon as the night was over and the pain and loneliness that were gnawing at her went away. I knew she was right, not because what she had said was true but because, deep down, we both believed it and it would always be the same. We hid like two thieves in one of the rooms without daring to light a single candle, without even daring to speak. I undressed her slowly, going over her skin with my lips, conscious that I would never do so again. Cristina gave herself with anger and abandon, and when we were overcome by exhaustion she fell asleep in my arms without feeling the need to say anything. I fought off sleep, enjoying the warmth of her body and thinking that if the following day death should come to take me away, I would go in peace. I caressed Cristina in the dark, listening to the storm outside as it left the city, knowing that I was going to lose her but also knowing that, for a few minutes, we had belonged to each other and to nobody else.

When the first light of dawn touched the windows I opened my eyes and found the bed empty. I went out into the corridor and as far as the gallery. Cristina had left the album and had taken Vidal's novel. I went through the whole house, which already smelled of her absence, and one by one blew out the candles I had lit the night before.

17

Nine weeks later I was standing in front of 17 Plaza de Cataluña, where the Catalonia bookshop had opened its doors two years earlier. I was staring in amazement at what seemed to be an endless display of copies of a novel called *The House of Ashes,* by Pedro Vidal. I smiled to myself. My mentor had even used the title I had suggested to him years before, when I had given him the idea for the story. I decided to go in and ask for a copy. I opened it at random and began to reread passages I knew by heart, for I had finished going over them only a couple of months earlier. I didn't find a single word in the whole book that I hadn't put there myself, except for the dedication: "For Cristina Sagnier, without whom . . ."

When I handed the book back to the shop assistant he told me not to think twice about buying it.

"We received it two days ago and I've already read it," he added. "A great novel. Take my advice and buy it now. I know the papers are praising it to the skies and that's usually a bad sign, but in this case it's the exception that proves the rule. If you don't like it, bring it to me and I'll give you your money back."

"Thanks," I replied. Knowing what I knew, his recommendation was flattering. "But I've read it too."

"May I interest you in something else?"

"You don't have a novel called *The Steps of Heaven?*"

The bookseller thought for a moment.

"That's the one by Martín, isn't it? I heard a rumor he also wrote *City*—"

I nodded.

"I've asked for it, but the publishers haven't sent me any copies. Let me have a good look."

I followed him to the counter, where he consulted with one of his colleagues, who shook his head.

"It was meant to arrive yesterday, but the publisher says he has no copies. I'm sorry. If you like, I'll reserve one for you when we get them."

"Don't worry. I'll come back another day. And thank you very much."

"I'm sorry, sir. I don't know what can have happened. As I say, I should have had it . . ."

I left the bookshop and went to a newspaper stand at the top of the Ramblas, where I bought a copy of every newspaper, from *La Vanguardia* to *The Voice of Industry.* I sat down in the Canaletas Café and began delving into their pages. Each paper carried a review of the novel I had written for Vidal, full page, with large headlines and a portrait of Don Pedro looking meditative and mysterious, wearing a new suit and puffing on a pipe with studied disdain. I began to read the headlines and then the first and last paragraphs of the reviews.

The first one I read opened with these words: *"The House of Ashes* is a mature, rich work of great quality that takes its place among the best examples of contemporary literature." Another paper informed the reader that "nobody in Spain writes better than Pedro Vidal, our most respected and noteworthy novelist," and a third asserted that this was a "superlative novel, of masterful craftsmanship and exquisite quality." A fourth newspaper summed up the great international success of Vidal and his work: "Europe bows to the master" (although the novel had come out in Spain only two days earlier and, were it to be translated, wouldn't appear in any other country for at least a year). The piece went into a long-winded ramble about the great international acclaim and huge respect that Vidal's name aroused among "the most famous international experts," even though, as far as I knew, none of his other books had been translated into any other language, except for a novel whose translation into French he himself had underwritten and that sold only 126 copies. Miracles aside, the consensus of the press was that "a classic has been born" and that the novel marked "the return of one of the greats, the best pen of our times: Vidal, undisputed master."

On the opposite page in some of those papers, covering a far more modest space of one or two columns, I also found a few reviews of a novel by someone called David Martín. The most favorable began like this: "A first novel written in a pedestrian style, *The Steps of Heaven* by David Martín shows the author's lack of skill and talent from the very first page." The last review I could bring myself to read, published in *The Voice of Industry,* opened succinctly with a short introduction in boldface that stated: "David Martín, a completely unknown author and writer of classified advertisements, surprises us with what is perhaps this year's worst literary debut."

I left the newspapers and the coffee I had ordered on the table and made my way down the Ramblas to the offices of Barrido & Escobillas. On the way I passed four or five bookshops, all of which were adorned with countless copies of Vidal's novel. In none did I see a single copy of mine. My experience in the Catalonia bookshop was repeated in each place.

"I'm sorry, I don't know what can have happened. It was meant to arrive the day before yesterday, but the publisher says he's run out of stock and doesn't know when he'll be reprinting. If you'd care to leave me your name and a telephone number, I can let you know if it arrives . . . Have you asked in Catalonia? Well, if they don't have it . . ."

The two partners received me with grim, unfriendly expressions, Barrido, behind his desk, stroking a fountain pen and Escobillas, standing behind him, boring through me with his eyes. Lady Venom, who sat on a chair next to me, was licking her lips in anticipation.

"I can't tell you how sorry I am, my dear Martín," Barrido was explaining. "The problem is as follows. The booksellers place their orders based on the reviews that appear in the papers, don't ask me why. If you go into the warehouse next door you'll see that we have three thousand copies of your novel just lying there."

"With all the expense and the loss which that entails," Escobillas added in a clearly hostile tone.

"I stopped by the warehouse before coming here and I've seen for myself that there are three *hundred* copies. The manager told me that's all they printed."

"That's a lie," Escobillas proclaimed.

Barrido interrupted him in a conciliatory tone.

"Please excuse my partner, Martín. You must understand that we're just as indignant as you, even more so, about the disgraceful treatment the press has given a book with which all of us at the firm were so in love. But I beg you to understand that, despite our faith in your talent, our hands are tied because of all the confusion created by the malicious press. Don't be disheartened. Rome was not built in a day. We're doing everything in our power to give your work the promotion its estimable literary merit deserves—"

"With a three-hundred-copy print run."

Barrido sighed, hurt by my lack of trust.

"It's a five-hundred-copy print run," Escobillas specified. "The other two hundred were collected by Barceló and Sempere in person yesterday. The rest will go out with our next delivery; they couldn't go out with this one because there were too many new titles. If you bothered to understand our problems and weren't so selfish you would recognize this."

I looked at the three of them in disbelief.

"Don't tell me you're not going to do anything."

Barrido gave me a mournful look.

"And what would you have us do, my friend? We have bet everything on you. Try to help us a little."

"If only you'd written a book like the one your friend Vidal has written," said Escobillas.

"Now that was one hell of a novel," Barrido asserted. "Even *The Voice of Industry* says so."

"I knew this was going to happen," Escobillas went on. "You're so ungrateful."

Lady Venom, sitting by my side, was looking at me sadly. I thought she was going to take my hand to comfort me so I quickly moved it away. Barrido gave me one of his unctuous smiles.

"Maybe it's all for the best, Martín. Maybe it's a sign from our Lord, who in his infinite wisdom wants to show you the way back to the work that has given so much happiness to the readers of *City of the Damned.*"

I burst out laughing. Barrido joined in and, at a signal from him, so did Escobillas and Lady Venom. I watched the choir of hyenas and told myself that, under other circumstances, this would have seemed a moment of delicious irony.

"That's better. I like to see you handling this with a positive attitude," Barrido said. "What do you say? When will we have the next installment by Ignatius B. Samson?"

The three of them looked at me expectantly. I cleared my throat so I could speak clearly and smiled at them.

"You can go screw yourselves."

18

On leaving, I wandered aimlessly for hours round the streets of Barcelona. I was finding it difficult to breathe, as if something were pressing down on my chest. A cold sweat covered my forehead and hands. When evening fell, not knowing where else to hide, I started to make my way back home. As I passed Sempere & Sons, I saw the bookseller filling his shop window with copies of my novel. It was already late and the shop was closed, but the light was still on. I tried to rush past, but Sempere noticed me and smiled with a sadness that I had never seen on his face before. He went over to the door and opened it.

"Come in for a while, Martín."

"Some other day, Señor Sempere."

"Do it for me."

He took me by the arm and dragged me into the bookshop. I followed him to the back room and he offered me a chair. He poured two glasses of something that looked thicker than tar and motioned to me to down it in one. He did the same.

"I've been glancing through Vidal's book," he said.

"This season's success story," I said.

"Does he know you wrote it?"

"What does it matter?" I asked.

Sempere looked at me the same way he'd looked at that eight-year-old boy who had come to his house one distant day, with a bruised face and broken teeth.

"Are you all right, Martín?"

"I'm fine."

Sempere shook his head, muttering to himself, and got up to take something from one of the shelves. It was a copy of my novel. He handed it to me with a pen and smiled.

"Please sign it for me."

When I'd finished writing something for him, Sempere took the book from my hands and placed it carefully in the glass case behind the counter where he displayed first editions that were not for sale. It was his private shrine.

"You don't have to do that, Señor Sempere," I mumbled.

"I'm doing it because I want to and because the occasion demands it. This book is a piece of your heart, Martín. And it is also a piece of my heart, for the small part I played in it. I'll place you between *Le Père Goriot* and *L'Éducation Sentimentale.*"

"That's a sacrilege."

"Nonsense. It's one of the best books I've sold in the last ten years, and I've sold a lot," old Sempere said.

Sempere's kind words could only scratch the surface of the cold, impenetrable calm that was beginning to invade me. I ambled back to my house, in no hurry.

When I walked into the tower house I poured myself a glass of water. As I drank it in the kitchen, in the dark, I began laughing.

. . .

The following morning I received two courtesy calls. The first one was from Pep, Vidal's new chauffeur. He was bringing a message from his boss, summoning me to a lunch at La Maison Dorée—doubtless the celebratory lunch he had promised me some time ago. Pep seemed a little stiff and anxious to leave as soon as possible. The air of complicity he'd once had with me had evaporated. He wouldn't come in, preferring to wait on the landing. Without looking straight at me, he handed me Vidal's note, and as soon as I told him I would go he left without saying good-bye.

The second visit, half an hour later, brought my two publishers to my door, accompanied by a forbidding-looking gentleman with piercing eyes, who identified himself as a lawyer. The formidable trio arrived displaying a mixture of mourning and belligerence, leaving me in no doubt as to the purpose of the occasion. I invited them into the gallery, where they proceeded to sit down on the sofa, lined up from left to right in descending order of height.

"May I offer you anything? A small glass of cyanide?"

I was not expecting a smile and I didn't get one. After a brief preamble from Barrido concerning the terrible losses that the fiasco associated with the failure of *The Steps of Heaven* was going to cause the publishing house, the lawyer went on to give a brisk exposition that in plain language said that if I didn't return to my work in the guise of Ignatius B. Samson and hand in a manuscript for the *City of the Damned* series within a month and a half, they would proceed to sue me for breach of contract, damages, and five or six other legal terms that escaped me because by then I wasn't paying attention. It was not all bad news. Despite the aggravations caused by my behavior, Barrido and Escobillas had found a pearl of generosity in their hearts to smooth away our differences and establish a new alliance, a friendship, that would benefit both sides.

"If you want, you can buy all the copies of *The Steps of Heaven* that haven't been distributed at a special rate of 75 percent of the cover price, since there is clearly no demand for the title and it will be impossible for us to include it in our next delivery," Escobillas explained.

"Why don't you give me back my rights? After all, you didn't pay a penny for the book and you're not planning on trying to sell a single copy."

"We can't do that, dear friend," Barrido assured me. "Even if no advance was paid out to you personally, the edition has required a huge outlay and the agreement you signed with us was for twenty years, automatically renewable under the same terms if our firm decides to exercise its rights. You have to understand that we are also entitled to something. The author can't get everything."

When he had finished his speech I invited the gentlemen to make their way to the exit, either willingly or with the help of a kick—they could choose. Before I slammed the door in their faces, Escobillas was good enough to cast me one of his evil-eyed looks.

"We demand a reply within a week or that will be the end of you," he muttered.

"In a week you and that idiot partner of yours will be dead," I replied calmly, without quite knowing why I'd uttered those words.

I spent the rest of the morning staring at the walls, until the bells of Santa María reminded me that it would soon be time for my meeting with Pedro Vidal.

He was waiting for me at the best table in the room, toying with a glass of white wine and listening to the pianist who was playing a piece by Granados with velvet fingers. When he saw me, he stood up and held out his hand.

"Congratulations," I said.

Vidal smiled, waiting for me to sit down before sitting down himself. We let a minute of silence go by, cocooned by the music and the glances of the distinguished people who greeted Vidal from afar or came up to the table to congratulate him on his success, which was the talk of the town.

"David, you can't imagine how sorry I am about what has happened," he began.

"Don't be sorry, enjoy it."

"Do you think this means anything to me? The flattery of a few poor devils? My greatest joy would have been to see you succeed."

"I'm sorry I've let you down once again, Don Pedro."

Vidal sighed.

"David, it's not my fault if they've gone after you. It's your fault. You were crying out for it. You're quite old enough to know how these things work."

"You tell me."

Vidal clicked his tongue, as if my naïveté offended him.

"What did you expect? You're not one of them. You never will be. You haven't wanted to be, and you think they're going to forgive you. You lock yourself up in that great rambling house and you think you can survive without joining the church choir and putting on the uniform. Well you're wrong, David. You've always been wrong. This isn't how you play the game. If you want to play alone, pack your bags and go somewhere where you can be in charge of your own destiny, if such a place exists. But if you stay here, you'd better join some parish or other—any one will do. It's that simple."

"Is that what you do, Don Pedro? Join the parish?"

"I don't have to, David. I feed them. That's another thing you've never understood."

"You'd be surprised how quickly I'm learning. But don't worry, the reviews are the least of it. For better or worse, tomorrow nobody will remember them, neither mine nor yours."

"What's the problem, then?"

"It doesn't matter."

"Is it those two sons of bitches? Barrido and the grave robber?"

"Forget it, Don Pedro. As you say, it's my fault. Nobody else's."

The head waiter came over to the table with an inquiring expression. I hadn't looked at the menu and wasn't going to.

"The usual, for both of us," Vidal told him.

The head waiter left with a bow. Vidal was observing me as if I were a dangerous animal locked in a cage.

"Cristina was unable to come," he said. "I brought this, so you could sign it for her."

He put on the table a copy of *The Steps of Heaven* wrapped in purple paper with the Sempere & Sons stamp on it and pushed it toward me. I made no move to pick it up. Vidal had gone pale. After his forceful remarks and his defensive tone, his manner seemed to have changed. Here comes the final thrust, I thought.

"Tell me once and for all whatever it is you want to say, Don Pedro. I won't bite."

Vidal downed his wine in one gulp.

"There are two things I've been wanting to tell you. You're not going to like them."

"I'm beginning to get used to that."

"One is to do with your father."

The bitter smile left my lips.

"I've wanted to tell you for years, but I thought it wouldn't do you any good. You're going to think I didn't tell you out of cowardice, but I swear, I swear on anything you hold sacred, that—"

"That what?" I cut in.

Vidal sighed.

"The night your father died—"

"The night he was murdered," I corrected him icily.

"It was a mistake. Your father's death was a mistake."

I looked at him, confused.

"Those men were not out to get him. They made a mistake."

I recalled the look in the three gunmen's eyes, in the fog the smell of gunpowder and the sight of my father's dark blood pouring through my hands.

"The person they wanted to kill was me," said Vidal almost inaudibly. "An old partner of my father's discovered that his wife and I . . ."

I closed my eyes and listened to the morbid laughter rising up inside me. My father had been riddled with bullets because of one of the great Pedro Vidal's bits of skirt.

"Please say something," Vidal pleaded.

I opened my eyes.

"What is the second thing you were going to tell me?"

I'd never seen Vidal look so frightened. It suited him.

"I've asked Cristina to marry me."

A long silence.

"She said yes."

Vidal looked down. One of the waiters came over with the starters. He left them on the table wishing us a *bon appétit*. Vidal did not dare look at me again. The starters were getting cold. After a while I took the copy of *The Steps of Heaven* and left.

. . .

That afternoon, after leaving La Maison Dorée, I found myself making my way down the Ramblas, carrying the copy of *The Steps of Heaven*. As I drew closer to the corner of Calle del Carmen my hands began to shake. I stopped by the window of the Bagués jewelry shop, pretending to be looking at some gold lockets in the shape of fairies and flowers, dotted with rubies. The ornate façade of El Indio was just a few meters away; anyone would have thought it was a grand bazaar full of wonders and extraordinary objects, not just a shop selling fabrics and linen. I approached the store slowly and stepped into the entrance hall that led to the main door. I knew that she wouldn't recognize me, that I might not recognize her, but even so I stood there for about five minutes before daring to go in. When I did, my heart was beating hard and my hands were sweating.

The walls were lined with shelves full of large fabric rolls of all types. Shop assistants armed with tape measures and special scissors tied to their belts spread the beautiful textiles on the tables and displayed them as if they were precious jewels to well-bred ladies who were there with their maids and seamstresses.

"Can I help you, sir?"

The words came from a heavily built man with a high-pitched voice, dressed in a flannel suit that looked as if it was about to burst at the seams and fill the shop with floating shreds of cloth. He observed me with a condescending air and a smile midway between forced and hostile.

"No," I mumbled.

Then I saw her. My mother was coming down a stepladder holding a handful of remnants. She wore a white blouse and I recognized her instantly. Her figure had grown a little fuller and her face, less well chiseled than it used to be, had that slightly defeated expression that comes with routine and disappointment. The shop assistant was annoyed and kept talking to me, but I hardly heard his voice. I only saw her drawing closer, then walking past me. She looked at me for a second, and when she saw that I was watching her, she smiled meekly, the way one smiles at a customer or at one's boss, and then continued with her work. I had such a lump in my throat that I almost wasn't able to open my mouth to silence the shop assistant and I hurried off toward the exit, my eyes full of tears. Once I was outside I crossed the street and went into a café. I sat at a table by the window from which I could see the door of El Indio, and I waited.

Almost an hour and a half had gone by when I saw the shop assistant who had tried to serve me come out and lower the entrance shutter. Soon afterwards the lights started to go out and some of the staff emerged. I got up and went outside. A boy of about ten was sitting by the entrance to the next-door building, looking at me. I beckoned him to come closer and when he did, I showed him a coin. He gave me a huge smile—I noticed he was missing a number of teeth.

"See this packet? I want you to give it to a lady who is about to come out right now. Tell her that a gentleman asked you to give it to her, but don't tell her it was me. Understood?"

The boy nodded. I gave him the coin and the book.

"Now we'll wait."

We didn't have to wait long. Three minutes later I saw her coming out. She was heading for the Ramblas.

"It's that lady, see?"

My mother stopped for a moment by the portico of the Church of Belén and I made a sign to the boy, who ran after her. I watched the scene from afar, but could not hear her words. The boy handed her the packet and she gave it a puzzled look, not sure whether to accept it or not. The boy insisted and finally she took the parcel in her hands and watched the boy run away. Disconcerted, she turned right and left, searching with her eyes. She weighed the packet, examining the purple wrapping paper. Finally curiosity got the better of her and she opened it.

I watched her take the book out. She held it with both hands, looking at the cover, then turning it over to examine the back. I could hardly breathe and wanted to go up to her and say something but couldn't. I stood there, only a few meters away from my mother, spying on her without her being aware of my presence, until she set off again, clutching the book, walking toward Colón. As she passed the Palace of La Virreina she went up to a waste bin and threw the book in it. I watched as she headed down the Ramblas until she was lost among the crowd, as if she had never been there at all.

19

Sempere was alone in the bookshop gluing down the spine of a copy of *Fortunata and Jacinta* that was coming apart. When he looked up, he saw me on the other side of the door. In just a few seconds he realized the state I was in and signaled to me to come in. As soon as I was inside, he offered me a chair.

"You don't look well, Martín. You should see a doctor. If you're scared, I'll come with you. Physicians make my flesh crawl too, with their white gowns and those sharp things in their hands, but sometimes you've got to go through with it."

"It's just a headache, Señor Sempere. It's already getting better."

Sempere poured me a glass of Vichy water.

"Here. This cures everything except stupidity, which is an epidemic on the rise."

I smiled weakly at Sempere's joke, then drank the water and sighed. I felt a wave of nausea and an intense pressure throbbed behind my left eye. For a moment I thought I was going to collapse and I closed my eyes. I took a deep breath, praying I wouldn't drop dead right there. Destiny couldn't have such a perverse sense of humor as to guide me to Sempere's bookshop so I that could present him with a corpse, after all he'd done for me. I felt a hand holding my head gently. Sempere. I opened my eyes and saw the bookseller and his son, who had popped in, watching me as if they were at a wake.

"Shall I call the doctor?" Sempere's son asked.

"I'm better, thanks. Much better."

"Your way of getting better makes one's hair stand on end. You look gray."

"A bit more water?"

Sempere's son rushed to fill me another glass.

"Forgive me for this performance," I said. "I can assure you I hadn't rehearsed it."

"Don't talk nonsense!"

"It might do you good to eat something sweet. Maybe it was a drop in your sugar levels . . ." the son suggested.

"Run over to the baker's on the corner and get him something," the bookseller agreed.

When we were alone, Sempere fixed his eyes on mine.

"I promise I'll go to the doctor," I said.

A few minutes later the bookseller's son returned with a paper bag full of the most select assortment of buns in the area. He handed it to me and I chose a brioche that any other time would have seemed to me as tempting as a chorus girl's backside.

"Bite," Sempere ordered.

I ate my brioche obediently, and slowly I began to feel better.

"He seems to be reviving," Sempere's son observed.

"What the corner shop buns can't cure . . ."

At that moment we heard the doorbell. A customer had come into the bookshop, and at Sempere's nod his son left us to serve him. The bookseller stayed by my side, trying to feel my pulse by pressing on my wrist with his index finger.

"Señor Sempere, do you remember many years ago when you said that if one day I needed to save a book, really save it, I should come to see you?"

Sempere glanced at the rejected book I had rescued from the bin, which I was still holding in my hands.

"Give me five minutes."

. . .

It was beginning to get dark when we walked down the Ramblas among a crowd who had come out for a stroll on a hot, humid evening. There was only the hint of a breeze; balconies and windows were wide open, with people leaning out of them, watching the human parade under an amber-colored sky. Sempere walked quickly and didn't slow down until we sighted an arcade of shadows at the entrance to Calle Arco del Teatro. Before crossing over he looked at me solemnly and said:

"Martín, you mustn't tell anyone what you're about to see. Not even Vidal. No one."

I nodded, intrigued by the bookseller's air of seriousness and secrecy. I followed him through the narrow street, barely a gap between bleak and dilapidated buildings that seemed to bend over like willows of stone, attempting to close the strip of sky between the rooftops. Soon we reached a large wooden door that looked as if it might be guarding the entrance to an old basilica that had spent a century at the bottom of a lake. Sempere went up the steps to the door and took hold of the brass knocker shaped like a smiling demon's face. He knocked three times, then came down the steps again to wait by my side.

"You can't tell anyone what you're about to see."

"No one. Not even Vidal. No one."

Sempere nodded severely. We waited for about two minutes until we heard what sounded like a hundred bolts being unlocked simultaneously. With a deep groan, the large door opened halfway and a middle-aged man with thick gray hair, a face like a vulture, and penetrating eyes stuck his head round it.

"We were doing just fine and now here's Sempere!" he snapped. "What are you bringing me today? Another aficionado who hasn't got himself a girlfriend because he'd rather live with his mother?"

Sempere paid no attention to this sarcastic greeting.

"Martín, this is Isaac Monfort, the keeper of this place. His friendliness has no equal. Do everything he says. Isaac, this is David Martín, a good friend, a writer, and a trustworthy person."

The man called Isaac looked me up and down without much enthusiasm and then exchanged a glance with Sempere.

"A writer is never trustworthy. Let's see, has Sempere explained the rules to you?"

"Only that I can never tell anyone what I will see here."

"That is the first and most important rule. If you don't observe it, I personally will wring your neck. Do you get the idea?"

"One hundred percent."

"Come on, then," said Isaac, motioning me to come in.

"I'll say good-bye now, Martín. You'll find a safe place here."

I realized that Sempere was referring to the book, not to me. He hugged me and disappeared into the night. I stepped inside and Isaac pulled a lever on the back of the door. A thousand mechanisms, knotted together in a web of rails and pulleys, sealed it up. Isaac took a lamp from the floor and raised it to my face.

"You don't look well," he pronounced.

"Indigestion," I replied.

"From what?"

"Reality."

"Join the queue."

We walked down a long corridor and on either side, through the shadows, I thought I could make out frescoes and marble staircases. We advanced farther into the palatial building and shortly there appeared in front of us what looked like the entrance to a large hall.

"What have you got there?" Isaac asked.

"The Steps of Heaven. A novel."

"What a preposterous title. Don't tell me you're the author."

"Who, me?"

Isaac sighed, shaking his head and mumbling to himself.

"And what else have you written?"

"City of the Damned, volumes one to twenty-seven, among other things."

Isaac turned round and smiled with satisfaction.

"Ignatius B. Samson?"

"May he rest in peace, and at your service."

At that point, the mysterious keeper stopped and left the lamp resting on what looked like a balustrade rising in front of a large vault. I looked up and was spellbound. There before me stood a colossal labyrinth of bridges, passages, and shelves full of hundreds of thousands of books, forming a gigantic library of seemingly impossible perspectives. Tunnels zigzagged through the immense structure, which seemed to rise in a spiral toward a large glass dome, curtains of light and darkness filtering through it. Here and there I could see isolated figures walking along footbridges and up stairs or carefully examining the contents of the passageways of that cathedral of books and words. I couldn't believe my eyes and I looked at Isaac Monfort in astonishment. He was smiling like an old fox enjoying his favorite game.

"Ignatius B. Samson, welcome to the Cemetery of Forgotten Books."

20

I followed the keeper to the foot of the large nave that housed the labyrinth. The floor we were stepping over was sown with tombstones, their inscriptions, crosses, and faces dissolving into the stone. The keeper stopped and lowered the gas lamp so that the light slid over some of the pieces of the macabre puzzle.

"The remains of an old necropolis," he explained. "But don't let that give you any ideas about dropping dead here."

We continued toward an area just before the central structure that seemed to form a kind of threshold. In the meantime Isaac was rattling off the rules and duties, fixing his gaze on me from time to time, while I tried to soothe him with docile assent.

"Article one: the first time somebody comes here he has the right to choose a book, whichever one he likes, from all the books there are in this place. Article two: upon adopting a book you undertake to protect it and do all you can to ensure it is never lost. For life. Any questions so far?"

I looked up toward the immensity of the labyrinth.

"How does one choose a single book among so many?"

Isaac shrugged.

"Some like to believe it's the book that chooses the person. Destiny, in other words. What you see here is the sum of centuries of books that have been lost and forgotten, books condemned to be destroyed and silenced forever, books that preserve the memory and soul of times and marvels that no one remembers anymore. None of us, not even the oldest, knows exactly when it was created or by whom. It's probably as old as the city itself and has been growing with it, in its shadow. We know the building was erected using the ruins of palaces, churches, prisons, and hospitals that may once have stood here. The origin of the main structure goes back to the beginning of the eighteenth century and has not stopped evolving since then. Before that, the Cemetery of Forgotten Books was hidden under the tunnels of the medieval town. Some say that during the Inquisition people who were learned and had free minds would hide forbidden books in sarcophagi or bury them in ossuaries all over the city to protect them, trusting that future generations would dig them up. In the middle of the last century a long tunnel was discovered leading from the bowels of the labyrinth to the basement of an old library that nowadays is sealed off, hidden in the ruins of an old synagogue in the Jewish quarter. When the last of the old city walls came down, there was a landslide and the tunnel was flooded with water from an underground stream that for centuries has run beneath what is now the Ramblas. It's inaccessible at present, but we imagine that for a long time the tunnel was one of the main entrance routes to this place. Most of the structure you can see was developed during the nineteenth century. Only about a hundred people know about it and I hope Sempere hasn't made a mistake by including you among them . . ."

I shook my head vigorously, but Isaac was looking at me with skepticism.

"Article three: you can bury your own book wherever you like."

"What if I get lost?"

"An additional clause, from my own stable: try not to get lost."

"Has anyone ever got lost?"

Isaac snorted.

"When I started here years ago there was a story doing the rounds about Darío Alberti de Cymerman. I don't suppose Sempere has told you this, of course."

"Cymerman? The historian?"

"No, the seal tamer. How many Darío Alberti de Cymermans do you know? What happened is that in the winter of 1889 Cymerman went into the labyrinth and disappeared for a whole week. He was found in one of the tunnels, half dead with fright. He had walled himself up behind a few rows of holy texts so he couldn't be seen."

"Seen by whom?"

Isaac looked at me for a long while.

"By the man in black. Are you sure Sempere hasn't told you anything about this?"

"I'm sure he hasn't."

Isaac lowered his voice, adopting a conspiratorial tone.

"Over the years, some members have occasionally seen the man in black in the tunnels of the labyrinth. They all describe him differently. Some even swear they have spoken to him. There was a time when it was rumored that the man in black was the ghost of a cursed author whom one of the members had betrayed after taking one of his books from here and not keeping the promise to protect it. The book was lost forever and the deceased author wanders eternally along the passages, seeking revenge—well, you know, the sort of Henry James touch people like so much."

"You're not saying you believe the rumors."

"Of course not. I have another theory. The Cymerman theory."

"Which is . . . ?"

"That the man in black is the master of this place, the father of all secret and forbidden knowledge, of wisdom and memory, the bringer of light to storytellers and writers since time immemorial. He is our guardian angel, the angel of lies and of the night."

"You're pulling my leg."

"Every labyrinth has its Minotaur," Isaac suggested. He smiled mysteriously and pointed toward the entrance to the stacks.

"It's all yours."

I set off along a footbridge then slowly entered a long corridor of books that formed a rising curve. When I reached the end of the curve the tunnel divided into four passages radiating out from a small circle from which a spiral staircase rose, vanishing upwards into the heights. I climbed the steps until I reached a landing that led into three different tunnels. I chose one of them, the one I thought would lead to the heart of the building, and entered. As I walked, I ran my fingers along the spines of hundreds of books. I let myself be imbued with the smell, with the light that filtered through the cracks or from the glass lanterns embedded in the wooden structure, floating among mirrors and shadows. I wandered aimlessly for almost half an hour until I reached a sort of closed chamber with a table and chair. The walls were made of books and seemed quite solid except for a small gap that looked as if someone had removed a book from it. I decided that this would be the new home for *The Steps of Heaven.* I looked at the cover for the last time and reread the first paragraph, imagining the moment when, many years after I was dead and forgotten, someone, if fortune would have it, would go down that same route and reach that room to find an unknown book into which I had poured everything I had. I placed it there, feeling that I was the one being left on the shelf. It was then that I felt the presence behind me and turned to find the man in black, his eyes fixed steadily on mine.

21

At first I didn't recognize my own eyes in the mirror, one of the many that formed a chain of muted light along the corridors of the labyrinth. What I saw in the reflection was my face and my skin, but the eyes were those of a stranger. Murky, dark, and full of malice. I looked away and felt the nausea returning. I sat on the chair by the table, imagining that even Dr. Trías might be amused at the thought that the tenant lodged in my brain—the tumorous growth, as he liked to call it—had decided to deal me the final blow in that place, thereby granting me the honor of being the first permanent citizen of the Cemetery of Forgotten Books buried in the company of his last and most ill-fated work, the one that had taken him to the grave. Someone would find me there in ten months, or ten years, or perhaps never. A grand finale worthy of *City of the Damned.*

I think I was saved by my bitter laughter. It cleared my head and reminded me of where I was and what I'd come to do. I was about to stand up again when I saw it. It was a rough-looking volume, dark, with no visible title on the spine. It lay on top of a pile of four other books at the end of the table. I picked it up. The covers were bound in what looked like leather, some sort of tanned hide darkened as a result of much handling rather than by dye. The title, which seemed to have been branded onto the cover, was blurred, but on the fourth page it could be clearly read:

Lux Aeterna
D.M.

I imagined that the initials, the same as mine, were those of the author, but there was no other indication in the book to confirm this. I turned a few pages quickly and recognized at least five different languages alternating through the text—Spanish, German, Latin, French, and Hebrew. Reading a paragraph at random, I was reminded of a prayer in the traditional liturgy that I couldn't quite remember. I wondered whether the notebook was perhaps some sort of missal or prayer book. The text was punctuated with numerals and verses, with the first words underlined, as if to indicate episodes or thematic divisions. The more I examined it, the more I realized it reminded me of the Gospels and catechisms of my school days.

I could have left, chosen any other tome from among the hundreds of thousands, and abandoned that place, never to return. I almost thought I had done just that, as I walked back through the tunnels and corridors of the labyrinth, until I became aware of the book in my hands, like a parasite stuck to my skin. For a split second the idea crossed my mind that the book had a greater desire to leave the place than I did, that it was somehow guiding my steps. After a few detours, in the course of which I passed the same copy of the fourth volume of LeFanu's complete works a couple of times, I found myself, without knowing how, by the spiral staircase, and from there I succeeded in locating the way out of the labyrinth. I had imagined Isaac would be waiting for me by the entrance, but there was no sign of him, although I was certain that somebody was observing me from the shadows. The large vault of the Cemetery of Forgotten Books was engulfed in silence.

"Isaac?" I called out.

My voice trailed off into the shadows. I waited in vain for a few seconds and then made my way toward the exit. The blue mist that filtered down from the dome began to fade until the darkness around me was almost absolute. A few steps farther on I made out a light flickering at the end of the gallery and realized that the keeper had left his lamp at the foot of the door. I turned to scan the dark gallery one last time, then pulled the handle that kick-started the mechanism of rails and pulleys. One by one, the bolts were released and the door yielded a few centimeters. I pushed it just enough to get through and stepped outside. A few seconds later the door began to close again, sealing itself with a sonorous echo.

22

As I walked away from that place I felt its magic leaving me and the nausea and pain took over once more. Twice I fell flat on my face, first in the Ramblas and the second time when I was trying to cross Vía Layetana, where a boy lifted me up and saved me from being run over by a tram. It was with great difficulty that I managed to reach my front door. The house had been closed all day and the heat—that humid, poisonous heat that seemed to suffocate the town a little more every day—floated on the air like dusty light. I went up to the study in the tower and opened the windows wide. Only the faintest of breezes blew and the sky was bruised by black clouds that moved in slow circles over Barcelona. I left the book on my desk and told myself there would be time enough to examine it in detail. Or perhaps not. Perhaps time was already coming to an end for me. It didn't seem to matter much anymore.

At that point I could barely stand and needed to lie down in the dark. I salvaged one of the bottles of codeine pills from the drawer and swallowed two or three. I kept the bottle in my pocket and made my way down the stairs, not quite sure whether I would be able to get to my room in one piece. When I reached the corridor I thought I noticed a flickering along the line of light coming from beneath the main door. I walked slowly to the entrance, leaning on the walls.

"Who's there?" I asked.

There was no reply, no sound at all. I hesitated for a moment, then opened the door and stepped out onto the landing. I leaned over to look down the stairs that descended in a spiral, merging into darkness. There was nobody there. When I turned back to face the door I noticed that the small lamp on the landing was blinking. I went back into the house and turned the key to lock the door, something I often forgot to do. Then I saw it. A cream-colored envelope with a serrated edge. Someone had slipped it under the door. I knelt down to pick it up. The paper was thick, porous. The envelope was sealed and had my name on it. The emblem on the wax was in the shape of the angel with its wings outspread.

I opened it.

> *Dear Señor Martín,*
>
> *I'm going to spend some time in the city and it would give me great pleasure to meet up with you and perhaps take the opportunity to revisit the subject of my proposal. I'd be very grateful if, unless you're otherwise engaged, you would care to join me for dinner this coming Friday the 13th at 10 o'clock, in a small villa I have rented for my stay in Barcelona. The house is on the corner of Calle Olot and Calle San José de la Montaña, next to the entrance to Güell Park. I trust and hope that you will be able to come.*
>
> *Your friend,*
> ANDREAS CORELLI

I let the note fall to the floor and dragged myself to the gallery. There I lay on the sofa, sheltering in the half-light. There were seven days to go before that meeting. I smiled to myself. I didn't think I was going to live seven more days. I closed my eyes and tried to sleep. The constant ringing in my ears seemed more deafening than ever and stabs of white light lit up my mind with every beat of my heart.

You won't even be able to think about writing.

I opened my eyes again and scanned the bluish shadow that veiled the gallery. Next to me, on the table, lay the old photograph album that

Cristina had left behind. I hadn't found the courage to throw it away, or even touch it. I reached for the album and opened it, turning the pages until I found the image I was looking for. I pulled it off the paper and examined it. Cristina, as a child, walking hand in hand with a stranger along the jetty that stretched out into the sea. I pressed the photograph to my chest and let exhaustion overcome me. Slowly, the bitterness and the anger of that day, of those years, faded and a warm darkness wrapped itself around me, full of voices and hands that were waiting for me. I had an overwhelming desire to surrender to it, but something held me back and a spear of light and pain wrenched me from that pleasant sleep that promised to have no end.

Not yet, the voice whispered, *not yet.*

. . .

I sensed the days were passing because there were times when I awoke and thought I could see sunlight coming through the slats of the shutters. Once or twice I was sure I heard someone knocking on the door and voices calling my name, but after a while they stopped. Hours or days later I got up and put my hands to my face and found blood on my lips. I don't know whether I went outside or whether I dreamed that I did, but without knowing how I had got there I found myself making my way up Paseo del Borne, toward the basilica of Santa María del Mar. The streets were deserted beneath a mercury moon. I looked up and thought I saw the ghost of a huge black storm spreading its wings over the city. A gust of white light split the skies and a mantle woven with raindrops cascaded down like a shower of glass daggers. A moment before the first drop touched the ground, time came to a standstill and hundreds of thousands of tears of light were suspended in the air like specks of dust. I knew that someone or something was walking behind me and could feel its breath on the nape of my neck, cold and filled with the stench of rotting flesh and fire. I could feel its fingers, long and pointed, hovering over my skin, and at that moment the young girl who lived only in the picture I held against my chest seemed to approach through the curtain of rain. She took me by the hand and pulled me, leading me back to the tower house, away from that icy presence that had crept along behind me. When I recovered consciousness, the seven days had passed.

Day was breaking on Friday, 13 July.

23

Pedro Vidal and Cristina Sagnier were married that afternoon. The ceremony took place at five o'clock in the chapel of the monastery of Pedralbes, attended by only a small section of the Vidal clan; the most select members of the family, including the father of the groom, were ominously absent. Had there been any gossip, people would have said that the youngest son's idea of marrying the chauffeur's daughter had fallen on the hosts of the dynasty like a jug of cold water. But there was none. Thanks to a discreet pact of silence, the chroniclers of society had better things to do that afternoon and not a single publication mentioned the ceremony. There was nobody there to relate how a bevy of Vidal's ex-lovers had clustered together by the church door, crying in silence like a sisterhood of faded widows still clinging to their last hope. Nobody was there to describe how Cristina held a bunch of white roses in her hand and wore an ivory-colored dress that matched her skin, making it seem as if the bride were walking naked up to the altar, with no other adornment than the white veil covering her face and an amber sky that appeared to be retreating into an eddy of clouds above the tall bell tower.

There was nobody there to recall how she stepped out of the car and how, for an instant, she stopped to look up at the square opposite the church door, until her eyes found the dying man whose hands shook and who was muttering words nobody could hear, words he would take with him to the grave.

"Damn you. Damn you both."

. . .

Two hours later, sitting in the armchair of my study, I opened the case that had come to me years before and that contained the only thing I had left of my father. I pulled out the pistol that was wrapped in a cloth and opened the barrel. I inserted six bullets and closed the weapon. I placed the barrel against my temple, drew back the hammer and shut my eyes. At that moment I felt a gust of wind whipping against the tower and the study windows burst open, hitting the wall with great force. An icy breeze touched my face, bringing with it the lost breath of great expectations.

24

The taxi slowly made its way up to the outskirts of the Gracia neighborhood, toward the solitary, somber grounds of Güell Park. The large houses that dotted the hill, peering through a grove that swayed in the wind like black water, had seen better days. I spied the large door of the estate high up on the hillside. Three years earlier, when Gaudí died, the heirs of Count Güell had sold the deserted grounds—whose sole inhabitant had been the estate's architect—to the town hall for one peseta. Now forgotten and neglected, the garden of columns and towers looked more like a cursed paradise. I told the driver to stop by the gates and paid my fare.

"Are you sure you wish to get out here, sir?" the driver asked, looking uncertain. "If you like, I can wait for you for a few minutes . . ."

"It won't be necessary."

The murmur of the taxi disappeared down the hill and I was left alone with the echo of the wind among the trees. Dead leaves trailed about the entrance to the park and swirled round my feet. I went up to the gates, which were closed with rusty chains, and scanned the grounds on the other side. Moonlight licked the outline of the dragon that presided over the staircase. A dark shape came slowly down the steps, watching me with eyes that shone like pearls under water. It was a black dog. The animal stopped at the foot of the steps and only then did I realize it was not alone. Two more animals were watching me. One of them had crept through the shadow cast by the guard's house, which stood at one side of the entrance. The other, the largest of the three, had climbed onto the wall and was looking down at me from barely two meters away, steaming breath pouring out between its bared fangs. I drew away very slowly, without taking my eyes off it and without turning round. Step by step I reached the pavement opposite the entrance. Another of the dogs had scrambled up the wall and was following me with its eyes. I quickly surveyed the ground in search of a stick or a stone to use in self-defense if they decided to attack, but all I could see were dry leaves. I knew that if I looked away and started to run, the animals would chase me and I wouldn't have gone more than twenty meters before they caught me and tore me to pieces. The largest dog advanced a few steps along the wall and I was sure it was going to pounce on me. The third one, the only one I had seen at first, which had probably acted as a decoy, was beginning to climb the lower part of the wall to join the other two. I'm done for, I thought.

At that moment, a flash lit up the wolfish faces of the three animals, and they stopped in their tracks. I looked over my shoulder and saw the mound that rose about fifty meters from the entrance to the park. The lights in the house had been turned on, the only lights on the entire hill. One of the animals gave a muffled groan and disappeared back into the park. The others followed it a few moments later.

Without thinking twice, I began to walk toward the house. It was a slender, angular three-story structure, shaped like a tower, its roof crowned with sharp gables, that looked down, like a sentinel, on the city with the ghostly park at its feet.

The house was at the end of a steep slope, with steps leading up to the front door. The large windows exhaled golden haloes of light. As I climbed the stone steps I thought I noticed the outline of a figure leaning on one of the balustrades on the second floor, as still as a spider waiting in its web. I climbed the last step and stopped to catch my breath. The main door was ajar and a sheet of light stretched out toward my feet. I approached slowly and stopped in the threshold. A smell of dead flowers emanated from within. I knocked gently on the door and it opened slightly. Before me was an entrance hall and a long corridor leading into the house. I heard a dry, repetitive sound, like that of a shutter banging against the window in the wind; it came from inside the house and reminded me of a heart beating. Advancing a few steps into the hall I saw a staircase on my left that led to the upper floors. I thought I heard light footsteps, a child's footsteps, climbing somewhere high above.

"Good evening?" I called out.

Before the echo of my voice had lost itself down the corridor, the percussive sound that was beating somewhere in the house stopped. Total silence now fell all around me and an icy draft kissed my cheek.

"Señor Corelli? It's Martín. David Martín."

I got no reply, so I ventured forward. The walls were covered with framed photographs of different sizes. From the poses and the clothes worn by the subjects I assumed they were all at least twenty or thirty years old. At the bottom of each frame was a small silver plaque with the name of the person in the photograph and the year it was taken. I studied those faces that were observing me from another time. Children and old people, ladies and gentlemen. They all bore the same shadow of sadness in their eyes, the same silent cry. They stared at the camera with a longing that chilled my blood.

"Does photography interest you, Martín, my friend?" said a voice next to me.

Startled, I turned round. Andreas Corelli was gazing at the photographs next to me with a smile tinged with melancholy. I hadn't seen or heard him approach and when he smiled at me I felt a shiver down my spine.

"I thought you wouldn't come."

"So did I."

"Then let me offer you a glass of wine and we'll drink a toast to our errors."

I followed him to a large room with wide French windows overlooking the city. Corelli pointed to an armchair and then filled two glasses from a decanter on a table. He handed me a glass and sat on the armchair opposite mine.

I tasted the wine. It was excellent. I almost downed it in one and soon felt the warmth sliding down my throat, calming my nerves. Corelli sniffed at his and watched me with a friendly, relaxed smile.

"You were right," I said.

"I usually am," Corelli replied. "It's a habit that rarely gives me any satisfaction. Sometimes I think that few things would give me more pleasure than being sure I had made a mistake."

"That's easy to resolve. Ask me. I'm always wrong."

"No, you're not wrong. I think you see things as clearly as I do and it doesn't give you any satisfaction either."

Listening to him it occurred to me that the only thing that could give me some satisfaction at that precise moment was to set fire to the whole world and burn along with it. As if he'd read my thoughts, Corelli smiled and nodded, baring his teeth.

"I can help you, my friend."

To my surprise, I found myself avoiding his eyes, concentrating instead on that small brooch with the silver angel on his lapel.

"Pretty brooch," I said, pointing at it.

"A family heirloom," Corelli replied.

I thought we'd exchanged enough pleasantries to last the whole evening.

"Señor Corelli, what am I doing here?"

Corelli's eyes shone the same color as the wine he was gently swilling in his glass.

"It's very simple. You're here because at last you've realized that this is the place you should be. You're here because I made you an offer a year ago. An offer that at the time you were not ready to accept but that you have not forgotten. And I'm here because I still think that you're the person I'm looking for and that is why I preferred to wait twelve months rather than let you go."

"An offer you never got round to explaining in detail."

"In fact, the only thing I gave you was the details."

"One hundred thousand francs in exchange for working for you for a whole year, writing a book."

"Exactly. Many people would think that was the essential information. But not you."

"You told me that when you described the sort of book you wanted me to write for you, I'd do it even if you didn't pay me."

Corelli nodded.

"You have a good memory."

"I have an excellent memory, Señor Corelli, so much so that I don't recall having seen, read, or heard about any book you've published."

"Do you doubt my solvency?"

I shook my head, trying not to let him notice my longing and greed that gnawed at my insides. The less interest I showed, the more tempted I felt by the publisher's promises.

"I'm simply curious about your motives," I said.

"As you should be."

"Anyhow, may I remind you that I have an exclusive contract with Barrido & Escobillas for five more years. The other day I received a very revealing visit from them, and from a litigious-looking lawyer. Still, I suppose it doesn't really matter, because five years is too long, and if there's one thing I'm certain of, it's that I have very little time."

"Don't worry about lawyers. Mine are infinitely more litigious-looking than the ones that couple of pustules use, and they've never lost a case. Leave all the legal details and litigation to me."

From the way he smiled when he uttered those words I thought it best never to have a meeting with the legal advisers for Éditions de la Lumière.

"I believe you. I suppose that leaves us with the question of what the other details of your offer are—the essential ones."

"There's no simple way of saying this, so I'd better get straight to the point."

"Please do."

Corelli leaned forward and locked his eyes on mine.

"Martín, I want you to create a religion for me."

At first I thought I hadn't heard him correctly.

"What did you say?"

Corelli held his gaze on mine, his eyes unfathomable.

"I said that I want you to create a religion for me."

I stared at him for a long moment, thunderstruck.

"You're pulling my leg."

Corelli shook his head, sipping his wine with relish.

"I want you to muster all your talent and devote yourself body and soul, for one year, to working on the greatest story you have ever created: a religion."

I couldn't help bursting out laughing.

"You're out of your mind. Is that your proposal? Is that the book you want me to write?"

Corelli nodded calmly.

"You've got the wrong writer. I don't know anything about religion."

"Don't worry about that. I do. I'm not looking for a theologian. I'm looking for a narrator. Do you know what a religion is, Martín, my friend?"

"I can barely remember the Lord's Prayer."

"A beautiful and well-crafted prayer. Poetry aside, a religion is really a moral code that is expressed through legends, myths, or any type of literary device in order to establish a system of beliefs, values, and rules with which to regulate a culture or a society."

"Amen," I replied.

"As in literature or any other act of communication, what confers effectiveness on it is the form and not the content," Corelli continued.

"You're telling me that a doctrine amounts to a tale."

"Everything is a tale, Martín. What we believe, what we know, what we remember, even what we dream. Everything is a story, a narrative, a sequence of events with characters communicating an emotional content. We only accept as true what can be narrated. Don't tell me you're not tempted by the idea."

"I'm not."

"Are you not tempted to create a story for which men and women would live and die, for which they would be capable of killing and allowing themselves to be killed, of sacrificing and condemning themselves, of handing over their souls? What greater challenge for your career than to create a story so powerful that it transcends fiction and becomes a revealed truth?"

We stared at each other for a few seconds.

"I think you know what my answer is," I said at last.

Corelli smiled.

"I do. But I think you're the one who doesn't yet know it."

"Thank you for your company, Señor Corelli. And for the wine and the speeches. Very stimulating. Be careful whom you throw them at. I hope you find your man and that the pamphlet is a huge success."

I stood up and turned to leave.

"Are you expected somewhere, Martín?"

I didn't reply, but I stopped.

"Don't you feel anger, knowing there could be so many things to live for, with good health and good fortune and no ties?" said Corelli from behind me. "Don't you feel anger when these things are being snatched from your hands?"

I turned back slowly.

"What is a year's work compared with the possibility of having everything you desire come true? What is a year's work compared with the promise of a long and fulfilling existence?"

Nothing, I said to myself, despite myself. Nothing.

"Is that your promise?"

"You name the price. Do you want to set fire to the whole world and burn with it? Let's do it together. You set the price. I'm prepared to give you what you most want."

"I don't know what it is that I want most."

"I think you do know."

The publisher smiled and winked at me. He stood up and went over to a chest of drawers that had a gas lamp resting on it. He opened the first drawer and pulled out a parchment envelope. He handed it to me but I didn't take it, so he left it on the table that stood between us and sat down again, without saying a word. The envelope was open and inside I could just make out what looked like a few wads of one-hundred-franc notes. A fortune.

"You keep all this money in a drawer and leave the door open?" I asked.

"You can count it. If you think it's not enough, name an amount. As I said, I'm not going to argue with you over money."

I looked at the small fortune for a long moment, and in the end I shook my head. At least I'd seen it. It was real. The offer and the vanity he had awoken in me in those moments of misery and despair were real.

"I cannot accept it," I said.

"Do you think it's dirty money?"

"All money is dirty. If it were clean nobody would want it. But that's not the problem."

"So?"

"I cannot accept it because I cannot accept your proposal. I couldn't even do so if I wanted to."

Corelli considered my words.

"May I ask why?"

"Because I'm dying, Señor Corelli. Because I have only a few weeks left to live, perhaps only days. Because I have nothing left to offer."

Corelli looked down, silent. I heard the wind scratching at the windows and sliding over the house.

"Don't tell me you didn't know," I added.

"I sensed it."

Corelli remained seated, not looking at me.

"There are plenty of writers who can write this book for you, Señor Corelli. I am grateful for your offer. More than you can imagine. Good night."

I began to walk away.

"Let's say I was able to help you get over your illness," he said.

I stopped halfway down the corridor and turned round. Corelli was barely a meter away, staring straight at me. I thought he was a bit taller, there in the corridor, than when I'd first seen him and that his eyes were larger and darker. I could see my reflection in his pupils getting smaller as they dilated.

"Does my appearance worry you, Martín, my friend?"

I swallowed hard.

"Yes," I confessed.

"Please come back and sit down. Give me the opportunity to explain some more. What have you got to lose?"

"Nothing, I suppose."

He put his hand gently on my arm. His fingers were long and pale.

"You have nothing to fear from me, Martín. I'm your friend."

His touch was comforting. I allowed him to guide me back to the sitting room and sat down meekly, like a child waiting for an adult to speak. Corelli knelt down by my armchair and fixed his eyes on mine. He took my hand and pressed it tightly.

"Do you want to live?"

I wanted to reply but couldn't find the words. I realized that my eyes were filling with tears. Until then I had not understood how much I longed to keep on breathing, to keep on opening my eyes every morning and be able to go out into the street, to step on stones and look at the sky, and, above all, to keep on remembering.

I nodded.

"I'm going to help you, Martín, my friend. All I ask of you is that you trust me. Accept my offer. Let me help you. Let me give you what you most desire. That is my promise."

I nodded again.

"I accept."

Corelli smiled and bent over to kiss me on the cheek. His lips were icy cold.

"You and I, my friend, are going to do great things together. You'll see," he whispered.

He offered me a handkerchief to dry my tears. I did so without feeling the silent shame of weeping before a stranger, something I had not done since my father died.

"You're exhausted, Martín. Stay here for the night. There are plenty of bedrooms in this house. I can assure you that tomorrow you'll feel better and that you'll see things more clearly."

I shrugged my shoulders, though I realized that Corelli was right. I could barely stand and all I wanted to do was sleep deeply. I couldn't even bring myself to get up from the armchair, the most comfortable and most comforting in the universal history of all armchairs.

"If you don't mind, I'd rather stay here."

"Of course. I'm going to let you rest. Very soon you'll feel better. I give you my word."

Corelli went over to the chest of drawers and turned off the gas lamp. The room was submerged in a bluish dusk. My eyelids were pressing down heavily and a sense of intoxication filled my head, but I managed to make out Corelli's silhouette crossing the room and disappearing into the shadows. I closed my eyes and heard the murmur of the wind behind the windowpanes.

25

I dreamed that the house was slowly sinking. At first, little teardrops of dark water began to appear through the cracks in the tiles, in the walls, in the relief on the ceiling, through the holes of the door locks. It was a cold liquid that crept slowly and heavily, like mercury, and gradually formed a layer covering the floor and climbing up the walls. I felt the water going over my feet, rising fast. I stayed in the armchair, watching as the water level rose to my throat and then, in just a few seconds, reached the ceiling. I felt myself floating and could see pale lights rising and falling behind the windows. There were human figures also suspended in that watery darkness. Trapped in the current as they floated by, they stretched their hands out to me, but I could not help them and the water dragged them away inexorably. Corelli's one hundred thousand francs flowed around me, undulating like paper fish. I crossed the room to a closed door at the other end. A thread of light shone through the lock. I opened the door and saw that it led to a staircase descending to the deepest part of the house. I went down.

At the bottom of the stairs an oval room opened up, and in its center I could distinguish a group of figures gathered in a circle. When they became aware of my presence they turned round and I saw that they were dressed in white and wore masks and gloves. Strong white lights burned over what seemed to be an operating table. A man whose face had no features or eyes was arranging the objects on a tray of surgical instruments.

One of the figures stretched out his hand to me, inviting me to draw closer. I went over to them and felt them take hold of me, grabbing my head and my body and lifting me onto the table. The lights were blinding, but I managed to see that all the figures were identical and had the face of Dr. Trías. I laughed to myself. One of the doctors was holding a syringe and injected it into my neck. I didn't feel the prick, just a pleasant, muzzy sensation of warmth spreading through my body. Two of the doctors placed my head in some holding contraption and proceeded to adjust the crown of screws that held a padded plate at one end. I felt them tying down my arms and legs with straps. I put up no resistance. When my whole body had been immobilized from head to toe, one of the doctors handed a scalpel to another of his twins, who then leaned over me. I felt someone take my hand and hold it. It was a boy who looked at me tenderly and had the same face I had on the day my father was killed.

I saw the blade of the scalpel coming down in the liquid darkness and felt the metal making a cut across my forehead. There was no pain. I could feel something issuing out of the cut and saw a black cloud bleeding slowly from the wound and spreading into the water. The blood rose toward the lights in spirals, like smoke, twisting into ever-changing shapes. I looked at the boy, who was smiling at me and holding my hand tightly. Then I noticed it. Something was moving inside me. Something that, until just a minute ago, had been gripping my mind like pincers. I felt it being dislodged, like a thorn stuck right into the marrow that was being pulled out with pliers. I panicked and wanted to get up, but I was immobilized. The boy kept his eyes on mine and nodded. I thought I was going to faint or wake up, when I saw something reflected in the lights of the operating theater. Two black filaments were emerging from the wound, creeping over my skin. It was a black spider the size of a fist. It ran across my face and before it could jump onto the table, one of the surgeons skewered it with a scalpel. He lifted it up so that I could see it. The spider kicked its legs and bled, silhouetted against the light. A white stain covered its carapace suggesting the shape of wings spread open. An angel. After a while the spider's legs went limp and its body withered. It was still held aloft and when the boy reached out to touch it, it crumbled into dust. The doctors undid my ties and loosened the contraption that had gripped my skull. With their help I sat up on the table and put my hand on my forehead. The wound was closing. When I looked around me once more, I realized I was alone.

The lights of the operating theater went out and the room was dark. I went back to the staircase and ascended the steps that led back to the sitting room. The light of dawn was filtering through the water, trapping a thousand floating particles. I was tired. More than I'd ever been in my whole life. I dragged myself to the armchair and let myself fall into it. My body collapsed and when I was finally resting on the chair I could see a trail of tiny bubbles beginning to move around the ceiling. A small air chamber was being formed at the top and I realized that the water level was starting to come down. The water, thick and shiny like jelly, gushed out through the cracks in the windows as if the house were a submarine emerging from the deep. I curled up in the armchair, succumbing to a sense of weightlessness and peace that I hoped would never end. I closed my eyes and listened to the murmur of the water around me. I opened them again and saw drops raining down from on high, slowly, like tears caught in midflight. I was tired, very tired, and all that I wanted to do was fall into a deep sleep.

· · ·

I opened my eyes to the intense brightness of a warm noon. Light fell like dust through the French windows. The first thing I noticed was that the hundred thousand francs were still on the table. I stood up and went over to the window. I drew aside the curtain and an arm of blinding light inundated the room. Barcelona was still there, shimmering like a mirage. I realized that the humming in my ears, which only the sounds of the day used to disguise, had disappeared completely. I heard an intense silence, as pure as crystal water, which I didn't remember ever having experienced before. Then I heard myself laughing. I brought my hands to my head and touched my skin: I felt no pressure whatsoever. I could see clearly and felt as if my five senses had only just awoken. I could even smell the old wood of the coffered ceiling and columns. I looked for a mirror but there wasn't one in the sitting room. I went out in search of a bathroom or another room where I might find a mirror and be able to see that I hadn't woken up in a stranger's body, that the skin I could feel and the bones were my own. All the rooms in the house were locked. I went through the whole floor without being able to open a single door. When I returned to the sitting room I noticed that where I had dreamed there was a door leading to the basement there was only a painting of an angel crouching on a rock that looked out over an endless lake. I went to the stairs that led to the upper floors, but as soon as I'd gone up one flight I stopped. A heavy, impenetrable darkness seemed to reside beyond.

"Señor Corelli?" I called out.

My voice was lost as if it had hit something hard, without leaving an echo or a trace. I went back to the sitting room and gazed at the money on the table. One hundred thousand francs. I took the money and felt its weight. The paper begged to be stroked. I put it in my pocket and set off again down the passage that led to the exit. The dozens of faces in the portraits were still staring at me with the intensity of a promise. I preferred not to confront their looks and continued walking toward the door, but just as I was nearing the end of the passage I noticed that among the frames there was an empty one, with no inscription or photograph. I became aware of a sweet scent, a scent of parchment, and realized it was coming from my fingers. It was the perfume of money. I opened the main door and stepped out into the daylight. The door closed heavily behind me. I turned round to look at the house, dark and silent, oblivious to the radiant clarity of the day, the blue skies and brilliant sun. I checked my watch. It was after one o'clock. I had slept more than twelve hours straight on an old armchair and yet I had never felt better in all my life. I walked down the hill toward the city with a smile on my face, certain that, for the first time in a long while, perhaps for the first time in my whole life, the world was smiling at me.

Act Two

Lux
Aeterna

I celebrated my return to the world of the living by paying homage to one of the most influential temples in town: the main offices of the Banco Hispano Colonial on Calle Fontanella. The sight of a hundred thousand francs sent the manager, the auditors, and the army of cashiers and accountants into ecstasy and elevated me to the ranks of clients who inspired a devotion and warmth that was almost saintly. Having sorted out formalities with the bank, I decided to deal with another Horseman of the Apocalypse by walking to a newspaper stand in Plaza Urquinaona. There I opened a copy of *The Voice of Industry* and looked for the local news section, which had once been mine. Don Basilio's expert touch was still apparent in the headlines and I recognized almost all of the bylines, as if not a day had gone by. Six years of General Primo de Rivera's lukewarm dictatorship had brought to the city a poisonous, murky calm unconducive to the reporting of crime and sensational stories. I was about to close the newspaper and collect my change when I saw it. Just a brief news item on the last page of the section in a column highlighting four different incidents:

MIDNIGHT FIRE IN THE RAVAL QUARTER.
ONE DEAD AND TWO BADLY INJURED

Joan Marc Huguet/Barcelona

A serious fire started in the early hours of Friday morning at 6 Plaza dels Àngels, main office of the publishing firm of Barrido & Escobillas. The firm's director, Don José Barrido, died in the blaze, and his partner, Don José Luis López Escobillas, was seriously injured. An employee, Don Ramón Guzmán, was also badly injured, trapped by the flames as he attempted to rescue the other two men. Firefighters are speculating that the blaze may have been started by a chemical product that was being used for renovation work in the offices. Other causes are not being ruled out, however, as eyewitnesses claim to have seen a man leaving the building moments before the fire began. The victims were taken to the Clínico hospital, where one was pronounced dead on arrival. The other two remain in critical condition.

I got there as quickly as I could. The smell of burning reached as far as the Ramblas. A group of neighbors and onlookers had congregated in the square opposite the building, and plumes of white smoke rose from the rubble by the entrance. I saw some of the firm's employees trying to salvage what little remained from the ruins. Boxes of scorched books and furniture bitten by flames were piled up in the street. The façade of the building was blackened and the windows had been blasted out by the fire. I broke through the circle of bystanders and went in. A powerful stench stuck in my throat. Some of the staff from the publishing house who were busy rescuing their belongings recognized me and mumbled a greeting, their heads bowed.

"Señor Martín . . . what a tragedy."

I crossed what had once been the reception area and went into Barrido's office. The flames had devoured the carpets and reduced the furniture to glowing skeletons. In one corner, the coffered ceiling had collapsed, opening a pathway of light toward the rear patio along which floated a bright beam of ashes. One chair had miraculously survived the fire. It was in the middle of the room and sitting on it was Lady Venom, crying, her eyes downcast. I knelt in front of her. She recognized me and smiled through her tears.

"Are you all right?" I asked.

She nodded.

"He told me to go home, you know? He said it was late and I should get some rest because today was going to be a very long day. We were finishing the monthly accounts. If I'd stayed another minute . . ."

"What happened, Herminia?"

"We were working late. It was almost midnight when Señor Barrido told me to go home. The publishers were expecting a gentleman—"

"At midnight? What gentleman?"

"A foreigner, I think. It had something to do with a proposal. I'm not sure. I would happily have stayed on, but Señor Barrido told me—"

"Herminia, that gentleman, do you remember his name?"

She gave me a puzzled look.

"I've already told the inspector who came here this morning everything I can remember. He asked for you."

"An inspector? For me?"

"They're talking to everyone."

"Of course."

Lady Venom looked straight at me, eyeing me with distrust.

"They don't know whether he'll come out of this alive," she murmured, referring to Escobillas. "We've lost everything—the archives, the contracts, everything. The publishing house is finished."

"I'm sorry, Herminia."

A crooked, malicious smile appeared.

"You're sorry? Isn't this what you wanted?"

"How can you think that?"

She looked at me suspiciously.

"Now you're free."

I was about to touch her arm but Herminia stood up and took a step back, as if my presence scared her.

"Herminia—"

"Go away," she said.

I left Herminia among the smoking ruins. When I went back outside I bumped into a group of children who were rummaging through the rubble. One of them had disinterred a book from the ashes and was examining it with a mixture of curiosity and disdain. The cover had been disfigured by the fire and the edges of the pages were charred, but otherwise the book was unspoiled. From the lettering on the spine, I knew that it was one of the installments of *City of the Damned*.

"Señor Martín?"

I turned to find three men wearing cheap suits that were a bad choice for a humid, sticky day. One of them, who seemed to be in charge, stepped forward and proffered me the friendly smile of an expert salesman. The other two, who stood as rigid and unyielding as a hydraulic press, glued their openly hostile eyes on mine.

"Señor Martín, I'm Inspector Víctor Grandes and these are my colleagues Officers Marcos and Castelo from the investigation and security squad. I wonder if you would be kind enough to spare us a few minutes."

"Of course," I replied.

The name Víctor Grandes rang a bell from my days as a reporter. Vidal had devoted some of his columns to him, and I particularly recalled one in which he described Grandes as a harbinger, a solid figure whose presence in the squad confirmed the arrival of a new generation of elite professionals, better prepared than their predecessors, incorruptible and tough as steel. The adjectives and the hyperbole were Vidal's, not mine. I imagined that Inspector Grandes would have moved up the ranks since then, and his presence was proof that the police were taking the fire at Barrido & Escobillas seriously.

"If you don't mind, we can go to a nearby café so that we can talk undisturbed," said Grandes, his obliging smile not diminishing one inch.

"As you wish."

Grandes took me to a small bar on the corner of Calle Doctor Dou and Calle Pintor Fortuny. Marcos and Castelo walked behind us, never taking their eyes off me. Grandes offered me a cigarette, which I refused. He put the pack back in his pocket and didn't open his mouth again until we reached the café and I was escorted to a table at the back, where the three men positioned themselves around me. Had they taken me to a dark, damp dungeon the meeting would have seemed more friendly.

"Señor Martín, you must already know what happened early this morning."

"Only what I've read in the paper. And what Lady Venom told me—"

"Lady Venom?"

"I'm sorry. Miss Herminia Duaso, the directors' assistant."

Marcos and Castelo exchanged glances that were priceless. Grandes smiled.

"Interesting nickname. Tell me, Señor Martín, where were you last night?"

How naïve of me; the question caught me by surprise.

"It's a routine question," Grandes explained. "We're trying to establish the whereabouts of anyone who might have been in touch with the victims during the last few days. Employees, suppliers, family . . ."

"I was with a friend."

As soon as I opened my mouth I regretted my choice of words. Grandes noticed it.

"A friend?"

"Well, he's actually someone connected with my work. A publisher. Last night I'd arranged a meeting with him."

"Can you tell me until what time you were with this person?"

"Until late. In fact, I ended up sleeping at his house."

"I see. And this person you describe as being connected with your work, what is his name?"

"Corelli. Andreas Corelli. A French publisher."

Grandes wrote the name down in a little notebook.

"The name sounds Italian," he remarked.

"As a matter of fact, I don't really know what his nationality is."

"That's understandable. And this Señor Corelli, whatever his nationality may be, would he be able to corroborate the fact that last night you were with him?"

"I suppose so."

"You suppose so?"

"I'm sure he would. Why wouldn't he?"

"I don't know, Señor Martín. Is there any reason you would think he might not?"

"No."

"That's settled then."

Marcos and Castelo were looking at me as if I'd done nothing but tell lies since we sat down.

"One last thing. Could you explain the nature of the meeting you had last night with this publisher of indeterminate nationality?"

"Señor Corelli had arranged to meet me because he wanted to make me an offer."

"What type of offer?"

"A professional one."

"I see. To write a book, perhaps?"

"Exactly."

"Tell me, is it usual after a business meeting to spend the night in the house of, how shall I put it, the contracting party?"

"No."

"But you say you spent the night in this publisher's house."

"I stayed because I wasn't feeling well and I didn't think I'd be able to get back to my house."

"The dinner upset you, perhaps?"

"I've had some health problems recently."

Grandes nodded, looking duly concerned.

"Dizzy spells, headaches . . ." I added.

"But it's reasonable to assume that now you're feeling better?"

"Yes. Much better."

"I'm glad to hear it. In fact, you're looking enviably well. Don't you agree?"

Castelo and Marcos nodded.

"Anyone would think you've had a great weight taken off your shoulders," the inspector pointed out.

"I don't understand."

"I'm talking about the dizzy spells and the aches and pains."

Grandes was handling this farce with an exasperating sense of timing.

"Forgive my ignorance regarding your professional life, Señor Martín, but isn't it true that you signed an agreement with the two publishers that didn't expire for another six years?"

"Five."

"And didn't this agreement tie you, so to speak, exclusively to Barrido & Escobillas?"

"Those were the terms."

"Then why would you need to discuss an offer with a competitor if your agreement didn't allow you to accept it?"

"It was just a conversation. Nothing more."

"Which nevertheless turned into a soirée at this gentleman's house."

"My agreement doesn't forbid me to speak to third parties. Or spend the night away from home. I'm free to sleep wherever I wish and to speak to whomever I want."

"Of course. I wasn't trying to imply that you weren't, but thank you for clarifying that point."

"Can I clarify anything else?"

"Just one small detail. Now that Señor Barrido has passed away, and supposing that, God forbid, Señor Escobillas does not recover from his injuries and also dies, the publishing house would be dissolved and so would your contract. Am I wrong?"

"I'm not sure. I don't really know how the company was set up."

"But would you say that it was likely?"

"Possibly. You'd have to ask the publishers' lawyer."

"In fact, I already have. And he has confirmed that, if what nobody wants to happen does happen and Señor Escobillas passes away, that is exactly how things will stand."

"Then you already have the answer."

"And you would have complete freedom to accept the offer of Señor . . ."

"Corelli."

"Tell me, have you accepted it already?"

"May I ask what this has to do with the cause of the fire?" I snapped.

"Nothing. Simple curiosity."

"Is that all?" I asked.

Grandes looked at his colleagues and then at me.

"As far as I'm concerned, yes."

I made as if to stand up, but the three policemen remained in their seats.

"Señor Martín, before I forget," said Grandes. "Can you confirm whether you remember that a week ago Señor Barrido and Señor Escobillas paid you a visit at your home, at number 30 Calle Flassaders, in the company of the aforementioned lawyer?"

"They did."

"Was it a social or a courtesy call?"

"The publishers came to express their wish that I return to my work on a series of books I'd put aside for a few months while I devoted myself to another project."

"Would you describe the conversation as friendly and relaxed?"

"I don't remember anyone raising his voice."

"And do you remember replying to them, and I quote, 'In a week you'll both be dead'? Without raising your voice, of course."

I sighed.

"Yes," I admitted.

"What were you referring to?"

"I was angry and said the first thing that came into my head, Inspector. That doesn't mean that I was serious. Sometimes one says things one doesn't mean."

"Thank you for your candor, Señor Martín. You have been very helpful. Good afternoon."

I walked away from that place with all three sets of eyes fixed like daggers on my back, and with the firm belief that if I'd replied to every one of the inspector's questions with a lie I wouldn't have felt as guilty.

2

The meeting with Víctor Grandes and the couple of basilisks he used as escorts left a nasty taste in my mouth, but it had gone by the time I'd walked in the sun for a hundred meters or so, in a body I hardly recognized: strong, free of pain and nausea, with no ringing in my ears or agonizing pinpricks in my skull, no weariness or cold sweats. No recollection of that certainty of death that had suffocated me only twenty-four hours ago. The tragedy of the previous night, including the death of Barrido and the very likely demise of Escobillas, should have filled me with grief and anguish, but neither I nor my conscience was able to feel anything other than a pleasant indifference. That July morning, the Ramblas were in a party mood and I was their prince.

I took a stroll as far as Calle Santa Ana, with the idea of paying a surprise visit to Señor Sempere. When I walked into the bookshop, Sempere senior was behind the counter settling accounts; his son had climbed a ladder and was rearranging the bookshelves. The bookseller gave me a friendly smile and I realized that for a moment he hadn't recognized me. A second later his smile disappeared, his mouth dropped, and he came round the counter to embrace me.

"Martín? Is it really you? Holy Mother of God, you look completely different! I was so worried. We went round to your house a few times, but you didn't answer the door. I've even been to the hospitals and police stations."

His son stared at me in disbelief from the top of the ladder. I had to remind myself that only a week before they had seen me looking like one of the corpses in the local morgue.

"I'm sorry I gave you a fright. I was away for a few days on a work-related matter."

"But you did listen to me and go to the doctor, didn't you?"

I nodded.

"It turned out to be something very minor, to do with my blood pressure. I took a tonic for a few days and now I'm as good as new."

"Give me the name of the tonic—I might take a shower with it. What a joy it is, and a relief, to see you looking so well!"

These high spirits were soon punctured when he turned to the news of the day.

"Did you hear about Barrido and Escobillas?" he asked.

"I've just come from there. It's hard to believe."

"Who would have imagined it? It's not as if they aroused any warm feelings in me, but this . . . And tell me, from a legal point of view, how does it all leave you? I don't mean to sound crude."

"To tell you the truth, I don't know. I think the two partners owned the company. There must be heirs, I suppose, but it's conceivable that if they both die the company as such will cease to exist. And, with it, any agreement I had with them. Or at least that's what I think."

"In other words, if Escobillas, may God forgive me, kicks the bucket too, then you're a free man."

I nodded.

"What a dilemma," mumbled the bookseller.

"What will be will be," I said.

Sempere nodded, but I noticed that something was bothering him and he wanted to change the subject.

"Anyway. The thing is, it's wonderful that you've dropped by because I wanted to ask you a favor."

"Say no more, it's already done."

"I warn you, you're not going to like it."

"If I liked it, it wouldn't be a favor, it would be a pleasure. And if the favor is for you, it will be."

"It's not really for me. I'll explain and you decide. No obligation, all right?"

Sempere leaned on the counter and adopted his confidential manner, bringing back childhood memories of times I had spent in that shop.

"There's this young girl, Isabella. She must be seventeen. Bright as a button. She's always coming round here and I lend her books. She tells me she wants to be a writer."

"Sounds familiar."

"The thing is, a week ago she left one of her stories with me—just twenty or thirty pages, that's all—and asked for my opinion."

"And?"

Sempere lowered his tone, as if he were revealing a secret from an official inquiry.

"Masterly. Better than 99 percent of what I've seen published in the last twenty years."

"I hope you are including me in the remaining 1 percent or I'll consider my self-esteem well and truly trodden on."

"That's just what I was coming to. Isabella adores you."

"She adores me?"

"Yes, as if you were the Virgin of Montserrat and Infant Jesus all in one. She's read the whole of the *City of the Damned* series ten times over and when I loaned her *The Steps of Heaven* she told me that if she could write a book like that she'd die a peaceful death."

"You were right. I don't like the sound of this."

"I knew you'd try to wiggle out of it."

"I'm not wiggling out. You haven't told me what the favor is."

"You can imagine."

I sighed.

"I warned you."

"Ask me something else."

"All you have to do is talk to her. Give her some encouragement, some advice. Listen to her, read some of her stuff, and give her a little guidance. The girl has a mind as quick as a bullet. You're really going to like her. You'll become friends. She could even work as your assistant."

"I don't need an assistant. Still less someone I don't know."

"Nonsense. Besides, you do know her. Or at least that's what she says. She says she's known you for years but you probably don't remember her. It seems that the couple of simple souls she has for parents are convinced that this literature business will consign her to eternal damnation, or at least to a secular spinsterhood. They're wavering between locking her up in a convent or marrying her off to some fool who will give her eight children and bury her forever among pots and pans. If you do nothing to save her, it's tantamount to murder."

"Don't pull a Jane Eyre on me, Señor Sempere."

"Look. I wouldn't ask you, because I know that you like this altruism stuff about as much as you like dancing the sardana, but every time I see her come in here and look at me with those little eyes that seem to be popping with intelligence and enthusiasm, I think of the future that awaits her and it breaks my heart. I've already taught her all I can. The girl learns fast, Martín. She reminds me of you when you were a young lad."

I sighed again.

"Isabella what?"

"Gispert. Isabella Gispert."

"I don't know her. I've never heard that name in my life. Someone's been telling you a tall story."

The bookseller shook his head and mumbled under his breath.

"That's exactly what Isabella said you'd say."

"So, she's talented *and* she's psychic. What else did she say?"

"She suspects you're a much better writer than a person."

"What an angel, this Isabelita."

"Can I tell her to come see you? No obligation?"

I gave in. Sempere smiled triumphantly and wanted to seal the pact with an embrace, but I escaped before the old bookseller was able to complete his mission of trying to make me feel like a good Samaritan.

"You won't be sorry, Martín," I heard him say as I walked out the door.

3

When I got home, Inspector Víctor Grandes was sitting on the front step, calmly smoking a cigarette. With the poise of a matinee star he smiled when he saw me, as if he were an old friend making a courtesy call. I sat down next to him and he pulled out his cigarette case. Gitanes, I noticed. I accepted.

"Where are Hansel and Gretel?"

"Marcos and Castelo were unable to come. We received a tip, so they've gone to find an old acquaintance in Pueblo Seco who is probably in need of a little persuasion to jog his memory."

"Poor devil."

"If I'd told them I was coming here, they would probably have joined me. They think the world of you."

"Love at first sight, I noticed. What can I do for you, Inspector? May I invite you upstairs for a cup of coffee?"

"I wouldn't dare invade your privacy, Señor Martín. In fact, I simply wanted to give you the news personally before you found out from other sources."

"What news?"

"Escobillas passed away early this afternoon in the Clínico hospital."

"God. I didn't know," I said.

Grandes continued smoking in silence.

"I could see it coming. Nothing anyone could do about it."

"Have you discovered anything about the cause of the fire?" I asked.

The inspector looked at me, then nodded.

"Everything seems to indicate that somebody spilled petrol over Señor Barrido and then set fire to him. The flames spread when he panicked and tried to get out of his office. His partner and the employee who rushed over to help him were trapped."

I swallowed hard. Grandes smiled reassuringly.

"The publishers' lawyer was saying this afternoon that, given the personal nature of your agreement, it becomes null and void with the death of the publishers, although their heirs will retain the rights on all the works published until now. I suppose he'll write to you, but I thought you might like to know in advance, in case you need to take any decision concerning the offer from the other publisher you mentioned."

"Thank you."

"You're welcome."

Grandes took a last puff of his cigarette and threw the butt on the ground. He smiled affably and stood up. Then he patted me on the shoulder and walked off toward Calle Princesa.

"Inspector?" I called.

Grandes stopped and turned round.

"You don't think that . . ."

Grandes gave a weary smile.

"Take care, Martín."

. . .

I went to bed early and woke all of a sudden thinking it was the following day, only to discover that it was just after midnight.

In my dreams I had seen Barrido and Escobillas trapped in their office. The flames crept up their clothes until every inch of their bodies was covered. First their clothes, then their skin began to fall off in strips, and their panic-stricken eyes cracked under the heat. Their bodies shook in spasms of agony until they collapsed among the rubble. Flesh peeled off their bones like melted wax, forming a smoking puddle at my feet, in which I could see my own smiling reflection as I blew out the match I held in my fingers.

I got up to fetch a glass of water and, assuming I'd missed the train to sleep, I went up to the study, opened the drawer in my desk and pulled out the book I had rescued from the Cemetery of Forgotten Books. I turned on the reading lamp and twisted its flexible arm so that it focused directly on the book. I opened to the first page and began to read:

Lux Aeterna
D.M.

At first glance, the book was a collection of texts and prayers that seemed to make no sense. It was a manuscript, a handful of typed pages bound rather carelessly in leather. I went on reading and after a while I thought I sensed some sort of method in the sequence of events, songs, and meditations that punctuated the main body of the text. The language possessed its own cadence, and what had at first seemed like a complete absence of form or style gradually turned into a hypnotic chant that permeated the reader's mind, plunging him into a state somewhere between drowsiness and forgetfulness. The same thing was true of the content, whose central theme did not become apparent until well into the first section, or chant, for the work seemed to be structured in the manner of ancient poems written in an age when time proceeded at its own pace and was unending. I realized then that *Lux Aeterna* was, for want of a better description, a sort of book of the dead.

After reading the first thirty or forty pages of circumlocutions and riddles, I found myself caught up in a precise, extravagant, and increasingly disturbing puzzle of prayers and entreaties in which death, referred to at times—in awkwardly constructed verses—as a white angel with reptilian eyes and at other times as a luminous boy, was presented as a sole and omnipresent deity made manifest in nature, desire, and the fragility of existence.

Whoever the mysterious D.M. was, death hovered over his verses like an all-consuming and eternal force. A byzantine tangle of references to various mythologies of heaven and hell were knotted together here into a single plane. According to D.M., there was only one beginning and one end, only one creator and one destroyer who presented himself under different names to confuse men and tempt them in their weakness, a sole God whose true face was divided into two halves: one sweet and pious, the other cruel and demonic.

That much I was able to deduce, but no more, because beyond those principles the author seemed to have lost the course of his narrative and it was almost impossible to decipher the prophetic references and images that peppered the text. Storms of blood and fire pouring over cities and peoples. Armies of corpses in uniform running across endless plains, destroying all life as they passed. Babies strung up with torn flags at the gates of fortresses. Black seas where thousands of souls in torment were suspended for all eternity beneath icy, poisoned waters. Clouds of ashes and oceans of bones and rotten flesh infested with insects and snakes. The succession of hellish, nauseating images went on unabated.

As I turned the pages I had the feeling that, step by step, I was following the map of a sick and broken mind. Line after line, the author of those pages had, without being aware of it, been documenting his own descent into a chasm of madness. The last third of the book seemed to suggest an attempt at retracing his steps, a desperate cry from the prison of his insanity to escape the labyrinth of tunnels that had formed in his mind. The text ended suddenly, midway through an imploring sentence, offering no explanation.

By this time my eyelids were beginning to close. A light breeze wafted through the window. It came from the sea, sweeping the mist off the rooftops. I was about to close the book when I realized that something was trapped in my mind's filter, something connected to the type on those pages. I returned to the beginning and started to go over the text. I found the first example on the fifth line. From then on the same mark appeared every two or three lines. One of the characters, the capital S, was always slightly tilted to the right. I took a blank page from the drawer, slipped it in the roller of the Underwood typewriter on my desk, and wrote a sentence at random:

Sometimes I hear the bells of Santa María del Mar.

I pulled out the paper and examined it under the lamp:

Sometimes . . . of Santa María

I sighed. *Lux Aeterna* had been written on that very same typewriter and probably, I imagined, at that same desk.

4

The following morning I went out to have my breakfast in a café opposite Santa María del Mar. The Borne neighborhood was heaving with carts and people going to the market, with shopkeepers and wholesalers opening their stores. I sat at one of the outdoor tables, asked for a *café con leche,* and adopted an orphaned copy of *La Vanguardia* that was lying on the next table. While my eyes slid over the headlines and leads, I noticed a figure walking up the steps to the church door and sitting down at the top to observe me on the sly. The girl must have been about sixteen or seventeen and was pretending to jot things down in a notebook while she stole glances at me. I sipped my coffee calmly. After a while I beckoned to the waiter.

"Do you see that young lady sitting by the church door? Tell her to order whatever she likes. It's on me."

The waiter nodded and went up to her. When she saw him approaching she buried her head in her notebook, assuming an expression of total concentration that made me smile. The waiter stopped in front of her and cleared his throat. She looked up from her notebook and stared at him. He explained his mission and pointed in my direction. The girl looked at me in alarm. I waved at her. She went crimson. She stood up and came over to my table, with short steps, her eyes lowered.

"Isabella?" I asked.

The girl looked up and sighed, annoyed at herself.

"How did you know?" she asked.

"Supernatural intuition," I replied.

She held out her hand and I shook it without much enthusiasm.

"May I sit down?" she asked.

She sat down without waiting for a reply. In the next half a minute the girl changed positions about six times until she returned to the original one. I observed her with a calculated lack of interest.

"You don't remember me, do you, Señor Martín?"

"Should I?"

"For years I delivered your weekly order from Can Gispert."

The image of the girl who for so long had brought my food from the grocer's came into my mind, then dissolved into the more adult and slightly more angular features of this Isabella, a woman of soft shapes and steely eyes.

"The little girl I used to tip," I said, although there was little or nothing left of the girl in her.

Isabella nodded.

"I always wondered what you did with all those coins."

"I bought books at Sempere & Sons."

"If only I'd known . . ."

"I'll go if I'm bothering you."

"You're not bothering me. Would you like something to drink?"

The girl shook her head.

"Señor Sempere tells me you're talented."

Isabella smiled at me skeptically.

"Normally, the more talent one has, the more one doubts it," I said. "And vice versa."

"Then I must be quite something," Isabella replied.

"Welcome to the club. Tell me, what can I do for you?"

Isabella took a deep breath.

"Señor Sempere told me that perhaps you could read some of my work and give me your opinion and some advice."

I fixed my eyes on hers for a few seconds before replying. She held my gaze without blinking.

"Is that all?"

"No."

"I could see it coming. What is chapter 2?"

Isabella hesitated for only a second.

"If you like what you read and you think I have potential, I'd like you to allow me to become your assistant."

"What makes you think I need an assistant?"

"I can tidy up your papers, type them, correct errors and mistakes—"

"Errors and mistakes?"

"I didn't mean to imply that you make mistakes . . ."

"Then what did you mean to imply?"

"Nothing. But four eyes are better than two. And besides, I can take care of your correspondence, run errands, help with research. What's more, I know how to cook and I can—"

"Are you asking for a position as assistant or cook?"

"I'm asking you to give me a chance."

Isabella looked down. I couldn't help but smile. Despite myself, I really liked this curious creature.

"This is what we'll do. Bring me the best twenty pages you've written, the ones you think will show me what you are capable of. Don't bring any more because I won't read them. I'll have a good look at them and then, depending on what I think, we'll talk."

Her face lit up and for a moment the veil of tension and toughness disappeared.

"You won't regret it," she said.

She stood up and looked at me nervously.

"Is it all right if I bring the pages round to your house?"

"Leave them in my letter box. Is that all?"

She nodded vigorously and backed away with those short, nervous steps. When she was about to turn and start running, I called her.

"Isabella?"

Her meek eyes clouded with sudden anxiety.

"Why me?" I asked. "And don't tell me it's because I'm your favorite author or any of that other flattery Sempere advised you to use to soften me up, because if you do this will be the first and last conversation we ever have."

Isabella hesitated for a moment. Then she replied with disarming bluntness.

"Because you're the only writer I know."

She gave me an embarrassed smile and went off with her notebook, her unsteady walk, and her frankness. I watched her turn the corner of Calle Mirallers and vanish behind the cathedral.

When I returned home an hour later, I found her sitting on my doorstep clutching what I imagined must be her story. As soon as she saw me she stood up and forced a smile.

"I told you to leave it in my letter box," I said.

Isabella nodded and shrugged her shoulders.

"As a token of my gratitude I've brought you some coffee from my parents' shop. It's Colombian and really good. The coffee didn't fit through your letter box so I thought I'd better wait for you."

An excuse like that could have been invented only by a budding novelist. I sighed and opened the door.

"In."

I went up the stairs, Isabella following like a lapdog a few steps behind.

"Do you always take that long to have your breakfast? Not that it's any of my business, of course, but I've been waiting here for three-quarters of an hour, so I was beginning to worry. I said to myself, I hope he hasn't choked on something. It would be just my luck. The one time I meet a writer in the flesh and then he goes and swallows an olive the wrong way and bang goes my literary career," she rattled on.

I stopped halfway up the steps and looked at her with the most hostile expression I could muster.

"Isabella, for things to work out between us we're going to have to set down a few rules. The first is that I ask the questions and you just answer them. When there are no questions from me, you don't give me answers or spontaneous speeches. The second rule is that I can take as long as I damn well please to have breakfast, an afternoon snack, or to daydream, and that does not constitute a matter for debate."

"I didn't mean to offend you. I understand that slow digestion of food is an aid to inspiration."

"The third rule is that sarcasm is not allowed before noon. Understood?"

"Yes, Señor Martín."

"The fourth is that you must not call me Señor Martín, not even at my funeral. I might seem like a fossil to you, but I like to think that I'm still young. In fact, I am young."

"What should I call you?"

"By my name, David."

The girl nodded. I opened the door of the apartment and showed her in. Isabella hesitated for a moment, then slipped in, giving a little jump.

"I think you still look quite young for your age, David."

I stared at her in astonishment.

"How old do you think I am?"

Isabella looked me up and down, assessing.

"About thirty? But a young-looking thirty?"

"Just shut up and go and make some coffee with that concoction you've brought."

"Where is the kitchen?"

"Look for it."

We shared a delicious Colombian coffee sitting in the gallery. Isabella held her cup and watched me furtively as I read the twenty pages she had brought with her. Every time I turned a page and looked up I was confronted by her expectant gaze.

"If you're going to sit there looking at me like an owl, this will take a long time."

"What do you want me to do?"

"Didn't you want to be my assistant? Then assist. Look for something that needs tidying and tidy it, for example."

Isabella looked around.

"Everything is untidy."

"This is your chance then."

Isabella agreed and went off, with military determination, to confront the chaos that reigned in my home. I continued reading. The story she had brought me had almost no narrative thread. With a sharp sensitivity and an articulate turn of phrase, it described the feelings and longings of a girl confined to a cold room in an attic of the Ribera quarter from which she gazed at the city with its people coming and going along dark, narrow streets. The images and the sad music of her prose spoke of a loneliness that bordered on despair. The girl in the story spent hours trapped in her world; sometimes she would sit facing a mirror and slit her arms and thighs with a piece of broken glass, leaving scars like the ones just visible under Isabella's sleeves. I had almost finished my reading when I noticed that she was looking at me from the gallery door.

"What?"

"I'm sorry to interrupt, but what's in the room at the end of the corridor?"

"Nothing."

"It smells odd."

"Damp."

"I can clean it if you like . . ."

"No. That room is never used. And besides, you're not my maid. You don't need to clean anything."

"I'm only trying to help."

"You can help by getting me another cup of coffee."

"Why? Did the story make you drowsy?"

"What's the time, Isabella?"

"It must be about ten o'clock."

"And what does that mean?"

"No sarcasm before noon," Isabella replied.

I smiled triumphantly and handed her my empty cup. She took it and headed off toward the kitchen.

When she returned with the steaming coffee, I had just read the last page. Isabella sat down opposite me. I slowly sipped the delicious brew. The girl wrung her hands and gritted her teeth, glancing now and then at the pages of her story that I had left face down on the table. She held out for a couple of minutes without saying a word.

"And?" she said at last.

"Superb."

She beamed.

"My story?"

"The coffee."

She gave me a wounded look and went to gather up her pages.

"Leave them where they are."

"Why? It's obvious that you didn't like them and you think I'm nothing but a poor idiot."

"I didn't say that."

"You didn't say anything, which is worse."

"Isabella, if you really want to devote yourself to writing, or at least to writing something others will read, you're going to have to get used to sometimes being ignored, insulted, and despised and to almost always being considered with indifference. It's an occupational hazard."

Isabella looked down.

"I don't know if I have any talent. I only know that I like to write. Or, rather, that I need to write."

"Liar."

She looked up and gazed at me harshly.

"OK. I am talented. And I don't care two hoots if you think that I'm not."

I smiled.

"That's better. I couldn't agree with you more."

She seemed confused.

"In that I have talent or in that you think that I don't?"

"What do you think?"

"Then do you believe I have potential?"

"I think you are talented and passionate, Isabella. More than you think and less than you expect. But there are a lot of people with talent and passion, and many of them never get anywhere. This is only the first step toward achieving anything in life. Natural talent is like an athlete's strength. You can be born with more or less ability, but nobody can become an athlete just because he or she was born tall, or strong, or fast. What makes the athlete, or the artist, is the work, the vocation, and the technique. The intelligence you are born with is just ammunition. To achieve something with it you need to transform your mind into a high-precision weapon."

"Why the military metaphor?"

"Every work of art is aggressive, Isabella. And every artist's life is a small war or a large one, beginning with oneself and one's limitations. To achieve anything you must first have ambition and then talent, knowledge, and finally the opportunity."

Isabella considered my words.

"Do you hurl that speech at everyone, or have you just made it up?"

"The speech isn't mine. It was 'hurled' at me, as you put it, by someone whom I asked the same questions that you're asking me today. It was many years ago, but not a day goes by when I don't realize how right he was."

"So, can I be your assistant?"

"I'll think about it."

Isabella nodded, satisfied. On the table, close to where she was sitting, lay the photograph album Cristina had left behind. She opened it at random, starting from the back, and was soon staring at a picture of Señora de Vidal, taken by the gates of Villa Helius two or three years before she was married. Isabella closed the album and let her eyes wander around the gallery until they came to rest on me. I was observing her impatiently. She gave me a nervous smile, as if I'd caught her poking around where she had no business.

"Your girlfriend is very beautiful," she said.

The look I gave her removed the smile in an instant.

"She's not my girlfriend."

"Oh."

A long silence ensued.

"I suppose the fifth rule is that I'm not to meddle in anything that doesn't concern me, right?"

I didn't reply. Isabella nodded to herself and stood up.

"Then I'd better leave you in peace and not bother you anymore today. If you like, I can come back tomorrow and we'll start then."

She gathered her pages and I nodded.

Isabella left discreetly and disappeared down the corridor. I heard her steps as she walked away and then the sound of the door closing. Her absence made me aware, for the first time, of the silence that bewitched that house.

6

Perhaps there was too much caffeine coursing through my veins, or maybe it was just my conscience trying to return, like electricity after a power cut, but I spent the rest of the morning turning over in my mind an idea that was far from comforting. It was hard to imagine that there was no connection between the fire in which Barrido and Escobillas had perished, Corelli's proposal—I hadn't heard a single word from him, which made me suspicious—and the strange manuscript I had rescued from the Cemetery of Forgotten Books, which I suspected had been written within the four walls of my study.

The thought of returning to Corelli's house uninvited, to ask him about the fact that our conversation and the fire had occurred practically at the same time, was not appealing. My instinct told me that when the publisher decided he wanted to see me again he would do so *motu propio,* and I was in no great hurry to pursue our inevitable meeting. The investigation into the fire was already in the hands of Inspector Víctor Grandes and his two bulldogs, Marcos and Castelo, on whose list of favorite people I came highly recommended. The farther away I kept from them, the better. This left only the connection between the manuscript and the tower house. After years of telling myself it was no coincidence that I had ended up living here, the idea was beginning to take on a different significance.

I decided to start my own investigation in the place to which I had confined most of the belongings left behind by the previous inhabitants. I found the key to the room at the far end of the corridor in the kitchen drawer, where it had spent many years. I hadn't been in the room since the men from the electric company had wired the house. When I put the key in the lock, I felt a draft of cold air from the keyhole brush across my fingers, and I realized that Isabella was right: the room did give off a strange smell, reminiscent of dead flowers and freshly turned earth.

I opened the door and covered my mouth and nose. The stench was intense. I groped around the wall for the light switch, but the naked bulb hanging from the ceiling didn't respond. The light from the corridor revealed the outline of the boxes, books, and trunks I had banished to that room years before. I looked at everything with disgust. The wall at the end was completely covered by a large oak wardrobe. I knelt down by a box full of old photographs, spectacles, watches, and other personal items. I began to rummage without really knowing what I was looking for, but after a while I abandoned the undertaking. If I was hoping to discover anything I needed a plan. I was about to leave the room when I heard the wardrobe door slowly opening behind my back. A puff of icy, damp air touched the nape of my neck. I turned round slowly. The wardrobe door was half open and I could see the old dresses and suits that hung inside it, eaten away by time, fluttering like seaweed under water. The current of fetid cold air was coming from within. I stood up and walked toward the wardrobe. I opened the doors wide and pulled aside the clothes hanging on the rail. The wood at the back was rotten and had begun to disintegrate. Behind it I noticed what looked like a wall of plaster with a hole in it a few centimeters wide. I leaned in to see what was on the other side of the wall, but it was almost pitch dark. The faint glow from the corridor cast only a vaporous thread of light through the hole into the space beyond, and all I could perceive was a murky gloom. I put my eye closer, trying to make out some shape, but at that moment a black spider appeared at the mouth of the hole. I recoiled quickly and the spider ran into the wardrobe, disappearing among the shadows. I closed the wardrobe door, left the room, turned the key in the lock, and put it safely in the top of a chest of drawers in the corridor.

The stench that had been trapped in the room had spread down the passage like poison. I cursed the moment I had decided to open that door and went outside to the street hoping to forget, if only for a few hours, the darkness that throbbed at the heart of the tower house.

. . .

Bad ideas always come in twos. To celebrate the fact that I'd discovered some sort of camera obscura hidden in my home, I went to Sempere & Sons with the intention of taking the bookseller to lunch at La Maison Dorée. Sempere the elder was reading a beautiful edition of Potocki's *The Manuscript Found in Saragossa* and wouldn't even hear of it.

"I don't need to pay to see snobs and halfwits congratulating one another, Martín."

"Don't be grumpy. I'm buying."

Sempere declined. His son, who had witnessed the conversation from the entrance to the back room, looked at me, hesitating.

"What if I take your son with me? Will you stop talking to me?"

"It's up to you how you waste your time and money. I'm staying here to read. Life's too short."

Sempere's son was the very model of discretion. Even though we'd known each other since we were children, I couldn't remember having had more than three or four short conversations with him. I didn't know of any vices or weaknesses he might have, but I had it on good authority that among the girls in the quarter he was considered quite a catch, the official golden bachelor. More than one would drop by the bookshop with some excuse and stand sighing by the shop window. But Sempere's son, even if he noticed, never tried to cash in on those promises of devotion and parted lips. Anyone else would have made a brilliant career in seduction with only a tenth of the capital. Anyone but Sempere's son, who, one sometimes felt, deserved to be called a saint.

"At this rate, he's going to end up on the shelf," Sempere complained from time to time.

"Have you tried throwing a bit of chili pepper into his soup to stimulate the blood flow in key areas?" I would ask.

"You can laugh, you rascal. I'm close to seventy and I don't have a single grandson."

. . .

We were received by the head waiter I remembered from my last visit, but without the servile smile or welcoming gesture. When I told him we hadn't made a reservation he nodded disdainfully, clicking his fingers to summon a young waiter who guided us unceremoniously to what I imagined was the worst table in the room, next to the kitchen door and buried in a dark, noisy corner. Over the next twenty-five minutes nobody came near our table, not even to offer us the menu or pour us a glass of water. The staff walked past, banging the door and utterly ignoring our presence and our attempts to attract their attention.

"Don't you think we should leave?" Sempere's son said at last. "I'd be happy with a sandwich in any old place."

He'd hardly finished speaking when I saw them arrive. Vidal and his wife were advancing toward their table escorted by the head waiter and two other waiters who were falling over themselves to offer their congratulations. The Vidals sat down and a couple of minutes later the royal audience began: one after the other, all the diners in the room went over to congratulate Vidal. He received these obeisances with divine grace and sent each one away shortly afterwards. Sempere's son, who had become aware of the situation, was observing me.

"Martín, are you all right? Why don't we leave?"

I nodded slowly. We got up and headed for the exit, skirting the edges of the dining room on the opposite side from Vidal's table. Before we left the restaurant we passed the head waiter, who didn't even bother to look at us, and as we reached the main door I saw, in the mirror above the doorframe, that Vidal was leaning over and kissing Cristina on the lips. Once outside, Sempere's son looked at me, mortified.

"I'm sorry, Martín."

"Don't worry. Bad choice. That's all. If you don't mind, I'd prefer it if you didn't tell your father about all this . . ."

"Not a word," he assured me.

"Thanks."

"Don't mention it. What do you say if I treat you to something more plebeian? There's an excellent eatery in Calle del Carmen."

I'd lost my appetite, but I gladly accepted.

"Sounds like a plan."

The place was near the library and served good homemade meals at inexpensive prices for the people of the area. I barely touched my food, which smelled infinitely better than anything I'd ever smelled at La Maison Dorée, but by the time dessert came round I had already drunk, on my own, a bottle and a half of red wine and my head was spinning.

"Tell me something, Sempere. What have you got against improving the human race? How is it that a young, healthy citizen blessed by the Lord Almighty with as fine a figure as yours has not yet taken advantage of the best offers on the market?"

The bookseller's son laughed.

"What makes you think that I haven't?"

I touched my nose with my index finger and winked at him. Sempere's son nodded.

"You will probably take me for a prude, but I like to think that I'm waiting."

"Waiting for what? For your equipment to get rusty?"

"You sound just like my father."

"Wise men think and speak alike."

"There must be something else, surely?" he asked.

"Something else?"

Sempere nodded.

"What do I know?" I said.

"I think you do know."

"Fat lot of good it's doing me."

I was about to pour myself another glass when Sempere stopped me.

"Moderation," he murmured.

"See what a prude you are?"

"We all are what we are."

"That can be cured. What do you say you and I go out on the town?"

Sempere looked sorry for me.

"Martín, I think the best thing you can do is go home and rest. Tomorrow is another day."

"You won't tell your father I got plastered, will you?"

. . .

On my way home I stopped in at least seven bars to sample their most potent stock until, for one reason or another, I was thrown out; each time I walked on down the street in search of my next port of call. I had never been a big drinker and by the end of the afternoon I was so drunk I couldn't even remember where I lived. I recall that a couple of waiters from the Hostal Ambos Mundos in Plaza Real took me by the arms and dumped me on a bench opposite the fountain, where I fell into a deep, thick stupor.

I dreamed that I was at Vidal's funeral. A blood-filled sky glowered over the maze of crosses and angels surrounding the large mausoleum of the Vidal family in Montjuïc cemetery. A silent cortège of black-veiled figures encircled the amphitheater of darkened marble that formed the portico. Each carried a long white candle. The light from a hundred flames sculpted the contours of a great, grieving marble angel on a pedestal. At the angel's feet was the open grave of my mentor and, inside it, a glass sarcophagus. Vidal's body, dressed in white, lay under the glass, his eyes wide open. Black tears ran down his cheeks. The silhouette of his widow, Cristina, emerged from the cortège; she fell on her knees next to the body, drowning in grief. One by one, the members of the procession walked past the deceased and dropped black roses on his glass coffin, until it was completely covered and all one could see was his face. Two faceless gravediggers lowered the coffin into the grave, the base of which was flooded with a thick dark liquid. The sarcophagus floated on the sheet of blood, which slowly filtered through the cracks in the glass cover until little by little it filled the coffin, covering Vidal's dead body. Before his face was completely submerged, my mentor moved his eyes and looked at me. A flock of black birds took to the air and I started to run, losing my way among the paths of the endless city of the dead. Only the sound of distant crying enabled me to find the exit and to avoid the laments and pleadings of the dark, shadowy figures who waylaid me, begging me to take them with me, to rescue them from their eternal darkness.

. . .

Two policemen woke me, tapping my leg with their truncheons. Night had fallen and it took me a while to work out whether these were normal policemen on the beat or agents of the Fates on a special mission.

"Now, sir, go and sleep it off at home, understood?"

"Yes, Colonel!"

"Hurry up or you'll spend the night in jail. Let's see if you find that funny."

He didn't have to tell me twice. I got up as best I could and set off toward my house, hoping to get there before my feet led me off into some other seedy dive. The walk, which would normally have taken me ten or fifteen minutes, took three times as long. Finally, by some miracle, I arrived at my front door only to find Isabella sitting there, like a curse, this time inside the main entrance of the building, in the courtyard.

"You're drunk," said Isabella.

"I must be, because in mid delirium tremens I thought I discovered you sleeping in my doorway at midnight."

"I had nowhere else to go. My father and I quarreled and he's thrown me out."

I closed my eyes and sighed. My brain, dulled by alcohol and bitterness, was unable to release its torrent of denials and curses.

"You can't stay here, Isabella."

"Please, just for tonight. Tomorrow I'll look for a pension. I beg you, Señor Martín."

"Don't give me that doe-eyed look," I threatened.

"Besides, it's your fault that I've been thrown out," she added.

"My fault. I like that! I don't know whether you have any talent for writing, but you certainly have plenty of imagination. For what ill-fated reason, pray tell me, is it my fault that your dear father has chucked you out?"

"When you're drunk you have an odd way of speaking."

"I'm not drunk. I've never been drunk in my life. Now answer my question."

"I told my father you'd taken me on as your assistant and that from now on I was going to devote my life to literature and couldn't work in the shop."

"What?"

"Can we go in? I'm cold and my bum's turned to stone from sitting on the steps."

My head was going round in circles and I felt nauseated. I looked up at the faint glimmer that seeped through the skylight at the top of the stairs.

"Is this a punishment from above to make me repent my rakish ways?"

Isabella followed my eyes upwards, looking puzzled.

"Who are you talking to?"

"I'm not talking to anyone, I'm delivering a monologue. It's the inebriated man's prerogative. But tomorrow morning first thing I'm going to talk to your father and put an end to this absurdity."

"I don't think that's a good idea. He's sworn to kill you if he sees you. He's got a double-barrel shotgun hidden under the counter. He's like that. He once killed a mule with it. It was in the summer, near Argentona—"

"Shut up. Not another word. Silence."

Isabella nodded and looked at me expectantly. I began searching for my key. At that point I couldn't cope with this garrulous adolescent's drama. I needed to collapse onto my bed and lose consciousness, preferably in that order. I continued looking for a couple of minutes, in vain. Finally, without saying a word, Isabella came over to me and rummaged through the pocket of my jacket, which my hands had already explored a hundred times, and found the key. She showed it to me, and I nodded, defeated.

Isabella opened the door to the apartment, keeping me upright, then guided me to my bedroom as if I were an invalid, and helped me onto my bed. After settling my head on the pillows, she removed my shoes. I looked at her in confusion.

"Don't worry, I'm not going to take your trousers off."

She loosened my collar, sat down beside me, and smiled with a melancholy expression that belied her youth.

"I've never seen you so sad, Señor Martín. It's because of that woman, isn't it? The one in the photograph."

She held my hand and stroked it, calming me.

"Everything passes, believe me. Everything."

Despite myself, I could feel my eyes filling with tears and I turned my head so that she couldn't see my face. Isabella turned off the light on the bedside table and stayed there, sitting close to me in the dark, listening to the weeping of a miserable drunk, asking no questions, offering no opinion, offering nothing other than her company and her kindness, until I fell asleep.

7

I was woken by the agony of the hangover—a press clamping down on my temples—and the scent of Colombian coffee. Isabella had set a table by my bed with a pot of freshly brewed coffee and a plate with bread, cheese, ham, and an apple. The sight of the food made me nauseated, but I stretched out my hand to reach for the coffeepot. Isabella, who had been watching from the doorway, rushed forward, all smiles, and poured a cup for me.

"Drink it like this, good and strong. It will work wonders."

I accepted the cup and drank.

"What's the time?"

"One o'clock in the afternoon."

I snorted.

"How long have you been awake?"

"About seven hours."

"Doing what?"

"Cleaning, tidying up, but there's enough work here for a few months," Isabella replied.

I took another long sip of coffee.

"Thanks," I mumbled. "For the coffee. And for cleaning up, although you don't have to do it."

"I'm not doing it for you, if that's what you're worried about. I'm doing it for myself. If I'm going to live here, I'd rather not have to worry about getting stuck to something if I lean on it accidentally."

"Live here? I thought we'd said that—"

As I raised my voice, a stab of pain sliced through my brain.

"Shhhh," whispered Isabella.

I nodded, agreeing to a truce. I couldn't quarrel with Isabella now, and I didn't want to. There would be time enough to take her back to her family once the hangover had beaten a retreat. I finished my coffee in one long gulp and got up. Five or six thorns pierced my head. I groaned. Isabella caught hold of my arm.

"I'm not an invalid. I can manage on my own."

She let go of me tentatively. I took a few steps toward the corridor, with Isabella following close behind, as if she feared I was about to topple over at any moment. I stopped in front of the bathroom.

"May I pee on my own?"

"Mind how you aim," the girl murmured. "I'll leave your breakfast in the gallery."

"I'm not hungry."

"You have to eat something."

"Are you my apprentice or my mother?"

"It's for your own good."

I closed the bathroom door and sought refuge inside. It took a while for my eyes to adjust to what I was seeing. The bathroom was unrecognizable. Clean and sparkling. Everything in its place. A new bar of soap on the sink. Clean towels that I didn't even know I owned. A smell of bleach.

"Good God," I mumbled.

I put my head under the tap and let the cold water run for a couple of minutes, then went out into the corridor and slowly made my way to the gallery. If the bathroom was unrecognizable, the gallery now belonged to another world. Isabella had washed the windowpanes and the floor and tidied the furniture and armchairs. A diaphanous light filtered through the tall windows and the smell of dust had disappeared. My breakfast awaited on the table opposite the sofa, over which the girl had spread a clean throw. The books on the shelves seemed to have been reorganized and the glass cabinets had recovered their transparency. Isabella served me a second cup of coffee.

"I know what you're doing, and it's not going to work."

"Pouring you a coffee?"

She had tidied up the books that lay scattered around in piles on tables and in corners. She had emptied magazine racks that had been overflowing for ages. In just seven hours she had swept away years of darkness, and still she had the time and energy to smile.

"I preferred it as it was," I said.

"Of course you did, and so did the hundred thousand cockroaches you had as lodgers. I've sent them packing with the help of some ammonia."

"So that's the stink I smell?"

"This 'stink' is the smell of cleanliness," Isabella protested. "You could be a little bit grateful."

"I am."

"It doesn't show. Tomorrow I'll go up to the study and—"

"Don't even think about it."

Isabella shrugged but she still looked determined, and I knew that in twenty-four hours the study in the tower was going to suffer an irreparable transformation.

"By the way, this morning I found an envelope in the corridor. Somebody must have slipped it under the door last night."

I looked at her over my cup.

"The main door downstairs is locked," I said.

"That's what I thought. Frankly, I did find it rather odd and, although it had your name on it—"

"You opened it."

"I'm afraid so. I didn't mean to."

"Isabella, opening other people's letters is not a sign of good manners. In some places it's even considered a crime that can be punished with a prison sentence."

"That's what I tell my mother. She always opens my letters. And she's still free."

"Where's the letter?"

Isabella pulled an envelope out of the pocket of the apron she had donned and handed it to me, averting her eyes. The envelope had serrated edges and the paper was thick, porous, and ivory-colored, with an angel stamped on the red wax—now broken—and my name written in red perfumed ink. I opened it and pulled out a folded sheet.

> *Dear David,*
>
> *I hope this finds you in good health and that you have banked the agreed money without any problems. Do you think we could meet tonight at my house to start discussing the details of our project? A light dinner will be served around ten o'clock. I'll be waiting for you.*
>
> *Your friend,*
> ANDREAS CORELLI

I folded the sheet of paper and put it back in the envelope. Isabella looked at me with curiosity.

"Good news?"

"Nothing that concerns you."

"Who is this Señor Corelli? He has nice handwriting, not like yours."

I looked at her severely.

"If I'm going to be your assistant, it's only logical that I should know who your contacts are. In case I have to send them packing, that is."

I grunted.

"He's a publisher."

"He must be a good one—just look at the writing paper and envelope he uses. What book are you writing for him?"

"It's none of your business."

"How can I help you if you won't tell me what you're working on? No, don't answer. I'll shut up."

For ten miraculous seconds, Isabella was silent.

"What's this Señor Corelli like, then?"

I looked at her coldly.

"Peculiar," I ventured.

"Takes one to know one . . ."

Watching that girl with a noble heart I felt, if anything, more miserable and understood that the sooner I got her away from me, even at the risk of hurting her, the better it would be for both of us.

"Why are you looking at me like that?"

"I'm going out tonight, Isabella."

"Shall I leave some supper for you? Will you be back very late?"

"I'll be having dinner out and I don't know when I'll be back, but by the time I return, whenever it is, I want you to have left. I want you to collect your things and go. I don't care where to. There's no place for you here. Do you understand?"

Her face grew pale, and her eyes began to water. She bit her lip and smiled at me, her cheeks lined with falling tears.

"I'm not needed here. Understood."

"And don't do any more cleaning."

I got up and left her alone in the gallery. I hid in the study, up in the tower, and opened the windows. From down in the gallery I could hear Isabella sobbing. I gazed at the city stretching out under the midday sun, then turned my head to look in the other direction, where I thought I could almost see the shining tiles covering Villa Helius. I imagined Cristina, Señora de Vidal, standing by the windows of her tower, looking down at the Ribera quarter. Something dark and murky filled my heart. I forgot Isabella's weeping and wished only for the moment when I would meet Corelli, so that we could discuss his accursed book.

. . .

I stayed in the study as the afternoon spread over the city like blood floating in water. It was hot, hotter than it had been all summer, and the rooftops of the Ribera quarter seemed to shimmer like a mirage. I went down to the lower floor and changed my clothes. The house was silent, and in the gallery the shutters were half closed and the windows tinted with an amber light that seeped down the corridor.

"Isabella?" I called.

There was no reply. I went to the gallery and saw that the girl had left. First, though, she had cleaned off and put in order a collection of the complete works of Ignatius B. Samson. For years they had collected dust and sunk into oblivion in a glass cabinet that now shone immaculately. She had taken one of the books and left it open on a lectern. I read a line at random and felt as if I were traveling back to a time when everything seemed simple and inevitable.

"Poetry is written with tears, fiction with blood, and history with invisible ink," said the cardinal, as he spread poison on the knife edge by the light of a candelabra.

The studied naïveté of those lines made me smile and brought back a suspicion that had never really left me: perhaps it would have been better for everyone, especially for me, if Ignatius B. Samson had never committed suicide and David Martín had never taken his place.

8

It was getting dark when I went out. The heat and humidity had encouraged many of my neighbors to bring their chairs out into the street, hoping for a breeze that never came. I dodged the improvised rings of people sitting around front doors and on street corners and made my way to the railway station, where there was always a queue of taxis waiting for customers. I got into the first cab in line. It took us about twenty minutes to cross the city and climb the hill on whose slopes lay Gaudí's ghostly forest. The lights in Corelli's house could be seen from afar.

"I didn't know anyone lived here," the driver remarked.

As soon as I'd paid for my ride, including a tip, he sped off, not wasting a second. I waited a few moments, savoring the strange silence that filled the place. Not a single leaf moved in the wood that covered the hill behind me. A starlit sky with wisps of cloud spread in every direction. I could hear the sound of my own breathing, of my clothes rustling as I walked, of my steps getting closer to the door. I rapped with the knocker, then waited.

The door opened a few moments later. A man with drooping eyes and drooping shoulders nodded when he saw me and beckoned me in. His outfit suggested that he was some sort of butler or servant. He made no sound at all. I followed him down the passageway with the portraits on either side, and when we came to the end he showed me into the large sitting room with its view over the whole city in the distance. He bowed slightly and left me on my own, walking away as slowly as he had when he brought me in. I went over to the French windows and looked through the net curtains, killing time while I waited for Corelli. A couple of minutes had gone by when I noticed that someone was observing me from a corner of the room. He was sitting in an armchair, completely still, half in darkness, the light from an oil lamp revealing only his legs and his hands as they rested on the arms of the chair. I recognized him by the glow of his unblinking eyes and by the angel-shaped brooch on his lapel. As soon as I looked at him he stood up and came over to me with quick steps—too quick—and a wolfish smile.

"Good evening, Martín."

I nodded, trying to smile back.

"I've startled you again," he said. "I'm sorry. May I offer you something to drink, or shall we go straight to dinner?"

"To tell you the truth, I'm not hungry."

"It's the heat, I'm sure. If you like, we can go into the garden and talk there."

The silent butler reappeared and proceeded to open the doors to the garden, where a path of candles placed on saucers led to a white metal table with two chairs facing each other. The flame from the candles burned bright and unflickering. The moon cast a soft bluish hue. I sat down, and Corelli followed suit, while the butler poured us two glasses from a decanter of what I thought must be wine or some sort of liqueur I had no intention of tasting. In the light of the waxing moon, Corelli seemed younger, his features sharper. He observed me with an intensity verging on greed.

"Something is bothering you, Martín."

"I suppose you've heard about the fire."

"A terrible end, and yet there was poetic justice in it."

"You think it just that two men should die in such a way?"

"Would a gentler way have seemed more acceptable? Justice is an affectation of perspective, not a universal value. I'm not going to pretend to feel dismayed when I don't, and I don't suppose you will either, however hard you try. But if you prefer, we can observe a moment's silence."

"That won't be necessary."

"Of course not. It's only necessary when one has nothing valid to say. Silence makes even idiots seem wise for a minute. Anything else worrying you, Martín?"

"The police seem to think I have something to do with what happened. They asked me about you."

Corelli nodded, unconcerned.

"The police must do their work and we must do ours. Shall we close this matter?"

I nodded. Corelli smiled.

"A while ago, as I was waiting for you, I realized that you and I have a small rhetorical conversation pending. The sooner we get it out of the way, the sooner we can get started. I'd like to begin by asking what faith means to you."

I pondered for a moment.

"I've never been a religious person. Rather than believe or disbelieve, I doubt. Doubt is my faith."

"Very prudent and very bourgeois. But you don't win a game by hitting the balls out of court. Why would you say that so many different beliefs have appeared and disappeared throughout history?"

"I don't know. Social, economic, or political factors, I suppose. You're talking to someone who left school at the age of ten. History has never been my strong point."

"History is biology's dumping ground, Martín."

"I think I wasn't in school the day that lesson was taught."

"This lesson is not taught in classrooms, Martín. It is taught through reason and the observation of reality. This lesson·is the one nobody wants to learn and is therefore the one we must examine carefully in order to be able to do our work. All business opportunities stem from someone else's inability to resolve a simple and inevitable problem."

"Are we talking about religion or economics?"

"You choose the label."

"If I understand you correctly, you're suggesting that faith, the act of believing in myths, ideologies, or supernatural legends, is the consequence of biology."

"That's exactly right."

"A rather cynical view, coming from a publisher of religious texts," I remarked.

"A dispassionate and professional view," Corelli explained. "Human beings believe just as they breathe—in order to survive."

"Is that your theory?"

"It's not a theory, it's a statistic."

"It occurs to me that at least three-quarters of the world would disagree with that assertion," I said.

"Of course. If they agreed they wouldn't be potential believers. Nobody can really be convinced of something he or she doesn't *need* to believe in through some biological imperative."

"Are you suggesting then that it is part of our nature to be deceived?"

"It is part of our nature to survive. Faith is an instinctive response to aspects of existence that we cannot explain by any other means, be it the moral void we perceive in the universe, the certainty of death, the mystery of the origin of things, the meaning of our lives, or the absence of meaning. These are basic and extremely simple aspects of existence, but our limitations prevent us from responding in an unequivocal way and for that reason we generate an emotional response, as a defense mechanism. It's pure biology."

"According to you, then, all beliefs or ideals are nothing more than fiction."

"All interpretation or observation of reality is necessarily fiction. In this case, the problem is that man is a moral animal abandoned in an amoral universe and condemned to a finite existence with no other purpose than to perpetuate the natural cycle of the species. It is impossible to survive in a prolonged state of reality, at least for a human being. We spend a good part of our lives dreaming, especially when we're awake. As I said, pure biology."

I sighed.

"And after all this, you want me to invent a fable that will make the unwary fall on their knees and persuade them that they have seen the light, that there is something to believe in, something to live and die for—even to kill for?"

"Exactly. I'm not asking you to invent anything that hasn't already been invented, one way or another. I'm only asking you to help me give water to the thirsty."

"A praiseworthy and pious proposition," I said with irony.

"No, simply a commercial proposition. Nature is one huge free market. The law of supply and demand is a molecular fact."

"Perhaps you should find an intellectual to do this job. I can assure you that most of them have never seen a hundred thousand francs in their lives. I bet they'd be prepared to sell their souls, or even invent them, for a fraction of that amount."

The metallic glow in his eyes made me suspect that Corelli was about to deliver another of his hard-hitting pocket sermons. I visualized the credit in my account at the Banco Hispano Colonial and told myself that a hundred thousand francs were well worth the price of listening to a mass or a collection of homilies.

"An intellectual is usually someone who isn't exactly distinguished by his intellect," Corelli asserted. "He claims that label to compensate for his inadequacies. It's as old as that saying: Tell me what you boast of and I'll tell you what you lack. Our daily bread. The incompetent always present themselves as experts, the cruel as pious, sinners as devout, usurers as benefactors, the small-minded as patriots, the arrogant as humble, the vulgar as elegant, and the feeble-minded as intellectual. Once again, it's all the work of nature. Far from being the sylph to whom poets sing, nature is a cruel, voracious mother who needs to feed on the creatures she gives birth to in order to stay alive."

Corelli and his fierce biological poetics were beginning to make me feel queasy. I was uncomfortable at the barely contained vehemence of his words, and I wondered whether there was anything in the universe that did not seem repugnant and despicable to him, including me.

"You should give inspirational talks in schools and churches on Palm Sunday. You'd be a tremendous success," I suggested.

Corelli laughed coldly.

"Don't change the subject. What I'm searching for is the opposite of an intellectual—in other words, someone intelligent. And I have found that person."

"You flatter me."

"Better still, I pay you. And I pay you very well, which is the only real form of flattery in this whorish world. Never accept medals unless they come printed on the back of a check. They benefit only those who give them. And since I'm paying you, I expect you to listen and follow my instructions. Believe me when I say that I have no interest at all in making you waste your time. While you're in my pay, your time is also my time."

His tone was friendly, but his eyes shone like steel and left no room for misunderstanding.

"You don't need to remind me every five minutes."

"Forgive my insistence, dear Martín. If I'm making your head spin with all these details it's only because I'm trying to get them out of the way sooner rather than later. What I want from you is the form, not the content. The content is always the same and has been in place since human life began. It's engraved in your heart with a serial number. What I want you to do is find an intelligent and seductive way of answering the questions we all ask ourselves, and you should do so using your own reading of the human soul, putting into practice your art and your profession. I want you to bring me a narrative that awakens the soul."

"Nothing more . . ."

"Nothing less."

"You're talking about manipulating feelings and emotions. Would it not be easier to convince people with a rational, simple, and straightforward account?"

"No. It's impossible to initiate a rational dialogue with someone about beliefs and concepts if he has not acquired them through reason. It doesn't matter whether we're looking at God, race, or national pride. That's why I need something more powerful than a simple rhetorical exposition. I need the strength of art, of stagecraft. We think we understand a song's lyrics, but what makes us believe in them, or not, is the music."

I tried to swallow his nonsense without choking.

"Don't worry, there'll be no more speeches for today," Corelli interjected. "Now let's discuss practical matters. We'll meet about once a fortnight. You will inform me of your progress and show me the work you've produced. If I have any changes or observations to make, I will point them out to you. The work will continue for twelve months or whatever fraction of that time you need to complete the job. At the end of that period you will hand in all the work and the documents it generated, with no exceptions: they belong to the sole proprietor and guarantor of the rights—in other words, me. Your name will not appear as the author of the document and you will agree not to claim authorship after delivery or discuss the work you have written or the terms of this agreement, either in private or in public, with anybody. In exchange, you have already received an initial payment of one hundred thousand francs, and upon delivery of the work to my satisfaction, you will receive a bonus of fifty thousand francs."

I gulped. One is never wholly conscious of the greed hidden in one's heart until one hears the sweet sound of silver.

"Don't you want to formalize the contract in writing?"

"Ours is a gentleman's agreement, based on honor, yours and mine. It has already been sealed. A gentleman's agreement cannot be broken without breaking the person who has entered into it," said Corelli in a tone that made me think it might have been better to sign a piece of paper, even in blood. "Any questions?"

"Yes. Why?"

"I don't follow you, Martín."

"Why do you want all this material, or whatever you wish to call it? What do you plan to do with it?"

"Problems of conscience at this stage, Martín?"

"Perhaps you think of me as someone with no principles, but if I'm going to take part in the project you're proposing, I want to know what the objective is. I think I have a right to know."

Corelli smiled and placed his hand on mine. I felt a shiver at the contact of his skin, which was icy cold and smooth as marble.

"Because you want to live."

"That sounds vaguely threatening."

"A simple and friendly reminder of what you already know. You'll help me because you want to live and because you don't care about the price or the consequences. Because not that long ago you saw yourself at death's door and now you have an eternity before you and the opportunity of a life. You will help me because you're human. And because, although you don't want to admit it, you have faith."

I withdrew my hand from his reach and watched him get up from his chair and walk to the end of the garden.

"Don't worry, Martín. Everything will turn out all right. Trust me," said Corelli in a sweet, almost paternal tone.

"May I leave now?"

"Of course. I don't want to keep you any longer than is necessary. I've enjoyed our conversation. I'll let you go now so you can start mulling over all the things we've discussed. You'll see that, once the indigestion has passed, the real answers will come to you. There is nothing in the path of life that we don't already know before we start. Nothing important is learned; it is simply remembered."

He signaled to the taciturn butler, who was waiting at the edge of the garden.

"A car will pick you up and take you home. We'll meet again in two weeks' time."

"Here?"

"It's in the lap of the Gods," Corelli said, licking his lips as if he'd made a delicious joke.

The butler came over and motioned for me to follow him. Corelli nodded and sat down, his eyes lost once more to the city below.

9

The car—for want of a better word—was waiting by the door of the large, old house. It was not an ordinary automobile but a collector's item. It reminded me of an enchanted carriage, a cathedral on wheels, its chrome and curves engineered by science, its hood topped by a silver angel like a ship's figurehead. In other words, a Rolls-Royce. The butler opened the door for me and took his leave with a bow. I stepped inside: it looked more like a hotel room than a motorcar. The engine started up as soon as I settled in the seat, and we set off down the hill.

"Do you know the address?" I asked.

The chauffeur, a dark figure on the other side of a glass partition, nodded vaguely. We crossed Barcelona in the narcotic silence of that metal carriage, barely touching the ground, or so it seemed. Streets and buildings flew past the windows like underwater cliffs. It was after midnight when the black Rolls-Royce turned off Calle Comercio and entered Paseo del Borne. The car stopped on the corner of Calle Flassaders, which was too narrow for it to pass. The chauffeur got out and opened my door with a bow. I stepped from the car and he closed the door and got in again without saying a word. I watched him leave, the dark silhouette blending into a veil of shadows. I asked myself what I had done, and, choosing not to seek an answer, I set off toward my house feeling as if the whole world were a prison from which there was no escape.

When I walked into the apartment I went straight up to the study.

I opened the windows on all four sides and let the humid breeze penetrate the room. I could see people lying on mattresses and sheets on some of the neighboring flat roofs, trying to escape the suffocating heat and get some sleep. In the distance, the three large chimneys in the Paralelo area rose like funeral pyres spreading a mantle of white ash over Barcelona. Nearer to me, on the dome of La Mercè church, the statue of Our Lady of Mercy, poised for ascension into heaven, reminded me of the angel on the Rolls-Royce and of the one on Corelli's lapel. After many months of silence it felt as if the city were speaking to me again, telling me its secrets.

Then I saw her, curled up on a doorstep in that miserable narrow tunnel between old buildings they called "Fly Alley." Isabella. I wondered how long she'd been there and told myself it was none of my business. I was about to close the window and walk over to the desk when I noticed that she was not alone. Two figures were slowly, perhaps too slowly, advancing toward her from the other end of the street. I hoped they would pass her by. They didn't. One of them took up a position on the other side, blocking the exit from the alley. The other knelt in front of the girl, stretching an arm out toward her. The girl moved. A few moments later the two figures closed in on Isabella and I heard her scream.

It took me about forty-five seconds to get there. When I did, one of the two men had grabbed Isabella by her arms and the other had pulled up her skirt. A terrified expression gripped the girl's face. The second man guffawed as he made his way between her thighs, holding a knife to her throat. Three lines of blood oozed from the cut. I looked around me. A couple of boxes of rubbish and a pile of cobblestones and building materials lay abandoned by the wall. I grabbed what turned out to be a metal bar, solid and heavy, about half a meter long. The first man to notice my presence was the one holding the knife. I took a step forward, brandishing the metal bar. His eyes jumped from the bar to my eyes and his smile disappeared. The other turned and saw me advancing toward them holding the bar up high. A nod from me was enough to make him let go of Isabella and quickly stand behind his companion.

"Come on, let's go," he whispered.

The other man ignored his words. He was looking straight at me with fire in his eyes, the knife still in his hand.

"Who asked you to stick your oar in, you son of a bitch?"

I took Isabella by the arm, lifting her up from the ground, without taking my eyes off the man with the knife. I searched for the keys in my pocket and gave them to her.

"Go home," I shouted. "Do as I say."

Isabella hesitated for a moment, but soon I heard her running toward Calle Flassaders. The guy with the knife saw her leave and smiled angrily.

"I'm going to slash you, you bastard."

I didn't doubt his ability or his wish to carry out his threat, but something in his eyes made me think that my opponent was not altogether stupid and if he had not done so already it was because he was wondering how much the metal bar I was holding might weigh and, above all, whether I'd have the strength, the courage, and the time to squash his skull with it before he could thrust his blade into me.

"Go on," I invited him.

The man held my eyes for a few seconds and then laughed. The other one sighed with relief. The first folded his blade and spat at my feet. Then he turned round and walked off into the shadows from which he had emerged, his companion running behind him like a puppy.

I found Isabella curled up at the bottom of the stairs in the inner courtyard of the tower house. She was trembling and held the keys with both hands. When she saw me come in she jumped up.

"Do you want me to call a doctor?"

She shook her head.

"Are you sure?"

"They hadn't managed to do anything to me yet," she mumbled, fighting away the tears.

"It didn't look that way."

"They didn't do anything, all right?" she protested.

"All right," I said.

I wanted to hold her arm as we went up the stairs, but she avoided any contact.

Once in the apartment I took her to the bathroom and turned on the light.

"Have you any clean clothes you can put on?"

Isabella showed me the bag she was carrying and nodded.

"Come on, you wash while I get something ready for dinner."

"How can you be hungry after what just happened?"

"Well, I am."

Isabella bit her lower lip.

"The truth is, so am I . . ."

"End of discussion then," I said.

I closed the bathroom door and waited until I heard the taps running, then returned to the kitchen and put some water on to boil. There was a bit of rice left, some bacon, and a few vegetables that Isabella had brought over the day before. I improvised a dish of leftovers and waited almost thirty minutes for her to come out of the bathroom, downing almost half a bottle of wine in that time. I heard her crying with anger on the other side of the wall. When she appeared at the kitchen door her eyes were red and she looked more like a child than ever.

"I'm not sure that I'm still hungry," she murmured.

"Sit down and eat."

We sat at the small table in the middle of the kitchen. Isabella examined her plate of rice and chopped-up bits with some suspicion.

"Eat," I ordered.

She brought a tentative spoonful to her lips.

"It's good," she said.

I poured her half a glass of wine and topped it up with water.

"My father doesn't let me drink wine."

"I'm not your father."

We had dinner in silence, exchanging glances. Isabella finished her plate and the slice of bread I'd given her. She smiled shyly. She didn't realize that the shock hadn't yet hit her. Then I went with her to her bedroom door and turned on the light.

"Try to get some rest," I said. "If you need anything, bang on the wall. I'm in the next room."

Isabella nodded. "I heard you snoring the other night."

"I don't snore."

"It must have been the pipes. Or maybe there's a neighbor with a pet bear."

"One more word and you're back in the street."

"Thanks," she whispered. "Don't close the door completely, please. Leave it ajar."

"Good night," I said, turning out the light and leaving Isabella in the dark.

Later, while I undressed in my bedroom, I noticed a dark mark on my cheek, like a black tear. I went over to the mirror and brushed it away with my fingers. It was dried blood. Only then did I realize that I was exhausted and my whole body was aching.

The following morning, before Isabella woke up, I walked over to her family's grocery shop on Calle Mirallers. It was just getting light and the security gate over the shop door was only half open. I slipped inside and found a couple of young boys piling up boxes of tea and other goods on the counter.

"It's closed," one of them said.

"Well, it doesn't look closed. Go and fetch the owner."

While I waited, I kept myself busy examining the family emporium of the ungrateful heiress Isabella, who in her infinite innocence had turned her back on the ambrosia of commerce to prostrate herself before the altar of literary misery. The shop was a small bazaar of marvels brought from every corner of the world. Jams, sweets, and teas. Coffees, spices, and tinned food. Fruit and cured meats. Chocolates and smoked ham. A Pantagruelian paradise for those with well-lined pockets. Don Odón, Isabella's father and the manager of the establishment, appeared presently, wearing blue overalls, a marshal's moustache, and an expression of alarm that seemed to herald an imminent heart attack. I decided to skip the pleasantries.

"Your daughter says you have a double-barreled shotgun with which you have sworn to kill me," I said. "Well, here I am."

"Who are you, you scoundrel?"

"I'm the scoundrel who's had to take in a young girl because her pathetic father was unable to keep her under control."

The shopkeeper's angry expression disappeared and was replaced with a timid smile.

"Señor Martín? I didn't recognize you . . . How is my child?"

"Your child is safe and sound in my house, snoring like a mastiff but with her honor and virtue intact."

The shopkeeper crossed himself twice, much relieved.

"God bless you."

"Thank you very much, but in the meantime I'm going to ask you to come collect her today without fail. Otherwise I'll smash your face in, shotgun or no shotgun."

"Shotgun?" the shopkeeper mumbled in confusion.

His wife, a small, nervous-looking woman, was spying on us from behind a curtain that concealed the back room. Something told me there would be no shots fired here. Don Odón huffed and puffed and looked as if he was on the point of collapse.

"Nothing would please me more, Señor Martín. But the girl doesn't want to be here," he countered, devastated.

When I realized the shopkeeper was not the rogue Isabella had painted him as, I was sorry for the way I'd spoken.

"You haven't thrown her out of your house?"

Don Odón opened his eyes wide and looked hurt. His wife stepped forward and took her husband's hand.

"We quarreled," he said. "Things were said that shouldn't have been said, on both sides. But that girl has such a temper, you wouldn't believe it . . . She threatened to leave us and said she'd never come back. Her saintly mother nearly passed away from the palpitations. I shouted at her and said I'd stick her in a convent."

"An infallible argument when reasoning with a seventeen-year-old girl," I pointed out.

"It was the first thing that came to mind," the shopkeeper said. "As if I would put her in a convent!"

"From what I've seen, you'd need the help of a whole regiment of infantry."

"I don't know what that girl has told you, Señor Martín, but you mustn't believe her. We might not be very refined, but we're not monsters either. I don't know how to deal with her anymore. I'm not the type of man who would pull out a belt and give her forty lashes. And my missus here doesn't dare even shout at the cat. I don't know where the girl gets it from. I think it's all that reading. Mind you, the nuns warned us. And my father, God rest his soul, used to say it too: the day women are allowed to learn to read and write the world will become ungovernable."

"A deep thinker, your father, but that doesn't solve your problem or mine."

"What can we do? Isabella doesn't want to be with us, Señor Martín. She says we're dim and we don't understand her. She says we want to bury her in this shop. There's nothing I'd like more than to understand her. I've worked in this shop since I was seven years old, from dawn to dusk, and the only thing I understand is that the world is a nasty place with no consideration for a young girl who has her head in the clouds," the shopkeeper explained, leaning on a barrel. "My greatest fear is that if I force her to return she might really run away and fall into the hands of any old . . . I don't even want to think about it."

"It's true," his wife said, with a slight Italian accent. "Believe me, the girl has broken our hearts, but this is not the first time she's gone away. She's turned out just like my mother, who had a Neapolitan temperament—"

"Oh, *la mamma,*" said Don Odón, shuddering even at the memory of his mother-in-law.

"When she told us she was going to stay at your house for a few days while she helped you with your work, well, we felt reassured," Isabella's mother went on, "because we know you're a good person and basically the girl is nearby, only two streets away. We're sure you'll be able to convince her to return."

I wondered what Isabella had told them about me to persuade them that yours truly could walk on water.

"Only last night, just round the corner from here, two laborers on their way home were given a terrible beating. Imagine! It seems they were battered with an iron pole, smashed to bits like dogs. One of them might not survive, and it looks like the other one will be crippled for life," said the mother. "What sort of world are we living in?"

Don Odón gave me a worried look.

"If I go and fetch her, she'll leave again. And this time I don't know whether she'll end up with someone like you. It's not right for a young girl to live in a bachelor's house, but at least you're honest and will know how to take care of her."

The shopkeeper seemed about to cry. I would have preferred if he'd rushed off to fetch the gun. There was still the chance that some Neapolitan cousin might turn up, armed with a blunderbuss, to save the girl's honor. *Porca miseria.*

"Do I have your word that you'll look after her for me until she comes to her senses?"

I grunted. "You have my word."

I returned home laden with superb delicacies that Don Odón and his wife insisted on foisting on me. I promised them I'd take care of Isabella for a few days, until she agreed to reason things out and understood that her place was with her family. The shopkeepers wanted to pay me for her keep, but I refused. My plan was that before the week was up Isabella would be back sleeping in her own home, even if I had to keep up the pretense that she was my assistant. Taller towers had toppled.

When I got home I found her sitting at the kitchen table. She had washed all the dishes from the night before, made coffee, and dressed and styled her hair so that she resembled a saint in a religious picture. Isabella, who was no fool, knew perfectly well where I'd been and looked at me like an abandoned dog, smiling meekly. I left the bags with the delicacies from Don Odón by the sink.

"Didn't my father shoot you with his gun?"

"He'd run out of bullets and decided to throw all these pots of jam and Manchego cheese at me instead."

Isabella pressed her lips together, trying to look serious.

"So the name Isabella comes from your grandmother?"

"*La mamma,*" she confirmed. "In the local area they called her Vesuvia."

"You don't say."

"They say I'm a bit like her. When it comes to persistence."

There was no need for a judge to pronounce on that, I thought.

"Your parents are good folk, Isabella. They don't misunderstand you any more than you misunderstand them."

The girl didn't say anything. She poured me a cup of coffee and waited for the verdict. I had two options: throw her out and give the two shopkeepers a fit or be bold and patient for two or three more days. I imagined that forty-eight hours of my most cynical and cutting performance would be enough to break the iron determination of the young girl and send her, on her knees, back to her mother, begging for forgiveness and full board.

"You can stay here for the time being—"

"Thank you!"

"Not so fast. You can stay here under the following conditions: one, that you go spend some time in the shop every day, to say hello to your parents and tell them you're well, and two, that you obey me and follow the rules of this house."

It sounded patriarchal but excessively fainthearted. I maintained my austere expression and decided to make my tone more severe.

"What are the rules of this house?" Isabella inquired.

"Basically, whatever I damn well please."

"Sounds fair."

"It's a deal, then."

Isabella came round the table and hugged me gratefully. I felt the warmth and the firm shape of her seventeen-year-old body against mine. I pushed her away delicately, keeping my distance.

"The first rule is that this is not *Little Women* and we don't hug each other or burst into tears at the slightest thing."

"Whatever you say."

"That will be the motto on which we'll build our coexistence: Whatever I say."

Isabella laughed and rushed off into the corridor.

"Where do you think you're going?"

"To tidy up your study. You don't mean to leave it like that, do you?"

I had to find a place where I could think, where I could escape from my new assistant's domestic pride and her obsession with cleanliness. So I went to the library in Calle del Carmen, set in a nave of Gothic arches that had once housed a medieval hospice. I spent the rest of the day surrounded by volumes that smelled like a papal tomb, reading about mythology and the history of religions until my eyes were about to fall out onto the table and roll away along the library floor. After hours of reading without a break, I worked out that I had barely scratched a millionth of what I could find beneath the arches of that sanctuary of books, let alone everything else that had been written on the subject. I decided to return the following day and the day after that: I would spend at least a week filling the cauldron of my thoughts with pages and pages about gods, miracles and prophecies, saints and apparitions, revelations and mysteries—anything rather than think about Cristina, Don Pedro, and their life as a married couple.

. . .

As I had an obliging assistant at my disposal, I instructed her to find copies of catechisms and schoolbooks currently used for religious instruction and to write me a summary of each one. Isabella did not dispute my orders, but she frowned when I gave them.

"I want to know, in numbing detail, how children are taught the whole business, from Noah's Ark to the Feeding of the Five Thousand," I explained.

"Why?"

"Because that's the way I am. I have a wide range of interests."

"Are you doing research for a new version of 'Away in a Manger'?"

"No. I'm planning a novel about the adventures of a second lieutenant nun. Just do as I say and don't question me or I'll send you back to your parents' shop to sell quince jelly galore."

"You're a despot."

"I'm glad to see we're getting to know each other."

"Does this have anything to do with the book you're writing for that publisher, Corelli?"

"It might."

"Well, I get the feeling it's not a book that will have much commercial appeal."

"And what would you know?"

"More than you think. And there's no need to get so worked up, either. I'm only trying to help you. Or have you decided to stop being a professional writer and change into an elegant amateur?"

"For the moment I'm too busy being a nanny."

"I wouldn't bring up the question of who is the nanny here, because I'd win that debate hands down."

"So what debate does Your Excellency fancy?"

"Commercial art versus stupid moral idiocies."

"Dear Isabella, my little Vesuvia, in commercial art—and all art that is worthy of the name is commercial sooner or later—stupidity is almost always in the eye of the beholder."

"Are you calling me stupid?"

"I'm calling you to order. Do as I say. And shush."

I pointed to the door and Isabella rolled her eyes, mumbling some insult or other that I didn't quite hear as she walked off down the passageway.

. . .

While Isabella went around schools and bookshops in search of textbooks and catechisms to summarize for me, I went back to the library in Calle del Carmen to further my theological education, an endeavor I undertook fueled by strong doses of coffee and stoicism. The first seven days of that strange creative process enlightened me only with more doubts. One of the few truths I discovered was that, although the vast majority of authors who felt a calling to write about the divine, the human, and the sacred must have been exceedingly learned and pious, as writers they were dreadful. For the long-suffering reader forced to skim their pages it was a real struggle not to fall into a coma induced by boredom with each new paragraph.

After surviving thousands of pages, I was beginning to get the impression that the hundreds of religious beliefs cataloged throughout the history of the printed letter were extraordinarily similar. I attributed this first impression to my ignorance or to a lack of adequate information, but I couldn't rid myself of the idea that I'd been going through the story lines of dozens of crime novels in which the murderer turned out to be either one person or another but the mechanics of the plot were, in essence, always the same. Myths and legends, either about divinities or about the origins and history of peoples and races, began to look like the images of a jigsaw puzzle, slightly different from one another but always constructed with the same pieces, though not in identical configurations.

After two days I had already become friends with Eulalia, the head librarian, who picked out texts and volumes from the ocean of paper in her care and from time to time came to see me at my table in the corner to ask whether I needed anything else. She must have been around my age and had wit to spare, generally expressed as sharp, somewhat poisonous jibes.

"You're reading a lot of hagiography, sir. Have you decided to become an altar boy now, at the threshold of maturity?"

"It's only research."

"Ah, that's what they all say."

The librarian's clever jokes provided an invaluable balm that enabled me to survive those texts that seemed to be carved in stone and to press on with my pilgrimage. Whenever Eulalia had a free moment she would come over to my table and help me classify all that bilge—pages abounding with stories of fathers and sons, of pure, saintly mothers, betrayals and conversions, prophets and martyrs, envoys from heaven, babies born to save the universe, evil creatures horrifying to look at and usually taking the form of animals, ethereal beings with racially acceptable features who acted as agents of good, and heroes subjected to terrible tests to prove their destiny. Earthly existence was always perceived as a temporary rite of passage that urged one to a docile acceptance of one's lot and the rules of the tribe, because the reward was always in the hereafter, a paradise brimming with all the things one had lacked in corporeal life.

On Thursday at midday, Eulalia came over to my table during one of her breaks and asked me whether, besides reading missals, I ate every now and then. So I asked her to lunch at nearby Casa Leopoldo, which had just opened to the public. While we enjoyed a delicious oxtail stew, she told me she'd been in the job for over two years and had spent two more years working on a novel that was proving difficult to finish. It was set in the library on Calle del Carmen and the plot was based on a series of mysterious crimes that took place there.

"I'd like to write something similar to those novels by Ignatius B. Samson," she said. "Ever heard of them?"

"Vaguely," I replied.

Eulalia couldn't quite find a way forward with her writing so I suggested she give it all a slightly sinister tone and focus the story on a secret book possessed by a tormented spirit, with subplots full of the seemingly supernatural.

"That's what Ignatius B. Samson would do, in your place," I suggested.

"And what are you doing reading all about angels and devils? Don't tell me you're a repentant ex-seminarist."

"I'm trying to find out what the origins of different religions and myths have in common," I explained.

"What have you discovered so far?"

"Almost nothing. I don't want to bore you with my lament."

"You won't bore me. Go on."

"Well, what I've found most interesting so far is that, generally speaking, beliefs arise from an event or character that may or may not be authentic and rapidly evolve into social movements that are conditioned and shaped by the political, economic, and societal circumstances of the group that accepts them. Are you still awake?"

Eulalia nodded.

"A large part of the mythology that develops around each of these doctrines, from its liturgy to its rules and taboos, comes from the bureaucracy generated as they develop and not from the supposed supernatural act that originated them. Most of the simple, well-intentioned anecdotes are a mixture of common sense and folklore, and all the belligerent force they eventually develop comes from a subsequent interpretation of those principles, or even their distortion, at the hands of bureaucrats. The administrative and hierarchic aspects seem to be crucial in the evolution of belief systems. The truth is first revealed to all men but very quickly individuals appear claiming sole authority and a duty to interpret, administer, and, if need be, alter this truth in the name of the common good. To this end they establish a powerful and potentially repressive organization. This phenomenon, which biology shows us is common to any social group, soon transforms the doctrine into a means of achieving control and political power. Divisions, wars, and breakups become inevitable. Sooner or later, the word becomes flesh and the flesh bleeds."

I thought I was beginning to sound like Corelli and I sighed. Eulalia gave a hesitant smile.

"Is that what you're looking for? Blood?"

"It's the caning that leads to learning, not the other way round."

"I wouldn't be so sure."

"I have a feeling you went to a convent school."

"The Sisters of the Holy Infant Jesus. The black nuns. Eight years."

"Is it true what they say, that girls from convent schools are the ones who harbor the darkest and most unmentionable desires?"

"I bet you'd love to find out."

"You can put all the chips on 'yes.' "

"What else have you learned in your crash course in theology?"

"Not much else. My initial conclusions have left an unpleasant aftertaste—it's so banal and inconsequential. All this seemed more or less evident already without the need to swallow whole encyclopedias and treatises on where to tickle angels—perhaps because I'm unable to understand beyond my own prejudices or because there is nothing else to understand and the crux of the matter lies in simply believing or not believing, without stopping to wonder why. How's my rhetoric? Are you still impressed?"

"It's giving me goose pimples. A shame I didn't meet you when I was a schoolgirl with dark desires."

"You're cruel, Eulalia."

The librarian laughed heartily, looking me in the eye.

"Tell me, Ignatius B., who has broken your heart and left you so angry?"

"I see books aren't the only things you read."

We sat awhile longer at the table, watching the waiters coming and going across the dining room of Casa Leopoldo.

"Do you know the best thing about broken hearts?" the librarian asked.

I shook my head.

"They can only really break once. The rest is just scratches."

"Put that in your book."

I pointed to her engagement ring.

"I don't know who the idiot is, but I hope he knows he's the luckiest man in the world."

Eulalia smiled a little sadly. We returned to the library and to our places: she went to her desk and I to my corner. I said good-bye to her the following day, when I decided that I couldn't, and wouldn't, read another line about revelations and eternal truths. On my way to the library I had bought her a white rose at one of the stalls on the Ramblas and I left it on her empty desk. I found her in one of the passages, sorting out some books.

"Are you abandoning me so soon?" she said when she saw me. "Who is going to flirt with me now?"

"Who isn't?"

She came with me to the exit and shook my hand at the top of the flight of stairs that led to the courtyard of the old hospital. Halfway down I stopped and turned round. She was still there, watching me.

"Good luck, Ignatius B. I hope you find what you're looking for."

12

While I was having dinner with Isabella at the gallery table, I noticed my new assistant was casting me a sidelong glance.

"Don't you like the soup? You haven't touched it," the girl ventured.

I looked at the plate I had allowed to grow cold, took a spoonful, and pretended I was tasting the most exquisite delicacy.

"Delicious," I remarked.

"And you haven't said a word since you returned from the library," Isabella added.

"Any other complaints?"

Isabella looked away, upset. Although I had little appetite, I ate some of the cold soup so as to have an excuse for not speaking.

"Why are you so sad? Is it because of that woman?"

I went on stirring my spoon around in the soup. Isabella didn't take her eyes off me.

"Her name is Cristina," I said eventually. "And I'm not sad. I'm pleased for her because she's married my best friend and she's going to be very happy."

"And I'm the Queen of Sheba."

"You're a busybody. That's what you are."

"I prefer you like this, when you're in a foul mood, because you tell the truth."

"Then let's see how you like this: clear off to your room and leave me in peace, for Christ's sake!"

She tried to smile, but by the time I stretched out my hand to her, her eyes had filled with tears. She took my plate and hers and fled to the kitchen. I heard the plates falling into the sink and then, a few moments later, the door of her bedroom slamming shut. I savored the glass of red wine left on the table, an exquisite vintage from Isabella's parents' shop. After a while I went along to her bedroom door and knocked gently. She didn't reply, but I could hear her crying. I tried to open the door, but the girl had locked herself in.

I went up to the study, which after Isabella's visit smelled of fresh flowers and looked like the cabin of a luxury cruiser. She had tidied up all the books, dusted and left everything shiny and unrecognizable. The old Underwood looked like a piece of sculpture and the letters on the keys were clearly visible again. A neat pile of paper, containing summaries of religious textbooks and catechisms, lay on the desk next to the day's mail. A couple of cigars on a saucer emitted a delicious scent: Macanudos, one of the Caribbean delicacies supplied to Isabella's father on the quiet by a contact in the state tobacco industry. I took one of them and lit it. It had an intense flavor that seemed to embody all the aromas and poisons a man could wish for in order to die in peace.

I sat at the desk and went through the day's letters, ignoring them all except one: ocher parchment embellished with the writing I would have recognized anywhere. The missive from my new publisher and patron, Andreas Corelli, summoned me to meet him on Sunday, midafternoon, at the top of the main tower of the new cable railway that had been launched to coincide with the International Exhibition.

. . .

The tower of San Sebastián stood one hundred meters high amid a jumble of cables and steel that induced vertigo if one merely looked at them. The cable railway crossed the docks from that first tower to a huge central structure reminiscent of the Eiffel Tower that served as the junction. From there the cable cars departed, suspended in midair, for the second part of the journey up to Montjuïc, where the heart of the exhibition was located. This technological marvel promised views of the city that until then had been the preserve only of airships, birds with a large wingspan, and hailstones. From my point of view, men and seagulls were not supposed to share the same air space and as soon as I set foot in the lift that went up the tower I felt my stomach shrink to the size of a marble. The journey up seemed endless, the jolting of that brass capsule an exercise in pure nausea.

I found Corelli gazing through one of the large windows that looked out over the docks, his eyes lost among watercolors of sails and masts as they slid across the water. He wore a white silk suit and was toying with a sugar lump, which he proceeded to swallow with an animal voracity. I cleared my throat and the boss turned round, smiling with pleasure.

"A marvelous view, don't you think?"

I nodded tentatively.

"You don't like heights?"

"I like to keep my feet on the ground as much as possible," I replied, maintaining a prudent distance from the window.

"I've gone ahead and bought return tickets," he informed me.

"What a kind thought."

I followed him to the footbridge from which one stepped into the cars that departed from the tower and traveled, suspended a sickening height above the ground, for what looked like a horribly long time.

"How did you spend the week, Martín?"

"Reading."

He glanced at me briefly.

"By your bored expression I suspect it was not Alexandre Dumas."

"A collection of dandruffy academics and their leaden prose."

"Ah, intellectuals. And you wanted me to sign one up. Why is it that the less one has to say the more one says it in the most pompous and pedantic way possible?" Corelli asked. "Is it to fool the world or just to fool themselves?"

"Probably both."

The boss handed me the tickets and signaled to me to go first. I showed the tickets to the person holding the cable car door open and entered unenthusiastically. I decided to stand in the center, as far as possible from the windows. Corelli smiled like an excited child.

"Perhaps part of your problem is that you've been reading the commentators and not the people they were commenting on. A common mistake but fatal when you're trying to learn something," Corelli observed.

The doors closed and a sudden jerk sent us into orbit. I held on to a metal pole and took a deep breath.

"I sense that scholars and theoreticians are no heroes of yours," I said.

"I have no heroes, my friend, still less those who cover themselves or one another in glory. Theory is the practice of the impotent. I suggest that you put aside the encyclopedists' accounts and go straight to the sources. Tell me, have you read the Bible?"

I hesitated for a moment. The cable car lurched on into the void. I looked at the floor.

"Fragments here and there, I suppose," I mumbled.

"You suppose. Like almost everyone. A serious mistake. Everyone should read the Bible. And reread it. Believers or nonbelievers, it doesn't matter. I read it at least once a year. It's my favorite book."

"And are you a believer or a skeptic?" I asked.

"I'm a professional. And so are you. What we believe or don't believe is irrelevant as far as our work is concerned. To believe or to disbelieve is a pointless act. Either one knows or one doesn't. And that's all there is to it."

"Then I confess that I don't know anything."

"Follow that path and you'll find the footsteps of the great philosophers. And along the way read the Bible from start to finish. It's one of the greatest stories ever told. Don't make the mistake of confusing the word of God with the missal industry that lives off it."

The longer I spent in the company of the publisher the less I understood him.

"I'm quite lost. We were talking about legends and fables and now you're telling me that I must think of the Bible as the word of God?"

A shadow of impatience and irritation clouded his eyes.

"I'm speaking figuratively. God isn't a charlatan. The word is human currency."

He smiled at me the way one smiles at a child who cannot understand the most elemental things. As I observed him, I realized that I found it impossible to know when he was talking seriously and when he was joking. As impossible as guessing at the purpose of the extravagant undertaking for which he was paying me such a princely sum. In the meantime the cable car was bobbing about like an apple on a tree lashed by a gale. Never had I thought so much about Isaac Newton.

"You're a coward, Martín. This machine is completely safe."

"I'll believe it when I'm back on firm ground."

We were nearing the midpoint of the journey, the tower of San Jaime, which rose up from the docks near the large Customs Building.

"Do you mind if we get off here?" I asked.

Corelli shrugged. I didn't feel at ease until I was inside the tower's lift and felt it touch the ground. When we walked out into the port we found a bench facing the sea and the slopes of Montjuïc. We sat down to watch the cable car flying high above us, me with a sense of relief, Corelli with longing.

"Tell me about your first impressions. What have these days of intensive study and reading suggested to you?"

I proceeded to summarize what I thought I'd learned, or unlearned, during those days. The publisher listened attentively, nodding and occasionally gesticulating with his hands. At the end of my report about the myths and beliefs of human beings, Corelli gave a satisfactory verdict.

"I think you've done an excellent work of synthesis. You haven't found the proverbial needle in the haystack, but you've understood that the only thing that really matters in the whole pile of hay is the damned needle—the rest is just fodder for asses. Speaking of donkeys, tell me, are you interested in fables?"

"When I was small, for about two months I wanted to be Aesop."

"We all give up great expectations along the way."

"What did you want to be as a child, Señor Corelli?"

"God."

He leered like a jackal, wiping the smile off my face.

"Martín, fables are possibly one of the most interesting literary forms ever invented. Do you know what they teach us?"

"Moral lessons?"

"No. They teach us that human beings learn and absorb ideas and concepts through narrative, through stories, not through lessons or theoretical speeches. This is what any of the great religious texts teach us. They're all tales about characters who must confront life and overcome obstacles, figures setting off on a journey of spiritual enrichment through exploits and revelations. All holy books are, above all, great stories whose plots deal with the basic aspects of human nature, setting them within a particular moral context and a particular framework of supernatural dogmas. I was content for you to spend a dismal week reading theses, speeches, opinions, and comments so that you could discover for yourself that there is nothing to learn from them, because they're nothing more than exercises in good or bad faith—usually unsuccessful—by people who are trying, in turn, to understand. The professorial conversations are over. From now on I'll ask you to start reading the stories of the Brothers Grimm, the tragedies of Aeschylus, the Ramayana, or the Celtic legends. Please yourself. I want you to analyze how these texts work. I want you to distill their essence and find out why they provoke an emotional reaction. I want you to learn the grammar, not the moral. And I want you to bring me something of your own in two or three weeks' time, the beginning of a story. I want you to make me believe."

"I thought we were professionals and couldn't commit the sin of believing in anything."

Corelli smiled, baring his teeth.

"One can convert only a sinner, never a saint."

13

The days passed. Accustomed as I was to years of living alone and to that state of methodical and undervalued anarchy common to bachelors, the continued presence of a woman in the house, even though she was an unruly adolescent with a volatile temper, was beginning to play havoc with my daily routine. I believed in controlled disorder; Isabella didn't. I believed that objects find their own place in the chaos of a household; Isabella didn't. I believed in solitude and silence; Isabella didn't. In just a couple of days I discovered that I was no longer able to find anything in my own home. If I was looking for a paper knife or a glass or a pair of shoes, I had to ask Isabella where Providence had kindly inspired her to hide them.

"I don't hide anything. I put things in their place. Which is different."

Not a day went by when I didn't feel the urge to strangle her half a dozen times. When I took refuge in my study, searching for peace and quiet in which to think, Isabella would appear after a few minutes, a smile on her face, bringing me a cup of tea or some biscuits. She would wander around the study, look out the window, tidy everything I had on my desk, and then would ask me what I was doing there, so quiet and mysterious. I discovered that seventeen-year-old girls have such huge verbal energy that their brains drive them to expend it every twenty seconds. On the third day I decided I had to find her a boyfriend—if possible a deaf one.

"Isabella, how is it that a girl as attractive as you has no suitors?"

"Who says I don't?"

"Isn't there any boy you like?"

"Boys my age are boring. They have nothing to say and half of them seem like complete idiots."

I was going to say that they didn't improve with age but didn't want to spoil her illusions.

"So what age do you like them?"

"Old. Like you."

"Do I seem old to you?"

"Well, you're not exactly a spring chicken."

It was preferable to think she was pulling my leg than to accept the blow to my vanity. I decided to respond with a few drops of sarcasm.

"The good news is that young girls like old men, and the bad news is that old men, especially decrepit, slobbering old men, like young girls."

"I know. I wasn't born yesterday."

Isabella observed me. She was scheming and smiled with a hint of malice.

"Do you like young girls too?"

The answer was on my lips before she had asked the question. I adopted a masterful, impartial tone, like a professor of geography.

"I liked them when I was your age. Now I generally like girls of my own age."

"At your age they're no longer girls. They're young women or, to be precise, ladies."

"End of argument. Have you nothing to do downstairs?"

"No."

"Then start writing. You're not here to wash the dishes and hide my things. You're here because you said you wanted to learn to write and I'm the only idiot you know who can help you."

"There's no need to get angry. It's just that I lack inspiration."

"Inspiration comes when you stick your elbows on the table and your bottom on the chair and start sweating. Choose a theme, an idea, and squeeze your brain until it hurts. That's called inspiration."

"I have a topic."

"Hallelujah."

"I'm going to write about you."

We exchanged glances, like opponents across a game board.

"Why?"

"Because I find you interesting. And strange."

"And old."

"And touchy. Almost like a boy my age."

Despite myself I was beginning to get used to Isabella's company, to her jibes and to the light she had brought into that house. If things continued this way, my worst fears were going to come true and we'd end up being friends.

"What about you? Have you found a subject with all those whopping great tomes you're consulting?"

I decided that the less I told Isabella about my commission, the better.

"I'm still at the research stage."

"Research? And how does that work?"

"Basically, you read thousands of pages to learn what you need to know and to get to the heart of a subject, to its emotional truth, and then you shed all that knowledge and start again at square one."

Isabella sighed.

"What is emotional truth?"

"It's sincerity within fiction."

"So, does one have to be an honest, good person to write fiction?"

"No. One has to be skilled. Emotional truth is not a moral quality. It's a technique."

"You sound like a scientist," protested Isabella.

"Literature, at least good literature, is science tempered with the blood of art. Like architecture or music."

"I thought it was something that sprang from the artist, just like that, spontaneously."

"The only things that spring spontaneously are unwanted body hair and warts."

Isabella considered these revelations without much enthusiasm.

"You're saying all this to discourage me and make me go home."

"I should be so lucky."

"You're the worst teacher in the world."

"It's the student who makes the teacher, not the other way round."

"It's impossible to argue with you because you know all the rhetorical tricks. It's not fair."

"Nothing is fair. The most one can hope is for things to be logical. Justice is a rare illness in a world that is otherwise a picture of health."

"Amen. Is that what happens as you grow older? Do people stop believing in things, as you have?"

"No. Most people, as they grow old, continue to believe in nonsense, usually even greater nonsense. I swim against the tide because I like to annoy."

"Tell me something I don't know! Well, when I'm older I'll go on believing in things," Isabella threatened.

"Good luck."

"And what's more, I believe in you."

She didn't look away as I fixed my eyes on hers.

"Because you don't know me."

"That's what you think. You're not as mysterious as you imagine."

"I don't pretend to be mysterious."

"That was a kind substitute for unpleasant. I also know a few rhetorical tricks."

"That isn't rhetoric. It's irony. They're two different things."

"Do you always have to win every argument?"

"When it's as easy as this, yes."

"And that man . . ."

"Corelli?"

"Corelli. Does he make it easy for you?"

"No. Corelli knows even more tricks than I do."

"That's what I thought. Do you trust him?"

"Why do you ask?"

"I don't know. Do you trust him?"

"Why shouldn't I trust him?"

Isabella shrugged.

"What exactly has he commissioned you to write? Aren't you going to tell me?"

"I told you. He wants me to write a book for his publishing company."

"A novel?"

"Not exactly. More like a fable. A legend."

"A book for children?"

"Something like that."

"And you're going to do it?"

"He pays very well."

Isabella frowned.

"Is that why you write? Because they pay you well?"

"Sometimes."

"And this time?"

"This time I'm going to write the book because I have to."

"Are you in debt to him?"

"You could put it that way, I suppose."

Isabella weighed the matter. She was about to say something but thought twice about it and bit her lip. Instead, she gave me an innocent smile and one of her angelic looks with which she was capable of changing the subject with a simple batting of her eyelids.

"I'd also like to be paid to write," she said.

"Anyone who writes would like the same, but it doesn't mean that he or she will achieve it."

"And how do you achieve it?"

"You begin by going down to the gallery, taking pen and paper—"

"Digging your elbows in and squeezing your brain until it hurts. I know."

She looked into my eyes, hesitating. She'd been staying in my house for a week and a half and I still showed no signs of sending her home. I imagined she was asking herself when I was going to do it or why I hadn't done it yet. I also asked myself that very question and could find no answer.

"I like being your assistant, even if you are the way you are," she said at last.

The girl was staring at me as if her life depended on a kind word. I yielded to temptation. Good words are a vain benevolence that demands no sacrifice and is more appreciated than real acts of kindness.

"I also like you being my assistant, Isabella, even if I am the way I am. And I will like it even more when there is no longer any need for you to be my assistant as you will have nothing more to learn from me."

"Do you think I have potential?"

"I have no doubt whatsoever. In ten years you'll be the teacher and I'll be the apprentice," I said, repeating words that still tasted of treason.

"You liar," she said, kissing me sweetly on the cheek before running off down the stairs.

14

That afternoon I left Isabella sitting at the desk we had set up for her in the gallery, facing her blank pages, while I went over to Gustavo Barceló's bookshop on Calle Fernando hoping to find a good, readable edition of the Bible. All the sets of New and Old Testaments I had in the house were printed in microscopic type on thin, almost translucent onionskin paper, and reading them induced not so much fervor and divine inspiration as migraines. Barceló, who among many other things was an avid collector of holy books and apocryphal Christian texts, had a private room at the back of his shop filled with a formidable assortment of Gospels, lives of saints and holy people, and all kinds of other religious texts.

When I walked into the bookshop, one of the assistants rushed into the backroom office to alert the boss. Barceló emerged looking euphoric.

"Bless my eyes! Sempere told me you'd been reborn, but this is quite something. Next to you, Valentino looks like someone just back from the salt mines. Where have you been hiding, you rogue?"

"Oh, here and there," I said.

"Everywhere except at Vidal's wedding party. You were sorely missed, my friend."

"I doubt that."

The bookseller nodded, implying that he understood my wish not to discuss the matter.

"Will you accept a cup of tea?"

"Or two. And a Bible. If possible, one that is easy to read."

"That won't be a problem," said the bookseller. "Dalmau?"

The shop assistant called Dalmau came over obligingly.

"Dalmau, our friend Martín here needs a Bible that is legible, not decorative. I'm thinking of Torres Amat, 1825. What do you think?"

One of the peculiarities of Barceló's bookshop was that books were spoken of as if they were exquisite wines, cataloged by bouquet, aroma, consistency, and vintage.

"An excellent choice, Señor Barceló, although I'd be more inclined toward the updated and revised edition."

"Eighteen sixty?"

"Eighteen ninety-three."

"Of course. That's it! Wrap it up for our friend Martín and put it on the house."

"Certainly not," I objected.

"The day I charge an unbeliever like you for the word of God will be the day I'm struck dead by lightning, and with good reason."

Dalmau rushed off in search of my Bible and I followed Barceló into his office, where the bookseller poured two cups of tea and offered me a cigar from his humidor. I accepted it and lit it with the flame of the candle he handed me.

"Macanudo?"

"I see you're educating your palate. A man must have vices, expensive ones if possible. Otherwise when he reaches old age he will have nothing to be redeemed from. In fact, I'm going to have one with you, what the hell!"

A cloud of exquisite cigar smoke covered us like high tide.

"I was in Paris a few months ago and took the opportunity to make some inquiries on the subject you talked about with our friend Sempere some time ago," Barceló said.

"Éditions de la Lumière."

"Exactly. I wish I'd been able to scratch a little deeper, but unfortunately, after the publishing house closed down, nobody, it seems, bought its inventory, so it was difficult to gather much information."

"You say it closed? When?"

"In 1914, I believe."

"There must be some mistake."

"Not if we're talking about the same Éditions de la Lumière, in Boulevard St.-Germain."

"That's the one."

"In fact, I made a note of everything so I wouldn't forget it when I saw you."

Barceló looked in the drawer of his desk and pulled out a small notebook.

"Here it is: 'Éditions de la Lumière, publishing house specializing in religious texts with offices in Rome, Paris, London, and Berlin. Founder and publisher, Andreas Corelli. Date of opening of first office in Paris, 1881—' "

"Impossible," I muttered.

"Of course, I could have got it wrong, but . . ."

"Did you get a chance to visit the offices?"

"As a matter of fact, I did try, because my hotel was opposite the Pantheon, very close by, and the former offices of the publishing house were on the southern side of the boulevard, between Rue St.-Jacques and Boulevard St.-Michel."

"And?"

"The building was empty, bricked up, and it looked as if there'd been a fire or something similar. The only thing remaining was the door knocker, an exquisite object in the shape of an angel. Bronze, I think. I would have taken it if a gendarme hadn't been watching me disapprovingly. I didn't have the courage to provoke a diplomatic incident—heaven forbid France should decide to invade us again!"

"The way things are going, they might be doing us a favor."

"Now that you mention it . . . But going back to the subject, when I saw what a state the place was in, I went to the café next door to make some inquiries and they told me the building had been like that for twenty years."

"Were you able to discover anything about the publisher?"

"Corelli? From what I gathered, the publishing house closed when he decided to retire, although he can't even have been fifty years old. I think he moved to a villa in the south of France, in the Lubéron, and died shortly afterwards. They say a snake bit him. A viper. That's what you get for retiring to Provence."

"Are you sure he died?"

"Père Coligny, an old competitor of Corelli's, showed me his death notice—he had it framed and treasures it like a trophy. He said he looks at it every day to remind himself that the damned bastard is dead and buried. His exact words, although in French they sounded much prettier and more musical."

"Did Coligny mention whether the publisher had any children?"

"I got the impression that Corelli was not his favorite topic, because as soon as he could he slipped away from me. It seems there was some scandal—Corelli stole one of his authors from him, someone called Lambert."

"What happened?"

"The funniest thing about all this is that Coligny had never actually set eyes on Corelli. His only contact with him was by correspondence. The root of the problem, I think, was that Monsieur Lambert signed an agreement to write a book for Éditions de la Lumière behind Coligny's back, when Coligny had sole rights to his work. Lambert was an opium addict and had accumulated enough debts to pave the Rue de Rivoli from end to end. Coligny suspected that Corelli had offered Lambert an astronomical sum and that the poor man, who was dying, had accepted it because he wanted to leave his children well provided for."

"What sort of book was it?"

"Something with a religious theme. Coligny mentioned the title, some fancy Latin expression that was fashionable at the time, but I can't remember it now. As you know, the titles of missals are all pretty much the same. *Pax Gloria Mundi* or something like that."

"And what happened to the book and Lambert?"

"That's where matters become complicated. It seems that poor Lambert, in a fit of madness, wanted to burn his manuscript, so he set fire to it, and to himself, in the offices of the publishing house. A lot of people thought the opium had frazzled his brain, but Coligny suspected that it was Corelli who pushed him toward suicide."

"Why would he want to do that?"

"Who knows? Perhaps he didn't want to pay him the sum he had promised. Perhaps it was all just Coligny's fantasy—he seemed to be a great fan of young Beaujolais twelve months a year. He told me that Corelli had tried to kill him in order to release Lambert from his contract and that Corelli left him in peace only when he decided to terminate the agreement and let Lambert go."

"Didn't you say he'd never seen him?"

"Exactly. I think Coligny must have been raving. When I visited him in his apartment I saw more crucifixes, Madonnas, and figures of saints than you'd find in a shop selling Christmas mangers. I got the impression that he wasn't all that well in the head. When I left he told me to stay away from Corelli."

"But hadn't he told you Corelli was dead?"

"*Ecco qua.*"

I fell silent. Barceló looked at me with curiosity.

"I have the feeling that my discoveries aren't a huge surprise to you."

I gave him a carefree smile, trying to make light of it all.

"On the contrary. Thank you for taking the time to investigate."

"Not at all. Going to Paris in search of gossip is a pleasure in itself. You know me."

Barceló tore the page with the information out of his notebook and handed it to me.

"In case it's of any use to you. I've noted down everything I was able to discover."

I stood up and we shook hands. He came with me to the door, where Dalmau had the parcel ready for me.

"How about a print of the Baby Jesus, one of those where he opens and closes his eyes depending how you look at it? Or one of the Virgin Mary surrounded by lambs that turn into rosy-cheeked cherubs when you move it? A wonder of stereoscopic technology."

"The revealed word is enough for the time being."

"Amen."

I was grateful to the bookseller for his attempts to cheer me up, but as I walked away from the shop I was beset by anxiety and I had the feeling that the streets and my destiny rested on nothing but quicksand.

15

On my way home I stopped by a stationer's in Calle Argenteria to look at the shop window. On a sheet of fabric was a case containing a set of nibs, an ivory pen, and a matching inkpot engraved with what looked like fairies or Muses. There was something melodramatic about the whole set, as if it had been stolen from the writing desk of some Russian novelist, the sort who would bleed to death over thousands of pages. Isabella had beautiful handwriting that I envied, as pure and clear as her conscience, and the set seemed to have been made for her. I went in and asked the shop assistant to show it to me. The nibs were gold-plated and the whole business cost a small fortune, but I decided that it would be a good idea to repay my young assistant's kindness and patience with this little gift. I asked the man to wrap it in bright purple paper with a ribbon the size of a carriage.

When I got home I was looking forward to the selfish satisfaction that comes from arriving with a gift in one's hand. I was about to call Isabella as if she were a faithful pet with nothing better to do than wait devotedly for her master's return, but what I saw when I opened the door left me speechless. The corridor was as dark as a tunnel. The door of the room at the other end was open, casting a square of flickering yellow light across the floor.

"Isabella?" I called out. My mouth was dry.

"I'm here."

The voice came from inside the room. I left the parcel on the hall table and walked down the corridor. I stopped in the doorway and looked inside. Isabella was sitting on the floor. She had placed a candle inside a tall glass and was earnestly devoting herself to her second vocation after literature: tidying up other people's belongings.

"How did you get in here?"

"I was in the gallery and I heard a noise. I thought it was you coming back, but when I went into the corridor I saw that this door was open. I thought you'd told me it was locked."

"Get out of here. I don't want you coming into this room. It's very damp."

"Don't be silly. With all the work there is to do here? Come on. Look at all the things I've found."

I hesitated.

"Here, come in."

I stepped into the room and knelt down beside her. Isabella had separated all the items and boxes into categories: books, toys, photographs, clothes, shoes, spectacles. I looked at all the objects with a certain apprehension. Isabella seemed to be delighted, as if she'd discovered King Solomon's mines.

"Is all of this yours?"

I shook my head.

"It belonged to the previous owner."

"Did you know him?"

"No. It had all been here for years when I moved in."

Isabella held a packet of letters out to me as if it were evidence in a magistrate's court.

"Well, I think I've discovered his name."

"You don't say."

Isabella smiled, clearly delighted with her detective work.

"Marlasca," she announced. "His name was Diego Marlasca. Don't you think it's odd?"

"What?"

"That his initials are the same as yours: D.M."

"It's just a coincidence. Tens of thousands of people in this town have the same initials."

Isabella winked at me. She was really enjoying herself.

"Look what else I've found."

Isabella had salvaged a tin box full of old photographs. They were images from another age, postcards of old Barcelona, of pavilions that had been demolished in Ciudadela Park after the 1888 Universal Exhibition, of large crumbling houses and avenues full of people dressed in the formal style of the time, of carriages and memories the color of my childhood. Faces with absent expressions stared at me from forty years back. In some of those photographs I thought I recognized the face of an actress who had been popular when I was a young boy and who had long since disappeared into obscurity. Isabella watched me in silence.

"Do you remember her?" she asked, after a time.

"I think her name was Irene Sabino. She was quite a famous actress in the Paralelo theaters. This was a long time ago. Before you were born."

"Just look at this, then."

Isabella handed me a photograph in which Irene Sabino appeared leaning against a window. It didn't take me long to identify it as the one in my study at the top of the tower.

"Interesting, isn't it?" Isabella asked. "Do you think she lived here?"

I shrugged my shoulders.

"Maybe she was Diego Marlasca's lover . . ."

"I don't think that's any of our business."

"Sometimes you're so boring."

Isabella put the photographs back in the box. As she did so, one of them slipped from her hands. The picture fell at my feet. I picked it up and examined it: Irene Sabino, wearing a dazzling black gown, posed with a group of people dressed for a party in what seemed to be the grand hall of the Equestrian Club. It was just a picture of a social gathering that wouldn't have caught my eye had I not noticed in the background, almost blurred, a gentleman with white hair standing at the top of a staircase. Andreas Corelli.

"You've gone pale," said Isabella.

She took the photograph from my hand and perused it silently. I stood up and made a sign to Isabella to leave the room.

"I don't want you to come in here again," I said weakly.

"Why?"

I waited for her to leave the room and closed the door behind us. Isabella looked at me as if I weren't altogether sane.

"Tomorrow you'll call the Sisters of Charity and tell them to come and collect all this. They're to take everything. What they don't want, they can throw away."

"But—"

"Don't argue with me."

I didn't want to face her and went straight to the stairs that led up to the study. Isabella watched me from the corridor.

"Who is that man, Señor Martín?"

"Nobody," I murmured. "Nobody."

16

I went up to the study. Night had fallen, but there was no moon or stars in the sky. I opened the windows and gazed at the city in shadows. Only a light breeze was blowing and the sweat tingled on my skin. I sat on the windowsill smoking the second of the cigars Isabella had left on my desk a few days before and waiting for a breath of fresh air or a more presentable idea than the collection of clichés with which I was supposed to begin work on the boss's commission. I heard the shutters in Isabella's bedroom opening on the floor below. A rectangle of light fell across the courtyard, punctured by the profile of her silhouette. Isabella went up to her window and gazed into the darkness without noticing my presence. I watched her slowly undress. I saw her walk over to the mirror and examine her body, stroking her belly with the tips of her fingers and going over the cuts she had made on the inside of her arms and thighs. She looked at herself for a long time, wearing nothing but a defeated air, then turned off the light.

I returned to my desk and sat in front of my pile of notes. I went over sketches of stories full of mystic revelations and prophets who survived extraordinary trials and who returned bearing the revealed truth; of messianic infants abandoned at the doors of humble families with pure souls, who were persecuted by evil, godless empires; of promised paradises for those who would accept their destiny and play the game with a sporting spirit; and of idle, anthropomorphic deities with nothing better to do than keep a telepathic watch on the consciences of millions of fragile primates—primates who learned to think just in time to discover that they had been abandoned to their lot in a remote corner of the universe and whose vanity, or despair, made them slavishly believe that heaven and hell were eager to know about their paltry little sins.

I asked myself if this was what the boss had seen in me, a mercenary mind with no qualms about hatching a narcotic story fit for sending small children to sleep or for convincing some poor hopeless devil to murder his neighbor in exchange for the eternal gratitude of some god who subscribed to rule of the gun. Some days earlier another letter had arrived, requesting that I meet with the boss to discuss the progress of my work. Setting aside my scruples, I realized that I had barely twenty-four hours until the meeting and at the rate I was going I'd arrive with my hands empty but with my head full of doubts and suspicions. Since there was no alternative, I did what I'd done for so many years in similar circumstances. I placed a sheet of paper in the Underwood and, with my hands poised on the keyboard like a pianist waiting for the beat, I began to squeeze my brain to see what would come out.

17

"Interesting," the boss pronounced when he'd finished the tenth and last page. "Strange, but interesting."

We were sitting on a bench in the gilded haze of the Shade House in Ciudadela Park. A vault of wooden strips filtered the sun until it was reduced to a golden shimmer, and all around us a garden of plants shaped the play of light and dark in the peculiar luminous gloom. I lit a cigarette and watched the smoke rise from my fingers in blue spirals.

"Coming from you, *strange* is a disturbing adjective," I noted.

"I meant strange as opposed to vulgar," Corelli specified.

"But?"

"There are no buts, Martín. I think you've found an interesting route with a lot of potential."

For a novelist, when someone comments that their pages are interesting and have potential, it is a sign that things aren't going well. Corelli seemed to read my anxiety.

"You've turned the question round. Instead of going straight for the mythological references you've started with the more prosaic. May I ask you where you got the idea of a warrior messiah instead of a peaceful one?"

"You mentioned biology."

"Everything we need to know is written in the great book of nature," Corelli agreed. "We only need the courage and the mental and spiritual clarity with which to read it."

"One of the books I consulted explained that among humans the male attains the plenitude of his fertility at the age of seventeen. The female attains it later and preserves it and somehow acts as selector and judge of the genes she agrees to reproduce. The male, on the other hand, simply offers himself and wastes away much faster. The age at which he reaches his maximum reproductive strength is also when his combative spirit is at its peak. A young man is the perfect soldier. He has great potential for aggression and a limited critical capacity—or none at all—with which to analyze it and judge how to channel it. Throughout history societies have found ways of using this store of aggression, turning their adolescents into soldiers, cannon fodder with which to conquer their neighbors or defend themselves against their aggressors. Our protagonist was an envoy from heaven, but an envoy who, in the first flush of youth, took arms and liberated truth with blows of iron."

"Have you decided to mix history with biology, Martín?"

"From what you said, I understood them to be one and the same thing."

Corelli smiled. I don't know whether he was aware of it, but when he smiled he looked like a hungry wolf. I swallowed hard and tried to ignore the goosebumps.

"I've given this some thought," I said, "and I realized that most of the great religions either were born or reached their apogee at a time when the societies that adopted them had a younger and poorer demographic base. Societies in which 70 percent of the population was under the age of eighteen—half of them males with their veins bursting with violence and the urge to procreate—were perfect breeding grounds for an acceptance and explosion of faith."

"That's an oversimplification, but I see where you're going, Martín."

"I know. But with these general ideas in mind, I asked myself, why not get straight to the point and establish a mythology around this warrior messiah? A messiah full of blood and anger, who saves his people, his genes, his womenfolk, and his patriarchs from the political and racial dogma of his enemies—that is to say, from anyone who does not subject himself to his doctrine."

"What about the adults?"

"We'll get to the adult by having recourse to his frustration. As life advances and we have to give up the hopes, dreams, and desires of our youth, we acquire a growing sense of being a victim of the world and of other people. There is always someone else to blame for our misfortunes or failures, someone we wish to exclude. Embracing a doctrine that will turn this grudge and this victim mentality into something positive provides comfort and strength. The adult then feels part of the group and sublimates his lost desires and hopes through the community."

"Perhaps," Corelli granted. "What about all this iconography of death and the flags and shields? Don't you find it counterproductive?"

"No. I think it's essential. Clothes maketh the man, but above all they maketh the churchgoer."

"And what do you say about women, the other half? I'm sorry, but I find it hard to imagine a substantial number of women in a society believing in pennants and shields. Boy Scout psychology is for children."

"The main pillar of organized religion, with few exceptions, is the subjugation, repression, even the annulment of women in the group. Woman must accept the role of an ethereal, passive, and maternal presence, never of authority or independence, or she will have to suffer the consequences. She might have a place of honor in the symbolism, but not in the hierarchy. Religion and war are male pursuits. And anyhow, woman sometimes ends up becoming the accomplice in her own subjugation."

"And the aged?"

"Old age is the lubricant of belief. When death knocks at the door, skepticism flies out the window. A serious cardiovascular fright and a person will even believe in Little Red Riding Hood."

Corelli laughed.

"Careful, Martín, I think you're becoming more cynical than I am."

I looked at him as if I were an obedient pupil eager for the approval of a demanding teacher. Corelli patted me on the knee, nodding with satisfaction.

"I like it. I like the flair of it. I want you to go on turning things round and finding a shape. I'm going to give you more time. We'll meet in two or three weeks. I'll let you know a few days beforehand."

"Do you have to leave the city?"

"Business matters concerning the publishing house. I'm afraid I have a few days of travel ahead of me, but I'm going away contented. You've done a good job. I knew I'd found my ideal candidate."

The boss stood up and put out his hand. I dried the sweat from my palm on my trouser leg and we shook hands.

"You'll be missed," I began.

"Don't exaggerate, Martín, you were doing very well."

I watched him leave and remained where I was a good while, wondering whether the boss had risen to the bait and swallowed the tall stories I'd fed him. I was sure that I'd told him exactly what he wanted to hear. I hoped so, and I also hoped that the string of nonsense would keep him satisfied for the time being, convinced that his servant, the poor failed novelist, had become a convert. I told myself that anything that bought me time in which to discover what I had got myself into was worth a try. When I stood up and left the Shade House, my hands were still shaking.

18

Years of experience writing thrillers provide one with a set of principles on which to base an investigation. One of them is that all moderately solid plots, including those seemingly about affairs of passion, bear the unmistakable whiff of money and property. When I left the Shade House I walked to the Land Registry in Calle Consejo de Ciento and asked whether I could consult the records in which the sales and ownership of my house were listed. Books in the Land Registry archive contain almost as much information on the realities of life as the complete works of the most respected philosophers—if not more.

I began by looking up the section containing the details of my lease of 30 Calle Flassaders. There I found the necessary data with which to trace the history of the property before the Banco Hispano Colonial took ownership in 1911, as part of the appropriation of the Marlasca family assets—apparently the family had inherited the building upon the death of the owner. A lawyer named S. Valera was mentioned as having represented the family. Another leap into the past allowed me to find information relating to the purchase of the building by Don Diego Marlasca Pongiluppi in 1902 from a certain Bernabé Massot y Caballé. I made a note of all this on a slip of paper, from the name of the lawyer and all those taking part in the transactions to the relevant dates.

One of the clerks announced in a loud voice that there were fifteen minutes to closing time so I got ready to leave, but before that I hurriedly tried to consult the records for Andreas Corelli's house next to Güell Park. After fifteen minutes of searching in vain, I looked up from the register and met the ashen eyes of the clerk. He was an emaciated character, pomade shining on moustache and hair, who oozed that belligerent apathy of those who turn their job into a platform for obstructing the lives of others.

"I'm sorry. I can't find a property," I said.

"That must be because it doesn't exist or because you don't know how to search properly. We've closed for today."

I repaid his kindness and efficiency with my best smile.

"I might find it with your expert help," I suggested.

He gave me a nauseating look and snatched the volume from my hands.

"Come back tomorrow."

My next stop was the ostentatious building of the Bar Association in Calle Mallorca, only a few streets away. I climbed the wide steps guarded by glass chandeliers and what looked like a statue of Justice but with the bosom and attitude of a Paralelo starlet. When I reached the secretary's office, a small, mousy-looking man welcomed me and asked how he could help.

"I'm looking for a lawyer."

"You've come to the right place. We don't know how to get rid of them here. There seem to be more every day. They multiply like rabbits."

"It's the modern world. The one I'm looking for is called, or was called, Valera, S. Valera, with a V."

The little man disappeared into a labyrinth of filing cabinets. I waited, leaning on the counter, my eyes wandering over a décor ponderous with the inexorable weight of the law. Five minutes later the man returned with a folder.

"I've found ten Valeras. Two with an S. Sebastián and Soponcio."

"Soponcio?"

"You're very young, but years ago that was a name with a certain cachet, and ideal for the legal profession. Then along came the Charleston and ruined everything."

"Is Don Soponcio still alive?"

"According to the folder and the date he stopped paying his dues, Soponcio Valera y Menacho was received into the glory of Our Lord in the year 1919. Memento mori. Sebastián is his son."

"Still practicing?"

"Fully and constantly. I sense you will want the address."

"If it's not too much trouble."

The little man wrote it down on a small piece of paper that he handed to me.

"442 Diagonal. It's just a stone's throw away. But it's two o'clock, and by now most top lawyers will be at lunch with rich widows or manufacturers of fabrics and explosives. I'd wait until four."

I put the address in my jacket pocket.

"I'll do that. Thank you for your help."

"That's what we're here for. God bless."

. . .

I had a couple of hours to kill before paying a visit to Señor Valera, so I took a tram down Vía Layetana and got off when it reached Calle Condal. The Sempere & Sons bookshop was close by and I knew from experience that—contravening the immutable tradition of local shops—the old bookseller didn't close at midday. I found him as usual, standing at the counter cataloging books and serving a large group of customers who were wandering around the tables and bookshelves hunting for treasure. He smiled when he saw me and came over to say hello. He looked thinner and paler than the last time I'd seen him. He must have noticed my anxiety because he immediately made light of the matter.

"Some win, others lose. You're looking fit and well and I'm all skin and bones, as you can see," he said.

"Are you all right?"

"Fresh as a daisy. It's the damned angina. Nothing serious. What brings you here, Martín, my friend?"

"I thought I'd take you out to lunch."

"Thank you, but I can't abandon ship. My son has gone to Sarriá to appraise a collection and business isn't so good that we can afford to close the shop when there are customers about."

"Don't tell me you're having financial problems."

"This is a bookshop, Martín, not an investment firm. The world of letters provides us with just enough to get by, and sometimes not even that."

"If you need help . . ."

Sempere held up his hand.

"If you want to help me, buy a book or two."

"You know that the debt I owe you can never be repaid with money."

"All the more reason not even to think about it. Don't worry about us, Martín. The only way they'll get me out of here is in a pine box. But if you like, you can come share a tasty meal of bread, raisins, and fresh Burgos cheese. With that, and *The Count of Monte Cristo,* anyone can live to a hundred."

19

Sempere hardly tasted his food. He smiled wearily and pretended to be interested in my comments, but I could see that from time to time he was having trouble breathing.

"Tell me, Martín, what are you working on?"

"It's difficult to explain. A book I've been commissioned to write."

"A novel?"

"Not exactly. I wouldn't know how to describe it."

"What's important is that you're working. I've always said that idleness dulls the spirit. We have to keep the brain busy, or at least the hands if we don't have a brain."

"But some people work more than is reasonable, Señor Sempere. Shouldn't you take a break? How many years have you been here, always hard at work, never stopping?"

Sempere looked around him.

"This place is my life, Martín. Where else would I go? To a sunny bench in the park, to feed pigeons and complain about my rheumatism? I'd be dead in ten minutes. My place is here. And my son isn't ready to take up the reins of the business, even if he thinks he is."

"But he's a good worker. And a good person."

"Between you and me, he's too good a person. Sometimes I look at him and wonder what will become of him the day I go. How is he going to cope?"

"All fathers say that, Señor Sempere."

"Did yours? Forgive me, I didn't mean to . . ."

"Don't worry. My father had enough worries of his own without having to worry about me as well. I'm sure your son has more experience than you think."

Sempere looked dubious.

"Do you know what I think he lacks?"

"Malice?"

"A woman."

"He'll have no shortage of girlfriends with all the turtledoves who cluster round the shop window to admire him."

"I'm talking about a real woman, the sort who makes you become what you're supposed to be."

"He's still young. Let him have fun for a few more years."

"That's a good one! If he'd at least have some fun. At his age, if I'd had that chorus of young girls after me, I'd have sinned like a cardinal."

"The Lord gives bread to the toothless."

"That's what he needs: teeth. And a desire to bite."

Something else seemed to be going round his mind. He was look-ing at me and smiling.

"Maybe you could help . . ."

"Me?"

"You're a man of the world, Martín. And don't give me that ex-pression. I'm sure that if you apply yourself you'll find a good woman for my son. He already has a pretty face. You can teach him the rest."

I was speechless.

"Didn't you want to help me?" the bookseller asked. "Well, there you are."

"I was talking about money."

"And I'm talking about my son, the future of this house. My whole life."

I sighed. Sempere took my hand and pressed it with what little strength he had left.

"Promise you'll not allow me to leave this world before I've seen my son set up with a woman worth dying for. And who'll give me a grandson."

"If I'd known this was coming, I'd have stayed at the Novedades Café for lunch."

Sempere smiled.

"Sometimes I think you should have been my son, Martín."

I looked at the bookseller, who seemed more fragile and older than ever before, barely a shadow of the strong, impressive man I remembered from my childhood, and I felt the world crumbling around me. I went up to him and before I realized it, did what I'd never done in all the years I'd known him. I gave him a kiss on his forehead, which was spotted with freckles and touched by a few gray hairs.

"Do you promise?"

"I promise," I said, as I walked to the door.

20

Señor Valera's office occupied the top floor of an extravagant Modernist building at 442 Avenida Diagonal, just round the corner from Paseo de Gracia. The building looked like a cross between a giant grandfather clock and a pirate ship and was adorned with huge French windows and a roof with green dormers. Anywhere else the baroque and byzantine structure would have been proclaimed either as one of the seven wonders of the world or as the freakish creation of a mad artist possessed by demons. In Barcelona's Ensanche quarter, where similar buildings cropped up everywhere like clover after rain, it barely raised an eyebrow.

I walked into the hallway and was shown to a lift that reminded me of something a giant spider might have left behind if it were weaving cathedrals instead of cobwebs. The doorman opened the cabin and imprisoned me in the strange capsule that began to rise through the middle of the stairwell. A severe-looking secretary opened the carved oak door at the top and showed me in. I gave her my name and explained that I had not made an appointment but that I was there to discuss a matter relating to the sale of a building in the Ribera quarter. Something changed in her expression.

"The tower house?" she asked.

I nodded. The secretary led me to an empty office. I sensed that this was not the official waiting room.

"Please wait, Señor Martín. I'll let Señor Valera know you're here."

I spent the next forty-five minutes in that office, surrounded by bookshelves packed with volumes the size of tombstones bearing inscriptions on the spines such as "1888–1889, B.C.A. Section One. Second Title." It seemed like irresistible reading matter. The office had a large window looking onto Avenida Diagonal that provided an excellent view over the city. The furniture smelled of fine wood, weathered and seasoned with money. Carpets and leather armchairs were reminiscent of those in a British club. I tried to lift one of the lamps presiding over the desk and guessed that it must have weighed at least thirty kilos. A huge oil painting, resting over a hearth that had never been used, portrayed the rotund and expansive presence of none other than Don Soponcio Valera y Menacho. The titanic lawyer sported a moustache and sideburns like the mane of an old lion, and his stern eyes, with the fire and steel of a hanging judge, dominated every corner of the room from the great beyond.

"He doesn't speak, but if you stare at the portrait for a while he looks as if he might do so at any moment," said a voice behind me.

Sebastián Valera was a man with a quiet demeanor who looked as if he'd spent the best part of his life attempting to crawl out from his father's shadow and now, at fifty plus, was tired of trying. He had penetrating, intelligent eyes and that exquisite manner enjoyed only by princesses and the most expensive lawyers. He offered me his hand and I shook it.

"I'm sorry to have kept you waiting, but I wasn't expecting your visit," he said, pointing to a seat.

"Not at all. Thank you for receiving me."

Valera gave me the smile of someone who knows how much he charges for every minute.

"My secretary tells me your name is David Martín. You're David Martín, the author?"

The look of surprise must have given me away.

"I come from a family of great readers," he explained. "How can I help?"

"I'd like to ask you about the ownership of a building in—"

"The tower house?" the lawyer interrupted politely.

"Yes."

"You know it?" he asked.

"I live there."

Valera looked at me for a while without abandoning his smile. He straightened up in his chair and seemed to go tense.

"Are you the present owner?"

"Actually I rent the place."

"And what is it you'd like to know, Señor Martín?"

"If possible, I'd like to know about the acquisition of the building by the Banco Hispano Colonial and gather some information on the previous owner."

"Don Diego Marlasca," the lawyer muttered. "May I ask the nature of your interest?"

"Personal. Recently, while I was doing some refurbishment on the building, I came across a number of items that I think belonged to him."

The lawyer frowned.

"Items?"

"A book. Or, rather, a manuscript."

"Señor Marlasca was a great lover of literature. In fact, he was the author of a large number of books on law and also on history and other subjects. A great scholar. And a great man, although at the end of his life there were those who wished to tarnish his reputation."

Again, my surprise must have been evident.

"I assume you're not familiar with the circumstances surrounding Señor Marlasca's death."

"I'm afraid not."

Valera looked as if he were debating whether or not to go on.

"You're not going to write about this, are you, or about Irene Sabino?"

"No."

"Do I have your word?"

I nodded.

"You couldn't say anything that wasn't already said at the time, I suppose," Valera said, more to himself than to me.

The lawyer looked briefly at his father's portrait and then fixed his eyes on me.

"Diego Marlasca was my father's partner and his best friend. Together they founded this law firm. Señor Marlasca was a brilliant lawyer. Unfortunately he was also a very complicated man, subject to long periods of melancholy. There came a time when my father and Señor Marlasca decided to dissolve their partnership. Señor Marlasca left the legal profession to devote himself to his first vocation, writing. They say most lawyers secretly wish to leave the profession and become writers—"

"Until they compare the salaries."

"The fact is that Don Diego had struck up a friendship with Irene Sabino, quite a popular actress at the time, for whom he wanted to write a play. That was all. Señor Marlasca was a gentleman and was never unfaithful to his wife, but you know what people are like. Gossip. Rumors and jealousy. Anyhow, word got round that Don Diego was having an affair with Irene Sabino. His wife never forgave him, and the couple separated. Señor Marlasca was shattered. He bought the tower house and moved in. Sadly, he'd been living there only a year when he died in an unfortunate accident."

"What sort of accident?"

"Señor Marlasca drowned. It was a tragedy."

Valera lowered his eyes.

"And the scandal?"

"Let's just say there were those with evil tongues who wanted people to believe that Señor Marlasca had committed suicide after an unhappy love affair with Irene Sabino."

"And was that so?"

Valera removed his spectacles and rubbed his eyes.

"To tell you the truth, I'm not sure. I don't know and I don't care. What happened, happened."

"What became of Irene Sabino?"

Valera put his glasses on again.

"I thought you were interested only in Señor Marlasca and the ownership of the house."

"It's simple curiosity. Among Señor Marlasca's belongings I found a number of photographs of Irene Sabino, as well as letters from her to Señor Marlasca . . ."

"What are you getting at?" Valera snapped. "Is it money you want?"

"No."

"I'm glad, because nobody is going to give you any. Nobody cares about the subject anymore. Do you understand?"

"Perfectly, Señor Valera. I had no intention of bothering you or in-sinuating that anything was untoward. I'm sorry if I offended you with my questions."

The lawyer smiled and let out a gentle sigh, as if the conversation had already ended.

"It doesn't matter. I'm the one who should apologize."

Taking advantage of the lawyer's conciliatory tone, I put on my sweetest expression.

"Perhaps his widow . . ."

Valera shrank into his armchair, visibly uncomfortable.

"Doña Alicia Marlasca? Señor Martín, please don't misunderstand me, but part of my duty as the family lawyer is to preserve their privacy. For obvious reasons. A lot of time has gone by and I wouldn't like to see old wounds reopened unnecessarily."

"I understand."

The lawyer was looking at me tensely.

"And you say you found a book?" he asked.

"Yes. A manuscript. It's probably not important."

"Probably not. What was the work about?"

"Theology, I'd say."

Valera nodded.

"Does that surprise you?"

"No. On the contrary. Diego was an authority on the history of re-ligion. A learned man. In this firm he is still remembered with great affection. Tell me, what particular aspects of the history of the property are you interested in?"

"I think you've already helped me a great deal, Señor Valera. I wouldn't like to take up any more of your time."

The lawyer nodded, looking relieved.

"It's the house, isn't it?" he asked.

"A strange place, yes," I agreed.

"I remember going there once when I was young, shortly after Don Diego bought it."

"Do you know why he bought it?"

"He said he'd been fascinated with it ever since he was a child and had always thought he'd like to live there. Don Diego was like that. Sometimes he acted like a young boy who would give everything up in exchange for a dream."

I didn't say anything.

"Are you all right?"

"Yes, fine. Do you know anything about the owner from whom Señor Marlasca bought the house? Someone called Bernabé Massot?"

"He'd made his money in the Americas. He didn't spend more than an hour in the house. He bought it when he returned from Cuba and kept it empty for years. He didn't say why. He lived in a mansion he had built in Arenys de Mar and sold the tower house for nothing. He didn't want to have anything to do with it."

"And before him?"

"I think a priest lived there. A Jesuit. I'm not sure. My father was the person who took care of Don Diego's business and when Don Diego died, he burned all of the files."

"Why would he do that?"

"Because of all the things I've told you. To avoid rumors and preserve the memory of his friend, I suppose. The truth is, he never told me. My father was not the sort of man to offer explanations, but he must have had his reasons. Good reasons, I'm sure. Diego had been a good friend to him, as well as being his partner, and all of it was very painful for my father."

"What happened to the Jesuit?"

"I believe he had disciplinary issues with the order. He was a friend of Father Cinto Verdaguer, and I think he was mixed up in some of his problems, if you know what I mean."

"Exorcisms."

"Gossip."

"How could a Jesuit who had been thrown out of the order afford a house like that?"

I sensed that I was scraping the bottom of the barrel.

"I'd like to be of further help, Señor Martín, but I don't know how. Believe me."

"Thank you for your time, Señor Valera."

The lawyer nodded and pressed a bell on the desk. The secretary who had greeted me appeared in the doorway. Valera and I shook hands.

"Señor Martín is leaving. See him to the door, Margarita."

The secretary inclined her head and led the way. Before leaving the office I turned round to look at the lawyer, who was standing crestfallen beneath his father's portrait. I followed Margarita out to the main door but just as she was about to close it I turned and gave her the most innocent of smiles.

"Excuse me. Señor Valera just told me Señora Marlasca's address, but now that I think of it I'm not sure I remember the street number correctly . . ."

Margarita sighed, eager to be rid of me.

"It's 13. Carretera de Vallvidrera, number 13."

"Of course."

"Good afternoon," said Margarita.

Before I was able to say good-bye, the door was shut in my face as solemnly as a holy sepulchre.

21

When I returned to the tower house, I looked with different eyes at the building that had been my home and my prison for too many years. I went through the front door feeling as if I were entering the jaws of a being made of stone and shadow and ascended the wide staircase, penetrating the bowels of this creature; when I opened the door of the main floor, the long corridor that faded into darkness seemed, for the first time, like the antechamber of a poisoned and distrustful mind. At the far end, outlined against the scarlet twilight that filtered through from the gallery, was the silhouette of Isabella advancing toward me. I closed the door and turned on the light.

Isabella had dressed as a refined young lady, with her hair up and a few touches of makeup that made her look ten years older.

"You're looking very attractive and elegant," I said coldly.

"Like a girl your age, don't you think? Do you like the dress?"

"Where did you find it?"

"It was in one of the trunks in the room at the end. I think it belonged to Irene Sabino. What do you think? Doesn't it fit me well?"

"I told you to get someone to take everything away."

"And I did. This morning I went to the parish church but they told me they couldn't collect and we'd have to take it to them ourselves."

I looked at her but didn't say anything.

"It's the truth," she added.

"Take that off and put it back where you found it. And wash your face. You look like—"

"A tart?" Isabella said.

I shook my head and sighed.

"No. You could never look like a tart, Isabella."

"Of course. That's why you don't fancy me," she muttered, turning round and heading for her room.

"Isabella," I called.

She ignored me.

"Isabella," I repeated, raising my voice.

She threw me a hostile glance before slamming the bedroom door. I heard her beginning to move things about. I walked over to the door and rapped with my knuckles. There was no reply. I rapped again. Not a word. I opened the door and found her gathering the few things she'd brought with her and putting them in her bag.

"What are you doing?" I asked.

"I'm leaving, that's what I'm doing. I'm going and I'm leaving you in peace. Or in war, because with you one never knows."

"May I ask where you're going?"

"What do you care? Is that a rhetorical or an ironic question? It's obvious that you don't give a damn about anything, but as I'm such an idiot I can't tell the difference."

"Isabella, wait a moment—"

"Don't worry about the dress, I'm taking it off right now. And you can return the nibs, because I haven't used them and I don't like them. They're corny and childish."

I moved closer and put a hand on her shoulder. She jumped away, as if a snake had brushed against her.

"Don't touch me."

I withdrew to the doorway in silence. Isabella's hands and lips were shaking.

"Isabella, forgive me. Please. I didn't mean to offend you."

She looked at me tearfully.

"You've done nothing but that. Ever since I got here. You've done nothing but insult me and treat me as if I were a poor idiot who didn't understand a thing."

"I'm sorry," I repeated. "Leave your things. Don't go."

"Why not?"

"Because I'm asking you, please, not to go."

"If I need pity and charity, I can find it elsewhere."

"It's not pity or charity, unless that's what you feel for me. I'm asking you to stay because I'm the idiot here and I don't want to be alone. I can't be alone."

"Great. Always thinking of others. Buy yourself a dog."

She let the bag fall on the bed and faced me, drying her tears as the pent-up anger slowly dissipated.

"Well then, since we're playing at telling the truth, let me tell you that you're always going to be alone. You'll be alone because you don't know how to love or how to share. You're like this house. It makes my hair stand on end. I'm not surprised your lady in white left you or that everyone else has too. You don't love and you don't allow yourself to be loved."

I stared at her, crushed, as if I'd just been given a beating and didn't know where the blows had come from. I searched for words but could only stammer.

"Is it true you don't like the pen set?" I managed at last.

Isabella rolled her eyes, exhausted.

"Don't look at me like a beaten dog. I might be stupid, but not that stupid."

I didn't reply but remained leaning against the doorframe. Isabella observed me with an expression somewhere between suspicion and pity.

"I didn't mean to say what I said about your friend, the one in the photographs. I'm sorry," she mumbled.

"Don't apologize. It's the truth."

I left the room, eyes downcast, and escaped to the study, where I gazed at the dark city buried in mist. After a while I heard her hesitant footsteps on the staircase.

"Are you up there?" she called out.

"Yes."

Isabella came into the room. She had changed her clothes and washed the tears from her face. She smiled and I smiled back at her.

"Why are you like that?"

I shrugged my shoulders. Isabella came over and sat next to me, on the windowsill. We enjoyed the play of silence and shadows over the rooftops of the old town. After a while, she grinned at me and said, "What if we were to light one of those cigars my father gives you and share it?"

"Certainly not."

Isabella sank back into silence, but every now and then she glanced at me and smiled. I watched her out of the corner of my eye and realized that just by looking at her it was easier to believe there might be something good and decent left in this lousy world and, with luck, in myself.

"Are you staying?" I asked.

"Give me a good reason why I should. An honest reason. In other words, coming from you, a selfish one. And it had better not be a load of drivel or I'll leave right away."

She barricaded herself behind a defensive look, waiting for one of my usual flattering remarks. I looked down and for once I spoke the truth, even if it was only to hear it myself.

"Because you're the only friend I have left."

The hard expression in her eyes disappeared, and before I could discern any pity I looked away.

"What about Señor Sempere and that pedant Barceló?"

"You're the only one who has dared tell me the truth."

"What about your friend, the boss, doesn't he tell you the truth?"

"The boss is not my friend. And I don't think he's ever told the truth in his entire life."

Isabella looked at me closely.

"You see? I knew you didn't trust him. I noticed it in your face from the very first day."

I tried to recover some of my dignity, but all I found was sarcasm.

"Have you added face reading to your list of talents?"

"You don't need any talent to read a face like yours," Isabella said. "It's like reading Tom Thumb."

"And what else can you read in my face, dearest fortune-teller?"

"That you're scared."

I tried to laugh, without much enthusiasm.

"Don't be ashamed of being scared. To be afraid is a sign of common sense. Only complete idiots are not afraid of anything. I read that in a book."

"The coward's handbook?"

"You needn't admit it if it's going to undermine your sense of masculinity. I know you men believe that the size of your stubbornness should match the size of your privates."

"Did you also read that in your book?"

"No, that wisdom's homemade."

I let my hands fall, surrendering in the face of the evidence.

"All right. Yes, I admit that I do feel a vague sense of anxiety."

"You're the one who's being vague. You're scared stiff. Admit it."

"Don't get things out of proportion. Let's say that I have some reservations concerning my publisher that, given my experience, are understandable. As far as I know, Corelli is a perfect gentleman and our professional relationship will be fruitful and positive for both parties."

"That's why your stomach rumbles every time his name crops up."

I sighed. I had no arguments left.

"What can I say, Isabella?"

"That you're not going to work for him anymore."

"I can't do that."

"And why not? Can't you just give him back his money and send him packing?"

"It's not that simple."

"Why not? Have you got yourself into trouble?"

"I think so."

"What sort of trouble?"

"That's what I'm trying to find out. In any case, I'm the only one to blame, so I must be the one to solve it. It's nothing that should worry you."

Isabella looked at me, resigned for the time being but not convinced.

"You really are a hopeless person. Did you know that?"

"I'm getting used to the idea."

"If you want me to stay, the rules here must change."

"I'm all ears."

"No more enlightened despotism. From now on, this house is a democracy."

"Liberty, equality, and fraternity."

"Watch it where fraternity is concerned. But no more ordering around, and no more little Mr. Rochester numbers."

"Whatever you say, Miss Eyre."

"And don't get your hopes up, because I'm not going to marry you even if you go blind."

I put out my hand to seal our pact. She shook it with some hesitation and then gave me a hug. I let myself be wrapped in her arms and leaned my face on her hair. Her touch was full of peace and welcome, the life light of a seventeen-year-old girl, and I wanted to believe that it resembled the embrace my mother had never had time to give me.

"Friends?" I whispered.

"Till death do us part."

22

The new regulations of the Isabellian reign came into effect at nine o'clock the following morning, when my assistant turned up in the kitchen and informed me how things were going to be from then on.

"I've been thinking that you need a routine in your life. Otherwise you get sidetracked and act in a dissolute manner."

"Where did you get that expression from?"

"From one of your books. Dis-so-lute. It sounds good."

"And it's great for rhymes."

"Don't change the subject."

During the day we would both work on our respective manuscripts. We would have dinner together and then she'd show me the pages she'd written that day and we'd discuss them. I swore I would be frank and give her appropriate suggestions, not just empty words to keep her happy. Sundays would be our day off and I'd take her to the pictures, to the theater, or out for a walk. She would help me find documents in libraries and archives and it would be her job to make sure the larder was always well stocked thanks to her connection with the family emporium. I would make breakfast and she'd make dinner. Lunch would be prepared by whoever was free at the moment. We divided up the chores and I promised to accept the irrefutable fact that the house needed to be cleaned regularly. I would not attempt to find her a boyfriend under any circumstances and she would refrain from questioning my motives for working for the boss and from expressing her opinion on the matter unless I asked for it. The rest we would make up as we went along.

I raised my cup of coffee and we toasted my unconditional surrender.

In just a couple of days I had given myself over to the peace and tranquillity of the vassal. Isabella awoke slowly and by the time she had emerged from her room, her eyes half closed, wearing a pair of my slippers that were much too big for her, I had breakfast ready, with coffee and the morning paper, a different one each day.

. . .

Routine is the housekeeper of inspiration. Only forty-eight hours after the establishment of the new regime, I discovered that I was beginning to recover the discipline of my most productive years. The hours of being locked up in the study crystallized into pages and more pages in which, not without some anxiety, I began to see the work taking shape, reaching the point at which it stopped being an idea and became a reality.

The text flowed, brilliant, electric. It read like a legend, a mythological saga about miracles and hardships, peopled with characters and scenes that were knotted around a prophecy of hope for the race. The narrative prepared the way for the arrival of a warrior savior who would liberate the nation of all pain and injustice in order to give it back the pride and glory that had been snatched away by its enemies, foes who had conspired since time immemorial against the people, whoever that people might be. The mechanics of the plot were impeccable and would work equally well for any creed, race, or tribe. Flags, gods, and proclamations were the jokers in a pack that always dealt the same cards. Given the nature of the work, I had chosen one of the most complex and difficult techniques to apply to any literary text: the apparent absence of technique. The language resounded plain and simple, the voice was honest and clean, a consciousness that did not narrate but simply revealed. Sometimes I would stop to reread what I'd written and, overcome with blind vanity, I'd feel that the mechanism I was setting up worked with perfect precision. I realized that for the first time in a long while I had spent whole hours without thinking about Cristina or Pedro Vidal. Life, I told myself, was improving. Perhaps for that very reason, because it seemed that at last I was going to get out of the predicament into which I'd fallen, I did what I've always done when I've got myself back on the rails: I ruined it all.

. . .

One morning, after breakfast, I donned one of my respectable suits. I stepped into the gallery to say good-bye to Isabella and saw her leaning over her desk, rereading pages from the day before.

"Are you not writing today?" she asked without looking up.

"I'm taking a day off for meditation."

I noticed the set of pen nibs and the inkpot decorated with Muses next to her notebook.

"I thought you considered them corny," I said.

"I do, but I'm a seventeen-year-old girl and I have every right in the world to like corny things. It's like you with your cigars."

The smell of eau de cologne reached her and she looked at me questioningly. When she saw that I'd dressed to go out, she frowned.

"You're off to do some more detective work?" she asked.

"A bit."

"Don't you need a bodyguard? A Dr. Watson? Someone with a little common sense?"

"Don't learn how to find excuses for not writing before you learn how to write. That's a privilege of professionals and you have to earn it."

"I think that if I'm your assistant that should cover everything."

"Actually, there *is* something I wanted to ask you. No, don't worry. It's to do with Sempere. I've heard that he's hard up and that the bookshop is at risk."

"That can't be true."

"Unfortunately it is, but it's all right because we're not going to allow matters to get any worse."

"Señor Sempere is very proud and he's not going to let you . . . You've already tried, haven't you?"

I nodded.

"That's why I thought we need to be a little shrewder and resort to something more cunning."

"Your speciality."

I ignored her disapproving tone. "This is what I've planned: you drop by the bookshop, as if you just happened to be passing, and tell Sempere that I'm an ogre, that you're sick of me—"

"Up to now it sounds 100 percent credible."

"Don't interrupt. You tell him all that and also tell him that what I pay you to be my assistant is a pittance."

"But you don't pay me a penny."

I sighed. This required patience.

"When he says he's sorry to hear it, and he will, make yourself look like a damsel in distress and confess, if possible with a tear or two, that your father has disinherited you and wants to send you to a nunnery. Tell him you thought that perhaps you could work in his shop for a few hours a day, for a trial period, in exchange for a 3 percent commission on what you sell. That way, you can carve out a future for yourself far from the convent, as a liberated woman devoted to the dissemination of literature."

Isabella grimaced.

"Three percent? Do you want to help Sempere or fleece him?"

"I want you to put on a dress like the one you wore the other night, get yourself all dolled up, as only you know how, and pay him a visit while his son is in the shop, which is usually in the afternoons."

"Are we talking about the handsome one?"

"How many sons does Señor Sempere have?"

Isabella made her calculations and, when she began to understand what was going on, she looked annoyed.

"If my father knew the kind of perverse mind you have, he'd buy himself that shotgun."

"All I'm saying is that the son must see you. And the father must see the son seeing you."

"You're even worse than I imagined. Now you're devoting yourself to the white slave trade."

"It's pure Christian charity. Besides, you were the first to admit that Sempere's son is good-looking."

"Good-looking and a bit slow."

"Don't exaggerate. Sempere junior is just shy in the presence of females, which does him credit. He's a model citizen who, despite being aware of his enticing appearance, exercises extreme self-control out of respect for and devotion to the immaculate purity of Barcelona's womenfolk. Don't tell me this doesn't bestow an aura of nobility that appeals to your instincts, both maternal and the rest."

"Sometimes I think I hate you, Señor Martín."

"Hold on to that feeling but don't blame poor young Sempere for my deficiencies as a human being because, strictly speaking, he's a saint."

"We agreed that you wouldn't try to find me a boyfriend."

"I've said nothing about a boyfriend. If you'll let me finish, I'll tell you the rest."

"Go on, Rasputin."

"When the older Sempere says yes to you, and he will, I want you to spend two or three hours a day at the counter in the bookshop."

"Dressed like what? Mata Hari?"

"Dressed with the decorum and good taste that is characteristic of you. Pretty, suggestive, but without standing out. As I've said, if necessary you can rescue one of Irene Sabino's dresses, but it must be modest."

"Two or three of them look fantastic on me," Isabella said eagerly.

"Then wear whichever one covers you the most."

"You're a reactionary. What about my literary education?"

"What better classroom than Sempere & Sons? You'll be surrounded by masterpieces from which you can learn in bulk."

"And what should I do? Take a deep breath to see if something sticks?"

"It's just for a few hours a day. After that you can continue your work here, as you have until now, receiving my advice, which is always priceless and will turn you into a new Jane Austen."

"And where's the cunning plan?"

"The cunning plan is that every day I'll give you a few pesetas and every time you are paid by a customer and open the till you'll slide them in discreetly."

"So that's your plan . . ."

"That's the plan. As you can see, there's nothing perverse about it."

Isabella frowned again.

"It won't work. He'll notice there's something wrong. Señor Sempere is nobody's fool."

"It will work. And if Sempere seems puzzled, you tell him that when customers see a pretty girl behind the counter they let go of the purse strings and become more generous."

"That might be so in the cheap haunts you frequent, not in a bookshop."

"I beg to differ. If I were to go into a bookshop and come across a shop assistant as pretty and charming as you are, I might even be capable of buying the latest national book award winner."

"That's because your mind is as filthy as a henhouse."

"I also have—or should I say we have—a debt of gratitude to Sempere."

"That's a low blow."

"Then don't make me aim even lower."

Every self-respecting persuasive ploy must first appeal to curiosity, then to vanity, and lastly to kindness or remorse. Isabella looked down and slowly nodded.

"And when were you planning to set this plan of the bounteous goddess in motion?"

"Don't put off for tomorrow what you can do today."

"Today?"

"This afternoon."

"Tell me the truth. Is this a strategy for laundering the money the boss pays you and for purging your conscience, or whatever it is you have where there should be one?"

"You know my motives are always selfish."

"And what if Señor Sempere says no?"

"Just make sure the son is there and you're dressed in your Sunday best, but not for Mass."

"It's a degrading and offensive plan."

"And you love it."

At last Isabella smiled, catlike.

"What if the son suddenly grows bold and allows his hands to wander?"

"I can guarantee the heir won't dare lay a finger on you unless it's in the presence of a priest waving a marriage certificate."

"That sounds a bit extreme."

"Will you do it?"

"For you?"

"For literature."

23

When I stepped outside I was greeted by an icy breeze sweeping up the streets, and I knew that autumn was tiptoeing its way into Barcelona. In Plaza Palacio I got on a tram that was waiting there, empty, like a large steel rat trap. I sat by the window and paid the conductor for my ticket.

"Do you go as far as Sarriá?" I asked.

"As far as the square."

I leaned my head against the window and soon the tram set off with a jerk. I closed my eyes and succumbed to one of those naps that can be enjoyed only on board some mechanical monstrosity, the sleep of modern man. I dreamed that I was traveling in a train made of black bones, its coaches shaped like coffins, crossing a deserted Barcelona that was strewn with discarded clothes, as if the bodies that had occupied them had simply evaporated. A wasteland of abandoned hats and dresses, suits and shoes that covered the silent streets. The engine gave off a trail of scarlet smoke that spread across the sky like spilled paint. A smiling boss traveled next to me. He was dressed in white and wore gloves. Something dark and glutinous dripped from the tips of his fingers.

What has happened to all the people?

Have faith, Martín. Have faith.

As I awoke, the tram was gliding slowly into Plaza de Sarriá. I jumped off before it reached the stop and made my way up Calle Mayor de Sarriá. Fifteen minutes later I arrived at my destination.

· · ·

Carretera de Vallvidrera started in a shady grove behind the red-brick castle of San Ignacio's school. The street climbed uphill, bordered by solitary mansions, and was covered with a carpet of fallen leaves. Low clouds slid down the mountainside, dissolving into puffs of mist. I walked along the pavement and tried to work out the street numbers as I passed garden walls and wrought-iron gates. Behind them, barely visible, stood houses of darkened stone and dried-up fountains beached between paths that were thick with weeds. I walked along a stretch of road beneath a long row of cypress trees and discovered that the numbers jumped from eleven to fifteen. Confused, I retraced my steps in search of number 13. I was beginning to suspect that Señor Valera's secretary was cleverer than she had seemed and had given me a false address, when I noticed an alleyway leading off the pavement. It ran for about fifty meters toward some dark iron railings that formed a crest of spears atop a stone wall.

I turned into the narrow cobbled lane and walked down to the railings. A thick, unkempt garden had crept toward the other side and the branches of a eucalyptus tree passed through the spearheads like the arms of prisoners pleading through the bars of a cell. I pushed aside the leaves that covered part of the wall and found the letters and numbers carved in the stone:

Casa Marlasca
13

As I followed the railings that ran round the edge of the garden, I tried to catch a glimpse of the interior. Some twenty meters along I discovered a metal door fitted into the stone wall. A large door knocker rested on the iron sheet, which was streaked with rust. The door was ajar. I pushed with my shoulder and managed to open it just enough to pass through without tearing my clothes on the sharp bits of stone that jutted out from the wall. The air was infused with the intense stench of wet earth.

A path of marble tiles led through the trees to a clearing covered with white stones. On one side stood a garage, its doors open, revealing the remains of what had once been a Mercedes-Benz and now looked like a hearse abandoned to its fate. The house was a three-story building in the Modernist style with curved lines and a crown of dormer windows coming together in a swirl beneath turrets and arches. Narrow windows opened on its façade, which was covered with reliefs and gargoyles. The glass panes reflected the silent passing of the clouds. I thought I could see the outline of a face behind one of the first-floor windows.

Without quite knowing why, I raised my arm and smiled faintly. I didn't want to be taken for a thief. The still figure remained there watching me. I looked down for a moment and when I looked up again it had disappeared.

"Good morning!" I called out.

I waited for a few seconds and when no reply came I proceeded slowly toward the house. An oval-shaped swimming pool flanked the eastern side, beyond which stood a glass conservatory. Frayed deck chairs surrounded the pool. A diving board, overgrown with ivy, was poised over the sheet of murky water. I walked to the edge and saw that it was littered with dead leaves and algae rippling over the surface. I was looking at my own reflection in the water when I noticed a dark figure hovering behind me.

I spun round and met with a pointed, somber face, examining me nervously.

"Who are you and what are you doing here?"

"My name is David Martín and Señor Valera, the lawyer, sent me."

Alicia Marlasca pressed her lips together.

"You're Señora de Marlasca? Doña Alicia?"

"What's happened to the one who usually comes?" she asked.

I realized that Señora Marlasca had taken me for one of the articled clerks from Valera's office and had assumed I was bringing papers to sign or some message from the lawyers. For a moment I considered adopting that identity, but something in the woman's face told me that she'd heard enough lies to last a lifetime.

"I don't work for the firm, Señora Marlasca. The reason for my visit is a personal matter. I wonder whether you would have a few minutes to speak about one of the old properties belonging to your deceased husband, Don Diego."

The widow turned pale and looked away. She was leaning on a stick and I noticed a wheelchair in the doorway of the conservatory. I assumed she spent more time in it than she would care to admit.

"None of the properties belonging to my husband remain, Señor . . ."

"Martín."

"The banks kept everything, Señor Martín. Everything except for this house, which, thanks to the advice of Señor Valera's father, was put in my name. The rest was taken by the scavengers."

"I'm referring to the tower house, in Calle Flassaders."

The widow sighed. I reckoned she was somewhere between sixty and sixty-five. The echo of what must once have been a dazzling beauty had scarcely faded.

"Forget that house. It's cursed."

"Unfortunately I can't. I live there."

Señora Marlasca frowned.

"I thought nobody wanted to live there. It stood empty for years."

"I've been renting it for some time. The reason for my visit is that, while I was doing some renovations, I came across a few personal items that I think belonged to your deceased husband and, I suppose, to you."

"There's nothing of mine in that house. Whatever you've found must belong to that woman . . ."

"Irene Sabino?"

Alicia Marlasca smiled bitterly.

"What do you really want to know, Señor Martín? Tell me the truth. You haven't come all this way to return some old things belonging to my husband."

We gazed at each other in silence and I knew that I couldn't, and didn't want to, lie to this woman, whatever the cost.

"I'm trying to find out what happened to your husband, Señora Marlasca."

"Why?"

"Because I think the same thing may be happening to me."

. . .

Casa Marlasca had the feel of an abandoned mausoleum that characterizes large houses sustained on absence and neglect. Far from its days of fortune and glory, when an army of servants kept it pristine and full of splendor, the house was now a ruin. Paint was peeling off the walls, the floor tiles were loose, the furniture was rotten and damp, the ceilings sagged, and the large carpets were threadbare and discolored. I helped the widow into her wheelchair and, following her instructions, pushed her to a reading room that contained hardly any books or pictures.

"I had to sell almost everything to survive," she explained. "If it hadn't been for Señor Valera, who still sends me a small pension every month on behalf of the firm, I wouldn't have known what to do."

"Do you live here alone?"

The widow nodded.

"This is my home. The only place where I've been happy, even though that was many years ago. I've always lived here and I'll die here. I'm sorry I haven't offered you anything. It's been so long since I last had visitors that I've forgotten how to treat a guest. Would you like a coffee or a tea?"

"I'm fine, thanks."

Señora Marlasca smiled and pointed to the armchair in which I was sitting.

"That was my husband's favorite. He used to sit by the fire and read until late. I sometimes sat here, next to him, and listened. He liked telling me things, at least he did back then. We were very happy in this house . . ."

"What happened?"

The widow stared at the ashes in the hearth.

"Are you sure you want to hear this story?"

"Please."

24

"To be honest, I'm not quite certain when my husband, Diego, met her. I just remember that one day he began to mention her in passing and that soon not a day went by without him saying her name, Irene Sabino. He told me he'd been introduced to her by a man called Damián Roures who organized séances somewhere on Calle Elisabets. Diego knew a great deal about religions and had gone to a number of séances as an observer. Irene Sabino was very popular in the Paralelo in those days. She was beautiful, I will not deny it. Apart from that, I think she was just about able to count up to ten. People said she'd been born in the shacks of Bogatell beach, that her mother had abandoned her in the Somorrostro shantytown and she'd grown up among beggars and fugitives. At fourteen she started to dance in cabarets and nightclubs in the Raval and the Paralelo. Dancing is one way of putting it. I suppose she began to prostitute herself before she learned to read and write, if she ever did learn, that is . . . For a while she was the main star at La Criolla, or that's what people said. Then she went on to fancier places. I think it was at the Apolo that she met a man called Juan Corbera, whom everyone called Jaco. Jaco was her manager and probably her lover. It was Jaco who came up with the name Irene Sabino and the legend that she was the secret offspring of a famous Parisian cabaret star and a prince of European nobility. I don't know what her real name was, or whether she ever had one. Jaco introduced her to the séances, at Roures's suggestion,

I believe, and the two men split the profits of selling her supposed virginity to wealthy, bored men who went along to those shams to kill the monotony. Her speciality was couples, they say.

"What Jaco and his partner, Roures, didn't suspect was that Irene was obsessed with the sessions and really believed she could make contact with the world of spirits. She was convinced that her mother sent her messages from the other side, and even when she became famous she continued attending the séances to try to establish contact with her. That is where she met Diego. I suppose we were going through a bad patch, like all marriages do. Diego had been wanting to leave the legal profession for some time to devote himself to writing. I admit that he didn't find the support he needed from me. I thought that if he did it, he would be throwing his life away, although probably what I really feared losing was all this—the house, the servants . . . I lost everything anyhow, and my husband too. What ended up separating us was the loss of Ismael. Ismael was our son. Diego was crazy about him. I've never seen a father so dedicated to his son. Ismael was his life, not I. We were arguing in the bedroom on the first floor. I began to reproach him for the time he spent writing and for the fact that Valera, tired of having to shoulder Diego's work as well as his own, had sent him an ultimatum and was thinking about dissolving their partnership and setting himself up independently. Diego said he didn't care, he was ready to sell his share in the business so that he could dedicate himself to his vocation. That afternoon we couldn't find Ismael. He wasn't in his room or in the garden. I thought that when he'd heard us arguing he must have been frightened and left the house. It wasn't the first time he'd done that. Some months earlier he'd been found on a bench in Plaza de Sarriá, crying. We went out to look for him as it was getting dark, but there was no sign of him anywhere. We went to our neighbors' houses, to hospitals . . . When we returned at dawn, after spending all night looking for him, we found his body at the bottom of the pool. He'd drowned the previous afternoon and we hadn't heard his cries for help because we were too busy shouting at each other. He was seven years old.

"Diego never forgave me, or himself. Soon we were unable to bear each other's presence. Every time we looked at each other, every time we touched, we saw our dead son's body at the bottom of that damned pool. One day I woke up and knew that Diego had abandoned me. He left the law firm and went to live in a rambling old house in the Ribera quarter that he had been obsessed with for years. He said he was writing and he'd received a very important commission from a publisher in Paris, so I didn't need to worry about money. I knew he was with Irene, even if he didn't admit it. He was a broken man and was convinced that he had only a short time to live. He thought he'd caught some illness, a sort of parasite that was eating him up. All he ever spoke about was death. He wouldn't listen to anyone. Not to me, not to Valera—only to Irene and Roures, who poisoned his mind with stories about spirits and extracted money from him by promising to put him in touch with Ismael. On one occasion I went to the tower house and begged him to open the door. He wouldn't let me in. He told me he was busy, said he was working on something that was going to enable him to save Ismael. I realized then that he was beginning to lose his mind. He believed that if he wrote that wretched book for the Parisian publisher our son would return from the dead. I think that between the three of them—Irene, Roures, and Jaco— they managed to get their hands on what little money he had left, we had left . . . He no longer saw anybody and spent his time locked up in that horrible place.

"Months later they found him dead. The police said it was an accident, but I never believed it. Jaco had disappeared and there was no trace of the money. Roures maintained he didn't know anything. He declared that he hadn't had any contact with Diego for months because Diego had gone mad, and he scared him. He said that in his last appearances at the séances, Diego had frightened the customers with stories of accursed souls so Roures had not allowed him to return. Diego said there was a huge lake of blood under the city, that his son spoke to him in his dreams, that Ismael was trapped by a shadow with a serpent's skin who pretended to be another boy and played with him . . . Nobody was surprised when they found him dead.

"Irene said Diego had taken his own life because of me; she said that his cold and calculating wife, who had allowed his son to die because she didn't want to give up her life of luxury, had pushed him to his death. She said she was the only one who had truly loved him and that she'd never accepted a penny from him. And I think, at least in that respect, she was telling the truth. I'm sure Jaco used her to seduce Diego in order to rob him of everything. Later, when matters came to a head, Jaco left her and fled without sharing a single thing. That's what the police said, or at least some of them. I always felt that they didn't want to stir things up and the suicide version of events turned out to be very convenient. But I don't believe Diego took his own life. I didn't believe it then and I don't believe it now. I think Irene and Jaco murdered him. And not just for the money. There was something else. I remember that one of the policemen assigned to the case, a young man called Salvador, Ricardo Salvador, thought the same. He said there was something that didn't add up in the official version of events and that somebody was covering up the real cause of Diego's death. Salvador tried very hard to establish the facts but he was removed from the case and was eventually thrown out of the police force.

"Even then he continued to investigate on his own. He came to see me sometimes and we became good friends. I was a woman on my own, ruined and desperate. Valera kept telling me I should remarry. He, too, blamed me for what had happened to my husband and even insinuated that there were plenty of unmarried shopkeepers around who wouldn't mind having a pleasant-looking widow with aristocratic airs warm their beds in their golden years. Eventually even Salvador stopped visiting me. I don't blame him. By trying to help me he had ruined his own life. Sometimes I think that the only thing I've ever managed to do for others is destroy their lives . . . I hadn't told anybody this story until today, Señor Martín. If you want some advice, forget that house; forget me, my husband, and this whole story. Go away, far away. This city is damned. Damned."

25

I left Casa Marlasca in low spirits and wandered aimlessly through the maze of lonely streets that led to Pedralbes. The sky was covered with a mesh of clouds that barely allowed the sun to filter through. Needles of light perforated the gray shroud and swept across the hillside. I followed them with my eyes and saw how, in the distance, they caressed the enameled roof of Villa Helius. The windows shone in the distance. Ignoring common sense, I set off in that direction. As I drew near, the sky darkened and a cutting wind lifted the fallen leaves into spirals. I stopped when I reached Calle Panamá. Villa Helius rose before me. I didn't dare cross the road and approach the wall surrounding the garden. Instead, I stood there for God knows how long, unable to leave or to go over to the door and knock. Then I saw her through one of the large windows on the second floor, walking across a room. An intense cold invaded me. I was about to leave when she turned and stopped. She went up to the window and I felt her eyes resting on mine. She raised her hand as if she were about to greet me but didn't spread her fingers. I didn't have the courage to hold her gaze: I turned round and walked off down the street. My hands were shaking and I thrust them into my pockets. Before turning the corner I looked back and saw that she was still there, watching me. I tried to hate her, but I couldn't find the strength.

I arrived home feeling chilled to the bone. As I walked through the front door I noticed the top of an envelope peeping out of the letter box.

Parchment and sealing wax. News from the boss. I opened it while I dragged myself up the stairs. His elegant handwriting summoned me to a meeting the following day. When I reached the landing, the door was already ajar and Isabella was waiting for me with a smile.

"I was in the study and saw you coming," she said.

I tried to smile back at her but can't have been very convincing. She looked me in the eye and her face took on a worried expression.

"Are you all right?"

"It's nothing. I think I've caught a bit of a chill."

"I have some broth on the stove. It'll work wonders. Come in."

Isabella took my arm and led me to the gallery.

"I'm not an invalid, Isabella."

She let go of me and looked down.

"I'm sorry."

I didn't feel like a confrontation with anybody, least of all my obstinate assistant, so I allowed her to guide me to one of the gallery armchairs, which I fell into limply. Isabella sat opposite me and looked at me with alarm.

"What happened?"

I smiled reassuringly.

"Nothing. Nothing has happened. Weren't you going to give me a bowl of soup?"

"Right away."

She shot off toward the kitchen and I heard her rushing about. I took a deep breath and closed my eyes until I heard her footsteps approaching.

She handed me an enormous steaming bowl.

"It looks like a chamber pot," I said.

"Drink it and don't be so rude."

I sniffed at the broth. It smelled good, but I didn't want to seem too docile.

"It smells odd," I said. "What's in it?"

"It smells of chicken because it's made of chicken, salt, and a dash of sherry. Drink it."

I took a sip and gave the bowl back to Isabella. She shook her head. "All of it."

I sighed and took another sip. It was good, whether I wanted to admit it or not.

"So, how was your day?" Isabella asked.

"It had its moments. How did you get on?"

"You're looking at the new star shop assistant of Sempere & Sons."

"Excellent."

"By five o'clock I'd already sold two copies of *The Picture of Dorian Gray* and a set of the complete works of Kipling to a very distinguished gentleman from Madrid who gave me a tip. Don't look at me like that; I put the tip in the till."

"What about Sempere's son? What did he say?"

"He didn't actually say very much. He was like a stuffed dummy the whole time, pretending he wasn't looking, but he couldn't take his eyes off me. I can hardly sit down my bum's so sore from him staring at it every time I went up the ladder to bring down a book. Happy?"

I smiled and nodded.

"Thanks, Isabella."

She looked straight into my eyes.

"Say that again."

"Thank you, Isabella. From the bottom of my heart."

She blushed and looked away. We sat placidly for a while, enjoying that camaraderie which doesn't even require words. I drank my broth until I could barely swallow another drop and then showed her the empty bowl. She nodded.

"You've been to see her, haven't you? That woman, Cristina," said Isabella, trying not to meet my eyes.

"Isabella, the reader of faces . . ."

"Tell me the truth."

"I only saw her from a distance."

Isabella looked at me cautiously, as if she were debating whether or not to say something that was stuck in her conscience.

"Do you love her?" she finally asked.

For a moment there was silence.

"I don't know how to love anybody. You know that. I'm a selfish person and all that. Let's talk about something else."

Isabella's eyes settled on the envelope sticking out of my pocket.

"News from the boss?"

"The monthly call. His Excellency Señor Andreas Corelli is pleased to ask me to attend a meeting tomorrow at seven o'clock in the morning by the entrance to the Pueblo Nuevo cemetery. He couldn't have chosen a better place."

"And you plan to go?"

"What else can I do?"

"You could take a train this very evening and disappear forever."

"You're the second person to suggest that to me today. To disappear from here."

"There must be a reason."

"And who would be your guide through the disasters of literature?"

"I'd go with you."

I smiled and took her hand in mine.

"With you to the ends of the earth and back, Isabella."

Isabella withdrew her hand suddenly and looked offended.

"You're making fun of me."

"Isabella, if I ever decide to make fun of you, I'll shoot myself."

"Don't say that. I don't like it when you talk like that."

"I'm sorry."

My assistant turned to her desk. I watched her going over her day's pages, making corrections and crossing out whole paragraphs with the pen set I had given her.

"I can't concentrate with you looking at me."

I stood up and went past her desk.

"Then I'll leave you to work and after dinner you can show me what you've written."

"It's not ready. I have to correct it all and rewrite it and—"

"It's never ready, Isabella. Get used to it. We'll read it together after dinner."

"Tomorrow."

I gave in.

"Tomorrow."

I walked away, leaving her alone with her words. I was just closing the door of my bedroom when I heard her voice calling me.

"David?"

I stopped on the other side of the door but didn't say anything.

"It's not true. It's not true that you don't know how to love anyone."

I closed the door, lay down on the bed, curled up, and closed my eyes.

26

I left the house after dawn. Dark clouds crept over the rooftops, stealing the color from the streets. As I crossed Ciudadela Park I saw the first drops hitting the trees and exploding on the path like bullets, raising eddies of dust. On the other side of the park a forest of factories and gas towers multiplied toward the horizon, the soot from the chimneys diluted in the black rain that plummeted from the sky like tears of tar. I walked along the uninviting avenue of cypress trees leading to the gates of the cemetery, the same route I had taken so many times with my father. The boss was already there. I saw him from afar, waiting patiently in the rain, at the foot of one of the large stone angels that guarded the main entrance to the graveyard. He was dressed in black, and the only thing that set him apart from the hundreds of statues on the other side of the cemetery railings was his eyes. He didn't move an eyelash until I was a few meters away. Not quite sure what to do, I raised my hand to greet him. It was cold and the wind smelled of lime and sulfur.

"Visitors naïvely think that it's always sunny and warm in this town," said the boss. "But I say that sooner or later Barcelona's ancient, murky soul will be reflected in the sky."

"You should publish tourist guides instead of religious texts," I suggested.

"It comes to the same thing, more or less. How have these peaceful, calm days been? Have you made progress with the work? Do you have good news for me?"

I opened my jacket and handed him a sheaf of pages. We entered the cemetery in search of a place to shelter from the rain. The boss chose an old mausoleum with a dome held up by marble columns and surrounded by angels with sharp faces and fingers that were too long. We sat on a cold stone bench. The boss gave me one of his canine smiles, his shining pupils contracting to a black point in which I could see the reflection of my uneasy expression.

"Relax, Martín. You make too much of the props."

Calmly, the boss began to read the pages I had brought.

"I think I'll go for a walk while you read," I said.

Corelli didn't bother to look up.

"Don't escape from me," he murmured.

I got away as fast as I could without making it obvious that I was doing just that, and wandered among the paths with their twists and turns. I skirted obelisks and tombs as I entered the heart of the necropolis. The tombstone was still there, marked by a vase containing only the skeleton of shriveled flowers. Vidal had paid for the funeral and had even commissioned a Pietà from a sculptor of some repute in the undertakers' guild. She guarded the tomb, eyes looking heavenward, her hands on her chest in supplication. I knelt down by the tombstone and cleaned away the moss that had covered the letters chiseled on it.

JOSÉ ANTONIO MARTÍN CLARÉS
1875–1908
Hero of the Philippines War
His country and his friends will never forget him

"Good morning, Father," I said.

I watched the black rain as it slid down the face of the Pietà, listened to the sound of the drops hitting the tombstones, and offered a smile to the health of those friends he'd never had and that country that had consigned him to a living death in order to enrich a handful of caciques who never knew he existed. I sat on the gravestone and put my hand on the marble.

"Who would have guessed, eh?"

My father, who had lived on the verge of destitution, rested eternally in a bourgeois tomb. As a child I had never understood why the newspaper had decided to give him a funeral with a smart priest and hired mourners, with flowers and a resting place fit for a sugar merchant. Nobody told me it was Vidal himself who paid for the lavish funeral of the man who had died in his place, although I had always suspected as much and had attributed the gesture to that infinite kindness and generosity with which the heavens had blessed my mentor and idol.

"I must beg your forgiveness, Father. For years I hated you for leaving me here alone. I told myself you'd got the death you deserved. That's why I never came to see you. Forgive me."

My father had never liked tears. He thought a man never cried for others, only for himself. And if he did cry, he was a coward and deserved no pity. I didn't want to cry for my father and betray him yet again.

"I would have liked you to have seen my name in a book, even if you couldn't read it. I would have liked you to have been here with me, to see that your son is managing to get on in life and has been able to do things that you were never allowed to do. I would have liked to have known you, Father, and for you to have known me. I turned you into a stranger in order to forget you and now I'm the stranger."

I didn't hear the boss approaching, but when I raised my head I saw him watching me from just a few meters away. I stood up and went over to him, like a well-trained dog. I wondered whether he knew my father was buried there and whether he had asked me to meet him in the graveyard for that very reason. My expression must have betrayed me, because the boss shook his head and put a hand on my shoulder.

"I didn't know, Martín. I'm sorry."

I was not going to open that door of friendship to him. I turned away to rid myself of his gesture of sympathy and pressed my eyes shut to contain the tears of anger. I started to walk toward the exit, without him. The boss waited a few seconds and then followed me. He walked beside me in silence until we reached the main gates. There I stopped and glared at him impatiently.

"Well? Any comments?"

The boss ignored my hostile tone and smiled indulgently.

"The work is excellent."

"But . . ."

"If I had any observation to make it would be that you've gotten the matter exactly right by constructing the whole story from the point of view of a witness to the events, someone who feels like a victim and speaks on behalf of a people awaiting the warrior savior. I want you to continue along those lines."

"You don't think it sounds forced, contrived?"

"On the contrary. Nothing makes us believe more than fear, the certainty of being threatened. When we feel like victims, all our actions and beliefs are legitimized, however questionable they may be. Our opponents, or simply our neighbors, stop sharing common ground with us and become our enemies. We stop being aggressors and become defenders. The envy, greed, or resentment that motivates us becomes sanctified, because we tell ourselves we're acting in self-defense. Evil, menace—those are always the preserve of the other. The first step for believing passionately is fear. Fear of losing our identity, our life, our status, or our beliefs. Fear is the gunpowder and hatred is the fuse. Dogma, the final ingredient, is only a lighted match. That is where I think your work has a hole or two."

"Please clarify one thing. Are you looking for a faith or a dogma?"

"It's not enough that people should believe. They must believe what we want them to believe. And they must not question it or listen to the voice of whoever questions it. Dogma must form part of identity itself. Whoever questions it is our enemy. He is evil. And it is our right and our duty to confront and destroy him. It is the only road to salvation. Believe in order to survive."

I sighed and looked away, nodding reluctantly.

"You don't look convinced, Martín. Tell me what you're thinking. Do you think I'm mistaken?"

"I don't know. I think you are simplifying things in a dangerous way. Your whole speech sounds like a stratagem for generating and channeling hatred."

"The adjective you were going to use was not *dangerous* but *repugnant,* but I won't hold that against you."

"Why should we reduce faith to an act of rejection and blind obedience? Is it not possible to believe in values of acceptance, of harmony?"

The boss smiled. He was enjoying himself.

"It is possible to believe in anything, Martín, be it the free market or even the tooth fairy. We can even believe that we don't believe in anything, as you do, which is the greatest credulity of them all. Am I right?"

"The customer is always right. What is the other hole you see in the story?"

"I miss having a villain. Whether we realize it or not, most of us define ourselves by opposing rather than by favoring something or someone. To put it another way, it is easier to react than to act. Nothing arouses a passion for dogma more than a good antagonist. And the more unlikely the better."

"I thought that role would work better in the abstract. The antagonist would be the nonbeliever, the alien, the one outside the group."

"Yes, but I'd like you to be more specific. It's difficult to hate an idea. That requires a certain intellectual discipline and a slightly obsessive, sick mind. There aren't too many of those. It's much easier to hate someone with a recognizable face whom we can blame for everything that makes us feel uncomfortable. It doesn't have to be an individual character. It could be a nation, a race, a group . . . anything."

The boss's flawless cynicism could get the better even of me. I gave a despondent sigh.

"Don't pretend to be a model citizen now, Martín. It's all the same to you, and we need a villain in this vaudeville. You should know that better than anyone. There is no drama without a conflict."

"What sort of villain would you like? A tyrant invader? A false prophet? The bogeyman?"

"I'll leave the outfit to you. Any of the usual suspects suits me. One of the functions of our villain must be to allow us to adopt the role of the victim and claim our moral superiority. We project onto him all those things we are incapable of recognizing in ourselves, things we demonize according to our particular interests. It's the basic arithmetic of the Pharisees. I keep telling you, you need to read the Bible. All the answers you're looking for are in there."

"I'm on the case."

"All you have to do is convince the sanctimonious that they are free of all sin and they'll start throwing stones, or bombs, with gusto. In fact, it doesn't take much, because they can be convinced with the bare minimum of encouragement and excuses. I don't know whether I'm making myself clear."

"You are making yourself abundantly clear. Your arguments have the subtlety of a blast furnace."

"I'm not sure I like that condescending tone, Martín. Does this mean you think this project isn't on a par with your moral or intellectual purity?"

"Not at all," I mumbled faintheartedly.

"What is it, then? Something tickling your conscience, dear friend?"

"The usual thing. I'm not sure I'm the nihilist you need."

"Nobody is. Nihilism is an attitude, not a doctrine. Place the flame from a candle under the testicles of a nihilist and notice how quickly he sees the light of existence. Something else is bothering you."

I raised my head and summoned up the most defiant manner I was capable of.

"Perhaps what's bothering me is that I understand everything you say, but I don't feel it."

"Do I pay you to have feelings?"

"Sometimes feeling and thinking are one and the same. The idea is yours, not mine."

The boss smiled and allowed a dramatic pause, like a schoolteacher preparing the lethal sword thrust with which to silence an unruly pupil.

"And what do you feel, Martín?"

The irony and disdain in his voice encouraged me and I gave vent to the humiliation accumulated during all those months in his shadow. Anger and shame at feeling terrified by his presence and allowing his poisonous speeches. Anger and shame because he had proved to me that, even if I would rather believe the only thing I had in me was despair, my soul was as petty and miserable as his sewer humanism claimed. Anger and shame at feeling, knowing, that he was always right, especially when it hurt to accept that.

"I've asked you a question, Martín. What is it you *feel*?"

"I feel that the best course would be to leave things as they are and give you back your money. I feel that, whatever it is you are proposing with this absurd venture, I'd rather not take part in it. And, above all, I feel regret for ever having met you."

The boss lowered his eyelids. He turned and walked a few steps toward the cemetery gates. I watched his dark silhouette outlined against the marble garden, a motionless shape in the rain. I felt murky fear grow inside me, inspiring a childish wish to beg forgiveness and accept any punishment in exchange for not having to bear that silence. And I felt disgust. At his presence and, in particular, at myself.

The boss turned round and came over to me again. He stopped just centimeters from me and put his face close to mine. I felt his cold breath on my skin and drowned in his black, bottomless eyes. This time his voice and his tone were like ice, devoid of that studied humanity that informed his conversation and his gestures.

"I will tell you only once. You fulfill your obligations and I'll fulfill mine. It's the only thing you can and must feel."

I was not aware that I was nodding repeatedly until the boss pulled the sheaf of papers from his pocket and handed it to me. He let the pages fall before I was able to catch them and a gust of wind swept them away, scattering them near the cemetery gates. I rushed to recover them from the rain, but some of the pages had fallen into puddles and were bleeding in the water. I gathered them together in a fistful of wet paper. When I looked up again, the boss had gone.

27

If ever I had needed to see a friendly face, it was then. The old building of *The Voice of Industry* peered over the cemetery walls. I headed there, hoping to find my former master Don Basilio, one of those rare souls immune to the world's stupidity, who always had good advice. When I walked into the newspaper offices I discovered that I still recognized most of the staff. It seemed as if not a minute had passed since I'd left the place so many years before. Those who, in turn, recognized me, gave me suspicious looks and turned their heads to avoid having to greet me. I slipped into the editorial department and went straight to Don Basilio's office, which was at the far end. It was empty.

"Who are you looking for?"

I turned round and saw Rosell, one of the journalists who'd already seemed old to me even when I was working there. Rosell had penned the poisonous review of *The Steps of Heaven,* describing me as a "writer of classified advertisements."

"Señor Rosell, I'm Martín. David Martín. Don't you remember me?"

Rosell spent a few moments inspecting me, pretending to have great difficulty in recognizing me, but finally he nodded.

"Where's Don Basilio?"

"He left two months ago. You'll find him at the offices of *La Vanguardia.* If you see him, give him my regards."

"I'll do that."

"I'm sorry about your book," said Rosell with an obliging smile.

I crossed the editorial department cutting a path among the unfriendly looks, twisted smiles, and venomous whispers. Time cures all, I thought, except the truth.

. . .

Half an hour later, a taxi dropped me off at the door of the main offices of *La Vanguardia* in Calle Pelayo. In contrast to the rather forbidding shabbiness of my old newspaper, everything here spoke of elegance and opulence. I made myself known at the reception and a chirpy young boy who looked like an unpaid intern, reminding me of myself in my youth, was dispatched to let Don Basilio know he had a visitor. My old friend's leonine presence remained unchanged; if anything, with his new attire matching the impressive setting, Don Basilio struck as formidable a figure as he had in his days at *The Voice of Industry*. His eyes lit up with joy when he saw me, and, breaking his iron protocol, he greeted me with an embrace that could easily have lost me two or three ribs had there not been an audience—happy or not, Don Basilio had to keep up appearances.

"Getting a little respectable, are we, Don Basilio?"

My old boss shrugged his shoulders, making a gesture to play down the new décor.

"Don't let it impress you."

"Don't be modest, Don Basilio, you've ended up with the jewel in the crown. Are you taking them in hand?"

Don Basilio pulled out his perennial red pencil and showed it to me, winking as he did so.

"I go through four a week."

"Two fewer than at *The Voice*."

"Give me time. I have one or two experts here who punctuate with a pistol and think that an intro is an orthopedic contraption."

Despite his words, it was obvious that Don Basilio felt comfortable in his new home, and he looked healthier than ever.

"Don't tell me you've come to ask me for work, because I might even give it to you," he threatened.

"That's very kind of you, Don Basilio, but you know I gave up the cloth and journalism·isn't for me."

"Then let me know how this grumpy old man can be of service."

"I need some information about an old case for a story I'm working on. The death of a well-known lawyer called Marlasca. Diego Marlasca."

"What year are we talking about?"

"Nineteen hundred and four."

Don Basilio sighed.

"That's going back a long way. A lot of water under the dam."

"Not enough to wash the matter away."

Don Basilio put a hand on my shoulder and asked me to follow him to the editorial department.

"Don't worry, you've come to the right place. These good people maintain an archive that would be the envy of the Vatican. If there was anything in the press, we'll find it for you. Besides, the archivist is a good friend of mine. Let me warn you that next to him I'm Snow White. Pay no attention to his unfriendly disposition. Deep down—very deep down—he's kindness itself."

I followed Don Basilio through a wide hall with fine wood paneling. On one side was a circular room with a large round table and a series of portraits of an illustrious group of frowning members of the aristocracy.

"The room for the witches' Sabbaths," Don Basilio explained. "All the section heads meet here with the deputy editor, yours truly, and the editor, and like good Knights of the Round Table, we find the Holy Grail every evening at seven o'clock."

"Impressive."

"You ain't seen nothing yet," said Don Basilio, winking at me. "Look at this."

Don Basilio stood beneath one of the august portraits and pushed the wooden panel covering the wall. The panel, yielding with a creak, revealed a hidden corridor.

"What do you say, Martín? And this is only one of the many secret passages in the building. Not even the Borgias had a setup like this."

Don Basilio led me down the corridor to a large reading room surrounded by glass cabinets, the repository of *La Vanguardia*'s secret library. At one end of the room, under the beam emanating from a lampshade of green glass, a middle-aged man was sitting at a table examining a document with a magnifying glass. When he saw us come in he raised his head and gave us a look that would have made anyone young or sensitive turn to stone.

"Let me introduce you to José María Brotons, lord of the underworld, chief of the catacombs of this holy house," Don Basilio announced.

Without letting go of the magnifying glass, Brotons observed me with eyes that seemed to go rusty on contact. I went up to him and shook his hand.

"This is my old apprentice, David Martín."

Brotons reluctantly shook my hand and glanced at Don Basilio.

"Is this the writer?"

"The very one."

Brotons nodded.

"He's certainly courageous, stepping out into the street after the thrashing they gave him. What's he doing here?"

"He's come to plead for your help, your blessing, and your advice on an important matter of documental archaeology," Don Basilio explained.

"And where's the blood sacrifice?" Brotons spat out.

"Sacrifice?" I asked.

Brotons looked at me as if I were an idiot.

"A goat, a lamb, a capon, if pressed . . ."

My mind went blank. For an endless moment, Brotons kept his eyes fixed on mine. Then, just as I started to feel the prickle of sweat down my back, the archivist and Don Basilio roared with laughter. I let them laugh as much as they wanted at my expense, until they couldn't breathe and had to dry their tears. Clearly, Don Basilio had found a soul mate in his new colleague.

"Come this way, young man," Brotons said, doing away with his fierce countenance. "Let's see what we can find."

28

The newspaper archives were located in one of the basements, under the floor that housed the huge rotary press, the product of post-Victorian technology. It looked like a cross between a monstrous steam engine and a machine for making lightning.

"Let me introduce you to the rotary press, better known as Leviathan. Mind how you go: they say it has already swallowed more than one unsuspecting person," said Don Basilio. "It's like the story of Jonah and the whale, only what comes out again is minced meat."

"Surely you're exaggerating."

"One of these days we could throw in that new trainee, the smart aleck who likes to say that print is dead," Brotons proposed.

"Set a time and a date and we'll celebrate with a stew," Don Basilio agreed.

They laughed like schoolchildren. Two of a kind.

The archive was a labyrinth of corridors bordered by three-meter-high shelves. A couple of pale creatures who looked as if they hadn't left the cellar in fifteen years officiated as Brotons's assistants. When they saw him, they rushed over, awaiting instructions. Brotons looked at me inquisitively.

"What is it we're looking for?"

"Nineteen hundred and four. The death of a lawyer called Diego

Marlasca. A pillar of Barcelona society, founder-member of the Valera, Marlasca & Sentís legal firm."

"Month?"

"November."

At a signal from Brotons, the two assistants ran off in search of copies dating back to November 1904. It was a time when each day was so stained with the presence of death that most newspapers ran large obituaries on their front pages. A character as important as Marlasca would probably have generated more than a simple death notice in the city's press and his obituary would have been first-page material. The assistants returned with a few volumes and placed them on a large desk. We divided up the task among all five present and found Diego Marlasca's obituary on the front page, just as I'd imagined. The edition was dated 23 November 1904. It was Brotons who made the discovery.

"*Habemus cadaver,*" he announced.

There were four obituary notices devoted to Marlasca. One from the family, another from the law firm, one from the Barcelona Bar Association, and the last from the cultural association of the Ateneo Barcelonés.

"That's what comes from being rich. You die five or six times," Don Basilio remarked.

The announcements were not in themselves very interesting—pleadings for the immortal soul of the deceased, a note explaining that the funeral would be for close friends and family only, grandiose verses lauding a great, erudite citizen, an irreplaceable member of Barcelona society, and so on.

"The type of thing you're interested in probably appeared a day or two earlier, or later," Brotons said.

We checked through the papers covering the week of Marlasca's death and found a sequence of news items relating to the lawyer. The first reported that the distinguished lawyer had died in an accident. Don Basilio read the text out loud.

"This was written by a chimp," he pronounced. "Three redundant paragraphs that don't say anything and only at the end does it explain that the death was accidental, but without saying what sort of accident it was."

"Here we have something more interesting," said Brotons.

An article published the following day explained that the police were investigating the circumstances of the accident. The most revealing piece of information was that, according to the forensic evidence, Marlasca had drowned.

"Drowned?" interrupted Don Basilio. "How? Where?"

"It doesn't say. Perhaps they had to shorten the item to include this urgent and extensive defense of the sardana, a three-column article entitled 'To the Strains of the *Tenora:* Spirit and Mettle,' " Brotons remarked.

"Does it say who was in charge of the investigation?" I asked.

"It mentions someone called Salvador. Ricardo Salvador," said Brotons.

We went over the rest of the news items related to the death of Marlasca, but there was nothing of any substance. The texts parroted one another, repeating a chorus that sounded too much like the official line supplied by the law firm of Valera & Co.

"This has the distinct whiff of deception," said Brotons.

I sighed, disheartened. I had hoped to find something more than sentimental remembrances and empty news items that threw no new light on the facts.

"Didn't you have a good contact in police headquarters?" Don Basilio asked. "What was his name?"

"Víctor Grandes," Brotons said.

"Perhaps he could put Martín in touch with this person Salvador."

I cleared my throat and the two hefty men looked at me with frowns.

"For reasons that have nothing to do with this matter, or perhaps because they're too closely related, I'd rather not involve Inspector Grandes," I said.

Brotons and Don Basilio exchanged glances.

"Right. Any other names that should be deleted from the list?"

"Marcos and Castelo."

"I see you haven't lost your talent for making friends," offered Don Basilio.

Brotons rubbed his chin.

"Let's not worry too much. I think I might be able to find another way that will not arouse suspicion."

"If you find Salvador for me, I'll sacrifice whatever you want, even a pig."

"With my gout I've given up pork, but I wouldn't say no to a good cigar," Brotons replied.

"Make it two," added Don Basilio.

While I rushed off to a tobacconist on Calle Tallers in search of two specimens of the most exquisite and expensive Havana cigars, Brotons made a few discreet calls to police headquarters and confirmed that Salvador had left the force, or rather that he had been made to leave, and was now working as a bodyguard as well as conducting investigations for various law firms in the city. When I returned to the newspaper offices to present my benefactors with their two cigars, the archivist handed me a note with an address:

Ricardo Salvador
Calle de la Lleona, 21. Top floor.

"May the publisher in chief of *La Vanguardia* bless you," I said.

"And may you live to see it."

29

Calle de la Lleona, better known to locals as the Street of the Three Beds in honor of the notorious brothel it harbored, was an alleyway almost as dark as its reputation. It started in the shadowy arches of Plaza Real and extended into a damp crevice, far from sunlight, between old buildings piled on top of one another and sewn together by a perpetual web of clotheslines. The crumbling, ocher façades were dilapidated, and the slabs of stone covering the ground had been bathed in blood during the years when the city had been ruled by the gun. More than once I'd used the setting as a backdrop to my stories in *City of the Damned* and even now, deserted and forgotten, it still smelled of crime and gunpowder. The grim surroundings seemed to indicate that Superintendent Salvador's premature retirement from the police force had not been a step up.

Number 21 was a modest property squeezed between two buildings that held it together like pincers. The main door was open, revealing a pool of shadows from which a steep, narrow staircase rose in a spiral. The floor was flooded with a dark, slimy liquid oozing from the cracks in the tiles. I climbed the steps as best I could, without letting go of the handrail, but not trusting it either. There was only one door on every landing. Judging by the appearance of the building, I didn't think that any of the apartments could be larger than forty square meters. A small skylight crowned the stairwell and bathed the upper floors in a tenuous light. The door to the top-floor apartment was at the end of a short corridor and I was surprised to find it open. I rapped with my knuckles but got no reply. The door opened onto a small sitting room containing an armchair, a table, and a bookshelf filled with books and brass boxes. A sort of kitchen-cum-washing-area occupied the adjoining room. The saving grace in that cell was a terrace that led to the flat roof. The door to the terrace was also open and a fresh breeze blew through it, bringing with it the smell of cooking and laundry from the rooftops of the old town.

"Is anyone home?" I called out.

Nobody answered, so I walked over to the terrace door and stepped outside. A jungle of roofs, towers, water tanks, lightning conductors, and chimneys spread out in every direction. Before I was able to take another step, I felt the touch of cold metal on the back of my neck and heard the metallic click of a revolver as the hammer was cocked. All I could think to do was raise my hands and not move even an eyebrow.

"My name is David Martín. I got your address from police headquarters. I wanted to speak to you about a case you handled."

"Do you usually go into people's homes uninvited, Señor David Martín?"

"The door was open. I called out but you can't have heard me. Can I put my hands down?"

"I didn't tell you to put them up. Which case?"

"The death of Diego Marlasca. I rent the house that was his last home. The tower house in Calle Flassaders."

He said nothing. I could still feel the revolver pressing against my neck.

"Señor Salvador?" I asked.

"I'm wondering whether it wouldn't be better to blow your head off right now."

"Don't you want to hear my story first?"

The pressure from the revolver seemed to lessen and I heard the hammer being uncocked. I slowly turned round. Ricardo Salvador was an imposing figure, with gray hair and pale blue eyes that penetrated like needles. I guessed that he must have been about fifty but it would have been difficult to find men half his age who would dare get in his way. I gulped. Salvador lowered the revolver and turned his back to me, returning to the apartment.

"I apologize for the welcome," he mumbled.

I followed him to the minute kitchen and stopped in the doorway. Salvador left the pistol on the sink and lit the stove with bits of paper and cardboard. He pulled out a coffeepot and looked at me questioningly.

"No, thanks."

"It's the only good thing I have, I warn you," he said.

"Then I'll have one with you."

Salvador put a couple of generous spoonfuls of coffee into the pot, filled it with water, and put it on the flame.

"Who has spoken to you about me?"

"A few days ago I visited Señora Marlasca, the widow. She's the one who told me about you. She said you were the only person who had tried to discover the truth and it had cost you your job."

"That's one way of describing it, I suppose," he said.

I noticed that at my mention of the widow his expression darkened and I wondered what might have happened between them during those unfortunate days.

"How is she?" he asked. "Señora Marlasca."

"I think she misses you."

Salvador nodded, his fierce manner crumbling.

"I haven't been to see her for a long time."

"She thinks you blame her for what happened. I think she'd like to see you again, even though so much time has gone by."

"Perhaps you're right. Maybe I should pay her a visit . . ."

"Can you talk to me about what happened?"

Salvador recovered his severe expression.

"What do you want to know?"

"Marlasca's widow told me that you never accepted the official line that her husband took his life. She said you had suspicions."

"More than suspicions. Has anyone told you how Marlasca died?"

"All I know is that people said it was an accident."

"Marlasca died by drowning. At least, that's what the police report said."

"How did he drown?"

"There's only one way of drowning, but I'll come back to that later. The curious thing is where he drowned."

"In the sea?"

Salvador smiled. It was a dark, bitter smile, like the coffee that was brewing.

"Are you sure you want to hear this?"

"I've never been surer of anything in my life."

He handed me a cup and looked me up and down, assessing me.

"I assume you've visited that son of a bitch Valera."

"If you mean Marlasca's partner, he's dead. The one I spoke to was his son."

"Another son of a bitch, except he has less guts. I don't know what he told you, but I'm sure he didn't say that between them they managed to get me thrown out of the police force and turned me into a pariah who couldn't even beg for money in the streets."

"I'm afraid he forgot to include that in his version of events," I conceded.

"It doesn't surprise me."

"You were going to tell me how Marlasca drowned."

"That's where it gets interesting," said Salvador. "Did you know that Señor Marlasca, apart from being a lawyer, a scholar, and a writer, had, as a young man, won the annual Christmas swim across the port organized by the Barcelona Swimming Club?"

"How can a champion swimmer drown?" I asked.

"The question is where did he drown. Señor Marlasca's body was found in the pond on the roof of the water reservoir building in Ciudadela Park. Do you know the place?"

I swallowed and nodded. It was there that I first encountered Corelli.

"If you know it, you'll know that when it's full it's barely a meter deep. It's essentially a basin. The day the lawyer was found dead, the reservoir was half empty and the water level was no more than sixty centimeters."

"A champion swimmer doesn't drown in sixty centimeters of water, just like that," I observed.

"That's what I said to myself."

"Were there other points of view?"

"For a start, it's doubtful whether he drowned at all. The pathologist who carried out the autopsy found water in the lungs, but his report said that death had occurred as a result of heart failure."

"I don't understand."

"When Marlasca fell into the pond, or when he was pushed, he was on fire. His body had severe burns on the torso, arms, and face. According to the pathologist, the body could have been on fire for almost a minute before it came into contact with the water. The remains of the lawyer's clothes showed the presence of some type of solvent on the fabrics. Marlasca was burned alive."

It took me a few minutes to digest all this.

"Why would anyone want to do something like that?"

"A settling of scores? Pure cruelty? You choose. My opinion is that somebody wanted to delay the identification of Marlasca's body in order to gain time and confuse the police."

"Who?"

"Jaco Corbera."

"Irene Sabino's agent."

"Who disappeared the same day Marlasca died, together with the balance from a personal account in the Banco Hispano Colonial that his wife didn't know about."

"A hundred thousand French francs," I said.

Salvador looked at me, intrigued.

"How did you know?"

"It's not important. What was Marlasca doing on the roof of the reservoir anyway? It's not exactly on the way to anywhere."

"That's another confusing point. We found a diary in Marlasca's study in which he had written down an appointment there at five in the afternoon. Or that's what it looked like. In the diary he'd only specified a time, a place, and an initial. *C.* Probably for Corbera."

"Then what do you think happened?" I asked.

"What I think, and what the evidence suggests, is that Jaco fooled Irene into manipulating Marlasca. As you probably know, the lawyer was obsessed with all that mumbo jumbo about séances, especially after the death of his son. Jaco had a partner, Damián Roures, who was mixed up in that world. A real fraud. Between the two of them, and with the help of Irene Sabino, they conned Marlasca, promising that they could help him make contact with the boy in the spirit world. Marlasca was a desperate man, ready to believe anything. That trio of vermin had organized the perfect sting but then Jaco became too greedy for his own good. Some think that Sabino didn't act in bad faith, that she genuinely was in love with Marlasca and believed in all that supernatural nonsense, just as he did. It is a possibility,but I don't buy it, and seeing how things turned out, it's irrelevant. Jaco knew that Marlasca had those funds in the bank and decided to get him out of the way and disappear with the money, leaving a trail of chaos behind him. The appointment in the diary may well have been a red herring left by Sabino or Jaco. There was no way at all of knowing whether Marlasca himself had noted it down."

"And where did the hundred thousand francs Marlasca had in the Hispano Colonial come from?"

"Marlasca had paid that money into the account himself, in cash, the year before. I haven't the faintest idea where he could have laid hands on a sum of that size. What I do know is that the remainder was withdrawn, in cash, on the morning of the day Marlasca died. Later, the lawyers said that the money had been transferred to some sort of discretionary fund and had not disappeared; they said Marlasca had simply decided to reorganize his finances. But I find it hard to believe that a man would reorganize his finances, moving almost one hundred thousand francs in the morning, and be discovered, burned alive, in the afternoon, without there being some connection. I don't believe this money ended up in some mysterious fund. To this day, there has been nothing to convince me that the money didn't end up in the hands of Jaco Corbera and Irene Sabino. At least at first, because I doubt that she saw any of it after Jaco disappeared."

"What happened to Irene?"

"That's another aspect that makes me think Jaco tricked both of his accomplices. Shortly after Marlasca's death, Roures left the afterlife industry and opened a shop selling magic tricks on Calle Princesa. As far as I know, he's still there. Irene Sabino worked for a couple more years in increasingly tawdry clubs and cabarets. The last thing I heard, she was prostituting herself in El Raval and living in poverty. She obviously didn't get a single franc. Nor did Roures."

"And Jaco?"

"He probably left the country under a false name and is living comfortably somewhere off the proceeds."

The whole story, far from clarifying things in my mind, only raised more questions. Salvador must have noticed my unease and gave me a commiserating smile.

"Valera and his friends in the town hall managed to persuade the press to publish the story about an accident. He resolved the matter with a grand funeral: he didn't want to muddy the reputation of the law firm, whose client list included many members of the town hall and the city council. Nor did he wish to draw attention to Marlasca's strange behavior during the last twelve months of his life, from the moment he abandoned his family and associates and decided to buy a ruin in a part of town he had never set his well-shod foot in so that he could devote himself to writing—or at least that's what his partner said."

"Did Valera say what sort of thing Marlasca wanted to write?"

"A book of poems or something like that."

"And you believed him?"

"I've seen many strange things in my work, my friend, but a wealthy lawyer who leaves everything to go write sonnets is not part of the repertoire."

"So?"

"So the reasonable thing would have been for me to forget the whole matter and do as I was told."

"But that's not what happened."

"No. And not because I'm a hero or an idiot. I did it because every time I saw the suffering of that poor woman, Marlasca's widow, it made my stomach turn and I couldn't look at myself in the mirror without doing what I was supposedly being paid to do."

He pointed around the miserable, cold place that was his home.

"Believe me, if I'd known what was coming I would have preferred to be a coward and wouldn't have stepped out of line. I can't say I wasn't warned at police headquarters. With the lawyer dead and buried, it was time to turn the page and put all our efforts into the pursuit of starving anarchists and schoolteachers of suspicious ideology."

"You say buried . . . Where is Diego Marlasca buried?"

"In the family vault in San Gervasio cemetery, I think, not far from the house where the widow lives. May I ask you why you are so interested in this matter? And don't tell me your curiosity was aroused just because you live in the tower house."

"It's hard to explain."

"If you want a friendly piece of advice, look at me and learn from my mistakes. Let it go."

"I'd like to. The problem is that I don't think the matter will let *me* go."

Salvador watched me for a long time. Then he took a piece of paper and wrote down a number.

"This is the telephone number of the downstairs neighbors. They're good people and the only ones who have a telephone in the whole building. You can get hold of me there or leave me a message. Ask for Emilio. If you need any help, don't hesitate to call. And watch out. Jaco disappeared from the scene many years ago, but there are still people who don't want this business stirred up again. A hundred thousand francs is a lot of money."

I took the note and put it away.

"Thank you."

"Not at all. Anyhow, what more can they do to me now?"

"Would you have a photograph of Diego Marlasca? I haven't found one anywhere in the tower house."

"I don't know . . . I think I must have one somewhere. Let me have a look."

Salvador walked over to a desk in a corner of the sitting room and pulled out a brass box full of bits of paper.

"I still have things from the case. As you see, even after all these years I haven't learned my lesson. Here. Look. This photograph was given to me by the widow."

He handed me an old studio portrait of a tall, good-looking man in his forties posed against a velvet backdrop and smiling for the camera. I tried to read those clear eyes, wondering how they could possibly conceal the dark world I had found in the pages of *Lux Aeterna*.

"May I keep it?"

Salvador hesitated.

"I suppose so. But don't lose it."

"I promise I'll return it."

"Promise me you'll be careful and I'd be much happier. And that if you're not, and you get into a mess, you'll call me."

We shook on it.

"I promise."

30

The sun was setting as I left Ricardo Salvador on his cold roof terrace and returned to Plaza Real. The square was bathed in a dusty light that tinted the figures of passersby with a reddish hue. From there I set off walking and ended up at the only place in town where I always felt welcome and protected. When I reached Calle Santa Ana, the Sempere & Sons bookshop was about to close. Twilight was advancing over the city and the sky was breached by a line of blue and purple. I stopped in front of the shop window and saw that Sempere's son was saying good-bye to a customer at the front door. When he saw me he smiled and greeted me with a shyness that spoke of his innate decency.

"I was just thinking about you, Martín. Everything all right?"

"Couldn't be better."

"It shows in your face. Here, come in, I'll make you some coffee."

He held the shop door open and showed me in. I stepped into the bookshop and breathed in that perfume of paper and magic that strangely no one had ever thought of bottling. Sempere's son took me to the back room, where he set about preparing a pot of coffee.

"How is your father? He looked fragile the other day."

Sempere's son nodded, as if appreciative of my concern. I realized that he probably didn't have anyone to talk to about him.

"He's seen better times, that's for sure. The doctor says he has to be careful with his angina, but he insists on working more than ever. Sometimes I have to get angry with him, but he seems to think that if he leaves me to look after the shop the business will fail. This morning when I got up I asked him to stay in bed and not come down to work today. Well, would you believe it, three minutes later I found him in the dining room putting on his shoes."

"He's a man with fixed ideas," I agreed.

"He's as stubborn as a mule," replied Sempere's son. "Thank goodness we now have a bit of help, otherwise . . ."

I adopted my best expression of surprise and innocence, which always came in handy and needed little practice.

"The girl," Sempere's son explained. "Isabella, your apprentice. That's why I was thinking about you. I hope you don't mind if she spends a few hours here each day. The truth is, with the way things are I'm very grateful for the help, but if you have any objections . . ."

I suppressed a smile when I noticed how he savored Isabella's double *l*.

"Well, as long as it's only temporary. The truth is, Isabella is a good girl. Intelligent and hardworking," I said. "And trustworthy. We get on very well."

"She says you're a tyrant."

"Is that what she says?"

"In fact, she has a nickname for you. Mr. Hyde."

"How charming. Pay no attention to her. You know what women are like."

"Yes, I do," said Sempere's son in a tone that made it clear that he might know a lot of things but certainly hadn't the faintest clue about women.

"Isabella might say that about me, but don't think she doesn't tell me things about you," I countered.

I noticed a change in his expression and let my words sink through the layers of his armor. He handed me a cup of coffee with an attentive smile and rescued the conversation with a trick unworthy even of a second-rate operetta.

"Goodness knows what she says about me."

I left him to soak in uncertainty for a few moments.

"Would you like to know?" I asked casually, hiding a smile behind my cup.

Sempere's son shrugged.

"She says you're a good and generous man. She says that people don't understand you because you're shy and they can't see beyond that, and, I quote, you have the presence of a film star and a fascinating personality."

Sempere's son looked at me in astonishment.

"I'm not going to lie to you, Sempere, my friend. The truth is I'm glad you've brought up the subject because I've been wanting to talk to you about it and didn't know how."

"Talk about what?"

I lowered my voice.

"Between you and me, Isabella wants to work here because she admires you and, I fear, is secretly in love with you."

Sempere gulped.

"But pure love, eh? Spiritual. Like the love of a Dickens heroine, if you see what I mean. No frivolities or childish nonsense. Isabella might be young, but she's a real woman. You must have noticed, I'm sure . . ."

"Now that you mention it . . ."

"And I'm referring not to her—if you'll pardon me—exquisitely tender frame but to her kindness and the inner beauty that is just waiting for the right moment to emerge and make some fortunate man the happiest in the world."

Sempere didn't know where to look.

"Besides, she has hidden talents. She speaks languages. She plays the piano like an angel. She has a good head for numbers. And to cap it all she's a wonderful cook. Look at me. I've put on a few kilos since she started working for me. Delicacies that even at La Tour d'Argent . . . Don't tell me you haven't noticed?"

"She didn't mention that she can cook . . ."

"I'm talking about love at first sight."

"Well, really . . ."

"Do you know what the matter is? Deep down, although she gives the impression she's an untamed shrew, the girl is docile and shy to a pathological degree. I blame the nuns: they unhinge them with all those stories of hell and all those sewing lessons. Long live secular education."

"Well, I would have sworn she took me for a little less than an idiot," Sempere assured me.

"There you are. Irrefutable proof. Sempere, my friend, when a woman treats you like an idiot it means her hormones are racing!"

"Are you sure about that?"

"As sure as the Bank of Spain. Believe me, I know quite a lot about this subject."

"That's what my father says. And what am I to do?"

"Well, that depends. Do you like the girl?"

"Like her? I don't know. How do you know if . . . ?"

"It's very simple. Do you look at her furtively and feel like biting her?"

"Biting her?"

"On her backside, for example."

"Señor Martín!"

"Don't be bashful, we're among gentlemen. It's a known fact that we men are the missing link between the pirate and the pig. Do you like her or don't you?"

"Well, Isabella is an attractive girl."

"What else?"

"Intelligent. Pleasant. Hardworking."

"Go on."

"And a good Christian, I think. Not that I'm much of a practicing Catholic, but—"

"Don't I know it. Isabella almost lives in the church. Those nuns, I tell you!"

"But quite frankly, it had never occurred to me to bite her."

"It hadn't occurred to you until I mentioned it."

"I must say, I think talking about her like that—or about any other woman—shows a lack of respect. You should be ashamed," protested Sempere's son.

"Mea culpa," I intoned, raising my hands in a gesture of surrender. "But never mind—we each show our devotion in our own way. I'm a frivolous, superficial creature, hence my canine focus, but you, with that *aurea gravitas* of yours, are a man of mysterious and profound feelings. The important thing is that the girl adores you and that the feeling is mutual."

"Well . . ."

"Don't you 'well' me. Let's face it, Sempere. You're a respectable and responsible man. Had it been me, what can I say? But you're not a fellow to play fast and loose with the noble, pure feelings of a ripe young girl. Am I mistaken?"

"I suppose not."

"Well, that's it then."

"What is?"

"Isn't it obvious?"

"No."

"It's time to go courting."

"Excuse me?"

"Courting, or, in scientific terms, time for a kiss and a cuddle. Look here, Sempere, for some strange reason centuries of supposed civilization have brought us to a situation in which one cannot go sidling up to women on street corners or asking them to marry us, just like that. First there has to be courtship."

"Marry? Have you gone mad?"

"What I'm trying to say is that perhaps—and this is your idea even if you're not aware of it—today or tomorrow or the next day, when you get over all this shaking and dribbling over her, you could take Isabella out when she finishes work at the bookshop. Take her out for afternoon tea somewhere special, and you'll realize once and for all that you were made for each other. You could take her to Els Quatre Gats, where they're so stingy they dim the lights to save on electricity—that always helps in these situations. Ask for some curd cheese for the girl with a good spoonful of honey; that always whets the appetite. Then, casually, you let her have a swig or two of that muscatel that goes straight to the head. At that point, placing a hand on her knee, you stun her with that sweet talk you keep to yourself, you rascal."

"But I don't know anything about her, or what interests her, or—"

"She's interested in the same things as you. She's interested in books, in literature, in the very smell of the treasures you have here— and in the penny novels with their promise of romance and adventure. She's interested in casting aside loneliness and in not wasting time trying to understand that in this rotten world nothing is worth a single céntimo if there isn't someone to share it with. Now you know the essentials. The rest you can find out and enjoy as you go along."

Sempere looked thoughtful, glancing first at his cup of coffee, which he hadn't touched, then at me as I attempted with great difficulty to maintain the smile of a stockbroker.

"I'm not sure whether to thank you or report you to the police," he said at last.

Just then we heard footsteps in the bookshop. A few seconds later Sempere senior put his head round the door of the back room and stood there looking at us with a frown.

"What's going on? The shop is left unattended and you're sitting here chattering as if it were a bank holiday. What if a customer had come in? Or some scoundrel trying to make off with our goods?"

Sempere's son sighed, rolling his eyes.

"Don't worry, Señor Sempere. Books are the only things in this world that no one wants to steal," I said, winking at him.

His face lit up with a knowing smile. Sempere's son took the opportunity to escape from my clutches and slink off back to the bookshop. His father sat next to me and sniffed at the cup of coffee his son had left untouched.

"What does the doctor say about the effects of caffeine on the heart?" I asked.

"That man can't even find his backside with an anatomy book. What would he know about the heart?"

"More than you, I'm sure," I replied, snatching the cup from him.

"I'm as strong as an ox, Martín."

"You're a mule, that's what you are. Please go back upstairs and get into bed."

"It's only worth staying in bed if you're young and in good company."

"If you want company, I'll find someone for you, but I don't think your heart is up to it right now."

"Martín, at my age, eroticism is reduced to enjoying flan and staring at widows' necks. The one I'm worried about here is my heir. Any progress on that score?"

"We're fertilizing the soil and sowing the seeds. We'll have to see if the weather is favorable and we reap a harvest. In two or three days I'll be able to give you a report on the first shoots that is 60 to 70 percent reliable."

Sempere gave a satisfied smile.

"A stroke of genius, sending Isabella to be our shop assistant," he said. "But don't you think she's a bit young for my son?"

"He's the one who seems a bit green, if I may be frank. He's got to pull himself together or Isabella will eat him alive. Thank goodness he's a decent sort, otherwise . . ."

"How can I repay you?"

"By going upstairs and getting into bed. If you need some spicy company, take a copy of *Moll Flanders*."

"You're right. Good old Defoe never lets you down."

"Not even if he tries. Go on, off to bed."

Sempere stood up. He moved with difficulty and his breathing was labored, with a hoarse rattle that frightened me. I took his arm and noticed that his skin was cold.

"Don't be alarmed, Martín. It's my metabolism; it's a little slow."

"Today it's as slow as *War and Peace*."

"A little nap and I'll be as good as new."

I decided to go up with him to the apartment where father and son lived, above the bookshop, and make sure he got under the blankets. It took us a quarter of an hour to negotiate the stairs. On the way we met one of the neighbors, an affable schoolteacher called Don Anacleto, who taught language and literature at the Jesuit school in Calle Caspe.

"How's life looking today, Sempere, my friend?"

"Rather steep, Don Anacleto."

With the teacher's help I managed to reach the first floor with Sempere practically hanging from my neck.

"If you will forgive me, I must retire to rest after a long day spent fighting that pack of primates I have for pupils," the teacher announced. "I'm telling you, this country is going to disintegrate within one generation. They'll tear one another to pieces like rats."

Sempere made a gesture to indicate that I shouldn't pay too much attention to Don Anacleto.

"He's a good man," he whispered, "but he drowns in a glass of water."

When I stepped into the apartment I was suddenly reminded of that distant morning when I had arrived there covered in blood, holding a copy of *Great Expectations.* I recalled how Sempere had carried me up to his home and given me a cup of hot cocoa after the doctor left and how he'd whispered soothing words, cleaning the blood off my body with a warm towel and a gentleness that nobody had ever shown me before. At that time Sempere was a strong man and to me he seemed like a giant in every way; without him I don't think I would have survived those years of scant hope. Little or nothing remained of that strength as I held him in my arms to help him into bed and covered him with a couple of blankets. I sat down next to him and took his hand, not knowing what to do.

"Listen, if we're both going to start crying our eyes out you'd better leave," he said.

"Take care, you hear me?"

"I'll wrap myself in cotton wool, don't worry."

I nodded and started toward the door.

"Martín?"

At the doorway I turned round. Sempere was looking at me with the same anxiety he had shown that morning long ago, when I'd lost a few teeth and much of my innocence. I left before he could ask me what was wrong.

31

One of the first expedients of the professional writer that Isabella had learned from me was the art of procrastination. Every veteran in the trade knows that any activity, from sharpening a pencil to cataloging daydreams, takes precedence over sitting down at one's desk and squeezing one's brain. Isabella had absorbed this fundamental lesson by osmosis and when I got home, instead of finding her at her desk, I surprised her in the kitchen as she was giving the last touches to a dinner that smelled and looked as if its preparation had been a question of a few hours.

"Are we celebrating something?" I asked.

"With that face of yours, I don't think so."

"What's the smell?"

"Caramelized duck with baked pears and chocolate sauce. I found the recipe in one of your cookbooks."

"I don't own any cookbooks."

Isabella got up and brought over a leather-bound volume, which she placed on the table: *The 101 Best Recipes of French Cuisine,* by Michel Aragon.

"That's what you think. On the second row of the library book-shelves, I've found all sorts of things, including a handbook on marital hygiene by Dr. Pérez-Aguado with some very suggestive illustrations and gems such as 'Woman, in accordance with the divine plan, has no knowledge of carnal desire and her spiritual and sentimental fulfillment is sublimated in the natural exercise of motherhood and household chores.' You've got a veritable King Solomon's mine there."

"Can you tell me what you were looking for on the second row of the shelves?"

"Inspiration. Which I found."

"But of a culinary persuasion. We'd agreed that you were going to write every day, with or without inspiration."

"I'm stuck. And it's your fault, because you've got me working two jobs and mixed up in your schemes with the immaculate son of Sempere."

"Do you think it's right to make fun of the man who's madly in love with you?"

"What?"

"You heard me. Sempere's son confessed to me that you've robbed him of sleep. Literally. He can't sleep, he can't eat, and he can't even pee, poor guy, for thinking so much about you all day."

"You're delirious."

"The one who is delirious is poor Sempere. You should have seen him. I came very close to shooting him, to put an end to his pain and misery."

"But he pays no attention to me whatsoever," Isabella protested.

"Because he doesn't know how to open his heart and find the words with which to express his feelings. We men are like that. Brutish and primitive."

"He had no trouble finding words to tell me off for not putting a collection of the *National Episodes* in the right order!"

"That's not the same. Administrative procedure is one thing, the language of passion another."

"Nonsense."

"There's no nonsense in love, my dear assistant. Changing the subject, are we having dinner or aren't we?"

Isabella had set a table to match her banquet, using a whole arsenal of dishes, cutlery, and glasses I'd never seen before.

"I don't know why, if you have all these beautiful things, you don't use them. They were all in boxes, in the room next to the laundry," said Isabella. "Typical man!"

I picked up one of the knives and examined it in the light of the candles that Isabella had placed on the table. I realized these household utensils belonged to Diego Marlasca and it made me lose my appetite altogether.

"Is anything the matter?" asked Isabella.

I shook my head. My assistant served the food and stood there looking at me expectantly. I tasted a mouthful and smiled.

"Very good," I said.

"It's a bit leathery, I think. The recipe said you had to cook it over a low flame for goodness knows how long, but on your stove the heat is either nonexistent or scorching, with nothing in between."

"It's good," I repeated, eating without appetite.

Isabella kept giving me furtive looks. We continued to eat in silence, the tinkling of the cutlery and plates our only company.

"Were you serious about Sempere's son?"

I nodded, without glancing up from my plate.

"And what else did he say about me?"

"He said you have a classical beauty, you're intelligent, intensely feminine—that's how old-fashioned he is—and he feels there's a spiritual connection between you."

"Swear you're not making this up," she said.

I put my right hand on the cookbook and raised my left hand.

"I swear on *The 101 Best Recipes of French Cuisine,*" I declared.

"One usually swears with the other hand."

I changed hands and repeated the performance with a solemn expression. Isabella puffed.

"What am I going to do?"

"I don't know. What do people do when they're in love? Go for a stroll, go dancing . . ."

"But I'm not in love with this man."

I went on sampling the caramelized duck, ignoring her insistent stare. After a while, Isabella banged her hand on the table.

"Will you please look at me? This is all your fault."

I calmly put down my knife and fork, wiped my mouth with the napkin, and looked at her.

"What am I going to do?" she asked again.

"That depends. Do you like Sempere or don't you?"

A cloud of doubt crossed her face.

"I don't know. To begin with, he's a bit old for me."

"He's practically my age," I pointed out. "One or two years older, at the most. Maybe three."

"Or four or five."

I sighed.

"He's in the prime of life. Hadn't we decided that you like them to be mature?"

"Don't tease me."

"Isabella, who am I to tell you what to do?"

"That's a good one!"

"Let me finish. What I mean is that this is something between Sempere's son and you. I'd say give him a chance. Nothing else. If one of these days he decides to take the first step and asks you, let's say, to have tea, accept the invitation. Perhaps you'll get talking and you'll end up being friends, or maybe you won't. But I think Sempere is a good man, his interest in you is genuine, and I dare say, if you think about it, you feel something for him too."

"You're mad."

"But Sempere isn't. And I think that not to respect the affection and admiration he feels for you would be mean. And you're not mean."

"This is blackmail."

"No, it's life."

Isabella looked daggers at me. I smiled.

"Will you at least finish your dinner?" she asked.

I bolted down the food on my plate, mopped it up with bread, and let out a sigh of satisfaction.

"What's for dessert?"

. . .

After dinner I left a pensive Isabella mulling over her doubts and anxieties in the reading room and went up to the study in the tower. I pulled out the photograph of Diego Marlasca lent to me by Salvador and left it by the base of the table lamp. Then I looked through the small citadel of writing pads, notes, and sheets of paper I had been accumulating for the boss. Still feeling the chill of Diego Marlasca's cutlery in my hands, I did not find it hard to imagine him sitting there gazing at the same view over the rooftops of the Ribera quarter. I took one of my pages at random and began to read. I recognized the words and sentences because I'd composed them, but the troubled spirit that fed them felt more remote than ever. I let the sheet of paper fall to the floor and looked up only to meet my own reflection in the windowpane, a stranger in the blue darkness burying the city. I knew I was not going to be able to work that night, that I would be incapable of putting together a single paragraph for the boss. I turned off the lamp and stayed there in the dark, listening to the wind scratching at the windows and imagining Diego Marlasca in flames, throwing himself into the water of the reservoir, while the last bubbles of air left his lips and the freezing liquid filled his lungs.

I awoke at dawn, my body aching from being encased in the armchair. As I got up I heard the grinding of two or three cogs in my anatomy. I dragged myself to the window and opened it wide. The flat rooftops in the old town shone with frost and a purple sky wreathed itself around Barcelona. At the sound of the bells of Santa María del Mar, a cloud of black wings took to the air from a dovecote. The smell of the docks and the coal ash issuing from neighboring chimneys was borne on a biting, cold wind.

I went down to the kitchen to make some coffee. I glanced at the larder and was astonished. Since Isabella's arrival in the house, it looked more like the Quílez grocer's in Rambla de Cataluña. Among the parade of exotic delicacies imported by Isabella's father, I found a tin of English chocolate biscuits and decided to have some. Half an hour later, my veins pumping with sugar and caffeine, my brain started to work and I had the brilliant idea of beginning the day by complicating my existence even further, if that was possible. As soon as the shops opened, I'd pay a visit to the one selling items for conjurers and magicians in Calle Princesa.

"What are you doing up so early?"

Isabella, the voice of my conscience, was observing me from the doorway.

"Eating biscuits."

Isabella sat at the table and poured herself a cup of coffee. She looked as if she hadn't slept all night.

"My father says this was the Queen Mother's favorite brand."

"No wonder she looked so strapping."

Isabella took one of the biscuits and bit into it distractedly.

"Have you thought about what you're going to do? About Sempere, I mean."

She threw me a venomous look.

"And what are you going to do today? Nothing good, I'm sure."

"A couple of errands."

"Right."

"Right, right? Or 'Right, I don't believe you'?"

Isabella set the cup on the table.

"Why do you never talk about whatever it is you're involved in with that man, the boss?"

"Among other things, for your own good."

"For my own good. Of course. How stupid could I be? By the way, I forgot to mention that your friend the inspector came by yesterday."

"Grandes? Was he on his own?"

"No. He came with two thugs as large as wardrobes with faces like pointers."

The thought of Marcos and Castelo at my door tied my stomach in knots.

"And what did Grandes want?"

"He didn't say."

"What *did* he say, then?"

"He asked me who I was."

"And what did you reply?"

"I said I was your lover."

"Outstanding."

"Well, one of the large ones seemed to find it very amusing."

Isabella took another biscuit and devoured it in two bites. She noticed me looking at her and immediately stopped chewing.

"What did I say?" she asked, projecting a shower of biscuit crumbs.

32

A sliver of light fell through the blanket of clouds, illuminating the red paintwork of the shop front in Calle Princesa. The establishment selling conjuring tricks stood behind a carved wooden canopy. Its glass doors revealed only the bare outlines of the gloomy interior. Black velvet curtains were draped across showcases displaying masks and Victorian-style apparatus: marked packs of cards, weighted daggers, books on magic, and bottles of polished glass containing a rainbow of liquids labeled in Latin and probably bottled in Albacete. The bell tinkled as I came through the door. An empty counter stood at the far end of the shop. I waited a few seconds, examining the collection of curiosities. I was searching for my face in a mirror that reflected everything in the shop except me, when I glimpsed, out of the corner of my eye, a small figure peeping round the curtain of the back room.

"An interesting trick, don't you think?" said the little man.

I nodded.

"How does it work?"

"I don't yet know. It arrived a few days ago from a manufacturer of trick mirrors in Constantinople. The creator calls it refractory inversion."

"It reminds one that nothing is as it seems," I said.

"Except for magic. How can I help you, sir?"

"Am I speaking to Señor Damián Roures?"

The little man nodded slowly. I noticed that his lips were set in a bright smile that, like the mirror, was not what it seemed. Beneath it, his expression was cold and cautious.

"Your shop was recommended to me."

"May I ask by whom?"

"Ricardo Salvador."

Any pretense of a smile disappeared from his face.

"I didn't know he was still alive. I haven't seen him for twenty-five years."

"What about Irene Sabino?"

Roures sighed. He came round the counter and went over to the door. After hanging up the Closed sign he turned the key.

"Who are you?"

"My name is Martín. I'm trying to clarify the circumstances surrounding the death of Señor Diego Marlasca, whom I understand you knew."

"As far as I know, they were clarified many years ago. Señor Marlasca committed suicide."

"That was not my understanding."

"I don't know what that policeman has told you. Resentment affects one's memory, Señor . . . Martín. At the time, Salvador tried to peddle a conspiracy for which he had no proof. Everyone knew he was warming the widow Marlasca's bed and trying to set himself up as the hero of the hour. As expected, his superiors made him toe the line, and when he didn't they threw him out of the police force."

"He thinks there was an attempt to hide the truth."

Roures scoffed.

"The truth . . . don't make me laugh. What they tried to hide was a scandal. Valera and Marlasca's law firm had its fingers stuck in almost every pie that was being baked in this town. Nobody wanted a story like that to be uncovered. Marlasca had abandoned his position, his work, and his marriage to lock himself up in that rambling old house doing God knows what. Anyone with a half a brain could see that it wouldn't end well."

"That didn't stop you and your partner, Jaco, from profiting from his madness by promising him he'd be able to make contact with the hereafter during your séances . . ."

"I never promised him a thing. Those sessions were a simple amusement. Everyone knew. Don't try to saddle me with the man's death—because all I was doing was earning an honest living."

"And Jaco?"

"I answer only for myself. What Jaco might have done is not my responsibility."

"Then he did do something."

"What do you want me to say? That he went off with the money Salvador insisted Marlasca had in a secret account? That he killed Marlasca and fooled us all?"

"And that's not what happened?"

Roures stared at me.

"I don't know, I haven't seen him since the day Marlasca died. I told Salvador and the rest of the police everything I knew. I never lied. If Jaco did do something, I never knew about it or got anything out of it."

"What can you tell me about Irene Sabino?"

"Irene loved Marlasca. She would never have plotted anything that might hurt him."

"Do you know what happened to her? Is she still alive?"

"I think so. I was told she was working in a laundry in the Raval quarter. Irene was a good woman. Too good. That's why she's ended up the way she has. She believed in those things. She believed in them with all her heart."

"And Marlasca? What was he looking for in that world?"

"Marlasca was involved in something, but don't ask me what. Something that neither Jaco nor I had sold him. All I know is that I once heard Irene say that apparently Marlasca had found someone, someone I didn't know—and, believe me, I knew everyone in the profession—who had promised him that if he did something, I don't know what, he would recover his son, Ismael, from the dead."

"Did Irene say who that someone was?"

"She'd never seen him. Marlasca didn't let her. But she knew that he was afraid."

"Afraid of what?"

Roures clicked his tongue.

"Marlasca thought that he was cursed."

"Can you explain?"

"I've already told you. He was ill. He was convinced that something had got inside him."

"Something?"

"A spirit. A parasite. I don't know. Look, in this business you get to know a lot of people who are not exactly in their right mind. A personal tragedy hits them—they lose a lover or a fortune—and they fall down the hole. The brain is the most fragile organ in the body. Señor Marlasca was not of sound mind. Anyone could see that after talking to him for five minutes. That's why he came to me."

"And you told him what he wanted to hear."

"No. I told him the truth."

"Your truth?"

"The only truth I know. I thought he was seriously unbalanced and I didn't want to take advantage of him. That sort of thing never ends well. In this business there is a line you don't cross, if you know what's good for you. We offer our services to people who come to us looking for a bit of fun or some excitement and comfort from the world beyond, and we charge accordingly. But anyone who seems to be on the verge of losing his mind we send home. It is a show like any other. What you want are spectators, not visionaries."

"Exemplary ethics. So, what did you say to Marlasca?"

"I told him it was all a load of mumbo jumbo, I told him I was a trickster who made a living organizing séances for poor devils who had lost their loved ones and needed to believe that lovers, parents, and friends were waiting for them in the next world. I told him there was nothing on the other side, just a giant void, and this world was all we had. I told him to forget about the spirits and return to his family."

"And he believed you?"

"Obviously not. He stopped coming to the sessions and looked elsewhere for help."

"Where?"

"Irene had grown up in the shacks of Bogatell beach, and although she'd made a name for herself dancing and acting in the clubs on the Paralelo, she still belonged to that place. She told me she'd taken Marlasca to see a woman they called the Witch of Somorrostro, to ask for protection from the person to whom Marlasca was indebted."

"Did Irene mention the name of that person?"

"If she did I can't remember. As I said, they'd stopped coming to the séances."

"Andreas Corelli?"

"I've never heard that name."

"Where can I find Irene Sabino?"

"I've already told you all I know," Roures replied, exasperated.

"One last question and I'll go."

"Let's see if that's true."

"Do you remember ever hearing Marlasca mention something called *Lux Aeterna*?"

Roures frowned, shaking his head.

"Thanks for your help."

"You're welcome. And if at all possible, don't come back."

I started toward the door.

"Wait," Roures called suddenly.

The little man observed me, hesitating.

"I seem to remember that *Lux Aeterna* was the name of some sort of religious pamphlet we sometimes used in the sessions in Calle Elisabets. It was part of a collection of similar books, probably loaned to us by the Afterlife Society, which had a library specializing in the occult. I don't know if that's what you're referring to."

"Do you remember what the pamphlet was about?"

"The person who was most familiar with it was my partner, Jaco—

he managed the séances. But I seem to recall that *Lux Aeterna* was a poem about death and the seven names of the Son of Morning, Bringer of Light."

"Bringer of Light?"

Roures smiled.

"Lucifer."

33

When I left the shop I returned home, wondering what to do next. I was approaching the entrance to Calle Moncada when I saw him. Inspector Grandes was leaning against a wall and enjoying a cigarette. He smiled at me and waved and I crossed the street toward him.

"I didn't know you were interested in magic, Martín."

"Nor did I know that you were following me, Inspector."

"I'm not following you. It's just that you're a difficult man to find and I decided that if the mountain wouldn't come to me, I'd go to the mountain. Do you have five minutes to spare, for a drink? It's on police headquarters."

"In that case . . . No chaperones today?"

"Marcos and Castelo stayed behind doing paperwork, but if I'd told them I was coming to see you, I'm sure they'd have volunteered."

We walked through the canyon of old palaces until we reached the Xampañet tavern, where we found a table at the far end. A waiter, armed with a mop that stank of bleach, stared at us and Grandes asked for a couple of beers and a tapa of Manchego cheese. When the beers and the snack arrived, the inspector offered me the plate. I declined.

"Do you mind? I'm always starving at this time of day."

"Bon appétit."

Grandes wolfed down the cubes of cheese and licked his lips.

"Didn't anyone tell you that I came by your house yesterday?"

"I didn't get the message until later."

"I understand. Hey, she's gorgeous, the girl. What's her name?"

"Isabella."

"You rascal, some people have all the luck. I envy you. How old is the little sweetheart?"

I threw him a toxic look. The inspector smiled, obviously pleased.

"A little bird told me you've been playing at detectives lately. Aren't you going to leave anything to the professionals?"

"What's your little bird's name?"

"He's more of a big bird. One of my superiors is a close friend of Valera, the lawyer."

"Are you also on the payroll?"

"Not yet, my friend. You know me. I'm of the old school. Honor and all that shit."

"A shame."

"And tell me, how is poor Ricardo Salvador? Do you know? I haven't heard that name for over twenty years. Everyone assumed he was dead."

"A premature diagnosis."

"And how is he?"

"Alone, betrayed, and forgotten."

The inspector nodded slowly. "Makes one think of the future in this job, doesn't it?"

"I bet that in your case things will be different and your promotion to the top is just a question of a couple of years. I can imagine you as chief commissioner before the age of forty-five, kissing the hands of bishops and generals during the Corpus parade."

Grandes let my sarcasm pass.

"Speaking of hand kissing, have you heard about your friend Vidal?"

Grandes never started a conversation without having an ace hidden up his sleeve. He watched me with a smile, relishing my anxiety.

"What about him?" I mumbled.

"They say his wife tried to kill herself the other night."

"Cristina?"

"Of course, you know her . . ."

I didn't realize that I'd stood up and my hands were shaking.

"Calm down. Señora de Vidal is all right. Just a fright. It seems that she overdid it with the laudanum. Will you sit down, Martín? Please."

I sat down.

"When was this?"

"Two or three days ago."

My mind filled with the image of Cristina in the window of Villa Helius a few days earlier, waving at me while I avoided her eyes and turned my back on her.

"Martín?" the inspector asked, waving a hand in front of my face as if he feared I'd lost my mind.

"What?"

The inspector seemed to be genuinely worried.

"Have you anything to tell me? I know you won't believe me, but I'd like to help you."

"Do you still think it was me who killed Barrido and his partner?"

Grandes shook his head.

"I've never believed it was you, but there are others who would like to."

"Then why are you still investigating me?"

"Calm down. I'm not investigating you, Martín. I never have. The day I do investigate you, you'll know. For the time being I'm only observing you. Because I like you and I'm concerned that you're going to get yourself into a mess. Why won't you trust me and tell me what's going on?"

Our eyes met and for an instant I was tempted to tell him everything. I would have done so, had I known where to begin.

"Nothing is going on, Inspector."

Grandes nodded and looked at me with pity, or perhaps it was only disappointment. He finished his beer and left a few coins on the table. He gave me a pat on the back and got up.

"Look after yourself, Martín. And watch how you go. Not everyone holds you in the same esteem as I do."

"I'll keep that in mind."

. . .

It was almost midday when I got home, unable to stop thinking about what the inspector had told me. When I reached the tower house I climbed the steps slowly, as if my very soul were weighing me down. I opened the door of the apartment, fearing I'd find Isabella in the mood for conversation. The house was silent. I walked up the corridor until I reached the gallery and there I found her, asleep on the sofa, an open book on her chest—one of my old novels. I couldn't help but smile. The temperature inside the house had dropped considerably during those autumn days and I was afraid Isabella might catch a chill. Sometimes I'd see her wandering about the apartment wrapped in a wool shawl she wore over her shoulders. I went to her room to find the shawl, so that I could quietly cover her with it. Her door was ajar. Although I was in my own home, I'd rarely entered that room since Isabella had installed herself there and now I felt uneasy going in. I saw the shawl folded over a chair and went to fetch it. The room had Isabella's sweet, lemony scent. The bed was still unmade and I leaned over to smooth out the sheets and blankets. I knew that when I applied myself to these domestic chores my moral standing rose in the eyes of my assistant.

As I straightened up I noticed there was something wedged between the mattress and the base of the bed. The corner of a piece of paper stuck out from under the folded sheet. When I tugged at it I realized it was a bundle of papers. I pulled it out completely and found that I was holding what looked like about twenty blue envelopes tied together with a ribbon. My whole body felt cold. I untied the knot in the ribbon and took one of the envelopes. It had my name and address on it. Where the return address should have been, it simply said: Cristina.

I sat on the bed with my back to the door and examined the envelopes, one by one. The first letter was a few weeks old, the last had been posted three days ago. All of the envelopes were open. I closed my

eyes and felt the letters falling from my hands. I heard her breathing behind me, and when I opened my eyes she was standing motionless in the
doorway.

"Forgive me," whispered Isabella.

She walked over slowly and knelt down to pick up the letters.
When she'd gathered them together she handed them to me with a
wounded look.

"I did it to protect you," she said.

Her eyes filled with tears and she placed a hand on my shoulder.

"Leave," I said.

I pushed her away and stood up. Isabella collapsed onto the floor,
moaning as if something were burning inside her.

"Leave this house."

I left the apartment without even bothering to close the door behind me. Once outside, I faced a world of buildings and faces that
seemed strange and distant. I started to walk aimlessly, oblivious to the
cold and the rain-filled wind that was starting to lash the town with the
breath of a curse.

34

The tram stopped by the gates of Bellesguard, a mansion standing on the edge of the city, at the foot of the hill. I walked on toward the entrance to San Gervasio cemetery, following the yellowish beam projected through the rain by the tram lights. The walls of the graveyard rose some fifty meters ahead, a marble fortress from which emerged a mass of statues the color of the storm. I found a booth next to the entrance where a guard, wrapped in a coat, was warming his hands over a brazier. When he saw me appear in the rain he looked startled and stood up. He examined me for a few seconds before opening the door.

"I'm looking for the Marlasca family vault."

"It'll be dark in less than half an hour. You'd better come back another day."

"The sooner you tell me where it is, the sooner I'll leave."

The guard checked a list and showed me the site by pointing a finger to a map of the graveyard hanging on the wall. I walked off without thanking him.

It wasn't difficult to find the vault among the citadel of tombs and mausoleums crowded together inside the walls of the cemetery. The structure stood on a marble base. Modernist in style, the mausoleum was shaped like an arch formed by two wide flights of steps that spread out like an amphitheater. The steps led to a gallery held up by columns, inside which was an atrium flanked by tombstones. The gallery was crowned by a dome, and the dome, in turn, by a marble figure, sullied by the passage of time. Its face was hidden by a veil, but as I approached I had the impression that this sentinel from beyond the grave was turning its head to watch me. I went up one of the staircases and when I reached the entrance to the gallery, I stopped to look behind me. The distant city lights were just visible in the rain.

I stepped into the gallery. In the center stood a statue of a woman in prayer, embracing a crucifix. The face had been disfigured and someone had painted the eyes and lips black, giving her a wolfish aspect. That was not the only sign of desecration in the vault. The tombstones seemed to be covered in what looked like markings or scratches made with a sharp object, and some had been defaced with obscene drawings and words that were almost illegible in the failing light. Diego Marlasca's tomb was at the far end. I went up to it and put my hand on the tombstone. Then I pulled out the photograph of Marlasca that Salvador had given me and examined it.

At that moment I heard footsteps on the stairway to the vault. I put the photograph back into my coat pocket and turned, facing the entrance to the gallery. The footsteps stopped and all I could hear now was the rain beating against the marble. I went toward the entrance and looked out. The figure had its back to me and was gazing at the city in the distance. It was a woman dressed in white, her head covered by a shawl. Slowly she turned and looked at me. She was smiling. Despite the years, I recognized her instantly. Irene Sabino. As I took a step toward her I realized there was someone else behind me. The blow to the back of my neck fired off a spasm of white light. I felt myself falling to my knees. A second later I collapsed on the flooded marble. A dark silhouette stood over me in the rain. Irene knelt down beside me; I felt her hands surrounding my head and feeling the place where I'd been hit. I saw her fingers emerging, covered in blood. She stroked my face. The last thing I saw before I lost consciousness was Irene Sabino pulling out a razor and opening it, silvery drops of rain sliding across the blade's edge as it drew toward me.

. . .

I opened my eyes to the blinding glare of an oil lamp. The guard's face was watching impassively. I tried to blink while a flash of pain shot through my skull from the back of my neck.

"Are you alive?" the guard asked, without specifying whether the question was directed at me or was purely rhetorical.

"Yes," I groaned. "Don't you dare stick me in a hole."

The guard helped me sit up. Every time I moved I felt a stab of pain in my head.

"What happened?"

"You tell me. I should have locked this place up over an hour ago, but as I hadn't seen you leave, I came to investigate and found you sleeping it off."

"What about the woman?"

"What woman?"

"There were two."

"Two women?"

I sighed, shaking my head.

"Can you help me get up?"

With the guard's assistance I managed to stand. It was then that I felt a burning sensation and noticed that my shirt was open. There were a number of superficial cuts running in lines across my chest.

"Hey, that doesn't look good . . ."

I closed my coat and felt the inside pocket. Marlasca's photograph had disappeared.

"Do you have a telephone in the booth?"

"Sure, it's in the room with the Turkish baths."

"Can you at least help me reach Bellesguard, so that I can call from there?"

The guard swore and held me by the armpits.

"I did tell you to come back another day," he said, resigned.

35

A few minutes before midnight I finally reached the tower house. As soon as I opened the door I knew that Isabella had left. The echo of my footsteps down the corridor sounded different. I didn't bother to turn on the light. I went farther into the apartment and put my head round the door of what had been her room. Isabella had cleaned and tidied it. The sheets and blankets were neatly folded on a chair and the mattress was bare. Her smell still floated in the air. I went to the gallery and sat at the desk my assistant had used. She had sharpened the pencils and arranged them in a glass. The pile of blank sheets had been carefully stacked on a tray and the pen and nib set I had given her had been left on one side of the table. The house had never seemed so empty.

In the bathroom I removed my wet clothes and put a bandage with surgical spirit on the nape of my neck. The pain had subsided to a mute throb and a general feeling that was not unlike a monumental hangover. In the mirror, the cuts on my chest looked like lines drawn with a pen. They were clean, superficial cuts, but they stung a great deal. I cleaned them with the surgical spirit and hoped they wouldn't become infected.

I got into bed and covered myself up to the neck with two or three blankets. The only parts of my body that didn't hurt were those that the cold and the rain had numbed to the point that I couldn't feel them at all. I lay there slowly warming up, listening to that cold silence, a silence of absence and emptiness that smothered the house. Before leaving, Isabella had left the pile of Cristina's letters on the bedside table. I stretched out my hand and took one at random, dated two weeks earlier.

> *Dear David,*
>
> *The days go by and I keep on writing letters to you which I suppose you prefer not to answer—if you even open them, that is. I've started to think that I write them just for myself, to kill the loneliness and to believe for a moment that you're close to me. Every day I wonder what has happened to you and what you're doing.*
>
> *Sometimes I think you've left Barcelona and won't return, and I imagine you in some place surrounded by strangers, beginning a new life that I will never know. At other times I think you still hate me, that you destroy these letters and wish you had never known me. I don't blame you. It's curious how easy it is to tell a piece of paper what you don't dare say to someone's face.*
>
> *Things are not simple for me. Pedro couldn't be kinder and more understanding, so much so that sometimes his patience and his desire to make me happy irritate me, which only makes me feel miserable. He has shown me that my heart is empty, that I don't deserve to be loved by anyone. He spends most of the day with me and doesn't want to leave me alone.*
>
> *I smile every day and I share his bed. When he asks me whether I love him I say I do, and when I see the truth reflected in his eyes I feel like dying. He never reproaches me. He talks about you a great deal. He misses you. He misses you so much that sometimes I think you're the person he loves most in this world. I see him growing old, on his own, in the worst possible company—mine. I don't expect you to forgive me, but if there's one thing I wish for in this world, it is for you to forgive him. I'm not worth depriving him of your friendship and company.*
>
> *Yesterday I finished one of your books. Pedro has them all and I've been reading them because it's the only way I can feel that I'm with you. It was a sad, strange story, about two broken dolls abandoned in a traveling circus that come alive for one night, knowing they are going to die at dawn. As I read it I felt you were writing about us.*

A few weeks ago I dreamed that I saw you again. We passed in the street and you didn't remember me. You smiled and asked me what my name was. You didn't know anything about me. You didn't hate me. Every night when Pedro falls asleep next to me, I close my eyes and beg heaven or hell that I might dream the same dream again.

Tomorrow or perhaps the next day I'll write again to tell you that I love you, even if it means nothing to you.

CRISTINA

I let the letter fall to the floor, unable to read anymore. Tomorrow would be another day, I told myself. It could hardly be worse than this one. Little did I imagine the delights in store. I must have slept for a couple of hours at the most when, all of a sudden, I awoke. Dawn was far away. Somebody was banging on the door of my apartment. I spent a couple of seconds in a daze, looking for the light switch. Again, the knocking on the door. I must have forgotten to lock the main entrance to the street. I turned on the light, got out of bed, and walked along to the entrance hall. I slid open the peephole. Three faces in the shadows of the landing. Inspector Grandes and, behind him, Marcos and Castelo. All three with their eyes trained on the peephole. I took two deep breaths before opening.

"Good evening, Martín. I'm sorry about the time."

"And what time is this supposed to be?"

"Time to move your ass, you son of a bitch," Marcos muttered, drawing from Castelo a smile so cutting I could have shaved with it.

Grandes looked at them disapprovingly and sighed.

"A little after three in the morning," he said. "May I come in?"

I groaned but let him in. The inspector signaled to his men to wait on the landing. Marcos and Castelo agreed reluctantly, throwing me reptilian looks. I slammed the door in their faces.

"You should be more careful with those two," said Grandes, wandering up the corridor as if he owned the place.

"Please, make yourself at home . . ." I said.

I returned to the bedroom and dressed carelessly, putting on the first things I found—dirty clothes piled on a chair. When I came out, there was no sign of Grandes in the corridor.

I went over to the gallery and found him there, gazing through the windows at the low clouds that crept over the flat roofs.

"Where's the sweetheart?"

"In her own home."

Grandes turned round smiling.

"Wise man, you don't keep them full board," he said, pointing at the armchair. "Sit down."

I slumped into the chair. Grandes remained standing, his eyes fixed on me.

"What?" I finally asked.

"You don't look so good, Martín. Did you get into a fight?"

"I fell."

"I see. I understand that today you visited the magic shop owned by Señor Damián Roures in Calle Princesa."

"You saw me coming out of the shop at lunchtime. What's all this about?"

Grandes was gazing at me coldly.

"Fetch a coat and a scarf or something. It's cold outside. We're off to the police station."

"What for?"

"Do as I say."

A car from police headquarters was waiting for us in Paseo del Borne. Marcos and Castelo pushed me unceremoniously into the back, positioning themselves on either side.

"Is the gentleman comfortable?" asked Castelo, digging his elbow into my ribs.

The inspector sat in the front, next to the driver. None of them opened their mouths during the five minutes it took to drive up Vía Layetana, deserted and buried in an ocher mist. When we reached the central police station, Grandes got out and went in without waiting. Marcos and Castelo took an arm each, as if they were trying to crush my bones, and dragged me through a maze of stairs, passages, and cells until we reached a room with no windows that smelled of sweat and urine. In the center stood a worm-eaten table and two dilapidated chairs. A naked bulb hung from the ceiling and there was a grating over a drain in the middle of the room, where the two inclines of the floor met. It was bitterly cold. Before I realized what was happening, the door was shut behind me with a bang. I heard footsteps moving away. I walked round that dungeon a dozen times until I collapsed on one of the shaky chairs. For the next hour, apart from my breathing, the creaking of the chair, and the echo of water dripping, I didn't hear another sound.

. . .

An eternity later I heard footsteps approaching and shortly afterwards the door opened. Marcos stuck his head round and peered into the cell with a smile. He held the door open for Grandes, who came in without looking at me and sat on the chair on the other side of the table. Grandes nodded to Marcos and Marcos closed the door, but not without first blowing me a silent kiss. The inspector took a good thirty seconds before deigning to look me in the eye.

"If you were trying to impress me, you've done so, Inspector."

He ignored my irony and fixed his eyes on me as if he'd never seen me before in his life.

"What do you know about Damián Roures?" he asked.

I shrugged my shoulders.

"Not much. He owns a magic shop. In fact, I knew nothing about him until a few days ago, when Ricardo Salvador mentioned him. Today, or yesterday—I've lost track of time—I went to see him in search of information about the previous occupier of the house I live in. Salvador told me that Roures and the owner—"

"Marlasca."

"Yes, Diego Marlasca. As I was saying, Salvador told me that Roures had had dealings with him some years ago. I asked Roures a few questions and he replied as best he could. There's little else."

Grandes inclined his head.

"Is that your story?"

"I don't know. What's yours? Let's compare and perhaps I'll finally understand what the hell I'm doing here in the middle of the night, freezing to death in a basement that smells of shit."

"Don't raise your voice to me, Martín."

"I'm sorry, Inspector, but I think you could at least have the courtesy to tell me why I'm here."

"I'll tell you why you're here. About three hours ago, one of the residents of the apartment block in which Señor Roures's shop is located was returning home late when he found that the door of the shop was open and the lights were on. He was surprised, so he went in, and when he did not see the owner or hear him reply to his calls, he went into the back room, where he found Roures bound hands and feet with wire to a chair, over a pool of blood."

Grandes paused, his eyes boring into me. I imagined there was more to come. Grandes always liked to end on something dramatic.

"Dead?" I asked.

Grandes nodded.

"Quite dead. Someone had amused himself by pulling out the man's eyes and cutting out his tongue with a pair of scissors. The pathologist believes he died by choking on his own blood about half an hour later."

I felt I needed air. Grandes was walking around. He stopped behind my back and I heard him light a cigarette.

"How did you get that bruise? It looks recent."

"I slipped in the rain and hit the back of my neck."

"Don't treat me like an idiot, Martín. It's not advisable. Would you rather I left you for a while with Marcos and Castelo, to see if they can teach you some manners?"

"All right. Someone hit me."

"Who?"

"I don't know."

"This conversation is beginning to bore me, Martín."

"Well, just imagine what it's doing to me."

Grandes sat down in front of me again and offered a conciliatory smile.

"Surely you don't believe I had anything to do with the death of that man?"

"No, Martín, I don't. What I do believe is that you're not telling me the truth and that somehow the death of that poor wretch is related to your visit. Like the death of Barrido and Escobillas."

"What makes you think that?"

"Call it a hunch."

"I've already told you I don't know anything."

"And I've already warned you not to take me for an idiot, Martín. Marcos and Castelo are out there waiting for an opportunity to have a private conversation with you. Is that what you want?"

"No."

"Then help me get you out of this so that I can send you home before your sheets get cold."

"What do you want to hear?"

"The truth, for example."

I pushed the chair back and stood up, exasperated. I was cold and my head felt as if it were going to burst. I began to walk round the table in circles, spitting out the words as if they were stones.

"The truth? I'll tell you the truth. The truth is I don't know what the truth is. I don't know what to tell you. I don't know why I went to see Roures or Salvador, I don't know what I'm looking for or what is happening to me. That's the truth."

Grandes watched me stoically.

"Stop walking in circles and sit down. You're making me dizzy."

"I don't want to."

"Martín, you're not telling me anything. All I'm asking you to do is to help me so that I can help you."

"You wouldn't be able to help me even if you wanted to."

"Then who can?"

I dropped back into the chair.

"I don't know . . ." I murmured.

I thought I saw a hint of pity, or perhaps it was just tiredness, in the inspector's eyes.

"Look, Martín. Let's begin again. Let's do it your way. Tell me a story, and start at the beginning."

I stared at him in silence.

"Martín. Don't think that because I like you I'm not going to do my work."

"Do whatever you have to do. Call Hansel and Gretel, if you like."

At that moment I noticed a touch of anxiety on his face. Footsteps were advancing along the corridor and something told me the inspector wasn't expecting them. I heard voices and nervously Grandes went up to the door. He tapped three times with his knuckles and Marcos, who was on guard, opened up. A man dressed in a camel hair coat and a matching suit came into the room, looked around him in disgust, and then gave me a sweet smile while he calmly removed his gloves. I watched him in astonishment. It was Valera, the lawyer.

"Are you all right, Señor Martín?" he asked.

I nodded. The lawyer led the inspector over to a corner. I heard them whispering. Grandes gesticulated with suppressed fury. Valera watched him coldly and shook his head. The conversation went on for almost a minute. Finally Grandes huffed and let his hands fall to his sides.

"Pick up your scarf, Señor Martín. We're leaving," Valera ordered. "The inspector has finished his questioning."

Behind him, Grandes bit his lip, glaring at Marcos, who shrugged. Without losing his expert smile, Valera took me by the arm and led me out of the dungeon.

"I trust that the treatment you received from these police officers has been correct, Señor Martín."

"Yes," I managed to stammer.

"Just a moment," Grandes called out behind us.

Valera stopped and, motioning for me to be quiet, he turned round.

"If you have any more questions for Señor Martín you can direct them to our office and we will be glad to help you. In the meantime, and unless you have a more important reason for keeping Señor Martín on the premises, we shall retire. We wish you a good evening and thank you for your kindness, which I will certainly mention to your superiors, especially to Chief Inspector Salgado, who, as you know, is a dear friend."

Sergeant Marcos started to move toward us, but Inspector Grandes stopped him. I exchanged a last glance with him before Valera took me by the arm again and pulled me away.

"Don't wait about," he whispered.

We walked down the dimly lit passage until we came to a staircase that took us up to another long corridor. At the end of the second corridor a small door opened onto the ground-floor entrance hall and the main exit, where a chauffeur-driven Mercedes-Benz was waiting for us with its engine running. As soon as the chauffeur saw Valera, he jumped out and opened the door for us. I sat down on the backseat. The car was equipped with heating and the leather seats were warm. Valera sat next to me and, with a tap on the glass that separated the back from the driver's compartment, he instructed the chauffeur to set off. Once the car was en route and had settled in the center lane of Vía Layetana, Valera smiled at me as if nothing had happened. He pointed at the mist that parted like undergrowth as we drove through it.

"A disagreeable night, isn't it?" he said casually.

"Where are we going?"

"To your home, of course. Unless you'd rather go to a hotel or . . ."

"No. That's fine."

The car was rolling along down Vía Layetana. Valera gazed at the deserted streets with little interest.

"What are you doing?" I finally asked.

"What do you think I'm doing? Representing you and looking after your interests."

"Tell the driver to stop the car," I said.

The chauffeur looked at Valera's eyes in the mirror. Valera shook his head and gestured to him to continue.

"Don't talk nonsense, Señor Martín. It's late, it's cold, and I'm taking you home."

"I'd rather walk."

"Be reasonable."

"Who sent you?"

Valera sighed and rubbed his eyes.

"You have good friends, Señor Martín. It is important in life to have good friends and especially to know how to keep them," he said. "As important as knowing when one is stubbornly following the wrong path."

"Might that path be the one that goes past Casa Marlasca, number 13 Carretera de Vallvidrera?"

Valera smiled patiently, as if he were scolding an unruly child.

"Señor Martín, believe me when I say that the farther away you stay from that house and that business, the better for you. Do accept at least this piece of advice."

When the chauffeur reached Paseo de Colón, he turned and drove up to Calle Comercio and from there to the entrance of Paseo del Borne. The carts with meat and fish, ice and spices were beginning to accumulate opposite the large marketplace. As we drove past, four boys were unloading the carcass of a calf, leaving a trail of blood that could be smelled in the air.

"Your area is charming, full of picturesque scenes, Señor Martín."

The driver stopped on the corner of Calle Flassaders and got out of the car to open the door for us. The lawyer got out with me.

"I'll come with you to the door," he said.

"People will think we're lovers."

We entered the alleyway, a chasm of shadows, and headed toward my house. On reaching the front door, the lawyer offered me his hand with professional courtesy.

"Thanks for getting me out of that place."

"Don't thank me," replied Valera, pulling an envelope out of the inside pocket of his coat.

I recognized the wax seal with the angel even in the tenuous light that dripped from the streetlamp above our heads. Valera handed me the envelope and, with a final nod, walked back to the waiting car. I opened my front door and went up the steps to the apartment. When I got in I went straight to the study and placed the envelope on the desk. I opened it and pulled out the folded sheet of paper with the boss's writing.

> *Martín, dear friend,*
> *I trust this note finds you in good health and good spirits. I happen to be passing through the city and would love the pleasure of your company this Friday at seven o'clock in the evening in the billiard room of the Equestrian Club, where we can talk about the progress of our project.*
> *Until then, please accept my warm regards,*
> ANDREAS CORELLI

I folded the sheet of paper and put it carefully in the envelope. Then I lit a match and, holding the envelope by one corner, moved it closer to the flame. I watched it burn until the wax turned to scarlet tears that fell on the desk and my fingers were covered in ashes.

"Go to hell," I whispered. The night, darker than ever, leaned in against the windowpanes.

36

Sitting in the armchair in the study, I waited for a dawn that did not come, until anger got the better of me and I went out into the street ready to defy Valera's warning. A cold, biting wind was blowing, the sort that precedes dawn in wintertime. As I crossed Paseo del Borne I thought I heard footsteps behind me. I turned round for a moment but couldn't see anyone except for the market boys unloading carts so I continued walking. When I reached Plaza Palacio I saw the lights of the first tram of the day waiting in the mist that crept up from the port. Snakes of blue light crackled along the overhead power cable. I stepped into the tram and sat at the front. The same conductor as on my last trip took the money for my ticket. A dozen or so passengers dribbled in, each one alone. After a few minutes the tram set off and we began our journey. Across the sky stretched a web of red capillaries between black clouds. There was no need to be a poet or a wise man to know that it was going to be a bad day.

By the time we reached Sarriá, dawn had broken with a gray, dull light that robbed the morning of any color. I climbed the deserted, narrow streets of the neighborhood toward the lower slopes of the hillside. Occasionally I thought I again heard footsteps behind me, but each time I stopped and looked back there was nobody there. At last I reached the entrance to the passage leading to Casa Marlasca and made my way through a blanket of dead leaves that crunched under foot. Slowly, I crossed the courtyard and walked up the stairs to the front door, peering through the large windows of the façade. I rapped the door knocker three times and moved back a few steps. I waited for a moment, but no answer came. I knocked again and heard the echoes fading away inside the house.

"Good morning!" I called out.

The grove surrounding the property seemed to absorb the sound of my voice. I went around the house, past the swimming pool area, and then on to the conservatory. Its windows were darkened by closed wooden shutters that made it impossible to see inside, but one of the windows next to the glass door was slightly open. The bolt securing the door was just visible through the gap. I put my arm through the window and slid open the bolt. The door gave way with a metallic creak. I looked behind me once more, to make sure there was nobody there, and went in.

. . .

As my eyes adjusted to the gloom, I began to distinguish a few outlines. I went over to the windows and half opened the shutters. A fan of light cut through the darkness, revealing the full profile of the room.

"Is anyone here?" I called out.

The sound of my voice sank into the bowels of the house like a coin falling into a bottomless well. I walked to the end of the conservatory, where an arch of carved wood led to a dim corridor lined with paintings that were barely visible on the velvet-covered walls. At the end of the corridor there was a large, round sitting room with a mosaic floor and a mural of enameled glass showing the figure of a white angel with one arm extended and fingers pointing like flames. A wide staircase rose around the room. I stopped at the foot of the stairs and called out again.

"Good morning! Señora Marlasca?"

The house drowned the dull echo of my words. I went up the stairs to the first floor and paused on the landing, looking down on the sitting room and the mural. From there I could see the trail my feet had left on the film of dust covering the ground. Apart from my footsteps, the only other sign of movement I could discern was parallel lines drawn in the dust, about half a meter apart, and a trail of footprints between them. Large footprints. I stared at those marks in some confusion until I understood what I was seeing: the movement of a wheelchair and the marks of the person pushing it.

I thought I heard a noise behind my back and turned. A half-open door at one end of the corridor was gently swinging and I could feel a breath of cold air. I moved slowly toward the door, glancing at the rooms on either side, bedrooms with dust sheets covering the furniture. The closed windows and heavy darkness suggested these rooms had not been used in a long time, except for one, which was larger than the others, the master bedroom. It smelled of that odd mixture of perfume and illness associated with elderly people. I imagined this must be the room of Marlasca's widow, but there was no sign of her.

The bed was neatly made. Opposite it stood a chest of drawers with a number of framed photographs on it. In all of them, without exception, was a boy with fair hair and a cheerful expression. Ismael Marlasca. In some pictures he posed next to his mother or other children. There was no sign of Diego Marlasca in any of them.

The sound of a door banging in the corridor startled me again and I exited the bedroom, leaving the pictures as I'd found them. The door to the room at the end was still swinging back and forth. I walked up to it and stopped for a second before entering, taking a deep breath.

Inside, everything was white. The walls and the ceiling were painted an immaculate white. White silk curtains. A small bed covered with white sheets. A white carpet. White shelves and cupboards. After the darkness that had prevailed throughout the house, the contrast dazzled my vision for a few seconds. The room seemed to be straight out of a fairy tale. There were toys and storybooks on the shelves. A life-size china harlequin sat at a dressing table, looking at himself in the mirror. A mobile of white birds hung from the ceiling. At first sight it looked like the room of a spoiled child, Ismael Marlasca, but it had the oppressive air of a funeral chamber.

I sat on the bed and sighed. Something in the room, I now noticed, seemed out of place. Beginning with the smell, a sickly, sweet stench. I stood up and looked around me. On a chest of drawers I saw a china plate with a black candle, its wax melted into beads. I turned round. The smell seemed to be coming from the head of the bed. I opened the drawer of the bedside table and found a crucifix broken in three. The stench grew stronger. I walked around the room a few times but was unable to find the source. Then I saw it. There was something under the bed. A tin box, the sort that children use to hold their childhood treasures. I pulled out the box and placed it on the bed. The stench was now more powerful, and penetrating. I ignored my nausea and opened the box. Inside was a white dove, its heart pierced by a needle. I took a step back, covering my mouth and nose, and retreated to the corridor. The harlequin with its jackal smile observed me in the mirror. I ran back to the staircase and hurtled down the stairs, looking for the passage that led to the reading room and the door to the garden. At one point I thought I was lost and the house, like a creature capable of moving its passageways and rooms at will, was trying to prevent me from escaping. At last I sighted the conservatory and ran to the door. Only then, while I was struggling to release the bolt, did I hear malicious laughter behind me and know I was not alone in the house. I turned for an instant and saw a dark figure watching me from the end of the corridor, carrying a shining object in its hand. A knife.

The bolt yielded and I pushed open the door, falling headlong onto the marble tiles surrounding the swimming pool. My face was barely centimeters from the surface and I could smell the stench of stagnant water. For a moment I peered into the shadows at the bottom of the pool. There was a short break in the clouds and a shaft of sunlight pierced the water, touching the floor, with its loose fragments of mosaic. The vision was over in a second: the wheelchair, tilted forward, stranded on the pool floor. The sunlight continued its journey to the deep end and it was there that I saw her: lying against the wall was what looked like a body shrouded in a threadbare white dress. At first I thought it was a doll, with scarlet lips shriveled by the water and eyes as bright as sapphires. Her red hair undulated gently in the rancid water and her skin was blue. It was Marlasca's widow. A second later the gap in the clouds closed again and the water was once more a clouded mirror in which I could glimpse only my face and a form that appeared in the doorway of the conservatory behind me, holding a knife. I shot up and ran straight into the garden, crossing the grove, scratching my face and hands on the bushes, until I reached the iron door and was out in the alleyway. I didn't stop running until I reached the main road. There I turned, out of breath, and saw that Casa Marlasca was once again hidden down its long alleyway, invisible to the world.

37

I returned home on the same tram, crossing a city that was growing darker by the minute. An icy wind lifted the fallen leaves from the streets. When I got out in Plaza Palacio I heard two sailors who were walking up from the docks talking about a storm that was approaching from the sea and would hit the town before nightfall. I looked up and saw a blanket of reddish clouds beginning to cover the sky. In the streets surrounding the Borne Market people were rushing to secure doors and windows, shopkeepers were closing early, and children came outside to play in the wind, lifting their arms and laughing at the distant roar of thunder. Streetlamps flickered and a flash of lightning bathed the buildings in a sudden white light. I hurried to the door of the tower house and rushed up the steps. The rumble of the storm could be felt through the walls, getting closer.

It was so cold indoors that I could see my breath as I stepped into the corridor. I went straight to the room with an old charcoal stove that I had used only four or five times since I'd lived there and lit it with a wad of old newspapers. I also lit the wood fire in the gallery and sat on the floor facing the flames. My hands were shaking, I didn't know whether from the cold or from fear. I waited until I had warmed up, staring out at the web of white light traced by lightning across the sky.

. . .

The rain didn't arrive until nightfall, and when it did, it plummeted in curtains of furious drops that quickly blinded the night and flooded rooftops and alleyways, hitting walls and windowpanes with tremendous force. Little by little, with the help of the stove and the fireplace, the house started to warm up, but I was still cold. I got up and went to the bedroom in search of blankets to wrap around myself. I opened the wardrobe and started to rummage in the two large drawers at the bottom. The case was still there, hidden at the back. I picked it up and placed it on the bed.

I opened the case and stared at my father's old revolver, the only thing I had left of him. I held it, stroking the trigger with my thumb. I opened the drum and inserted six bullets from the ammunition box in the false bottom of the case. I left the box on the bedside table and took the gun and a blanket back to the gallery. Lying on the sofa wrapped in the blanket, with the gun against my chest, I abandoned myself to the storm behind the windowpanes. I could hear the ticking of the clock on the mantelpiece but didn't need to look at it to realize that there was barely half an hour to go before my meeting with the boss in the billiard room at the Equestrian Club.

I closed my eyes and imagined him traveling through the deserted streets of the city, sitting in the backseat of his car, his golden eyes shining in the dark, the silver angel on the hood of the Rolls-Royce plunging through the storm. I imagined him motionless, like a statue, not breathing or smiling, with no expression at all. I heard the crackle of burning wood and the sound of the rain on the windows; I fell asleep with the weapon in my hands and the certainty that I was not going to keep my appointment.

· · ·

Shortly after midnight I opened my eyes. The fire was almost out and the gallery was submerged in the flickering half-light projected by the last blue flames in the embers. It continued to rain heavily. The revolver was still in my hands: it felt warm. I remained like that for a few seconds, barely blinking. I knew that there was someone at the door before I heard the knock.

I pushed aside the blanket and sat up. I heard the knock again. Knuckles on the front door. I stood up, the gun in my hands, and went into the corridor. Again the knock. I took a few steps toward the door and stopped. I imagined him smiling on the landing, the angel on his lapel gleaming in the dark. I pulled back the hammer on the gun. Once again the sound of a hand knocking on the door. I tried to turn the light on, but there was no power. I kept walking. I was about to slide the peephole open but didn't dare. I stood there stock-still, hardly daring to breathe, with the gun raised and pointing toward the door.

"Go away," I called out, with no strength in my voice.

Then I heard a sob on the other side of the door and lowered the gun. I opened the door and found her there in the shadows. Her clothes were soaking and she was shivering. Her skin was frozen. When she saw me, she almost collapsed into my arms. I could find no words, I just held her tight. She smiled weakly at me and when I put my hand on her cheek she kissed it and closed her eyes.

"Forgive me," whispered Cristina.

She opened her eyes and gave me a broken look that would have stayed with me even in hell. I smiled at her.

"Welcome home."

38

I undressed her by candlelight. I removed her shoes and dress, which were soaking wet, and her laddered stockings. I dried her body and her hair with a clean towel. She was still shaking with cold when I put her to bed and lay down next to her, hugging her to give her warmth. We stayed like that for a long time, not saying anything, just listening to the rain. Slowly I felt her body warming up and her breathing become deeper. I thought she had fallen asleep when I heard her speak.

"Your friend came to see me."

"Isabella."

"She told me she'd hidden my letters. She said she hadn't done it in bad faith. She thought she was doing it for your own good. Perhaps she was right."

I leaned over and searched her eyes. I caressed her lips and for the first time she smiled weakly.

"I thought you'd forgotten me," she said.

"I tried."

Her face was marked by tiredness. The months I had not seen her had drawn lines on her skin and her eyes had an air of defeat and emptiness.

"We're no longer young," she said, reading my thoughts.

"When have we ever been young, you and I?"

I pulled away the blanket and looked at her naked body stretched out on the white sheet. I stroked her neck and her breasts, barely touching her skin with my fingertips. I drew circles on her belly and traced the outline of the bones of her hips. I let my fingers play with the almost transparent hair between her thighs.

Cristina watched me without saying a word, her smile sad and her eyes half open.

"What are we going to do?" she asked.

I bent over her and kissed her lips. She embraced me and we remained like that as the light from the candle sputtered, then went out.

"We'll think of something," she whispered.

. . .

I woke up shortly after dawn and discovered I was alone in the bed. I sat up abruptly, fearing that Cristina had left again in the middle of the night. Then I saw her clothes and shoes on the chair and let out a deep sigh. I found her in the gallery, wrapped in a blanket, sitting on the floor by the fireplace, where a breath of blue fire emerged from a smoldering log. I sat down next to her and kissed her on the neck.

"I couldn't sleep," she said, her eyes fixed on the fire.

"You should have woken me."

"I didn't dare. You looked as if you were sleeping for the first time in months. I preferred to explore your house."

"And?"

"This house is cursed with sadness," she said. "Why don't you set fire to it?"

"And where would we live?"

"In the plural?"

"Why not?"

"I thought you'd stopped writing fairy tales."

"It's like riding a bike. Once you learn . . ."

Cristina looked at me.

"What's in that room at the end of the corridor?"

"Nothing. Junk."

"It's locked."

"Do you want to see it?"

She shook her head.

"It's only a house, Cristina. A pile of stones and memories. That's all."

Cristina nodded but looked unconvinced.

"Why don't we go away?" she asked.

"Where to?"

"Far away."

I couldn't help smiling, but she didn't smile back.

"How far?" I asked.

"Far enough that people won't know who we are, and won't care, either."

"Is that what you want?" I asked.

"Don't you?"

I hesitated for a second.

"What about Pedro?" I asked, almost choking on the words.

She let the blanket fall from her shoulders and looked at me defiantly. "Do you need his permission to sleep with me?"

I bit my tongue.

Cristina looked at me, her eyes full of tears.

"I'm sorry," she whispered. "I had no right to say that."

I picked up the blanket and tried to cover her, but she moved away, rejecting my gesture.

"Pedro has left me," she said in a broken voice. "He went to the Ritz yesterday to wait until I'd gone. He said he knew I didn't love him, that I married him out of gratitude or pity. He said he doesn't want my compassion and that every day I spend with him pretending to love him only hurts him. Whatever I did he would always love me, he said, and that is why he doesn't want to see me again."

Her hands were shaking.

"He's loved me with all his heart and all I've done is make him miserable," she murmured.

She closed her eyes and her face twisted in pain. A moment later she let out a deep moan and began to hit her face and body with her fists. I threw myself on her and put my arms around her, holding her still.

Cristina struggled and shouted. I pressed her against the floor, restraining her. Slowly she gave in, exhausted, her face covered in tears, her eyes reddened. We remained like that for almost half an hour, until I felt her body relaxing. I covered her with the blanket and embraced her, hiding my own tears.

"We'll go far away," I whispered in her ear, not knowing whether she could hear or understand me. "We'll go far away where nobody will know who we are, and won't care, either. I promise."

Cristina tilted her head and looked at me, her face robbed of all expression, as if her soul had been smashed to pieces with a hammer. I held her tight and kissed her on the forehead. The rain was still whipping against the windowpanes. Trapped in that gray, pale light of a dead dawn, it occurred to me for the first time that we were sinking.

39

That same morning I abandoned my work for the boss. While Cristina slept I went up to the study and put the folder containing all the pages, notes, and drafts for the project in an old trunk by the wall. I wanted to set fire to it, but I didn't have the courage. I had always felt that the pages I left behind were a part of me. Normal people bring children into the world; we novelists bring books. We are condemned to put our whole lives into them, even though they hardly ever thank us for it. We are condemned to die in their pages and sometimes even to let our books be the ones who, in the end, will take our lives. Among all the strange creatures made of paper and ink that I'd brought into the world, this one, my mercenary offering to the promises of the boss, was undoubtedly the most grotesque. There was nothing in those pages that deserved anything better than to be burned, and yet they were still flesh of my flesh and I couldn't find the courage to destroy them. I abandoned the work in the bottom of that trunk and left the study with a heavy heart, almost ashamed of my cowardice and the murky sense of paternity inspired in me by that manuscript of shadows. The boss would probably have appreciated the irony of the situation. All it inspired in me was disgust.

. . .

Cristina slept well into the afternoon. I took advantage of her sleep to go to the grocer's shop next to the market and buy some milk, bread, and cheese. The rain had stopped at last, but the streets were full of puddles and you could feel the dampness in the air, like a cold dust that permeated your clothes and your bones. While I waited for my turn in the shop I had the feeling that someone was watching me. When I went outside again and crossed Paseo del Borne, I turned and saw that a boy was following me. He could not have been more than five years old. I stopped and looked at him. The boy held my gaze.

"Don't be afraid," I said. "Come here."

The boy came closer, until he was standing about two meters away. His skin was pale, almost blue, as if he'd never seen the sunlight. He was dressed in black and wore shiny new patent leather shoes. His eyes were dark, with pupils so large they left no space for the whites.

"What's your name?" I asked.

The boy smiled and pointed at me with his finger. I was about to take a step toward him but he ran off, disappearing into Paseo del Borne.

When I got back to my front door I found an envelope stuck in it. The red wax seal with the angel was still warm. I looked up and down the street but couldn't see anybody. I went in and closed the main door behind me with a double lock. Then I paused at the foot of the staircase and opened the envelope.

> *Dear friend,*
>
> *I deeply regret that you were unable to come to our meeting last night. I trust you are well and there has been no emergency or setback. I am sorry I couldn't enjoy the pleasure of your company, but I hope that whatever it was that did not allow you to join me is quickly and favorably resolved and that next time it will be easier for us to meet. I must leave the city for a few days, but as soon as I return I'll send word. Hoping to hear from you and to learn about your progress in our joint project, please accept, as always, my friendship and affection,*
>
> ANDREAS CORELLI

I crushed the letter in my fist and put it in my pocket, then went quietly into the apartment and closed the door. I peeked into the bedroom and saw that Cristina was still asleep. Then I went to the kitchen and began to prepare coffee and a light lunch. A few minutes later I heard Cristina's footsteps behind me. She was looking at me from the doorway, clad in an old sweater of mine that went halfway down her thighs. Her hair was a mess and her eyes were still swollen. Her lips and cheeks had dark bruises, as if I'd hit her hard. She avoided my eyes.

"I'm sorry," she whispered.

"Are you hungry?" I asked.

She shook her head, but I ignored the gesture and motioned for her to sit at the table. I poured her a cup of coffee with milk and sugar and gave her a slice of freshly baked bread with some cheese and a little ham. She made no move to touch her plate.

"Just a bite," I suggested.

She nibbled the cheese and smiled.

"It's good," she said.

We ate in silence. To my surprise, Cristina finished off half the food on her plate. Then she hid behind the cup of coffee and gave me a fleeting look.

"If you want, I'll leave today," she said at last. "Don't worry. Pedro gave me money and—"

"I don't want you to go anywhere. I don't want you to go away ever again. Do you hear me?"

"I'm not good company, David."

"That makes two of us."

"Did you mean it? What you said about going far away?"

I nodded.

"My father used to say that life doesn't give second chances."

"Only to those who never had a first chance. Actually, they're secondhand chances that someone else hasn't made use of, but that's better than nothing."

She smiled faintly.

"Take me for a walk," she suddenly said.

"Where do you want to go?"

"I want to say good-bye to Barcelona."

40

Halfway through the afternoon the sun appeared from behind the blanket of clouds left by the storm. The shining streets were transformed into mirrors, on which pedestrians walked, reflecting the amber of the sky. I remember that we went to the foot of the Ramblas where the statue of Columbus peered out through the mist. We walked in silence, gazing at the buildings and the crowds as if they were a mirage, as if the city were already deserted and forgotten. Barcelona had never seemed so beautiful and so sad to me as it did that afternoon. When it began to grow dark we walked to the Sempere & Sons bookshop and stood in a doorway on the opposite side of the street, where nobody could see us. The shop window of the old bookshop cast a faint light over the damp, gleaming cobblestones. Inside we could see Isabella standing on a ladder, sorting out the books on the top shelf, as Sempere's son pretended to be going through an accounts book, looking furtively at her ankles all the while. Sitting in a corner, old and tired, Señor Sempere watched them both with a sad smile.

"This is the place where I've found almost all the good things in my life," I said without thinking. "I don't want to say good-bye."

. . .

When we returned to the tower house it was already dark. As we walked in we were greeted by the warmth of the fire that I had left burning when we went out. Cristina went ahead down the corridor and, without saying a word, began to get undressed, leaving a trail of clothes on the floor. I found her lying on the bed, waiting. I lay down beside her and let her guide my hands. As I caressed her I could feel her muscles tensing. There was no tenderness in her eyes, just a longing for warmth, and an urgency. I abandoned myself to her body, charging at her with anger, feeling her nails dig into my skin. I heard her moan with pain and with life, as if she lacked air. At last we collapsed, exhausted and covered in sweat. Cristina leaned her head on my shoulder and looked into my eyes.

"Your friend told me you'd got yourself into trouble."

"Isabella?"

"She's very worried about you."

"Isabella has a tendency to believe she's my mother."

"I don't think that's what she was getting at."

I avoided her eyes.

"She told me you were working on a new book commissioned by a foreign publisher. She calls him the boss. She says he's paying you a fortune but you feel guilty for having accepted the money. She says you're afraid of this man, the boss, and there's something murky about the whole business."

I sighed with annoyance.

"Is there anything Isabella hasn't told you?"

"The rest is between us," she answered, winking at me. "Was she lying?"

"She wasn't lying. She was speculating."

"And what's the book about?"

"It's a story for children."

"Isabella told me you'd say that."

"If Isabella has already given you all the answers, why are you questioning me?"

Cristina looked at me severely.

"For your peace of mind, and Isabella's, I've abandoned the book. *C'est fini,*" I assured her.

Cristina frowned and looked dubious.

"And this man, the boss, does he know?"

"I haven't spoken to him yet. But I suppose he has a good idea. And if he doesn't, he soon will."

"So you'll have to give him back the money?"

"I don't think he's bothered about the money in the least."

Cristina fell into a long silence.

"May I read it?" she asked at last.

"No."

"Why not?"

"It's a draft and it doesn't make any sense yet. It's a pile of ideas and notes, loose fragments. Nothing readable. It would bore you."

"I'd still like to read it."

"Why?"

"Because you've written it. Pedro always says that the only way you can truly get to know an author is through the trail of ink he leaves behind him. The person you think you see is only an empty character: truth is always hidden in fiction."

"He must have read that on a postcard."

"In fact he took it from one of your books. I know because I've read it too."

"Plagiarism doesn't prevent it being nonsense."

"I think it makes sense."

"Then it must be true."

"May I read it then?"

"No."

. . .

That evening, sitting opposite each other at the kitchen table, looking up occasionally, we ate the remains of the bread and cheese. Cristina had little appetite and examined every morsel of bread in the light of the oil lamp before putting it in her mouth.

"There's a train leaving the Estación de Francia for Paris tomorrow at midday," she said. "Is that too soon?"

I couldn't get the image of Andreas Corelli out of my mind; I imagined him coming up the stairs and calling at my door at any moment.

"I suppose not," I agreed.

"I know a little hotel opposite the Luxembourg Gardens where they rent out rooms by the month. It's a bit expensive, but . . ." she added.

I preferred not to ask her how she knew of the hotel.

"The price doesn't matter, but I don't speak French."

"I do."

I looked down.

"Look at me, David."

I raised my eyes reluctantly.

"If you'd rather I left . . ."

I shook my head. She held my hand and brought it to her lips.

"It'll be fine. You'll see," she said. "I know. It will be the first thing in my life that will work out all right."

I looked at her, a broken woman with tears in her eyes, and didn't wish for anything in the world other than the ability to give her back what she'd never had.

We lay down on the sofa in the gallery under a couple of blankets, staring at the embers in the fireplace. I fell asleep stroking Cristina's hair, thinking it was the last night I would spend in that house, the prison in which I had buried my youth. I dreamed that I was running through the streets of a Barcelona strewn with clocks whose hands were turning backwards. Alleyways and avenues twisted as I ran, as if they had a will of their own, creating a living labyrinth that blocked me at every turn. Finally, under a midday sun that burned in the sky like a red-hot metal sphere, I managed to reach the Estación de Francia and sped toward the platform where the train was beginning to pull away. I ran after it but the train gathered speed and, despite my efforts, all I managed to do was touch it with the tips of my fingers. I kept on running until I was out of breath, and when I reached the end of the platform I fell into a void.

When I glanced up it was too late. The train was disappearing into the distance, Cristina's face staring back at me from the last window.

. . .

I opened my eyes and knew that Cristina was not there. The fire was reduced to a handful of ashes. I stood up and looked through the windows. Dawn was breaking. I pressed my face against the glass and noticed a flickering light shining from the windows of the study. I went to the spiral staircase that led up to the tower. A copper-colored glow spilled down over the steps. I climbed them slowly. When I reached the study I stopped in the doorway. Cristina was sitting on the floor with her back to me. The trunk by the wall was open. Cristina was holding the folder containing the boss's manuscript and was untying the ribbon.

When she heard my footsteps she stopped.

"What are you doing up here?" I asked, trying to hide the note of alarm in my voice.

Cristina turned and smiled.

"Nosing around."

She followed the direction of my gaze to the folder in her hands and adopted a mischievous expression.

"What's in here?"

"Nothing. Notes. Comments. Nothing of any interest . . ."

"You liar. I bet this is the book you've been working on," she said, "I'm dying to read it."

"I'd rather you didn't," I said in the most relaxed tone I could muster.

Cristina frowned. I took advantage of the moment to kneel down beside her and delicately snatch the folder away.

"What's the matter, David?"

"Nothing's the matter," I assured her with a stupid smile plastered across my lips.

I tied the ribbon again and put the folder back in the trunk.

"Aren't you going to lock it?" asked Cristina.

I turned round, ready to offer some excuse, but Cristina had already disappeared down the stairs. I sighed and closed the lid of the trunk.

I found her in the bedroom. For a moment she looked at me as if I were a stranger.

"Forgive me," I began.

"You don't have to ask me to forgive you," she replied. "I shouldn't have stuck my nose in where I have no business."

"No, it's not that."

"It doesn't matter," she said icily, her tone cutting the air.

I put off a second remark for a more auspicious moment.

"The ticket office at the Estación de Francia will be open soon," I said. "I thought I'd go there so that I can buy the tickets first thing. Then I'll go to the bank and withdraw some money."

"Very good."

"Why don't you get a bag ready in the meantime? I'll be back in a couple of hours at the most."

Cristina barely smiled.

"I'll be here."

I went over to her and held her face in my hands.

"By tomorrow night we'll be in Paris," I said.

I kissed her on the forehead and left.

41

The large clock suspended from the ceiling of the Estación de Francia was reflected in the shining surface of the floor beneath my feet. The hands pointed to seven thirty-five in the morning, but the ticket offices hadn't opened yet. A porter, armed with a large broom and an exaggerated manner, was polishing the floor, whistling a popular folk song and, within the limits imposed by his limp, jauntily moving his hips. As I had nothing better to do, I stood there observing him. He was a small man who looked as if the world had wrinkled him up to such a degree that it had taken everything from him except his smile and the pleasure of being able to clean that bit of floor as if it were the Sistine Chapel. There was nobody else around, but finally he realized that he was being watched. When his fifth pass over the floor brought him to my observation post on one of the wooden benches surrounding the vestibule, the porter stopped and leaned on his mop with both hands.

"They never open on time," he explained, pointing toward the ticket offices.

"Then why do they have a notice saying they open at seven?"

The little man sighed philosophically.

"Well, they also have timetables and in the fifteen years I've been here I haven't seen a single train leave on time," he remarked.

The porter continued with his cleaning and fifteen minutes later I heard the window of a ticket office opening. I walked over and smiled at the clerk.

"I thought you opened at seven," I said.

"That's what the notice says. What do you want?"

"Two first-class tickets to Paris on the midday train."

"For today?"

"If that's not too much trouble."

It took him almost a quarter of an hour. Once he had finished his masterpiece, he dropped the tickets on the counter disdainfully.

"One o'clock. Platform 4. Don't be late."

I paid and, as I didn't then leave, he gave me a hostile look.

"Anything else?"

I smiled and shook my head, at which point he closed the window in my face. I turned and crossed the immaculate vestibule, its brilliant shine courtesy of the porter, who waved at me from afar and wished me a *bon voyage.*

. . .

The central offices of the Banco Hispano Colonial on Calle Fontanella were reminiscent of a temple. A huge portico gave way to a nave, which was flanked by statues and extended as far as a row of windows that looked like an altar. On either side of this altar, like side-chapels and confessionals, were oak tables and easy chairs fit for a general, with a small army of auditors and other staff in attendance, neatly dressed and sporting friendly smiles. I withdrew four thousand francs and received instructions on how to take out money at their Paris branch, at the intersection of Rue de Rennes and Boulevard Raspail, near the hotel Cristina had mentioned. With that small fortune in my pocket I said good-bye, disregarding the warning given to me by the manager about the risks of walking the streets with that amount of cash in my pocket.

The sun was rising in a blue sky the color of good luck and a clean breeze brought with it the smell of the sea. I was walking briskly, as if relieved of a tremendous burden, and I began to think that the city had decided to let me go without any ill feeling. In Paseo del Borne I stopped to buy flowers for Cristina, white roses tied with a red ribbon. I climbed the steps to the apartment, two at a time, with a smile on my lips, certain that this would be the first day of a life I thought I had lost forever. I was about to open the door when, as I put the key in the lock, it gave way. It was open.

I stepped into the hall. The house was silent.

"Cristina?"

I left the flowers on a shelf and put my head round the door of the bedroom. Cristina wasn't there. I walked up the corridor to the gallery. There was no sign of her. I went to the staircase that led up to the study and called out in a loud voice.

"Cristina?"

Nothing but an echo. I checked the clock on one of the glass cabinets in the gallery. It was almost nine. I imagined that Cristina must have gone out to get something and, being used to leaving such matters as doors and keys to the servants in Pedralbes, she had left the front door open. While I waited, I decided to lie down on the sofa in the gallery. The sun poured in through the large windows, a clean, bright winter sun that felt like a warm caress. I closed my eyes and tried to think about what I was going to take with me. I'd spent half my life surrounded by all these objects and now, when it was time to part from them, I felt incapable of making a short list of the ones I considered essential. Slowly, without noticing, lying in the warmth of the sun and lulled by tepid hope, I fell asleep.

· · ·

When I woke up and looked at the clock, it was twelve thirty. There was barely half an hour before the train was due to leave. I jumped up and ran to the bedroom.

"Cristina?"

This time I went through the whole house, room by room, until I reached the study. There was nobody, but I thought I could smell something odd. Phosphorous. The light from the windows trapped a faint web of blue filaments of smoke suspended in the air. I found a couple of burned matches on the study floor. Feeling a pang of anxiety, I knelt down by the trunk. I opened it and sighed with relief. The folder containing the manuscript was still there. I was about to close the lid when I noticed something: the red ribbon of the folder was undone. I picked the folder up and opened it, leafing through the pages, but nothing seemed to be missing. I closed it again, this time tying the ribbon with a double knot, and put it back in its place. After closing the trunk, I went down to the lower floor. I sat on a chair in the gallery, facing the long corridor that led to the front door, and waited. The minutes went by with infinite cruelty.

Slowly, the awareness of what had happened fell all upon me and my desire to believe and to trust turned to bitterness. I heard the bells of Santa María strike two o'clock. The train to Paris had left the station and Cristina had not returned. I realized then that she had gone, that those brief hours we had shared were nothing but a mirage. I went up to the study again and sat down. The dazzling day I saw through the windowpanes was no longer the color of luck; I imagined her back in Villa Helius, seeking the shelter of Pedro Vidal's arms. Resentment slowly poisoned my blood and I laughed at myself and my absurd hopes. I remained there, incapable of taking a single step, watching the city grow dark as the afternoon went by and the shadows lengthened. Finally I stood up and went to the window, I opened it wide and looked out. Beneath me, a sheer drop, sufficiently high. Sufficiently high to crush my bones, to turn them into daggers that would pierce my body and let it die in a pool of blood on the courtyard below. I wondered whether the pain would be as bad as I imagined it or whether the impact would be enough to numb the senses and offer a quick, efficient death.

Then I heard three knocks on the door. One, two, three. Insistent. I turned, still dazed by my thoughts. The knocks came again. My heart skipped a beat and I rushed downstairs, convinced that Cristina had returned, that something had happened along the way that had detained her, that my miserable, despicable feelings of betrayal were unjustified and that today was, after all, the first day of that promised life. I ran to the door and opened it. She was there in the shadows, dressed in white. I was about to embrace her, but then I saw her face, wet with tears. It was not Cristina.

"David," Isabella whispered in a broken voice. "Señor Sempere has died."

Act Three

The Angel's
Game

I

Night had fallen by the time we reached the bookshop. A golden glow broke through the blue of the night outside Sempere & Sons, where about a hundred people had gathered holding candles. Some cried quietly, others looked at one another, not knowing what to do. I recognized some of the faces—friends and customers of Sempere, people to whom the old bookseller had given books as presents, readers who had been initiated into the art of reading through him. As the news spread through the area, more people arrived, all finding it hard to believe that Señor Sempere had died.

The shop lights were on and I could see Don Gustavo Barceló inside, embracing a young man who could hardly stand. I didn't realize it was Sempere's son until Isabella pressed my hand and led me into the bookshop. When Barceló saw me come in, he looked up and smiled dolefully. The bookseller's son was weeping in his arms and I didn't have the courage to go and greet him. It was Isabella who went over and put her hand on his back. Sempere's son turned round and I saw his distraught face. Isabella led him to a chair and helped him sit down; he collapsed like a rag doll and Isabella knelt down beside him and hugged him. I had never felt as proud of anyone as I was that day of Isabella. She seemed no longer a girl but a woman, stronger and wiser than any of the rest us.

Barceló held out a trembling hand. I shook it.

"It happened a couple of hours ago," he explained in a hoarse voice.

"He'd been left alone in the bookshop for a moment and when his son returned . . . They say he was arguing with someone . . . I don't know. The doctor said it was his heart."

I swallowed hard.

"Where is he?"

Barceló nodded toward the door of the back room. I walked over, but before going in I took a deep breath and clenched my fists. Then I walked through the doorway and saw him: he was lying on a table, his hands crossed over his belly. His skin was as white as paper and his features seemed to have sunk in on themselves. His eyes were still open. I found it hard to breathe and felt as if I'd been dealt a strong blow to the stomach. I leaned on the table and tried to steady myself. Then I bent over him and closed his eyelids. I stroked his cheek, which was cold, and looked around me at that world of pages and dreams he had created. I wanted to believe that Sempere was still there, among his books and his friends. I heard steps behind me and turned. Barceló was accompanied by two somber-looking men, both dressed in black.

"These gentlemen are from the undertaker's," said Barceló.

They nodded with professional gravitas and went over to examine the body. One of them, who was tall and gaunt, took a brief measurement and said something to his colleague, who wrote down his instructions in a little notebook.

"Unless there is any change, the funeral will be tomorrow afternoon, in the Pueblo Nuevo cemetery," said Barceló. "I thought it best to take charge of the arrangements because his son is devastated, as you can see. And with these things, the sooner—"

"Thank you, Don Gustavo."

The bookseller glanced at his old friend and smiled tearfully.

"What are we going to do now that the old man has left us?" he said.

"I don't know . . ."

One of the undertakers discreetly cleared his throat.

"If it's all right with you, in a moment my colleague and I will go and fetch the coffin and—"

"Do whatever you have to do," I cut in.

"Any preferences regarding the ceremony?"

I stared at him, not understanding.

"Was the deceased a believer?"

"Señor Sempere believed in books," I said.

"I see," he replied as he left the room.

I looked at Barceló, who shrugged his shoulders.

"Let me ask his son," I added.

I went back to the front of the bookshop. Isabella glanced at me inquisitively and stood up. She left Sempere's son and came over to me and I whispered the problem to her.

"Señor Sempere was a good friend of the local parish priest—from the church of Santa Ana right next door. People say the bigwigs in the diocese have been wanting to get rid of him for years because they consider him a rebel in the ranks, but he's so old they decided to wait for him to die instead. He's too tough a nut for them to crack."

"Then he's the man we need," I said.

"I'll speak to him," said Isabella.

I pointed toward Sempere's son.

"How is he?"

Isabella met my gaze.

"And how are you?" she replied.

"I'm fine," I lied. "Who's going to stay with him tonight?"

"I am," she said, without a moment's hesitation.

I kissed her on the cheek and returned to the back room. Barceló was sitting in front of his old friend, and while the two undertakers took further measurements and debated about suits and shoes, he poured two glasses of brandy and offered one to me. I sat down next to him.

"To the health of our friend Sempere, who taught us all how to read, and even how to live," he said.

We toasted and drank in silence. We remained there until the undertakers returned with the coffin and the clothes in which Sempere was going to be buried.

"If it's all right with you, we'll take care of this," the one who seemed to be the brighter of the two suggested. I agreed. Before leaving the room and going back to the front of the shop, I picked up the old copy of *Great Expectations,* which I'd never come back to collect, and put it in Sempere's hands.

"For the journey," I said.

A quarter of an hour later, the undertakers brought out the coffin and placed it on a large table that had been set up in the middle of the bookshop. A multitude had been gathering in the street, waiting in silence. I went over to the door and opened it. One by one, the friends of Sempere & Sons filed through. Some were unable to hold back the tears, and such were the scenes of grief that Isabella took the bookseller's son by the hand and led him up to the apartment above the bookshop, where he had lived all his life with his father. Barceló and I stayed in the shop, keeping old Sempere company while people came in to say their farewells. Those closest to him stayed on.

The wake lasted the entire night. Barceló remained until five in the morning and I didn't leave until Isabella came down to the shop shortly after dawn and ordered me to go home, if only to change my clothes and freshen up.

I looked at poor Sempere and smiled. I couldn't believe I'd never see him again, standing behind the counter, when I came through that door. I remembered the first time I'd visited the bookshop, when I was just a child and the bookseller had seemed tall and strong. Indestructible. The wisest man in the world.

"Go home, please," murmured Isabella.

"What for?"

"Please . . ."

She came out into the street with me and hugged me.

"I know how fond you were of him and what he meant to you," she said.

Nobody knew, I thought. Nobody. But I nodded and, after kissing her on the cheek, I wandered off, walking through streets that seemed emptier than ever, thinking that if I didn't stop, if I kept on walking, I wouldn't notice that the world I thought I knew was no longer there.

2

The crowd had gathered by the cemetery gates to await the arrival of the hearse. Nobody dared speak. We could hear the murmur of the sea in the distance and the echo of a freight train rumbling toward the city of factories that spread out beyond the graveyard. It was cold and snowflakes drifted in the wind. Shortly after three o'clock in the afternoon, the hearse, pulled by a team of black horses, turned into Avenida de Icaria, which was lined by rows of cypress trees and old storehouses. Sempere's son and Isabella traveled with it. Six colleagues from the Barcelona booksellers' guild, Don Gustavo among them, lifted the coffin onto their shoulders and carried it into the cemetery. The crowd followed, forming a silent cortege that advanced through the streets and mausoleums of the cemetery beneath a blanket of low clouds that rippled like a sheet of mercury. I heard someone say that the bookseller's son looked as if he'd aged fifteen years in one night. They referred to him as Señor Sempere, because he was now the person in charge of the bookshop; for four generations that enchanted bazaar in Calle Santa Ana had never changed its name and had always been managed by a Señor Sempere. Isabella held his arm—without her support he looked as if he might have collapsed like a puppet with no strings.

The parish priest of Santa Ana, a veteran the same age as the deceased, waited at the foot of the tomb, a sober slab of marble without decorative elements that could almost have gone unnoticed. The six booksellers who had carried the coffin left it resting beside the grave. Barceló noticed me and greeted me with a nod. I preferred to stay toward the back of the crowd, I'm not sure whether out of cowardice or respect. From there I could see my father's grave, some thirty meters away.

Once the congregation had spread out, the parish priest looked up and smiled.

"Señor Sempere and I were friends for almost forty years, and in all that time we spoke about God and the mysteries of life on only one occasion. Almost nobody knows this, but Sempere had not set foot in a church since the funeral of his wife, Diana, to whose side we bring him today so that they might lie next to each other forever. Perhaps for that reason people assumed he was an atheist, but he was truly a man of faith. He believed in his friends, in the truth of things, and in something to which he didn't dare put a name or a face because he said as priests that was our job. Señor Sempere believed that we are all a part of something and that when we leave this world our memories and our desires are not lost but go on to become the memories and desires of those who take our place. He didn't know whether we created God in our own image or whether God created us without quite knowing what he was doing. He believed that God, or whatever brought us here, lives in each of our deeds, in each of our words, and manifests himself in all those things that show us to be more than mere figures of clay. Señor Sempere believed that God lives, to a smaller or greater extent, in books, and that is why he devoted his life to sharing them, to protecting them, and to making sure their pages, like our memories and our desires, are never lost. He believed, and he made me believe it too, that as long as there is one person left in the world who is capable of reading them and experiencing them, a small piece of God, or of life, will remain. I know that my friend would not have liked us to say our farewells to him with prayers and hymns. I know that it would have been enough for him to realize that his friends, many of whom have come here today to say goodbye, will never forget him. I have no doubt that the Lord, even though old Sempere was not expecting it, will receive our dear friend at his side, and I know that he will live forever in the hearts of all those who are here today, all those who have discovered the magic of books thanks to him, and all those who, without even knowing him, will one day go through the door of his little bookshop, where, as he liked to say, the story has only just begun. May you rest in peace, Sempere, dear friend, and may God give us all the opportunity to honor your memory and feel grateful for the privilege of having known you."

An endless silence fell over the graveyard when the priest finished speaking. He retreated a few steps, blessing the coffin, his eyes downcast. At a sign from the chief undertaker, the gravediggers moved forward and slowly lowered the coffin with ropes. I remember the sound as it touched the bottom and the stifled sobs among the crowd. I remember that I stood there, unable to move, watching the gravediggers cover the tomb with the large slab of marble on which a single word was written, "Sempere," the tomb in which his wife, Diana, had lain buried for twenty-six years.

The congregation shuffled away toward the cemetery gates, where they separated into groups, not quite knowing where to go, because nobody wanted to leave the place and abandon poor Señor Sempere. Barceló and Isabella led the bookseller's son away, one on each side of him. I stayed on until I thought everyone else had left; only then did I dare go up to Sempere's grave. I knelt and put my hand on the marble.

"See you soon," I murmured.

I heard him approaching and knew who it was before I saw him. I got up and turned round. Pedro Vidal offered me his hand and the saddest smile I have ever seen.

"Aren't you going to shake my hand?" he asked.

I didn't and a few seconds later Vidal nodded to himself and pulled his hand away.

"What are you doing here?" I spat out.

"Sempere was my friend too," replied Vidal.

"I see. And are you here alone?"

Vidal looked puzzled.

"Where is she?" I asked.

"Who?"

I let out a bitter laugh. Barceló, who had noticed us, was coming over, looking concerned.

"What did you promise her, to buy her back?"

Vidal's eyes hardened.

"You don't know what you're saying, David."

I drew closer, until I could feel his breath on my face.

"Where is she?" I insisted.

"I don't know," said Vidal.

"Of course," I said, looking away.

I was about to walk toward the exit when Vidal grabbed my arm and stopped me.

"David, wait—"

Before I realized what I was doing, I turned and hit him as hard as I could. My fist crashed against his face and he fell backwards. I noticed that there was blood on my hand and heard steps hurrying toward me. Two arms caught hold of me and pulled me away from Vidal.

"For God's sake, Martín . . ." said Barceló.

The bookseller knelt down next to Vidal, who was gasping as blood streamed from his mouth. Barceló cradled his head and threw me a furious look. I fled, passing some of the people who had been present at the graveside and who had stopped to watch the altercation. I didn't have the courage to look them in the eye.

3

I didn't leave the house for several days, sleeping at odd times and barely eating. At night I would sit in the gallery by the open fire and listen to the silence, hoping to hear footsteps outside the door, thinking that Cristina would return, that as soon as she heard about the death of Señor Sempere she'd come back to me, if only out of compassion, which by now would have been enough for me. When almost a week had gone by since the death of the bookseller and I realized that Cristina was not going to return, I began to visit the study again. I rescued the boss's manuscript from the trunk and started to reread it, savoring every phrase, every paragraph. Reading it produced in me both nausea and a dark satisfaction. When I thought of the hundred thousand francs that at first had seemed so much, I smiled and reflected that I'd sold myself to that son of a bitch too cheaply. Vanity papered over my bitterness, and pain closed the door of my conscience. In an act of pure arrogance, I reread my predecessor Diego Marlasca's *Lux Aeterna* and then threw it into the fire. Where he had failed, I would triumph. Where he had lost his way, I would find the path out of the labyrinth.

I went back to work on the seventh day. I waited until midnight and sat down at my desk. A clean sheet in the old Underwood typewriter and the city black behind the windowpanes. The words and images sprang forth from my hands as if they'd been waiting angrily in the prison of my soul. The pages flowed from me without thought or measure, with nothing more than the desire to bewitch, or poison, hearts and minds. I stopped thinking about the boss, about his reward or his demands. For the first time in my life I was writing for myself and nobody else. I was writing to set the world on fire and be consumed along with it. I worked every night until I collapsed from exhaustion. I banged the typewriter keys until my fingers bled and fever clouded my vision.

One morning in January, when I'd lost all notion of time, I heard someone knocking on the door. I was lying on my bed, my eyes lost in the old photograph of Cristina as a small child, walking hand in hand with a stranger along a jetty that reached out into a sea of light. That image seemed to be the only good thing I had left, the key to all mysteries. I ignored the knocking for a few minutes, until I heard her voice and knew she was not going to give up.

"Open the door, damn you! I know you're there and I'm not leaving until you open it or I knock it down."

When she saw me Isabella stepped back and looked horrified.

"It's only me, Isabella."

She pushed me aside and made straight for the gallery, where she flung open the windows. Then she went to the bathroom and started filling the tub. She took my arm and dragged me there, then made me sit on the edge of the bath and examined my eyes, lifting my eyelids with her fingertips and muttering to herself. Without saying a word she began to remove my shirt.

"Isabella, I'm not in the mood."

"What are all these cuts? But . . . what have you done to yourself?"

"They're just scratches."

"I want a doctor to see you."

"No."

"Don't you dare say no to me," she replied harshly. "You're getting into this bathtub right now; you're going to wash yourself with soap and water and you're going to have a shave. You have two options: either you do it or I will. And don't imagine for one second that I won't."

I smiled.

"I know."

"Do as I say. In the meantime I'm going to find a doctor."

I was about to reply, but she raised her hand to silence me.

"Don't say another word. If you think you're the only person for whom life is painful, you're wrong. And if you don't mind letting yourself die like a dog, at least have the decency to remember that there are those of us who do care—although, to tell the truth, I don't see why."

"Isabella—"

"Into the water. And please remove your trousers and underpants."

"I know how to take a bath."

"I'd never have guessed."

While Isabella went off in search of a doctor, I submitted to her orders and subjected myself to a baptism of cold water and soap. I hadn't shaved since the funeral and when I looked in the mirror I was greeted by the face of a wolf. My eyes were bloodshot and my skin had an unhealthy pallor. I put on clean clothes and went to wait in the gallery. Isabella returned twenty minutes later with a physician I thought I'd seen in the area once or twice.

"This is the patient. Pay no attention whatsoever to anything he says to you. He's a liar," Isabella announced.

The doctor glanced at me, calibrating the extent of my hostility.

"It's over to you, doctor," I said. "Just imagine I'm not here."

We went to my bedroom and he began the subtle rituals that form the basis of medical science: he took my blood pressure, listened to my chest, examined my pupils and my mouth, and asked me questions of a mysterious nature. When he inspected the razor cuts Irene Sabino had made on my chest, he raised an eyebrow.

"What's this?"

"It's a long story, doctor."

"Did you do it to yourself?"

I shook my head.

"I'm going to give you an ointment for the cuts, but I'm afraid you'll be left with some scars."

"I think that was the idea."

He continued with his examination and I submitted to everything obediently, my eye on Isabella, who was watching anxiously from the doorway. I understood then how much I had missed her and how much I appreciated her company.

"What a fright you gave me," she mumbled with disapproval.

The doctor frowned when he saw the raw wounds on the tips of my fingers. He proceeded to bandage them one by one.

"When did you last eat?"

I didn't reply. The doctor exchanged glances with Isabella.

"There is no cause for alarm, but I'd like to see him in my office tomorrow at the latest."

"I'm afraid that won't be possible, doctor," I said.

"He'll be there," Isabella assured him.

"In the meantime I recommend that he begins by eating something warm, first broth and then solids. A lot of water but no coffee or other stimulants, and above all he must get lots of rest. Let him go out for a little fresh air and sunshine, but he mustn't overexert himself. He is showing the classic symptoms of exhaustion and dehydration and the beginnings of anemia."

Isabella sighed.

"It's nothing," I remarked.

The doctor looked at me, unconvinced, and stood up.

"Tomorrow afternoon in my office, at four o'clock. I don't have the correct instruments or environment for a proper examination here."

He closed his bag and politely said good-bye. Isabella accompanied him to the door and I heard them murmuring on the landing for a few minutes. I got dressed again and waited, like a good patient, sitting on the bed. I heard the front door close and the doctor's steps as he descended the stairs. I knew that Isabella was in the entrance hall, pausing before she came into the bedroom. When at last she did, I greeted her with a smile.

"I'm going to prepare something for you to eat."

"I'm not hungry."

"I couldn't care less. You're going to eat and then we're going to go out so that you get some fresh air."

Isabella prepared some broth for me, to which I added morsels of bread. I then forced myself to swallow it with a cheerful face, although to me it tasted like grit. Eventually I cleaned my bowl and showed it to Isabella, who had been standing on guard duty while I ate. Next she took me to the bedroom, searched for a coat in the wardrobe, equipped me with gloves and a scarf, and pushed me toward the front door. When we stepped outside a cold wind was blowing, but the sky shone with an evening sun that turned the streets the color of amber. She put her arm in mine and we set off.

"As if we were engaged," I said.

"Very funny."

We walked to Ciudadela Park and into the gardens surrounding the Shade House. When we reached the pond by the large fountain we sat down on a bench.

"Thank you," I murmured.

Isabella didn't reply.

"I haven't asked you how you are," I volunteered.

"That's nothing new."

"So how are you?"

Isabella paused.

"My parents are delighted that I've returned. They say you've been a good influence. If only they knew . . . The truth is, we do get on better than before. Not that I see that much of them. I spend most of my time in the bookshop."

"How's Sempere? How is he taking his father's death?"

"Not very well."

"And how are you taking him?"

"He's a good man," she said.

Isabella fell silent and lowered her eyes.

"He proposed to me," she said after a while. "A couple of days ago, in Els Quatre Gats."

I contemplated her profile, serene and robbed of the youthful innocence that I had wanted to see in her and that had probably never been there.

"And?" I finally asked.

"I've told him I'll think about it."

"And will you?"

Isabella's gaze was lost in the fountain.

"He told me he wanted to have a family, children. He said we'd live in the apartment above the bookshop, that somehow we'd make a go of it, despite Señor Sempere's debts."

"Well, you're still young . . ."

She tilted her head and looked me in the eye.

"Do you love him?" I asked.

She gave a smile that seemed endlessly sad.

"How do I know? I think so, although not as much as he thinks he loves me."

"Sometimes, in difficult circumstances, one can confuse compassion with love," I said.

"Don't you worry about me."

"All I ask is that you give yourself some time."

We looked at each other, bound by an infinite complicity that needed no words, and I hugged her.

"Friends?"

"Till death do us part."

4

On our way home we stopped at a grocer's in Calle Comercio to buy some milk and bread. Isabella told me she was going to ask her father to deliver an order of fine foods and I'd better eat everything up.

"How are things in the bookshop?" I asked.

"Sales have gone right down. I think people feel sad about coming to the shop, because they remember poor Señor Sempere. As things stand, it's not looking good."

"How are the accounts?"

"Below the waterline. In the weeks I've been working there I've gone through the ledgers and realized that Señor Sempere, God rest his soul, was a disaster. He'd simply give books to people who couldn't afford them. Or he'd lend them out and never get them back. He'd buy collections he knew he wouldn't be able to sell just because the owners had threatened to burn them or throw them away. He supported a whole host of second-rate bards who didn't have a penny to their name by giving them small sums of money. You can imagine the rest."

"Any creditors in sight?"

"Two a day, not counting letters and final demands from the bank. The good news is that we're not short of offers."

"To buy the place?"

"A couple of sausage merchants from Vic are very interested in the premises."

"And what does Sempere's son say?"

"He just says that pork can be mightier than the sword. Realism isn't his strong point. He says we'll stay afloat and I should have faith."

"And do you?"

"I have faith in arithmetic, and when I do the sums they tell me that in two months' time the bookshop window will be full of chorizo and slabs of bacon."

"We'll find a solution."

Isabella smiled.

"I was hoping you'd say that. And speaking of unfinished business, please tell me you're no longer working for the boss."

I showed her my hands were clean.

"I'm a free agent once more."

She accompanied me up the stairs and was about to say good-bye when she appeared to hesitate.

"What?" I asked her.

"I'd decided not to tell you, but . . . I'd rather you heard it from me than from someone else. It's about Señor Sempere."

We went into the house and sat down in the gallery by the open fire, which Isabella revived by throwing on a couple of logs. The ashes of Marlasca's *Lux Aeterna* were still visible and my former assistant threw me a glance I could have framed.

"What were you going to tell me about Sempere?"

"It's something I heard from Don Anacleto, one of the neighbors in the building. He told me that on the afternoon Señor Sempere died he saw him arguing with someone in the shop. Don Anacleto was on his way back home and he said that their voices could be heard from the street."

"Whom was he arguing with?"

"It was a woman. Quite old. Don Anacleto didn't think he'd ever seen her around there, though he did say she looked vaguely familiar. But you never know with Don Anacleto. He likes to chatter on more than he likes sugared almonds."

"Did he hear what they were arguing about?"

"He thought they were talking about you."

"About me?"

Isabella nodded.

"Sempere's son had gone out for a moment to deliver an order in Calle Canuda. He wasn't away for more than ten or fifteen minutes. When he got back he found his father lying on the floor, behind the counter. Señor Sempere was still breathing but he was cold. By the time the doctor arrived, it was too late . . ."

I felt the whole world collapsing on top of me.

"I shouldn't have told you," whispered Isabella.

"No. You did the right thing. Did Don Anacleto say anything else about the woman?"

"Only that he heard them arguing. He thought it was about a book. Something she wanted to buy and Señor Sempere didn't want to sell her."

"And why did he mention me? I don't understand."

"Because it was your book. *The Steps of Heaven.* It was Señor Sempere's only copy, in his personal collection, and not for sale."

I was filled with a dark certainty.

"And the book . . . ?" I began.

"It's no longer there. It disappeared," Isabella explained. "I checked the sales ledger, because Señor Sempere always made a note of every book he sold, with the date and the price, and this one wasn't there."

"Does his son know?"

"No. I haven't told anybody except you. I'm still trying to understand what happened that afternoon in the bookshop. And why. I thought perhaps you might know . . ."

"I suspect the woman tried to take the book by force, and in the quarrel Señor Sempere suffered a heart attack. That's what happened," I said. "And all over a damned book of mine."

I could feel my stomach churning.

"There's something else," said Isabella.

"What?"

"A few days later I bumped into Don Anacleto on the stairs and he told me he'd remembered how he knew that woman. He said that at first he couldn't put his finger on it, but now he was sure he'd seen her, many years ago, in the theater."

"In the theater?"

Isabella nodded.

I was silent for a long while. Isabella watched me anxiously.

"Now I'm not happy about leaving you here. I shouldn't have told you."

"No, you did the right thing. I'm fine. Honestly."

Isabella shook her head.

"I'm staying with you tonight."

"What about your reputation?"

"It's your reputation that's in danger. I'll just go to my parents' store to phone the bookshop and let him know."

"There's no need, Isabella."

"There would be no need if you'd accepted that we live in the twentieth century and had installed a telephone in this mausoleum. I'll be back in a quarter of an hour. No arguments."

. . .

During Isabella's absence, the death of my friend Sempere began to weigh on my conscience. I recalled how the old bookseller had always told me that books have a soul, the soul of the person who wrote them and of those who read them and dream about them. I realized that until the very last moment he had fought to protect me, giving his own life for a bundle of paper and ink in which, he felt, my soul had been inscribed. When Isabella returned, carrying a bag of delicacies from her parents' shop, she only needed to take one look at me.

"You know that woman," she said. "The woman who killed Sempere."

"I think so. Irene Sabino."

"Isn't she the one in the old photographs we found? The actress?"

I nodded.

"Why would she want your book?"

"I don't know."

Later, after sampling one or two treats from Can Gispert, we sat together in the large armchair in front of the hearth. We were both able to fit on it, and Isabella leaned her head on my shoulder while we stared at the flames.

"The other night I dreamed that I had a son," she said. "I dreamed that he was calling to me but I couldn't reach him because I was trapped in a place that was very cold and I couldn't move. He kept calling me and I couldn't go to him."

"It was only a dream."

"It seemed real."

"Maybe you should write it as a story," I suggested.

Isabella shook her head.

"I've been thinking about that. And I've decided that I'd rather live my life than write about it. Please don't take it badly."

"I think it's a wise decision."

"What about you? Are you going to live your life?"

"I'm afraid I've already lived quite a lot of it."

"What about that woman? Cristina?"

I took a deep breath.

"Cristina has left. She's gone back to her husband. Another wise decision."

Isabella pulled away and frowned at me.

"What?" I asked.

"I think you're mistaken."

"What about?"

"The other day Gustavo Barceló came by and we talked about you. He told me he'd seen Cristina's husband, what's his name . . ."

"Pedro Vidal."

"That's the one. And Señor Vidal had told him that Cristina had gone off with you, that he hadn't seen her or heard from her in over a month. As a matter of fact, I was surprised not to find her here, but I didn't dare ask."

"Are you sure that's what Barceló said?"

Isabella nodded.

"Now what have I said?" she asked in alarm.

"Nothing."

"There's something you're not telling me . . ."

"Cristina isn't here. I haven't seen her since the day Señor Sempere died."

"Where is she then?"

"I don't know."

Little by little we grew silent, curled up in the armchair by the fire, and in the small hours Isabella fell asleep. I put my arm round her and closed my eyes, thinking about all the things she had said and trying to find some meaning. When the light of dawn appeared through the windowpanes of the gallery, I opened my eyes and saw that Isabella was already awake.

"Good morning," I said.

"I've been meditating," she declared.

"And?"

"I'm thinking about accepting Sempere's proposal."

"Are you sure?"

"No." She laughed.

"What will your parents say?"

"They'll be upset, I suppose, but they'll get over it. They would prefer me to marry a prosperous merchant who sold sausages rather than books, but they'll just have to put up with it."

"It could be worse," I remarked.

Isabella agreed.

"Yes. I could end up with a writer."

We looked at each other for a long time, until she extracted herself from the armchair. She collected her coat and buttoned it up, her back turned to me.

"I must go," she said.

"Thanks for the company," I replied.

"Don't let her escape," said Isabella. "Search for her, wherever she may be, and tell her you love her, even if it's a lie. We girls like to hear that kind of thing."

She turned round and leaned over to brush my lips with hers. Then she squeezed my hand and left without saying good-bye.

I spent the rest of that week scouring Barcelona for anyone who might remember having seen Cristina over the last month. I visited the places I'd shared with her and traced Vidal's favorite route through cafés, restaurants, and elegant shops, all in vain. I showed everyone I met a photograph from the album Cristina had left in my house and asked whether they had seen her recently. Somewhere, I forget where, I came across a person who recognized her and remembered having seen her with Vidal sometime or other. Other people even remembered her name, but nobody had seen her in weeks. On the fourth day, I began to suspect that Cristina had left the tower house that morning after I went to buy the train tickets and had evaporated off the face of the earth.

Then I remembered that Vidal's family kept a room permanently reserved at Hotel España, on Calle Sant Pau, behind the Liceo theater. It was used whenever a member of the family visited the opera and didn't feel like returning to Pedralbes in the early hours. I knew that Vidal and his father had also used it, at least in their golden years, to enjoy the company of young ladies whose presence in their official residences in Pedralbes would have led to undesirable rumors—due to either the low or the high birth of the lady in question. More than once Vidal had offered the room to me when I still lived in Doña Carmen's pension in case, as he put it, I felt like undressing a damsel somewhere that wasn't quite so alarming. I didn't think Cristina would have chosen the hotel room as a refuge—if she knew of its existence, that is—but it was the only place left on my list and nowhere else had occurred to me.

It was getting dark when I arrived at Hotel España and asked to speak to the manager, presenting myself as Señor Vidal's friend. When I showed him Cristina's photograph, the manager, a gentleman who mistook frostiness for discretion, smiled politely and told me that "other" members of Vidal's staff had already been there a few weeks earlier, asking after that same person, and he had told them what he was telling me now: he had never seen that lady in the hotel. I thanked him for his icy kindness and walked away in defeat.

As I passed the glass doors that led into the dining room, I thought I registered a familiar profile. The boss was sitting at one of the tables, the only guest there, eating what looked like lumps of sugar. I was about to make a quick getaway when he turned and waved at me, smiling. I cursed my luck and waved back. He signaled for me to join him. I walked through the dining room door, dragging my feet.

"What a lovely surprise to see you here, dear friend. I was just thinking about you," said Corelli.

I shook hands with him reluctantly.

"I thought you were out of town," I said.

"I came back sooner than planned. Would you care for a drink?"

I declined. He asked me to sit down at his table and I obeyed. The boss wore his usual three-piece suit of black wool and a red silk tie. As always, he was impeccably attired, but something didn't quite add up. It took me a few seconds to notice what it was—the angel brooch was not in his lapel. Corelli followed the direction of my gaze.

"Alas, I've lost it, and I don't know where," he explained.

"I hope it wasn't too valuable."

"Its value was purely sentimental. But let's talk about more important matters. How are you, my dear friend? I've missed our conversations enormously, despite our occasional disagreements. It's difficult to find a good conversationalist."

"You overrate me, Señor Corelli."

"On the contrary."

A brief silence followed, those bottomless eyes drilling into mine. I told myself that I preferred him when he embarked on his usual banal conversations—when he stopped speaking his face seemed to change and the air thickened around him.

"Are you staying here?" I asked to break the silence.

"No, I'm still in the house by Güell Park. I arranged to meet a friend here this afternoon, but he seems to be late. The manners of some people are deplorable."

"There can't be many people who dare to stand you up, Señor Corelli."

The boss looked me straight in the eye.

"Not many. In fact, the only person I can think of is you."

The boss took a sugar lump and dropped it into his cup. A second lump followed, and then a third. He tasted the coffee and added four more lumps. Then he picked up yet another and popped it in his mouth.

"I love sugar," he said.

"So I see."

"You haven't told me anything about our project, Martín, dear friend," he cut in. "Is there a problem?"

I winced.

"It's almost finished," I said.

The boss's face lit up with a smile I tried to ignore.

"That is wonderful news. When will I be able to see it?"

"In a couple of weeks. I need to do some revisions. Pruning and finishing touches more than anything else."

"Can we set a date?"

"If you like."

"How about Friday? That's the twenty-fourth. Will you accept an invitation to dine and celebrate the success of our venture?"

Friday, 24 January, was exactly two weeks away.

"Fine," I agreed.

"That's confirmed, then."

He raised his sugar-filled cup as if he were drinking a toast and downed the contents in one gulp.

"How about you?" he asked casually. "What brings you here?"

"I was looking for someone."

"Someone I know?"

"No."

"And have you found the person?"

"No."

The boss savored my silence.

"I get the impression that I'm keeping you here against your will, dear friend."

"I'm just a little tired, that's all."

"Then I won't take up any more of your time. Sometimes I forget that although I enjoy your company, perhaps mine is not to your liking."

I smiled meekly and took the opportunity to stand up. I saw myself reflected in his pupils, a pale doll trapped in a dark well.

"Take care of yourself, Martín. Please."

"I will."

I took my leave with a quick nod and headed for the exit. As I walked away I heard him putting another sugar lump in his mouth and crunching it between his teeth.

. . .

When I turned into the Ramblas I noticed that the canopies outside the Liceo were lit up and a long row of cars, guarded by a small regiment of chauffeurs in uniform, was waiting by the pavement. The posters announced *Così fan tutte* and I wondered if Vidal had felt like forsaking his castle to attend. I scanned the circle of drivers that had formed on the central pavement and soon spotted Pep among them. I beckoned him over.

"What are you doing here, Señor Martín?"

"Where is she?"

"Señor Vidal is inside, watching the performance."

"Not 'he.' 'She.' Cristina. Señora de Vidal. Where is she?"

Poor Pep swallowed hard.

"I don't know. Nobody knows."

He told me that Vidal had been attempting to find her and that his father, the patriarch of the clan, had even hired various members of the police force to try to discover where she was.

"At first, Señor Vidal thought she was with you . . ."

"Hasn't she called or sent a letter, a telegram . . . ?"

"No, Señor Martín. I swear. We're all very worried, and Señor Vidal, well . . . I've never seen him like this in all the years I've known him. This is the first time he's gone out since Señorita Cristina, I mean Señora Cristina—"

"Do you remember whether Cristina said something, anything, before she left Villa Helius?"

"Well . . ." said Pep, lowering his voice to a whisper. "You could hear her arguing with Señor Vidal. She seemed sad to me. She spent a lot of time by herself. She wrote letters and every day she went to the post office in Paseo Reina Elisenda to post them."

"Did you ever speak to her alone?"

"One day, shortly before she left, Señor Vidal asked me to drive her to the doctor."

"Was she ill?"

"She couldn't sleep. The doctor prescribed laudanum."

"Did she say anything to you on the way there?"

Pep hesitated.

"She asked after you, in case I'd heard from you or seen you."

"Is that all?"

"She just seemed very sad. She started to cry, and when I asked her what was the matter she said she missed her father, Señor Manuel."

I suddenly understood, berating myself for not having figured things out sooner. Pep looked at me in surprise and asked me why I was smiling.

"Do you know where she is?" he asked.

"I think so," I murmured.

I thought I could hear a voice calling from the other side of the street and glimpsed a familiar figure in the Liceo foyer. Vidal hadn't even managed to last the first act. Pep turned to attend to his master's call, and before he had time to tell me to hide I had already disappeared into the night.

6

Even from afar it looked like bad news: the ember of a cigarette in the blue of the night, silhouettes leaning against a dark wall, the spiraling breath of three figures lying in wait by the main door of the tower house. Inspector Víctor Grandes, accompanied by his two guard dogs Marcos and Castelo, led the welcome committee. It wasn't hard to work out that they'd found Alicia Marlasca's body at the bottom of her pool in Sarriá and that my place on their list had gone up a few notches. The minute I caught sight of them I stopped and melted into the shadows, observing them for a few seconds to make sure they hadn't noticed me—I was only some fifty meters away. I could distinguish Grandes's profile in the thin light shed by the streetlamp on the wall. Retreating into the darkness, I slipped into the first alleyway I could find, disappearing into the mass of passages and arches of the Ribera quarter.

Ten minutes later I reached the main entrance to the Estación de Francia. The ticket offices were closed, but I could still see a few trains lined up by the platforms under the large vault of glass and steel. I checked the timetables. Just as I had feared, there were no departures scheduled until the following day and I couldn't risk returning home and bumping into Grandes and Co. Something told me that on this occasion my visit to police headquarters would include full board, and not even the good offices of the lawyer Señor Valera would get me out of there as easily as the last time.

I decided to spend the night in a cheap hotel opposite the old Stock Exchange, in Plaza Palacio. Legend had it that the building was inhabited by a number of walking cadavers, one-time speculators whose greed and poor arithmetic skills had proved their undoing. I chose this dump because I imagined that not even the Fates would come looking for me there. I registered under the name of Antonio Miranda and paid for the room in advance. The receptionist, who looked like a mollusk, seemed to be embedded in his cubbyhole, which also served as a linen closet and souvenir shop. Handing me the key and a bar of El Cid soap that stank of bleach and looked as if it had already been used, he informed me that if I wanted female company he could send up a serving girl nicknamed Cock-Eye as soon as she returned from a home visit.

"She'll make you as good as new," he assured me.

I turned down the offer, claiming the onset of lumbago, and hurried up the stairs, wishing him good night. The room had the appearance and shape of a sarcophagus. One quick look was enough to persuade me that I should lie on the old bed fully clothed rather than getting under the sheets to fraternize with whatever was growing there. I covered myself with a threadbare blanket I found in the wardrobe—which at least smelled of mothballs—and turned off the light, trying to imagine that I was actually in the sort of suite that someone with a hundred thousand francs in the bank could afford. I barely slept all night.

. . .

I left the hotel halfway through the morning and made my way to the station, where I bought a first-class ticket, hoping I'd be able to sleep on the train to make up for the dreadful night I'd spent in that dive. Seeing that there were still twenty minutes to go before the train's departure, I went over to the row of public telephones. I gave the operator the number Ricardo Salvador had given me—that of his downstairs neighbor.

"I'd like to speak to Don Emilio, please."

"Speaking."

"My name is David Martín. I'm a friend of Señor Ricardo Salvador. He told me I could call him at this number in an emergency."

"Let's see . . . Can you wait a moment while we get him?"

I looked at the station clock.

"Yes. I'll wait. Thanks."

More than three minutes went by before I heard the sound of footsteps and then Ricardo Salvador's voice.

"Martín? Are you all right?"

"Yes."

"Thank goodness. I read about Roures in the newspaper and was very concerned about you. Where are you?"

"Señor Salvador, I don't have much time now. I need to leave Barcelona."

"Are you sure you're all right?"

"Yes. Listen. Alicia Marlasca is dead."

"The widow? Dead?"

A long silence. I thought I could hear Salvador sobbing and cursed myself for having broken the news to him so bluntly.

"Are you still there?"

"Yes . . ."

"I'm calling to warn you. You must be careful. Irene Sabino is alive and she's been following me. There is someone with her. I think it's Jaco."

"Jaco Corbera?"

"I'm not sure it's him. I think they know I'm on their trail and they're trying to silence all the people I've been speaking to. I think you were right."

"Why would Jaco return now?" Salvador asked. "It doesn't make sense."

"I don't know. I have to go now. I just wanted to warn you."

"Don't worry about me. If that bastard comes to visit me, I'll be ready for him. I've been ready for twenty-five years."

The stationmaster blew the whistle: the train was about to leave.

"Don't trust anyone. Do you hear me? I'll call you as soon as I get back."

"Thanks for calling, Martín. Be careful."

7

The train was beginning to glide past the platform as I took refuge in my compartment and collapsed on the seat. I abandoned myself to the flow of tepid air from the heating and the gentle rocking of the train. We left the city behind us, crossing the forest of factories and chimneys and escaping the shroud of scarlet light that covered it. Slowly the wasteland of railway depots and trains abandoned on sidings dissolved into an endless plain of fields, woodlands, rivers, and hills crowned with large, run-down houses and watchtowers. The occasional covered wagon or hamlet peered through a bank of mist. Small railway stations slipped by; bell towers and farmhouses loomed up like mirages.

At some point in the journey I fell asleep, and when I woke the landscape had changed dramatically. We were now passing through steep valleys with rocky crags rising between lakes and streams. The train skirted great forests that climbed the soaring mountains. After a while, the tangle of hills and tunnels cut into the rock gave way to a large open valley with never-ending pastures where herds of wild horses galloped across the snow and small stone villages appeared in the distance. The peaks of the Pyrenees rose up on the other side, their snow-covered slopes set alight by the amber glow of evening. In front of us was a jumble of houses and buildings clustered around a hill. The ticket inspector put his head through the door of my compartment and smiled.

"Next stop, Puigcerdà," he announced.

. . .

The train stopped and let out a blast of steam that inundated the platform. When I got out I was enveloped in a thick mist that smelled of electricity. Shortly afterwards, I heard the stationmaster's bell and the train set off again. As the coaches filed past, the shape of the station began to emerge around me. I was alone on the platform. A fine curtain of snow was falling, and to the west a red sun peeped below the vault of clouds, scattering the snow with tiny bright embers. I went over to the stationmaster's office and knocked on the glass door. He looked up, opened the door, and gazed at me distractedly.

"Could you tell me how to find a place called Villa San Antonio?"

He raised an eyebrow.

"The sanatorium?"

"I think so."

The stationmaster adopted the pensive air of someone trying to work out how best to offer directions to a stranger. Then, with the help of a whole catalog of gestures and expressions, he came up with the following:

"You have to walk right through the village, past the church square, until you reach the lake. On the other side of the lake there's a long avenue with large houses on either side that leads to Paseo de la Rigolisa. There, on a corner, you'll find a three-story house surrounded by a garden. That's the sanatorium."

"And do you know of anywhere I might find accommodation?"

"On the way you'll pass Hotel del Lago. Tell them Sebas sent you."

"Thank you."

"Good luck . . ."

I walked through the lonely streets of the village beneath the falling snow, looking for the outline of the church tower. On the way I passed a few locals, who bobbed their heads and looked at me suspiciously. When I reached the square, two men who were unloading coal from a cart pointed me in the right direction, and a couple of minutes later I found myself walking down a road that bordered a large, frozen lake surrounded by stately-looking mansions with pointed towers. The great expanse of white was studded with small rowing boats trapped in the ice and around it, like a ribbon, ran a promenade punctuated by benches and trees. I walked to the edge and gazed at the ice spread out at my feet. It must have been almost twenty centimeters thick and in some places it shone like opaque glass, hinting at the current of black water that flowed under its shell.

Hotel del Lago, a two-story house painted dark red, stood at the end of the lake. Before continuing on my way, I stopped to book a room for two nights and paid in advance. The receptionist informed me that the hotel was almost empty and I could take my pick of rooms.

"Room 101 has spectacular views of the sunrise over the lake," he suggested. "But if you prefer a room facing north I have—"

"You choose," I cut in, indifferent to the majestic beauty of the landscape.

"Then Room 101 it is. In the summer, it's the honeymooners' favorite."

He handed me the keys of the nuptial suite and informed me of the hours for dinner. I told him I'd return later and asked if Villa San Antonio was far from there. The receptionist adopted the same expression I had seen on the face of the stationmaster, first shaking his head, then giving me a friendly smile.

"It's quite near, about ten minutes' walk. If you take the promenade at the end of this street, you'll see it a short distance away. You can't miss it."

. . .

Ten minutes later I was standing by the gates of a large garden strewn with dead leaves half buried in the snow. Beyond the garden, Villa San Antonio rose up like a somber sentinel wrapped in a halo of golden light that radiated from the windows. As I crossed the garden my heart was pounding and my hands perspired despite the bitter cold. I walked up the stairs to the main door. The entrance hall was covered in black and white floor tiles like a chessboard and led to a staircase at the far end. There I saw a young woman in a nurse's uniform holding the hand of a man who was trembling and seemed to be eternally suspended between two steps, as if his whole life had suddenly become trapped in that moment.

"Good afternoon?" said a voice to my right.

Her eyes were black and severe, her features sharp, without a trace of warmth, and she had the serious air of one who has learned not to expect anything but bad news. She must have been in her early fifties, and although she wore the same uniform as the young nurse, everything about her exuded authority and rank.

"Good afternoon. I'm looking for someone called Cristina Sagnier. I have reason to believe she is staying here . . ."

The woman observed me without batting an eyelid.

"Nobody *stays* here, sir. This place is not a hotel or a guesthouse."

"I'm sorry. I've just come on a long journey in search of this person . . ."

"Don't apologize," said the nurse. "May I ask you if you are family or a close friend?"

"My name is David Martín. Is Cristina Sagnier here? Please . . ."

The nurse's expression softened and there followed a tiny smile. I took a deep breath.

"I'm Teresa, the sister in charge of night duty. If you'd be so kind as to follow me, Señor Martín, I'll take you to the office of Dr. Sanjuán."

"How is Señorita Sagnier? Can I see her?"

Another faint and impenetrable smile.

"This way, please."

The rectangular room had four blue walls but no windows and was lit by two lamps that hung from the ceiling, giving off a metallic light. The only three objects in the room were an empty table and two chairs. It was cold and the air smelled of disinfectant. The nurse had described the room as an office, but after ten minutes of waiting on my own, anchored to one of the chairs, all I could see was a cell. Even though the door was shut I could hear voices, sometimes isolated shouts, on the other side of the wall. I was beginning to lose all notion of how long I'd been there when the door opened and a man came in. He was in his midthirties and wore a white coat. His smile was as cold as the air that filled the room. Dr. Sanjuán, I imagined. He walked round the table and sat on the other chair, planting his hands on the desk and observing me with vague curiosity for a few moments.

"I realize you must be tired after your journey but I'd like to know why Señor Pedro Vidal isn't here," he said at last.

"He wasn't able to come."

The doctor kept his gaze fixed on me, waiting. His eyes were cold and he seemed like the type of person who listens but does not hear.

"Can I see her?"

"You can't see anyone unless you tell me the truth about why you're here."

I surrendered. I hadn't traveled a hundred and fifty kilometers just to lie.

"My name is Martín, David Martín. I'm a friend of Cristina Sagnier."

"Here we call her Señora de Vidal."

"I don't care what you call her. I want to see her. Now."

The doctor sighed.

"Are you the writer?"

I stood up impatiently.

"What sort of place is this? Why can't I see her?"

"Sit down, please. I beg you."

He pointed to the chair and waited for me to sit down again.

"May I ask when was the last time you saw her or spoke to her?"

"Weeks ago," I replied. "Why?"

"Do you know anyone who might have seen or spoken to her since then?"

"No . . . I don't know. What's going on?"

The doctor put his fingertips to his lips, measuring his words.

"Señor Martín, I'm afraid I have bad news."

I felt a knot in the pit of my stomach.

"What's wrong with her?"

The doctor did not reply, but I glimpsed a shadow of doubt in his eyes.

"I don't know," he said.

. . .

We walked along a short corridor flanked by metal doors. Dr. Sanjuán went in front of me, holding a bunch of keys in his hands. As we passed I thought I could hear voices whispering, suppressed laughter and sobs. The room was at the end of the corridor. The doctor opened the door but stopped at the threshold, his expression unreadable.

"Fifteen minutes," he said.

I went in and heard the doctor shut the door behind me. Before me lay a room with a high ceiling and white walls reflected in a floor of shining tiles. On one side stood a bed—a metallic frame surrounded by a white gauze curtain. It was empty. Large French windows looked out over the snowy garden, trees, and in the distance the outline of the lake. I didn't notice her until I'd taken a few steps into the room.

She was sitting in an armchair by the window, wearing a white nightdress, her hair up in a plait. I went round in front of her and looked straight at her, but her eyes didn't move. I knelt down next to her, but she didn't even blink. I put my hand over hers, but she didn't move a single muscle. Then I noticed the bandages covering her arms, from her wrists to her elbows, and the straps that tied her to the chair. I stroked her cheek, gathering a tear that trickled down her face.

"Cristina," I whispered.

Her eyes were blank: she seemed completely unaware of my presence. I brought a chair over and sat opposite her.

"It's David," I murmured.

For a quarter of an hour we remained like that, not speaking, her hand in mine, her eyes lost, and my questions unanswered. At some point I heard the door open again and felt someone taking me gently by the arm and pulling me away. It was Dr. Sanjuán. I let myself be led to the corridor without offering any resistance. The doctor shut the door and took me back to his freezing office. I collapsed into a chair, unable to utter a single word.

"Would you like me to leave you alone for a few minutes?" he asked.

I nodded. The doctor left the room, closing the door behind him. I stared at my right hand, which was shaking, and clenched my fist. I hardly felt the cold of that room or heard the shouts and voices that filtered through the walls. I only knew that I needed some air and had to get out of that place.

8

Dr. Sanjuán found me in the hotel dining room, sitting by the fire next to a plate of food I hadn't touched. There was nobody else there except for a maid who was going round the deserted tables, polishing the cutlery. Outside it had grown dark and the snow was still falling, like a dusting of powdered blue glass. The doctor walked over to my table and smiled at me.

"I thought I'd find you here," he said. "All visitors end up in this hotel. It's where I spent my first night in the village when I arrived ten years ago. What room were you given?"

"It's supposed to be the newlyweds' favorite, with views over the lake."

"Don't you believe it. That's what they say about all the rooms."

Away from the sanatorium and without his white coat, Dr. Sanjuán looked more relaxed, even friendly.

"I hardly recognized you without your uniform," I remarked.

"Medicine is like the army. The cowl maketh the monk," he replied. "How are you feeling?"

"I'm all right."

"I see. I missed you earlier, when I went back to the office to look for you."

"I needed some air."

"I understand. I was hoping you wouldn't be affected quite so much."

"Why?"

"Because I need you. Or rather, Cristina needs you."

I gave a deep sigh.

"You must think I'm a coward," I said.

The doctor shook his head.

"How long has she been like this?"

"Weeks. Practically since she arrived here. And she's getting steadily worse."

"Is she aware of where she is?"

"It's hard to tell," the doctor replied with a shrug.

"What happened to her?"

Dr. Sanjuán exhaled.

"She was found, four weeks ago, not far from here—in the village graveyard, lying on her father's grave. She was delirious and suffering from hypothermia. They brought her to the sanatorium because one of the Civil Guards recognized her from last year, when she spent a few months here, because of her father. A lot of people in the village knew her. We admitted her and she was kept under observation for a night or two. She was dehydrated and had probably not slept in days. Every now and then she regained consciousness, and when she did, she spoke about you. She said you were in great danger. She made me swear I wouldn't call anyone, not even her husband, until she was capable of doing so herself."

"Even so, why didn't you let Vidal know what had happened?"

"I would have but . . . You'll think this is absurd."

"What?"

"I was convinced that she was fleeing from something and thought it was my duty to help her."

"Fleeing from what?"

"I'm not sure," he said with an ambiguous expression.

"What is it you're not telling me?"

"I'm just a doctor. There are things I don't understand."

"What things?"

Dr. Sanjuán smiled nervously.

"Cristina thinks that something, or someone, has got inside her and wants to destroy her."

"Who?"

"I only know that she thinks it has something to do with you and that it frightens her. That's why I think nobody else can help her. It's also why I didn't let Vidal know, as I ought to have done. Because I knew that sooner or later you would turn up here."

He looked at me with a strange mixture of pity and despair.

"I'm fond of her too, Señor Martín. The months Cristina spent visiting her father . . . we ended up being good friends. I don't suppose she talked to you about me—there was no reason she would have. It was a very difficult time for her. She confided a lot of things in me, and I in her, things I've never told anyone else. In fact, I even proposed to her. So you see, even the doctors here are slightly nuts. Of course she refused me. I don't know why I'm telling you this."

"But she'll be all right again, won't she, doctor? She'll recover . . ."

Dr. Sanjuán turned his head toward the fire.

"I hope so," he replied.

"I want to take her away from here."

The doctor raised his eyebrows.

"Take her away? Where to?"

"Home."

"Señor Martín, let me be frank. Aside from the fact that you're not a relative or, indeed, the patient's husband—which is a legal requirement—Cristina is in no state to go anywhere."

"She's better off here with you, locked up in a rambling old house, tied to a chair and full of drugs? Don't tell me you've proposed to her again."

The doctor observed me carefully, ignoring the offense my words had clearly caused him.

"Señor Martín, I'm glad you're here because I believe that together we can help Cristina. I think your presence will allow her to come out of the place into which she has retreated. I believe it, because the only word she has uttered in the last two weeks is your name. Whatever happened to her, I think it had something to do with you."

The doctor was watching me as if he expected something from me, something that would answer all his questions.

"I thought she had abandoned me," I began. "We were about to run away together, leaving everything behind. I had gone out for a moment to buy the train tickets and do an errand. I wasn't away for more than ninety minutes but when I returned home, Cristina had left."

"Did anything happen before she left? Did you have an argument?"

I bit my lip.

"I wouldn't call it an argument."

"What would you call it?"

"I caught her looking through some papers relating to my work and I think she was offended by what she must have taken as a lack of trust."

"Was it something important?"

"No. Just a manuscript, a draft."

"May I ask what type of manuscript it was?"

I hesitated.

"A fable."

"For children?"

"Let's say for a family audience."

"I see."

"No, I don't think you do. There was no argument. Cristina was slightly annoyed because I wouldn't let her have a look, but that was all. When I left, she was fine, packing a few things. That manuscript is not important."

The doctor acquiesced, more out of courtesy than conviction.

"Could it be that while you were out someone else visited her?"

"I was the only one who knew she was there."

"Can you think of any reason she would have decided to leave the house before you returned?"

"No. Why?"

"It's only a question, Señor Martín. I'm trying to understand what happened between the moment you last saw her and her appearance here."

"Did she say what, or who, had got inside her?"

"It's just a manner of speaking, Señor Martín. Nothing has got inside Cristina. It's not unusual for patients who have suffered a traumatic experience to feel the presence of dead relatives or imaginary people, or even to disappear into their own minds and close every door to the outside world. It's an emotional response, a form of self-defense against feelings or emotions that seem unacceptable. But you mustn't worry about that now. What matters and what's going to help is that, if there is anyone who is important to her right now, that person is you. From what Cristina confided in me at the time, I know that she loves you, Señor Martín. She loves you as she's never loved anyone else, and certainly as she'll never love me. That's why I'm asking you to help me. Don't let yourself be blinded by fear or resentment. Help me, because we both want the same thing. We both want Cristina to be able to leave this place."

I felt ashamed.

"I'm sorry if—"

The doctor raised his hand to silence me. Then he stood up and put on his overcoat.

"I'll see you tomorrow," he said.

"Thank you, doctor."

"Thank *you*. For coming here."

. . .

The following morning I left the hotel just as the sun was beginning to rise over the frozen lake. A group of children were playing by the shore, throwing stones at the hull of a small boat wedged in the ice. It had stopped snowing and white mountains were visible in the distance. Large clouds paraded across the sky like monumental cities built of mist.

I reached Villa San Antonio shortly before nine o'clock. Dr. Sanjuán was waiting for me in the garden with Cristina. They were sitting in the sun and the doctor held Cristina's hand as he spoke to her. She barely glanced at him. When he saw me crossing the garden, he beckoned me over to join them. He had kept a chair for me opposite Cristina. I sat down and looked at her, her eyes on mine without seeing me.

"Cristina, look who's here," said the doctor.

I took Cristina's hand and moved closer to her.

"Speak to her," said the doctor.

I nodded, lost in her absent gaze, but could find no words. The doctor stood up and left us alone. I saw him disappear into the sanatorium, but not without first asking a nurse to keep a close eye on us. Ignoring the presence of the nurse, I pulled my chair even closer to Cristina's. I brushed her hair from her forehead and she smiled.

"Do you remember me?" I asked.

I could see my reflection in her eyes but didn't know whether she could see me or hear my voice.

"The doctor says you'll get better soon and we'll be able to go home. Or wherever you like. I'll leave the tower house and we'll go far away, just as you wanted. A place where nobody will know us and nobody will care who we are or where we're from."

Her hands were covered with long woolen gloves that hid the bandages on her arms. She had lost weight and there were deep lines on her skin; her lips were cracked and her eyes dull and lifeless. All I could do was smile and stroke her cheek and her forehead, talking nonstop, telling her how much I'd missed her and how I'd looked for her everywhere. We spent a couple of hours like that, until the doctor returned and Cristina was taken indoors. I stayed there, sitting in the garden, not knowing where else to go, until I saw Dr. Sanjuán reappear at the door. He came over and sat down beside me.

"She didn't say a word," I said. "I don't think she was even aware that I was here."

"You're wrong, my friend," he replied. "This is a long process, but I can assure you that your presence helps her—a lot."

I accepted the doctor's meager reassurance and kindhearted lie.

"We'll try again tomorrow," he said.

It was only midday.

"And what am I going to do until tomorrow?" I asked him.

"Aren't you a writer? Then write. Write something for her."

9

I walked round the lake back to the hotel. The receptionist had told me where to find the only bookshop in the village, and I was able to buy some blank sheets of paper and a fountain pen that must have been there since time immemorial. Thus equipped, I locked myself in my room. I moved the table over to the window and asked for a flask of coffee. I spent almost an hour gazing at the lake and the mountains in the distance before writing a single word. I remembered the old photograph Cristina had given me, that image she had never been able to place, of a girl walking along a wooden jetty that stretched out to sea. I imagined myself walking down that pier, my steps following behind her, and slowly the words began to flow and the outline of a story emerged. I knew I was going to write the story that Cristina could never remember, the story that had led her, as a child, to walk over those shimmering waters holding on to a stranger's hand. I would write the tale of a memory that never was, the memory of a stolen life. The images and the light that began to appear between sentences took me back to the old, shadowy Barcelona that had shaped us both. I wrote until the sun had set and there was not a drop of coffee left in the flask, until the frozen lake was lit up by a blue moon and my eyes and hands were aching. I let the pen drop and pushed aside the sheets of paper lying on the table. When the receptionist came to knock on my door to ask if I was coming down for dinner, I didn't hear him. I had fallen fast asleep, for once dreaming and believing that words, even my own, had the power to heal.

. . .

Four days passed with the same rhythm. I rose at dawn and went out onto the balcony to watch the sun tint with scarlet the lake at my feet. I would arrive at the sanatorium around half past eight and usually find Dr. Sanjuán sitting on the entrance steps, gazing at the garden with a steaming cup of coffee in his hands.

"Do you never sleep, doctor?" I would ask.

"No more than you," he replied.

Around nine o'clock the doctor would take me to Cristina's room and open the door, then leave us. I always found her sitting in the same armchair facing the window. I would bring over a chair and take her hand. She was barely aware of my presence. Then I would read out the pages I'd written for her the night before. Every day I started again from the beginning. Sometimes, when I interrupted my reading and looked at her, I would be surprised to discover the hint of a smile on her lips. I spent the day with her until the doctor returned in the evening and asked me to leave. Then I would trudge back to the hotel through the snow, eat some dinner, and go up to my room to continue writing until I was overcome by exhaustion. The days ceased to have a name.

When I went into Cristina's room on the fifth day, as I did every morning, the armchair in which she was usually waiting for me was empty. I looked around anxiously and found her on the floor, curled up into a ball in a corner, clasping her knees, her face covered with tears. When she saw me she smiled, and I realized that she had recognized me. I knelt down next to her and hugged her. I don't remember ever having been as happy as I was during those miserable seconds when I felt her breath on my face and saw that a glimmer of light had returned to her eyes.

"Where have you been?" she asked.

That afternoon Dr. Sanjuán gave me permission to take her out for an hour. We walked down to the lake and sat on a bench. She started to tell me a dream she'd had, about a child who lived in the dark maze of a

town in which the streets and buildings were alive and fed on the souls
of its inhabitants. In her dream, as in the story I had been reading to her,
the girl managed to escape and came to a jetty that stretched out over an
endless sea. She was holding the hand of the faceless stranger with no
name who had saved her and who now went with her to the very end of
the wooden platform, where someone was waiting for her, someone she
would never see, because her dream, like the story I had been reading to
her, was unfinished.

. . .

Cristina had a vague recollection of Villa San Antonio and Dr. Sanjuán. She blushed when she told me she thought he'd proposed to her a
week ago. Time and space seemed to be confused in her mind. Sometimes she thought that her father had been admitted to one of the rooms
and she'd come to visit him. A moment later she couldn't remember how
she'd got there and at times she ceased to care. She remembered that I'd
gone out to buy the train tickets and referred to the morning she disappeared as if it were just the previous day. Sometimes she confused me
with Vidal and asked me to forgive her. At others, fear cast a shadow over
her face and she began to tremble.

"He's getting closer," she would say. "I have to go. Before he sees you."

Then she would grow silent, unaware of my presence, unaware of
the world itself, as if something had dragged her to some remote and inaccessible place.

After a few days, the certainty that Cristina had lost her mind began to affect me deeply. My initial hope became tinged with bitterness,
and on occasion, when I returned at night to my hotel cell, I felt that old
pit of darkness and hatred, which I had thought forgotten, opening up
inside me. Dr. Sanjuán, who watched over me with the same care and
tenacity with which he treated his patients, had warned me that this
would happen.

"Don't give up hope, my friend," he would say. "We're making
great progress. Have faith."

I nodded meekly and returned day after day to the sanatorium to take Cristina out for a stroll as far as the lake and listen to the dreamed memories that she'd already described dozens of times but that she discovered anew every day. Each day she would ask me where I'd been, why I hadn't come back to fetch her, and why I'd left her alone. Each day she looked at me from her invisible cage and asked me to hold her tight. Each day when I said good-bye to her, she asked me if I loved her and I always gave her the same reply.

"I'll always love you," I would say. "Always."

. . .

One night I was woken by the sound of someone knocking on my door. It was three in the morning. I stumbled over, in a daze, and found one of the nurses from the sanatorium standing in the doorway.

"Dr. Sanjuán has asked me to come and fetch you."

"What's happened?"

Ten minutes later I was walking through the gates of Villa San Antonio. The screams could be heard from the garden. Cristina had apparently locked the door of her room from the inside. Dr. Sanjuán, who looked as if he hadn't slept for a week, and two male nurses were trying to force the door open. Inside, Cristina could be heard shouting and banging on the walls, knocking down furniture as if she were destroying everything she could find.

"Who is in there with her?" I asked, petrified.

"Nobody," replied the doctor.

"But she's speaking to someone," I protested.

"She's alone."

An orderly rushed up, carrying a large crowbar.

"It's the only thing I could find," he said.

The doctor nodded and the orderly levered the crowbar between the door and the frame.

"How was she able to lock herself in?" I asked.

"I don't know."

For the first time I thought I saw fear in the doctor's face, and he avoided my eyes. The orderly was about to force the door when suddenly there was silence on the other side.

"Cristina?" called the doctor.

There was no reply. The door finally gave way and flew open with a bang. I followed the doctor into the room. It was dark. The window was open and an icy wind was blowing. The chairs, tables, and armchair had been knocked over and the walls were stained with an irregular line of what looked like black ink. It was blood. There was no trace of Cristina.

The male nurses ran out to the balcony and scanned the garden for footprints in the snow. The doctor looked right and left, searching for Cristina. Then we heard laughter coming from the bathroom. I went to the door and opened it. The floor was scattered with bits of glass. Cristina was sitting on the tiles, leaning against the metal bathtub like a broken doll. Her hands and feet were bleeding, covered in cuts and splinters of glass, and her blood still trickled down the cracks in the mirror she had destroyed with her fists. I put my arms around her and searched her eyes. She smiled.

"I didn't let him in," she said.

"Who?"

"He wanted me to forget, but I didn't let him in," she repeated.

The doctor knelt down beside me and examined the wounds covering Cristina's body.

"Please," he murmured, pushing me aside. "Not now."

One of the male nurses had rushed to fetch a stretcher. I helped him lift Cristina onto it and held her hand as they wheeled her to a treatment room. There, Dr. Sanjuán injected her with a sedative and in a matter of seconds her consciousness stole away. I stayed by her side, looking into her eyes until they became empty mirrors and one of the nurses led me gently from the room. I stood there, in the middle of a dark corridor that smelled of disinfectant, my hands and clothes stained with blood. I leaned against the wall and then slid to the floor.

· · ·

Cristina woke up the following morning to find herself lying on a bed, bound with leather straps, locked up in a windowless room with no other light than the pale glow from a bulb on the ceiling. I had spent the night in a corner, sitting on a chair, observing her, with no notion of time passing. Suddenly she opened her eyes and grimaced at the stabbing pain from the wounds that covered her arms.

"David?" she called out.

"I'm here," I replied.

When I reached the bed I leaned over so that she could see my face and the anemic smile I'd rehearsed for her.

"I can't move."

"They've strapped you down. It's for your own good. As soon as the doctor comes he'll take them off."

"You take them off."

"I can't. It must be the doctor—"

"Please," she begged.

"Cristina, it's better—"

"Please."

I saw pain and fear in her eyes but above all a lucidity and a presence that had not been there in all the days I had visited her in that place. She was herself again. I untied the first two straps, which crossed over her shoulders and waist, and stroked her face. She was shaking.

"Are you cold?"

She shook her head.

"Do you want me to call the doctor?"

She shook her head again.

"David, look at me."

I sat on the edge of the bed and met her gaze.

"You must destroy it," she said.

"I don't understand."

"You must destroy it."

"What must I destroy?"

"The book."

"Cristina, I'd better call the doctor—"

"No. Listen to me."

She grabbed my hand.

"The morning you went to buy the tickets, do you remember? I went up to your study again and opened the trunk."

I took a breath.

"I found the manuscript and began to read it."

"It's just a fable, Cristina . . ."

"Don't lie to me. I've read it, David. At least enough to know that I had to destroy it."

"You don't need to worry about that now. I told you: I've abandoned the manuscript."

"But it hasn't abandoned you. I tried to burn it . . ."

For a moment I let go of her hand when I heard those words, repressing the surge of anger I felt when I remembered the burned matches I'd found on the floor of the study.

"You tried to burn it?"

"But I couldn't," she muttered. "There was someone else in the house."

"There was no one in the house, Cristina. Nobody."

"As soon as I lit the match and held it close to the manuscript, I sensed him behind me. I felt a blow to the back of my neck and then I fell."

"Who hit you?"

"It was all very dark, as if the daylight had suddenly vanished. I turned round but could see only his eyes. Like the eyes of a wolf."

"Cristina . . ."

"He took the manuscript from my hands and put it back in the trunk."

"Cristina, you're not well. Let me call the doctor."

"You're not listening to me."

I smiled at her and kissed her on the forehead.

"Of course I'm listening to you. But there was no one else in the house."

She closed her eyes and tilted her head, moaning as if my words were like daggers cutting her inside.

"I'm going to call the doctor."

I bent over to kiss her again and then stood up. I went toward the door, feeling her eyes on my back.

"Coward," she said.

When I came back to the room with Dr. Sanjuán, Cristina had undone the last strap and was staggering round the room, leaving bloody footprints on the white tiles. We laid her back on the bed and held her down. Cristina shouted and fought with such anger it made my blood freeze. The noise alerted the other staff. An orderly helped us restrain her while the doctor tied the straps. Once she was immobilized, the doctor looked at me severely.

"I'm going to sedate her again. Stay here and this time don't even think of untying her straps."

I was left alone with her for a moment but could not calm her. Cristina went on fighting to escape. I held her face and tried to catch her eye.

"Cristina, please—"

She spat at me.

"Go away."

The doctor returned with a nurse who carried a metal tray with a syringe, dressings, and a glass bottle containing a yellowish solution.

"Leave the room," he ordered.

I went to the doorway. The nurse held Cristina against the bed and the doctor injected the sedative into her arm. Cristina's shrieks pierced the room. I covered my ears and went out into the corridor.

Coward, I told myself. Coward.

10

Beyond Villa San Antonio, a tree-lined path led out of the village, following an irrigation channel. The framed map in the hotel dining room
bestowed on it the saccharine name of Lovers' Lane. That afternoon, after
leaving the sanatorium, I ventured down the gloomy path, which was
suggestive more of loneliness than of romance. I walked for about half an
hour without meeting a soul, leaving the village behind, until the sharp
outline of Villa San Antonio and the large rambling houses that surrounded the lake were small cardboard cutouts on the horizon. I sat on
one of the benches dotting the path and watched the sun setting at the
other end of the Cerdanya valley. Some two hundred meters from where
I sat, I could see the silhouette of a small, isolated country chapel in the
middle of a snow-covered field. Without quite knowing why, I got up
and made my way toward it. When I was about a dozen meters away, I
noticed that the chapel had no door. The stone walls had been blackened
by the flames that had devoured the building. I climbed the steps to
what had once been the entrance and went in. The remains of burned
pews and loose pieces of timber that had fallen from the ceiling were
scattered among the ashes. Weeds had crept into the building and grown
up around the former altar. The fading light shone through the narrow
stone windows. I sat on what remained of a pew in front of the altar and
heard the wind whispering through the cracks in the burned-out vault. I
looked up and wished I had even a breath of the faith my old friend Sem-

pere had possessed—his faith in God or in books—with which I could pray to God, or to hell, to give me another chance and let me take Cristina away from that place.

"Please," I murmured, fighting back the tears, a defeated man pitifully begging a God in whom he had never trusted. I looked around at that holy site filled with nothing but ruins and ashes, emptiness and loneliness and knew that I would go back to fetch her that very night, with no more miracle or blessing than my own determination to tear her away from the clutches of that timid, infatuated doctor who had decided to turn her into his own Sleeping Beauty. I would set fire to the sanatorium rather than allow anyone to touch her again. I would take her home and die by her side. Hatred and anger would light my way.

. . .

I left the old chapel at nightfall and crossed the silvery field, which glowed in the moonlight, returning to the tree-lined path. In the dark, I followed the trail of the irrigation channel until I glimpsed the lights of Villa San Antonio in the distance and the citadel of towers and attic windows surrounding the lake. When I reached the sanatorium I didn't bother to ring the bell next to the wrought-iron gates. After jumping over the wall, I crept across the garden, then went round the building to one of the back entrances. It was locked from the inside but I didn't hesitate for a moment before smashing the glass with my elbow and grabbing hold of the door handle. I went down the corridor, listening to the voices and whisperings, catching the aroma of broth that rose from the kitchen, until I reached the room at the end where the good doctor had imprisoned Cristina, his fantasy princess, lying forever in a limbo of drugs and straps.

I had expected to find the door locked, but the handle yielded beneath my hand. I pushed the door open and went into the room. The first thing I noticed was that I could see my own breath floating in front of my face. The second thing was that the white-tiled floor was stained with bloody footprints. The large window that overlooked the garden was open and the curtains fluttered in the wind. The bed was empty. I drew closer and picked up one of the leather straps with which the doctor and the orderly had tied Cristina down. They had all been cleanly cut, as if they were paper. I went out into the garden, where I saw a trail of red footprints across the snow. I followed it to the stone wall surrounding the grounds and found yet more blood. I climbed up and jumped over to the other side. The erratic footprints led off toward the village. I remember that I began to run.

I followed the tracks as far as the park that bordered the lake. A full moon burned over the large sheet of ice. That is when I saw her. She was limping over the frozen lake, a line of blood behind her, the nightdress covering her body trembling in the breeze. By the time I reached the shore, Cristina had walked about thirty meters toward the center of the lake. I shouted her name and she stopped. Slowly she turned and I saw her smile as a cobweb of cracks began to weave itself beneath her feet. I jumped onto the ice, feeling the frozen surface buckle, and ran toward her. Cristina stood still, looking at me. The cracks under her feet were expanding into a mesh of black veins. The ice was giving way and I fell flat on my face.

"I love you," I heard her say.

I crawled toward her, but the web of cracks was growing and now encircled her. Barely a few meters separated us when I heard the ice finally break. Black jaws snapped open and swallowed her up into a pool of tar. As soon as she disappeared under the surface, the plates of ice began to join up, sealing the opening through which Cristina had plunged.

Caught by the current, her body slid a couple of meters toward me under the ice. I managed to pull myself to the place where she had become trapped and I pounded the ice frantically. Cristina, her eyes open and her hair streaming out around her, watched me from the other side of the translucent sheet. I hammered at the ice until I'd shattered my hands, but in vain. Cristina never let her eyes stray from mine. She placed her hand on the ice and smiled. The last bubbles of air were escaping from her lips and her pupils dilated a final time. A second later, she began to sink forever into the blackness.

11

I didn't return to my room to collect my things. From where I was hiding among the trees by the lake, I saw the doctor and a couple of Civil Guards approach the hotel, then spied them talking to the receptionist through the French windows. I crossed the village, stealing through the deserted streets, until I came to the station, which was buried in fog. Two gas lamps helped me distinguish the shape of a train waiting at the platform, its dark metal skeleton reflecting the red light of the stop signal at the end of the station. The locomotive had been shut down and tears of ice hung from its rails and levers. The carriages were in darkness, the windows veiled with frost. No light shone from the stationmaster's office. The train was not scheduled to leave for several hours, and the station was empty.

I went over to one of the carriages and tried the door but it was bolted shut. I stepped down onto the track and walked round the train. Under cover of darkness I climbed onto the platform linking the guard's van to the rear coach and tried my luck with the connecting door. It was open. I slipped into the coach and stumbled through the gloom until I reached one of the compartments. I went in and bolted the door. Trembling with cold, I collapsed onto the seat. I didn't dare close my eyes, fearing I would see Cristina's face again, looking at me from beneath the ice. Minutes went by, perhaps hours. At some point I asked myself why I was hiding and why I couldn't feel anything.

I cocooned myself in that void and waited, hidden away like a fugitive, listening to a thousand groans of metal and wood as they contracted in the cold. I scanned the shadows beyond the windows until finally the beam of a lamp glanced across the walls of the coach and I heard voices on the platform. I cleared a peephole with my fingers through the film of mist that coated the windowpane and saw the engine driver and a couple of railway workers making their way toward the front of the train. Some ten meters away, the stationmaster was talking to the two Civil Guards I'd seen with the doctor earlier. I saw him nod and extract a bunch of keys, then he walked toward the train, followed by the two guards. I pulled back from the window. A few seconds later I heard the click of the carriage door as it opened, then footsteps approaching. I unbolted the door, leaving the compartment unlocked, and lay down on the floor under one of the rows of seats, pressing my body against the wall. I heard the Civil Guards drawing closer and saw the beam from their flashlights drawing needles of blue light through the compartment window. When the steps stopped by my compartment I held my breath. The voices subsided. I heard the door being opened and a pair of boots passed within centimeters of my face. The guard remained there for a few seconds, then left and closed the door.

I stayed where I was, motionless, as he moved away down the carriage. Presently I heard a rattling and warm air breathed out through the radiator grille by my face. An hour later the first light of dawn crept slowly through the windows. I came out from my hiding place and looked outside. Travelers walked alone or in couples up the platform, dragging their suitcases and bundles. The rumble of the locomotive could be felt through the walls and floor of the coach. After a few minutes the travelers began to climb into the train and the ticket collector turned on the lights. I sat on the seat by the window and acknowledged some of the passengers who walked by my compartment. When the large clock in the station struck eight, the train began to move. Only then did I close my eyes and hear the church bells ringing in the distance, like the echo of a curse.

. . .

The return journey was plagued with delays. Some overhead power cables had fallen and we didn't reach Barcelona until the afternoon of that Friday, 24 January. The city was buried under a crimson sky across which stretched a web of black smoke. It was hot, as if winter had suddenly departed, and a dirty, damp smell rose from the sewers. When I opened the front door of the tower house I found a white envelope on the ground. I recognized the wax seal and didn't bother to pick it up because I knew exactly what it contained: a reminder of my meeting with the boss that very evening in his rambling old house by Güell Park, at which I was to hand over the manuscript. I climbed the stairs and opened the main door of the apartment. Without turning on the light I went straight up to the study, where I walked over to one of the windows and stared back at the room touched by the flames of that infernal sky. I imagined her there, just as she had described, kneeling by the trunk. Opening it and pulling out the folder with the manuscript. Reading those accursed pages with the certainty that she must destroy them. Lighting the matches and drawing the flame to the paper.

There was someone else in the house.

I went over to the trunk but stopped a few paces from it, as if I were standing behind her, spying on her. I leaned forward and opened it. The manuscript was still there, waiting for me. I stretched out my hand to touch the folder gently with my fingertips. Then I saw it. The silver shape shone at the bottom of the trunk like a pearl at the bottom of a lake. I picked it up between two fingers and examined it. The angel brooch.

"Son of a bitch," I heard myself say.

I pulled the box containing my father's old revolver from the back of the wardrobe and opened the cylinder to make sure it was loaded. I put the remaining contents of the ammunition box in the left pocket of my coat, then wrapped the weapon in a cloth and put in into my right-hand pocket. Before leaving I stopped for a moment to gaze at the stranger who looked at me from the mirror in the entrance hall. I smiled, a calm hatred burning in my veins, and went out into the night.

12

Andreas Corelli's house stood out on the hillside against the blanket of dark red clouds. Behind me, the dark forest of Güell Park gently swayed. A breeze stirred the branches, making the leaves hiss like snakes. I stopped by the entrance and looked up at the house. There was not a single light on in the whole building and the shutters on the French windows were closed. I could hear the panting of the dogs that prowled behind the walls of the park, following my scent. I pulled the revolver out of my pocket and turned back toward the park gates, where I could make out the shape of the animals, liquid shadows watching me from the blackness.

I walked up to the main door of the house and gave three dry raps with the knocker. I didn't wait for a reply. I would have blown it open with a shot, but that wasn't necessary: the door was already open. I turned the bronze handle, releasing the bolt, and the oak door slowly swung inward under its own weight. The long passage opened up before me, a sheet of dust covering the floor like fine sand. I took a few steps toward the staircase that rose up on one side of the entrance hall, disappearing in a spiral of shadows. Then I walked along the corridor that led to the sitting room. Dozens of eyes followed me from the gallery of old photographs covering the wall. The only sounds I could hear were my own footsteps and breathing. I reached the end of the corridor and stopped. The strange, reddish glow of the night filtered through the shutters in narrow blades of light. I raised the revolver and stepped into the sitting room, my eyes adjusting to the dark. The pieces of furniture were in the same places as before, but even in that faint light I noticed that they looked old and were covered in dust. Ruins. The curtains were frayed and the paint on the walls was peeling off in strips. I went over to one of the French windows to open the shutters and let in some light, but just before I reached it I realized I was not alone. I froze and then turned around slowly.

His silhouette, sitting in the usual armchair in the corner of the room, was unmistakable. The light that bled in through the shutters revealed his shiny shoes and the outline of his suit. His face was buried in shadows, but I knew he was looking at me. And I knew he was smiling. I raised the revolver and pointed it at him.

"I know what you've done," I said.

Corelli didn't move a muscle. His figure remained motionless, like a spider waiting to jump. I took a step forward, pointing the gun at his face. I thought I heard a sigh in the dark and, for a moment, the reddish light caught his eyes and I was certain he was going to pounce on me. I fired. The weapon's recoil hit my forearm like the blow of a hammer. A cloud of blue smoke rose from the gun. One of Corelli's hands fell from the arm of the chair and swung, his fingernails grazing the floor. I fired again. The bullet hit him in the chest and opened a smoking hole in his clothes. I was left holding the revolver with both hands, not daring to take a single step, transfixed in front of the motionless shape in the armchair. The swaying of his arm gradually came to a halt and his body was still. There was no sound at all, no hint of movement, from the body that had just received two bullet wounds—one in the face, the other in the chest. I moved back a few steps toward the French window and kicked it open, not taking my eyes off the armchair where Corelli lay. A column of hazy light cut a passageway through the room from the balustrade outside to the corner, revealing the face and body of the boss. I tried to swallow, but my mouth was dry. The first shot had ripped open a hole between his eyes. The second had pierced his lapel. Yet there was not a single drop of blood. In its place a fine, shiny dust spilled out down his clothes, like sand slipping through an hourglass. His eyes shone and his lips were frozen in a sarcastic smile. It was a dummy.

I lowered the revolver, my hands still shaking, and edged closer. I bent over the grotesque puppet and tentatively stretched my hand toward its face. For a moment I feared that those glass eyes would suddenly move or those hands with their long, polished fingernails would hurl themselves round my neck. I touched the cheek with my fingertips. Enameled wood. I couldn't help but let out a bitter laugh—one wouldn't expect anything less from the boss. Once again I confronted that mocking grin and I hit the puppet so hard with the gun that it collapsed to the ground and I started kicking it. The wooden frame began to lose its shape until arms and legs were twisted together in an impossible position. I moved back a few steps and looked around me. The large canvas with the figure of the angel was still on the wall: I tore it down with one great tug. Behind the picture was the door that led into the basement—I remembered it from the night I'd fallen asleep there. I tried the handle. The door was open. I looked down the staircase, which led into a well of darkness, then went back to the sitting room, to the chest of drawers from which I'd seen Corelli take the hundred thousand francs during our first meeting in that house. In one of the drawers I found a tin with candles and matches. For a moment I wavered, wondering whether the boss had also left those things there on purpose, hoping I would find them just as I had found the dummy. I lit one of the candles and crossed the sitting room to the door. I glanced at the fallen doll one last time and, holding the candle up high, my right hand firmly gripping the revolver, I prepared to go down.

I descended carefully, stopping on each step to look back over my shoulder. When I reached the basement I held the candle as far away from me as I could and moved it around in a semicircle. Everything was still there: the operating table, the gas lamps, and the tray with surgical instruments. Everything covered with a patina of dust and cobwebs. But there was something else. Other dummies could be seen leaning against the wall, as immobile as the puppet of the boss. I left the candle on the operating table and walked over to the inert bodies. Among them, I recognized the butler who had served us that night and the chauffeur who had driven me home after my dinner with Corelli in the garden. There were other figures I was unable to identify. One of them was turned against the wall, its face hidden. I poked it with the end of the gun, making it spin round, and a second later found myself staring at my own image. I felt a shiver down my spine. The doll that looked like me had only half a face. The other half was unfinished. I was about to crush it with my foot when I heard a child's laughter coming from the top of the steps.

I held my breath. Then came a few dry, clicking sounds. I ran back up the stairs, and when I reached the sitting room the figure of the boss was no longer where I'd left it. Footprints trailed off toward the corridor that led to the exit. I cocked the gun and followed the tracks, pausing at the entrance to the corridor. The footprints stopped halfway down. I searched for the hidden shape of the boss among the shadows but saw no sign of him. At the end, the main door was still open. I advanced cautiously toward the point where the trail gave out. It took me a few seconds to notice that the gap I remembered between the portraits on the wall was no longer there. Instead there was a new frame, and in that frame, in a photograph that looked as if it had been taken with the same camera as the rest of the macabre collection, I saw Cristina dressed in white, her gaze lost in the eye of the lens. She was not alone. Two arms enveloped her, holding her up. They were the arms of a smiling man: Andreas Corelli.

13

I set off down the hill toward the tangle of dark streets that formed the Gracia neighborhood. There I found a café in which a large group of locals had assembled and were angrily discussing politics or football—it was hard to tell which. I dodged in and out of the crowd, through a cloud of smoke and noise, until I reached the bar. The bartender gave me a vaguely hostile look with which I imagined he received all strangers—anyone living more than a couple of streets beyond his establishment, that is.

"I need to use a phone," I said.

"The telephone is for customers only."

"Then get me a brandy. And the telephone."

The bartender picked up a glass and pointed toward a corridor on the other side of the room with a sign above it saying TOILETS. At the end of the passage, opposite the entrance to the toilets, I found what was trying to pass for a telephone booth, exposed to the intense stench of ammonia and the noise that filtered through from the café. I took the receiver off the hook and waited until I had a line. A few seconds later an operator from the exchange replied.

"I need to make a call to a law firm. The name of the lawyer is Valera, number 442 Avenida Diagonal."

The operator took a couple of minutes to find the number and connect me. I waited, holding the receiver with one hand and blocking my left ear with the other. Finally she confirmed that she was putting my call through and moments later I recognized the voice of Valera's secretary.

"I'm sorry, but Señor Valera isn't here right now."

"It's important. Tell him my name is Martín. David Martín. It's a matter of life and death."

"I know who you are, Señor Martín. I'm sorry, but I can't put you through because he's not here. It's half past nine at night and he left the office a long time ago."

"Then give me his home address."

"I cannot give you that information, Señor Martín. I do apologize. If you wish, you can phone tomorrow morning and—"

I hung up and again waited for a line. This time I gave the operator the number Ricardo Salvador had given me. His neighbor answered the phone and told me he would go up to see whether the ex-policeman was in. Salvador was soon on the line.

"Martín? Are you all right? Are you in Barcelona?"

"I've just arrived."

"You must be careful. The police are looking for you. They came round here asking questions about you and Alicia Marlasca."

"Víctor Grandes?"

"I think so. He came with a couple of big guys I didn't like the look of. I think he wants to pin the deaths of Roures and Marlasca's widow on you. You'd better keep your eyes peeled—they're probably watching you. If you like, you could come here."

"Thanks, Señor Salvador. I'll think about it. I don't want to get you into any more trouble."

"Whatever you do, watch out. I think you were right: Jaco is back. I don't know why, but he's back. Do you have a plan?"

"I'm going to try to find Valera, the lawyer. I think the publisher for whom Marlasca worked is at the heart of all this, and I think Valera is the only person who knows the truth."

Salvador paused for a moment.

"Do you want me to come with you?"

"I don't think that will be necessary. I'll call you once I've spoken to Valera."

"As you wish. Are you armed?"

"Yes."

"I'm glad to hear that."

"Señor Salvador . . . Roures spoke to me about a woman in the Somorrostro area whom Marlasca had consulted. Someone he had met through Irene Sabino."

"The Witch of Somorrostro."

"What do you know about her?"

"There isn't much to know. I don't think she even exists, the same as this mysterious publisher. What you need to worry about is Jaco and the police."

"I'll bear that in mind."

"Call me as soon as you know anything, will you?"

"I will. Thanks."

I hung up and as I passed the bar I left a few coins to cover the calls and the glass of brandy, which was still there, untouched.

Twenty minutes later I was standing outside 442 Avenida Diagonal, looking up at the lights that were on in Valera's office, at the top of the building. The porter's lodge was closed, but I banged on the door until the porter peered out with a distinctly unfriendly expression on his face. As soon as he'd opened the door a little to get rid of me, I gave it a push and slipped into the hallway, ignoring his protests. I went straight to the lift. The porter tried to stop me by grabbing hold of my arm, but I threw him a look that quickly dissuaded him.

When Valera's secretary opened the door, her expression rapidly changed from surprise to fear, especially when I stuck my foot in the gap to make sure she didn't slam the door in my face and went in without being invited.

"Let the lawyer know I'm here," I said. "Now."

The secretary looked at me, her face completely white.

I took her by the elbow and pushed her into the lawyer's office. The lights were on, but there was no trace of Valera. The terrified secretary sobbed, and I realized that I was digging my fingers into her arm. I let go and she retreated a few steps. She was shaking. I sighed and tried to make some sort of calming gesture that only served to reveal the gun tucked into the waistband of my trousers.

"Please, Señor Martín. I swear that Señor Valera isn't here."

"I believe you. Calm down. I only want to talk to him. That's all."

The secretary nodded. I smiled at her.

"Please be so kind as to pick up the telephone and call him at home," I said firmly.

The secretary lifted the receiver and murmured the lawyer's number to the operator. When she got a reply she handed me the phone.

"Good evening," I ventured.

"Martín, what an unfortunate surprise," said Valera at the other end of the line. "May I know what you're doing in my office at this time of night, aside from terrorizing my employees?"

"My apologies for any trouble I may be causing, Señor Valera, but I urgently need to locate your client Señor Andreas Corelli, and you're the only person who can help me."

A long silence.

"I'm afraid you're mistaken, Señor Martín. I cannot help you."

"I was hoping to resolve this amicably, Señor Valera."

"You don't understand, Martín. I don't know Señor Corelli."

"Excuse me?"

"I've never seen him or spoken to him, and I certainly don't know where to find him."

"Let me remind you that he hired you to get me out of police headquarters."

"A couple of weeks before that, we received a check with a letter explaining that you were an associate of his, that Inspector Grandes was harassing you, and that we should take care of your defense if it became necessary to do so. With the letter came the envelope that he asked us to hand to you personally. All I did was deposit the check and ask my contact at police headquarters to let me know if you were ever taken there.

That's what happened, and you'll remember that I got you out by threatening Grandes with a whole storm of trouble if he didn't agree to expedite your release. I don't think you can complain about our services."

At that point the silence was mine.

"If you don't believe me, ask Señorita Margarita to show you the letter," Valera added.

"What about your father?" I asked.

"My father?"

"Your father and Marlasca had dealings with Corelli. He must have known something . . ."

"I can assure you that my father was never directly in touch with this Señor Corelli. All his correspondence, if indeed there was any—because there is absolutely nothing in the files at the office—was dealt with personally by the deceased Señor Marlasca. In fact, and since you ask, I can tell you that my father even doubted the existence of this Señor Corelli, especially during the final months of Señor Marlasca's life, when he began to—how shall I say it—have contact with that woman."

"What woman?"

"The chorus girl."

"Irene Sabino?"

I heard him give an irritated sigh.

"Before he died, Señor Marlasca arranged a fund, administered and managed by our firm, from which a series of payments were to be made to an account in the name of some people called Juan Corbera and María Antonia Sanahuja."

Jaco and Irene Sabino, I thought.

"What was the size of the fund?"

"It was a deposit in foreign currency. I seem to remember it was something like a hundred thousand French francs."

"Did Marlasca say where he'd obtained that money?"

"We're a law firm, not a detective agency. Our company merely followed the instructions stipulated in Señor Marlasca's last wishes; we did not question them."

"What other instructions did he leave?"

"Nothing special. Simple payments to third parties that had nothing to do with the office or with his family."

"Do you remember any one in particular?"

"My father took charge of these matters himself, to avoid any of the office employees having access to information that might be, let us say, awkward."

"And didn't your father find it odd that his ex-partner should wish to hand over that sum of money to strangers?"

"Of course he thought it was odd. A lot of things seemed odd to him."

"Do you remember where those payments were sent?"

"How could I possibly remember? It must have been twenty-five years ago."

"Make an effort," I said. "For Señorita Margarita's sake."

The secretary gave me a terrified look, to which I responded with a wink.

"Don't you dare lay a finger on her," Valera threatened.

"Don't give me ideas," I cut in. "How's your memory? Is it refreshed?"

"I could have a look at my father's private diaries."

"Where are they?"

"Here, among his papers. But it will take a few hours . . ."

I put down the phone and looked at Valera's secretary, who had burst into tears. I offered her a handkerchief and gave her a pat on the shoulder.

"Come on now, don't get all worked up. I'm leaving. See? I only wanted to talk to him."

She nodded tentatively, her eyes fixed on the revolver. I buttoned my coat and smiled.

"One last thing."

She looked up, fearing the worst.

"Write down the lawyer's address for me. And don't try to trick me, because if you lie I'll come back and you can be quite sure that I'll leave all my inherent good nature downstairs in the porter's lodge."

Before I left I asked Margarita to show me where the telephone cable was and I cut it, saving her from the temptation of warning Valera that I was on my way or of calling the police to inform them about our small disagreement.

14

Señor Valera lived in a palatial building situated on the corner of Calle Girona and Calle Ausiàs March that seemed to have pretensions to being a Norman castle. I imagined he must have inherited the monstrosity from his father, together with the firm, and that every stone in its structure derived from the blood and sweat of entire generations of Barcelona's inhabitants who could never have dreamed of even entering such a palace. I told the porter I was delivering some documents from the lawyer's office on behalf of Señorita Margarita. After a moment's hesitation, he allowed me to go up. I climbed the wide staircase at a leisurely pace, under the porter's attentive gaze. The first-floor landing was larger than most of the homes I remembered from my childhood days in the old Ribera quarter, which was only a short distance away. The door knocker was shaped like a bronze fist. I grasped it but the door was already open. I pushed it gently and looked inside. The entrance hall led to a long passageway, about three meters wide, its walls lined with blue velvet and covered with pictures. I closed the door behind me and scanned the warm half-light that was coming from the other end. Faint music floated in the air, a piano lament in a melancholic and elegant style: Granados.

"Señor Valera?" I called out. "It's Martín."

As there was no reply, I ventured down the passage, following the trace of that sad music. I passed paintings and recesses containing statuettes of Madonnas and saints and went through a series of arches, each one veiled by net curtains, until I came to the end of the corridor, where a large dark room spread out before me. The room was rectangular, its walls lined with bookshelves from floor to ceiling. At the far end I could make out a half-open door and, through it, the flickering orange shadows of an open fire.

"Valera?" I called again, raising my voice.

A silhouette appeared in the light projected through the door by the flames. Two shining eyes examined me suspiciously. A dog that looked like an Alsatian but whose fur was white padded toward me. I stood still, unbuttoning my coat and looking for the revolver. The animal stopped at my feet and peered up at me, then let out a whine. I stroked its head and it licked my fingers. Then it turned, walked back to the doorway, stopped again and looked back at me. I followed it.

On the other side of the door I discovered a reading room dominated by a large fireplace. The only light came from the flames, casting a dance of flickering shadows over the walls and ceiling. In the middle of the room there was a table with a large gramophone from which the music emanated. Opposite the fire, with its back to the door, stood a large leather armchair. The dog went over to the chair and turned to look at me again. I went closer, close enough to see a hand resting on the arm of the chair. The hand held a burning cigar from which rose a plume of blue smoke.

"Valera? It's Martín. The door was open . . ."

The dog lay down at the foot of the armchair, never taking its eyes off me. Slowly, I walked round in front of the chair. Señor Valera was sitting there, facing the fire, his eyes open and a faint smile on his lips. He was wearing a three-piece suit and his other hand rested on a leatherbound notebook. I drew closer and searched his face. He didn't blink. Then I noticed a red tear, a tear of blood, gliding down his cheek. I knelt down and removed the notebook from his hand. The dog gave me a distraught look. I stroked its head.

"I'm sorry," I whispered.

The book seemed to be some sort of diary, with its entries, each handwritten and dated, separated by a short line. Valera had it open at the middle. The first entry on the page was dated 23 November 1904:

Payment note (356 on 23/11/04), 7,500 pesetas, from the account of D.M. trust. Sent with Marcel (in person) to the address supplied by D.M. Alleyway behind old cemetery—stonemason's workshop Sanabre & Sons.

I reread the entry a few times, trying to scratch some meaning out of it. I knew the alleyway from my days at *The Voice of Industry*. It was a miserable, narrow street, sunk behind the walls of the Pueblo Nuevo cemetery, with a jumble of workshops where headstones and memorials were produced. It ended by one of the riverbeds that crossed Bogatell beach and the cluster of shacks stretching down to the sea: the Somorrostro. For some reason, Marlasca had given instructions to pay a considerable amount of money to one of those workshops.

On the same page under the same date was another entry relating to Marlasca, showing the start of the payments to Jaco and Irene Sabino:

Bank transfer from D.M. trust to account in Banco Hispano Colonial (Calle Fernando branch) no. 008965-2564-1. Juan Corbera–María Antonia Sanahuja. First monthly payment of 7,000 pesetas. Establish payment plan.

I went on leafing through the notebook. Most annotations concerned expenses and minor operations pertaining to the firm. I had to look over a number of pages full of cryptic reminders before I found another mention of Marlasca. Again, it referred to a cash payment made through a person called Marcel, who was probably one of the articled clerks in the office:

Payment note (379 on 29/12/04), 15,000 pesetas from D.M. trust account. Paid via Marcel. Bogatell beach, next to level crossing. 9 a.m. Contact will give name.

The Witch of Somorrostro, I thought. After his death, Diego Marlasca had been doling out large amounts of money through his partner. This contradicted Salvador's suspicion that Jaco had fled with the money. Marlasca had ordered the payments to be made in person and had left the money in a trust managed by the law firm. The other two payments suggested that shortly before his death Marlasca had been in touch with a stonemason's workshop and with some murky character from the Somorrostro neighborhood; the dealings had translated into a large amount of money changing hands. I closed the notebook feeling more confused than ever.

As I turned to leave, I noticed that one of the walls of the reading room was covered with neatly framed portraits set against a wine-colored velvet background. I went closer and recognized the dour and imposing face of Valera the elder, whose portrait still presided over his son's office. In most of the pictures the lawyer appeared in the company of the great and the good of Barcelona, at what seemed to be different social occasions and civic events. It was enough to examine a dozen or so of those pictures and identify the array of celebrities who posed, smiling, next to the old lawyer to understand that the firm of Valera, Marlasca & Sentís was a vital cog in the machinery of the city. Valera's son, much younger but still recognizable, also appeared in some of the photographs, always in the background, always with his eyes buried in the shadow of the patriarch.

I sensed it before I saw him. In the photograph were both Valeras, father and son. The picture had been taken by the door of the law firm, at 442 Avenida Diagonal. Next to them stood a tall, distinguished-looking man. His face had also been in many of the other photographs in the collection, always close to Valera. Diego Marlasca. I concentrated on those turbulent eyes, that sharp and serene profile staring at me from a picture taken twenty-five years ago. Just like the boss, he had not aged a single day. I smiled bitterly when I understood how easily he'd fooled me. That face was not the one that appeared in the photograph given to me by my friend the ex-policeman.

The man I knew as Ricardo Salvador was none other than Diego Marlasca.

15

The staircase was in darkness when I left the Valera family mansion. I groped my way toward the entrance and, as I opened the door, the street-lamps cast a rectangle of blue light back across the hall, at the end of which I spotted the stern eyes of the porter. I hurried away toward Calle Trafalgar, where the tram set out on its journey down to the gates of Pueblo Nuevo cemetery—the same tram I used to take with my father when I accompanied him on his night shifts at *The Voice of Industry*.

The tram was almost empty and I sat at the front. As we approached Pueblo Nuevo we entered a network of shadowy streets covered in large puddles. There were hardly any streetlamps and the tram's headlights revealed the contours of the buildings like a torch shining through a tunnel. At last I sighted the gates of the cemetery, its crosses and sculptures set against an endless horizon of factories and chimneys injecting red and black into the vault of the sky. A group of emaciated dogs prowled around the foot of the two large angels guarding the grave-yard. For a moment they stood still, staring into the lights of the tram, their eyes lit up like the eyes of jackals, before they scattered into the shadows.

I jumped from the tram while it was still moving and set off, skirt-ing the walls of the cemetery. The tram sailed away like a ship in the fog and I quickened my pace. I could hear and smell the dogs following be-hind me in the dark. When I reached the back of the cemetery I stopped on the corner of the alley and blindly threw a stone at them. I heard a sharp yelp and then the sound of paws galloping away into the night. The alley was just a narrow walkway trapped between the wall and the row of stonemasons' workshops, all jumbled together. The sign SANABRE & SONS swung in the dusty light of a streetlamp that stood a little farther on. I went to the door, just a grille secured with chains and a rusty lock, and blew it open with one shot.

The echo of the shot was swallowed by the wind as it gusted up the passageway, carrying salt from the breaking waves of the sea only a hundred meters away. I opened the grille and walked into the Sanabre & Sons workshop, drawing back the dark curtain that masked the interior so that the light from the streetlamp could penetrate. Beyond was a deep, narrow corridor populated by marble figures seemingly frozen in the shadows, their faces only half sculpted. I took a few steps past Madonnas cradling infants in their arms, white women holding marble roses and looking heavenward, and blocks of stone on which I could just make out the beginnings of an expression. The scent of dust from the stone filled the air. There was nobody there except for these nameless effigies. I was about to retrace my steps when I saw it. The hand peeped out from behind a tableau of figures covered with a cloth at the back of the workshop. As I walked toward it, the shape gradually revealed itself to me. Finally I stood in front of it and gazed up at that great angel of light, the same angel the boss had worn on his lapel and I had found at the bottom of the trunk in the study. The figure must have been two and a half meters high, and when I looked at its face I recognized the features, especially the smile. At its feet was a gravestone, with an inscription:

DAVID MARTÍN

1900–1930

I smiled. One thing I had to admit about my good friend Diego Marlasca was that he had a sense of humor and a taste for the unexpected. It shouldn't have surprised me, I told myself, that in his eagerness he'd got ahead of himself and prepared such a heartfelt send-off. I knelt down by the gravestone and stroked my name. Behind me I heard light footsteps. I turned and saw a familiar face. The boy wore the same black suit he had worn when he followed me weeks ago in Paseo del Borne.

"The lady will see you now," he said.

I nodded and stood up. The boy offered me his hand, and I took it.

"Don't be frightened," he said, as he led me toward the exit.

"I'm not," I whispered.

The boy took me to the end of the alleyway. From there I could make out the line of the beach, hidden behind a row of run-down warehouses and the remains of a cargo train abandoned on a weed-covered siding. Its coaches were eaten away by rust, and all that was left of the engine was a skeleton of boilers and metal struts waiting for the scrapyard.

Up above, the moon peeped through the gaps in a bank of leaden clouds. Out at sea, the blurred shapes of distant freighters appeared between the waves, and on the sands of Bogatell beach lay the skeletons of old fishing boats and coastal vessels, spewed up by storms. On the other side, like a mantle of rubbish stretching out from the great, dark fortress of industry, stood the shacks of the Somorrostro encampment. Waves broke only a few meters from the first row of huts made of cane and wood. Plumes of white smoke slithered among the roofs of the miserable hamlet growing between the city and the sea like an endless human dumping ground. We stepped into the streets of that forgotten city, passages that opened up between structures held together with stolen bricks, mud, and driftwood. The boy led me on, oblivious to the distrustful stares of the locals. Unemployed day laborers, Gypsies ousted from similar camps on the slopes of Montjuïc or opposite the communal graves of the Can Tunis cemetery, homeless old men, women, and children. They all observed me with suspicion. As we walked by, women of indeterminate age stood by fires outside their shacks, heating up water or food in tin canisters. We stopped in front of a whitish structure at the door of which we saw a girl with the face of an old woman, limping on a leg withered by polio. She was dragging a bucket with something gray and slimy moving about inside it. Eels. The boy pointed to the door.

"It's here," he said.

I took a last look at the sky. The moon was hiding behind the clouds again and a veil of darkness advanced toward us from the sea.

I went in.

16

Her face was lined with memories and the look in her eyes could have been ten or a hundred years old. She was sitting by a small fire watching the dancing flames with the fascination of a child. Her hair was the color of ash and she wore it tied up in a plait. Her figure was slim, austere, her movements subtle and unhurried. She was dressed in white and wore a silk scarf knotted round her throat. She smiled warmly and offered me a chair next to her. I sat down. We spent a couple of minutes in silence, listening to the crackle of the embers and the murmur of the sea. In her presence time seemed to stop, and the urgency that had brought me to her door had strangely disappeared. Slowly, as I absorbed the heat from the fire, the cold that had gripped my bones melted away. Only then did she turn her eyes from the flames and, holding my hand, open her lips.

"My mother lived in this house for forty-five years," she said. "It wasn't even a house then, just a hut made of cane and old rubbish washed up by the sea. Even when she had earned herself a reputation and had the chance to get out of this place, she refused. She always said that the day she left the Somorrostro she would die. She was born here, among the people of the beach, and she would remain here until her last day. Many things were said about her. Many people talked about her, but very few really knew her. Many feared and hated her. Even after her death. I'm telling you all this because I think it's fair that you should know I'm not the person you're looking for or you think you're looking for. The one many called the Witch of Somorrostro was my mother."

I looked at her in confusion.

"When . . . ?"

"My mother died in 1905," she said. "She was killed a few meters from here, by the sea—stabbed in the neck."

"I'm sorry. I thought that—"

"A lot of people do. The wish to believe can conquer even death."

"Who killed her?"

"You know who."

It took me a few seconds to reply.

"Diego Marlasca . . ."

She nodded.

"Why?"

"To silence her. To cover his tracks."

"I don't understand. Your mother had helped him. He even gave her a large amount of money in exchange."

"That's exactly why he wanted to kill her, so that she would take his secret to the grave."

She watched me, a half smile playing on her lips as if my confusion amused her and made her pity me at the same time.

"My mother was an ordinary woman, Señor Martín. She grew up in poverty and the only power she possessed was her will to survive. She never learned to read or write, but she knew how to see inside people. She felt what they felt, knew their secrets and their longings. She could read it in their eyes, in their gestures, in their voices, in the way they walked or their mannerisms. She knew what they were going to say or do before they did. That's why a lot of people called her a sorceress, because she was able to see in them what they refused to see themselves. She earned her living selling love potions and enchantments that she prepared with water from the riverbed, herbs, and a few grains of sugar. She helped lost souls believe what they wanted to believe. When she gained a certain popularity, a lot of people from well-to-do families began to pay her visits and seek her favors. The rich wanted to become even richer. The powerful wanted more power. The mean wanted to feel like saints, and the pious wanted to be punished for sins they regretted not having had the courage to commit. My mother listened to them all and accepted their coin. With this money she sent me and my siblings to the same schools as the sons of her customers. She bought us another name and another life far from this place. My mother was a good person, Señor Martín. Don't be fooled. She never took advantage of anyone, nor did she make them believe more than they needed to believe. Life had taught her that we all require big and small lies in order to survive, just as much as we need air. She used to say that if during one single day, from dawn to dusk, we could see the naked reality of the world, and of ourselves, we would either take our own lives or lose our minds."

"But—"

"If you've come here in search of magic, I'm sorry to disappoint you. My mother told me there was no magic; she said there was no more good or evil in this world than we imagine there to be, either out of greed or out of innocence. Or sometimes madness."

"That's not what she told Diego Marlasca when she accepted his money," I objected. "Seven thousand pesetas in those days must have bought quite a few years of a good name and good schools."

"Diego Marlasca needed to believe. My mother helped him to do so. That's all."

"Believe in what?"

"In his own salvation. He was convinced that he had betrayed himself and those he loved. He believed that he had placed his life on a path of evil and falsehood. My mother thought this didn't make him any different from most men who at some point in their lives stop to look at themselves in the mirror. The most despicable humans are the ones who always feel virtuous and look down on the rest of the world. But Diego Marlasca was a man with a conscience, and he was not satisfied with what he saw. That's why he went to my mother. Because he had lost all hope, and probably his mind."

"Did Marlasca say what he had done?"

"He said he'd handed his life over to a shadow."

"A shadow?"

"Those were his words. A shadow who followed him and possessed the same shape, face, and voice as his own."

"What did that mean?"

"Guilt and remorse have no meaning. They are feelings, emotions, not ideas."

It occurred to me that not even the boss could have explained this more clearly.

"And what was your mother able to do for him?" I asked.

"Only comfort him and help him find some peace. Diego Marlasca believed in magic and that's why my mother thought she should convince him that his road to salvation passed through her. She spoke to him of an ancient spell, a fisherman's legend she had heard as a child among the hovels by the sea. When a man lost his way in life and felt that death had put a price on his soul, the legend said that if he found a pure soul that would agree to be sacrificed in order to save him, he would be able to disguise his own black heart with it, and death, which cannot see, would pass him by."

"A pure soul?"

"Free of sin."

"And how was this to be carried out?"

"With pain, of course."

"What sort of pain?"

"A blood sacrifice. One soul in exchange for another. Death in exchange for life."

A long silence amid the whisper of the sea and the wind swirling among the shacks.

"Irene would have pulled out her own eyes and heart for Marlasca. He was her reason for living. She loved him blindly and, like him, believed that his only salvation lay in magic. At first she wanted to take her own life, offering it to him as a sacrifice, but my mother dissuaded her.

She told her what she already knew, that her soul was not free of sin and that her sacrifice would be in vain. She said that to save her. To save them both."

"From whom?"

"From themselves."

"But she made a mistake . . ."

"Even my mother couldn't see everything."

"What did Marlasca do?"

"My mother never wanted to tell me—she didn't want me and my siblings to be a part of it. She separated us and sent each of us far away to different boarding schools so that we would forget where we came from and who we were. She said that now we were the ones who were cursed. She died shortly afterwards, alone. We didn't find out until much later. When they discovered her body nobody dared touch it: they let the sea take it away. Nobody dared speak about her death either. But I knew who had killed her and why. Even today I believe my mother knew she was going to die soon and by whose hand. She knew and she did nothing about it because in the end she, too, believed. She believed because she was unable to accept what she'd done. She believed that by handing over her soul she would save ours, the soul of this place. That's why she didn't want to flee, because, as the legend says, the soul that sacrifices itself should always remain in the place where the treasonable act was committed, like a bandage over the eyes of death."

"And where is the soul that saved Diego Marlasca?"

The woman smiled.

"There are no souls or salvations, Señor Martín. That's just an old wives' tale, gossip. Only ashes and memories remain, but if there are any they will be in the place where Marlasca committed his crime, the secret he has hidden all these years to mock his own destiny."

"The tower house. I've lived there for almost ten years and there's nothing . . ."

She smiled again and, with her eyes fixed on mine, leaned toward me and kissed me on the cheek. Her lips were frozen, like the lips of a corpse, and her breath smelled of dead flowers.

"Perhaps you haven't been looking in the right place," she whispered in my ear. "Perhaps the trapped soul is your own."

Then she untied the scarf she wore round her neck and revealed a large scar across her throat. This time her smile was malicious and her eyes shone with a cruel, defiant light.

"Soon the sun will rise. Leave while you can," said the Witch of Somorrostro, turning her back to me and looking into the flames once more.

The boy in the black suit appeared in the doorway and offered me his hand, an indication that my time was up. I stood and followed him. When I turned I caught her reflection in a mirror hanging on the wall. In it I could see the profile of an old hag, dressed in rags, hunched over the fire. Her dark, cold laughter stayed with me until I was out of the door.

17

Dawn was breaking when I arrived at the tower house. The lock on the front door was broken. I pushed the door open and stepped into the courtyard. The locking mechanism on the back of the door was smoking and gave off an acrid smell. Acid. I climbed the stairs slowly, convinced that I would find Marlasca waiting for me in the shadows of the landing or that if I turned around he would be there, behind me, smiling. As I walked up the last flight of stairs I noticed that the keyhole on the apartment door also showed signs of acid. I put in the key and had to struggle with it for a couple of minutes; the lock was damaged but had apparently not yielded. Finally I succeeded and pulled out the key, which was slightly gnawed by the substance, and pushed open the door. I left it open behind me and headed down the corridor without taking off my coat. I pulled the revolver out of my pocket and unlocked the barrel, emptying it of the cartridges of the bullets I had fired and replacing them with new ones, just as I'd seen my father do so many times when he returned home at dawn.

"Salvador?" I called.

The echo of my voice spread through the house. I cocked the hammer and continued to advance until I reached the room at the end. The door was ajar.

"Salvador?" I asked.

I pointed my gun at the door and kicked it open. There was no trace of Marlasca inside, just the mountain of boxes and old objects piled up in a corner. Again I noticed the odd smell that seemed to filter through the walls. I went over to the wardrobe that covered the back wall and opened its doors wide, removing all the old clothes from the hangers. The cold, damp draft that came from the hole behind it caressed my face. Whatever it was that Marlasca had hidden in the house, it was on the other side of that wall.

I put the weapon in my coat pocket and removed my coat. Standing by a rear corner of the wardrobe, I put my arm into the space between the frame and the wall. I managed to grab the back of the wardrobe with my hand and I pulled it forward hard. The first pull allowed me to gain a few centimeters and secure my hold. I pulled it forward again. The wardrobe now moved almost a hand's width. I kept on pulling the end of the wardrobe until the wall behind it became visible and there was enough room for me to slip in. Once I was behind the wardrobe I pushed it with my shoulder, moving it against the adjacent wall. I stopped to recover my breath and examine my work. The wall was painted an ocher color, different from the rest of the room. Beneath the paint I could feel some sort of claylike mass. I rapped on it with my knuckles. The echo left no room for doubt. This was not a supporting wall. There was something on the other side. I leaned my head against the wall and listened carefully. Then I heard a noise. Steps along the corridor, approaching. I moved away and stretched out my hand toward the coat I had left on a chair, in order to grab the gun. A shadow filled the doorway. I held my breath. It peered into the room.

"Inspector," I whispered.

Víctor Grandes smiled at me coldly. I imagined he must have spent hours waiting for me, hiding in some doorway in the street.

"Are you refurbishing the house, Martín?"

"Just tidying up."

The inspector looked at the pile of clothes and boxes thrown on the floor and the displaced wardrobe.

"I've asked Marcos and Castelo to wait downstairs. I was going to knock, but the door was open so I took the liberty of coming straight in.

I said to myself, This must mean that my friend Martín is expecting me."

"What can I do for you, Inspector?"

"Come along with me to the police station, if you'd be so kind."

"Am I being arrested?"

"I'm afraid so. Are you going to make it easy for me or are we going to have to do this the hard way?"

"No, I'll come," I assured him.

"I appreciate that."

"May I get my coat?"

Grandes stared straight at me for a moment. Then I picked up the coat and he helped me put it on. I felt the weight of the revolver against my thigh. Before leaving the room, the inspector cast a last glance at the wall that had been revealed. Then he told me to go on out into the corridor. Marcos and Castelo had come up to the landing and were waiting for me with triumphant smiles. Just as we were about to leave I stopped for a second to look back inside the house, which seemed to withdraw into a well of shadows. I wondered if I would ever see it again. Castelo pulled out handcuffs, but Grandes stopped him.

"That won't be necessary, will it, Martín?"

I shook my head. Grandes closed the door and pushed me gently but firmly toward the stairs.

18

This time there were no dramatic effects, no sinister setting, no echoes of damp, dark dungeons. The room was large and full of light, with a high ceiling. It reminded me of a classroom in an exclusive religious school, crucifix on the wall included. It was on the first floor of police headquarters, with large French windows that offered views of people and trams beginning their morning procession along Vía Layetana. In the middle of the room were two chairs and a metal table that looked tiny stranded in such a large, empty space. Grandes led me to the table and told Marcos and Castelo to leave us. The two policemen took their time following the order. I could practically smell their anger in the air. Grandes waited for them to leave and then relaxed.

"I thought you were going to throw me to the lions," I said.

"Sit down."

I did as I was told. Had it not been for the expression on the faces of Marcos and Castelo as they left, the metal door, and the iron bars on the other side of the windowpanes, nobody would have guessed that my situation was grave. What finally convinced me was the thermos flask of hot coffee and the packet of cigarettes that Grandes left on the table, but above all his warm, confident smile. This time the inspector was deadly serious.

He sat opposite me, opened a file, and produced a few photographs that he proceeded to place on the table, one next to the other. The first picture was of Valera, the lawyer, seated in the armchair in his sitting room. Next to that was a photograph of the dead body of Marlasca's widow, or what remained of it, shortly after they pulled it out of the swimming pool at her house on Carretera de Vallvidrera. A third picture showed a little man with his throat slit open who looked like Damián Roures. The fourth picture was of Cristina Sagnier, taken on the day she married Pedro Vidal. The last two were studio portraits of my former publishers, Barrido and Escobillas. Once he had neatly lined up all six photographs, Grandes gave me an inscrutable look and let a couple of minutes go by, studying my reaction to the images, or the absence of one. Then he calmly poured two cups of coffee and pushed one toward me.

"Before we begin I'd like to give you the opportunity to tell me the whole story, Martín. In your own way, and no rush," he said at last.

"It won't be any use," I replied. "It won't change anything."

"Would you prefer us to interview the other people we think might be implicated? Your assistant, for example? What was her name? Isabella?"

"Leave her alone. She doesn't know anything."

"Convince me."

I turned my head toward the door.

"There's only one way of getting out of this room, Martín," said the inspector, showing me a key.

Once again, I felt the weight of the gun in my coat pocket.

"Where would you like me to start?"

"You're the narrator. All I ask of you is that you tell me the truth."

"I don't know what the truth is."

"The truth is what hurts."

. . .

For a little over two hours, Víctor Grandes didn't once open his mouth. He listened attentively, nodding every now and then and jotting in his notebook. At first I looked at him, but soon I forgot he was there and realized that I was telling the story to myself. The words made me travel to a time I had thought lost, to the night when my father was murdered at the gates of the newspaper building. I remembered my days in the offices of *The Voice of Industry,* the years I'd survived by writing stories through the night, and that first letter signed by Andreas Corelli promising me great expectations. I remembered my first meeting with the boss in the water reservoir building and the days in which the certainty of imminent death was the only horizon before me. I spoke to him about Cristina, about Vidal, and about a story whose end anyone might have guessed but me. I spoke to him about the two books I had written, one under my own name and the other using Vidal's, about the loss of those miserable expectations and about the afternoon when I saw my mother drop into a waste bin the one good thing I thought I'd done in my life. I wasn't looking for pity or understanding from the inspector. It was enough for me to try to trace an imaginary map of the events that had led me to that room, to that moment of complete emptiness. I returned to the house next to Güell Park and the night when the boss had made me an offer I could not refuse. I confessed my first suspicions, my discoveries about the history of the tower house, the strange death of Diego Marlasca, and the web of deceit in which I'd become ensnared— or which I had chosen in order to satisfy my vanity, my greed, and my desire to live at any price. To live so that I could tell the story.

I left nothing out. Nothing except the most important part, the part I did not even dare tell myself. In the account I gave Grandes, I returned to the sanatorium to look for Cristina but all I found was a trail of footsteps lost in the snow. Perhaps, if I repeated those words over and over again, even I would end up believing that was what had happened. My story ended that very morning, when I returned from the Somorrostro shacks to discover that Diego Marlasca wanted to add my portrait to the lineup the inspector had placed on the table.

When I finished my tale I fell into a deep silence. I had never felt as tired in all my life. I wanted to go to sleep and never wake again. Grandes was observing me from the other side of the table. He seemed confused, sad, angry—and lost.

"Say something," I said.

Grandes sighed. He got up from his chair and went over to the window, turning his back to me. I pictured myself pulling the gun out of my coat, shooting him in the neck, and getting out of there with the key he kept in his pocket. In sixty seconds I could be on the street again.

"The reason we're talking is because a telegram arrived yesterday from the Civil Guard barracks in Puigcerdà, stating that Cristina Sagnier has disappeared from the sanatorium and you're the main suspect. The doctor in charge of the center says that you'd wanted to take her away and that he'd refused to discharge her. I'm telling you all this so that you understand exactly why we're here in this room, with hot coffee and cigarettes, talking like old friends. We're here because the wife of one of the richest men in Barcelona has disappeared and you're the only person who knows where she is. We're here because the father of your friend Pedro Vidal, one of the most powerful men in this town, has taken a personal interest in the case. It appears that he's an old acquaintance of yours and has politely asked my superiors that we obtain the information we need before laying a finger on you, leaving other considerations for later. Had it not been for that and for my insistence that I wanted to try to clarify the matter in my own way, right now you'd be in a cell in Campo de la Bota. And instead of speaking to me you'd be talking directly to Marcos and Castelo, who, for your information, think any course of action that doesn't start with breaking your knees with a hammer is a waste of time and might put Señora de Vidal's life in danger. This is an opinion that my superiors, who think I'm giving you too much leeway, are endorsing more heartily with every passing minute."

Grandes turned and looked at me, restraining his anger.

"You haven't listened to me," I said. "You haven't listened to anything I've said."

"I've listened to you perfectly well, Martín. I've listened to how, when you were a desperate, dying man, you entered into a pact with a mysterious Parisian publisher whom nobody has ever heard of to invent, in your own words, a new religion in exchange for a hundred thousand French francs, only to discover that you had fallen into a sinister plot involving a lawyer, who faked his death twenty-five years ago to escape a destiny that is now your own, and this lawyer's lover, a chorus girl who had known better days. I have listened to how this destiny led you into the trap of an accursed old house that had already trapped your predecessor, Diego Marlasca; and how you found proof in that house that somebody was following you and murdering anyone who might reveal the secret of a man who, judging from your own words, is almost as mad as you. The man in the shadows, who adopted the identity of a former policeman to hide the fact that he is alive, has been committing a number of crimes with the help of his lover, and those include provoking the death of Señor Sempere, for some strange motive that not even you are able to explain."

"Irene Sabino killed Sempere when she was trying to steal a book from him. A book that she thought contained my soul."

Grandes hit his forehead with the palm of his hand as if he'd just stumbled on the crux of the matter.

"Of course. How stupid of me. That explains it all. Like that business about the terrible secret revealed to you by a sorceress on Bogatell beach. The Witch of Somorrostro. I like that. Very typical of you. Let's see whether I've understood this correctly. This Señor Marlasca has imprisoned a soul in order to mask his own soul and thus escape from some sort of curse. Tell me, did you get that out of *City of the Damned* or have you just invented it?"

"I haven't invented anything."

"Put yourself in my position and tell me whether you would have believed a single word you've said."

"I suppose I wouldn't. But I've told you everything I know."

"Of course. You've given me information and specific details so that I can check the truth of your story, from your visit to Dr. Trías to your account at Banco Hispano Colonial, your own gravestone waiting for you in a Pueblo Nuevo workshop, and even a legal connection between the man you call 'the boss' and Valera's law firm, not to mention many other clues that are not unworthy of your skill in spinning detective yarns. The only thing that you have not told me and that, in all frankness, for your good and mine, I was hoping to hear is where I can find Cristina Sagnier."

I realized that all that could save me at that moment was a lie. The moment I told him the truth about Cristina, my hours were numbered.

"I don't know where she is."

"You're lying."

"I told you that telling you the truth wouldn't be of any use," I answered.

"Except to make me look like an idiot for wanting to help you."

"Is that what you're trying to do, Inspector? Help me?"

"Yes."

"Then check out everything I've said. Find Marlasca and Irene Sabino."

"My superiors have given me twenty-four hours to question you. If after that I don't hand them Cristina Sagnier safe and sound, or at least alive, I'll be removed from the case and it will be passed on to Marcos and Castelo, who have been looking forward to a chance to prove themselves and are certainly not going to waste it."

"Then don't lose any time."

Grandes snorted.

"I hope you know what you're doing, Martín."

19

I worked out that it must have been nine o'clock in the morning when Inspector Víctor Grandes left me locked up in that room with no other company than a thermos flask of cold coffee and his packet of cigarettes. He posted one of his men by the door and I heard him ordering the man not to let anyone in under any circumstances. Five minutes after his departure I heard someone knocking and recognized Sergeant Marcos's face through the glass. I couldn't hear his words, but the movement of his lips made his meaning crystal clear:

Get ready, you bastard.

I spent the rest of the morning sitting on the windowsill watching people who thought themselves free walking past the iron bars, smoking, even eating sugar lumps with the same relish I'd seen the boss exhibit on more than one occasion. Tiredness, or perhaps it was just the final wave of despair, hit me by noon and I lay down on the floor, my face to the wall. I fell asleep in less than a minute. When I woke up, the room was in darkness. Night had fallen and the streetlamps along Vía Layetana cast shadows of cars and trams on the ceiling. I stood up, feeling the cold of the floor in every muscle, and walked over to a radiator in a corner of the room. It was even icier than my hands.

At that moment, I heard the door open behind me and I turned to find the inspector watching me. At a signal from Grandes, one of his men turned on the light and closed the door. The harsh metallic light blinded me for a moment. When I opened my eyes again, I saw that the inspector looked almost as bad as I did.

"Do you need to go to the bathroom?" he asked.

"No. Taking advantage of the circumstances, I decided to wet myself and practice for when you send me off to the chamber of horrors with those inquisitors Marcos and Castelo."

"I'm glad to see you haven't lost your sense of humor. You're going to need it. Sit down."

We resumed our earlier positions.

"I've been checking the details of your story."

"And?"

"Where would you like me to begin?"

"You're the policeman."

"My first visit was to Dr. Trías's office in Calle Muntaner. It was brief. Dr. Trías died twelve years ago and the office has belonged to a dentist called Bernat Llofriu for eight. Needless to say, he's never heard of you."

"Impossible."

"Wait, it gets better. On my way from there I went by the main offices of Banco Hispano Colonial. Impressive décor and impeccable service. I felt like opening a savings account. There, I was able to find out that you've never had an account with that bank, that they've never heard of anyone called Andreas Corelli, and that there is no customer who at this time has a foreign currency account with them to the tune of one hundred thousand French francs. Shall I continue?"

I pressed my lips together but let him go on.

"My next stop was the law firm of the deceased, Señor Valera. There I discovered that you do have a bank account, not with the Hispano Colonial but with Banco de Sabadell, from which you transferred two thousand pesetas to the lawyer's account about six months ago."

"I don't understand."

"Very simple. You hired Valera anonymously, or that's what you thought, because banks have total recall and once they've seen a penny fly away they never forget it. I confess that by this point I was beginning to enjoy myself and decided to pay a visit to the stonemasons' workshop, Sanabre & Sons."

"Don't tell me you didn't see the angel . . ."

"I saw it. Impressive. Like the letter signed in your own handwriting, dated three months ago, when you commissioned the work, and the receipt for the advance payment, which good old Sanabre has kept in his account books. A charming man, very proud of his work. He told me it was his masterpiece. He said he'd received divine inspiration."

"Didn't you ask about the money Marlasca paid him twenty-five years ago?"

"I did. He has also kept those receipts. They were for works to improve, maintain, and alter the family mausoleum."

"Someone is buried in Marlasca's tomb who isn't Marlasca."

"That's what you say. But if you want me to desecrate a grave, you must understand that you have to provide me with a more solid argument. Anyway, let me continue with my revision of your story."

I swallowed.

"Since I was there, I decided to walk over to Bogatell beach, where for one real I found at least ten people ready to reveal the huge secret of the Witch of Somorrostro. I didn't tell you this morning when you were narrating your story so as not to ruin the drama, but in fact the big, stout woman who called herself by that name died years ago. The old woman I saw this morning doesn't even frighten children and is laid up in a chair. And there's a detail you will love: she's dumb."

"Inspector—"

"I haven't finished. You can't say I don't take my work seriously. So much so that from there I went to the large old mansion you described to me next to Güell Park, which has been abandoned for at least ten years and in which I'm sorry to say there were no pictures or prints or anything else but cat shit. What do think?"

I didn't reply.

"Tell me, Martín. Put yourself in my position. What would you have done?"

"Given up, I suppose."

"Exactly. But I'm not you and, like an idiot, after such a fruitful tour I decided to follow your advice and look for the fearsome Irene Sabino."

"Did you find her?"

"Give the police some credit, Martín. Of course we found her. A complete wreck in a miserable pension in the Raval, where she's lived for years."

"Did you speak to her?"

Grandes nodded.

"At length."

"And?"

"She hasn't the faintest idea who you are."

"Is that what she told you?"

"Among other things."

"What things?"

"She told me that she met Diego Marlasca at a session organized by Roures in an apartment on Calle Elisabets, where a spiritualist group called the Afterlife Society held meetings in the year 1903. She told me she met a man who took refuge in her arms, a man who was destroyed by the loss of his son and trapped in a marriage that no longer made any sense. She told me that Marlasca was kindhearted but disturbed. He believed that something had got inside him and was convinced that he was soon going to die. She told me that before he died he left some money in a trust, so that she and the man she had abandoned to be with Marlasca—Juan Corbera, aka Jaco—would receive something once he was gone. She told me that Marlasca took his life because he couldn't bear the pain that was consuming him. She told me that she and Juan Corbera had lived off Marlasca's charity until the trust ran out, and soon afterwards the man you call Jaco dumped her. People say he died alone, an alcoholic, working as a night watchman in the Casaramona factory. She told me that she did take Marlasca to see the woman they called the Witch of Somorrostro, because she thought the woman might comfort him and make him believe he would be reunited with his son in the next life . . . Shall I continue?"

I unbuttoned my shirt and showed him the cuts Irene Sabino had engraved on my chest the night she and Marlasca had attacked me in the San Gervasio cemetery.

"A six-pointed star. Don't make me laugh, Martín. You could have made those cuts yourself. Irene Sabino is just a poor woman who earns her living in a laundry in Calle Cadena, not a sorceress."

"And what about Ricardo Salvador?"

"Ricardo Salvador was thrown out of the police force in 1906, after spending two years stirring up the case of Diego Marlasca's death while having an illicit relationship with the widow of the deceased. The last thing anyone knew about him was that he'd decided to take a ship to the Americas and start a new life."

I couldn't help but burst out laughing at the enormity of the deceit.

"Don't you realize, Inspector? Don't you realize you're falling into the same trap that was laid for me by Marlasca?"

Grandes looked at me with pity.

"You're the one who doesn't realize, Martín. The clock is ticking, and instead of telling me what you did with Cristina Sagnier, you persist in trying to convince me with a story that sounds like something from *City of the Damned*. There's only one trap here: the one you've laid for yourself. And every moment that goes by without you telling me the truth makes it more difficult for me to get you out of it."

Grandes waved his hand in front of my eyes a couple of times, as if he wanted to make sure that I could still see.

"No? Nothing? As you wish. Let me finish telling you what the day had to offer. After my visit to Irene Sabino I was beginning to feel rather tired, so I returned for a while to police headquarters, where I still found the time and the energy to call the Civil Guard barracks in Puigcerdà. They've confirmed that you were seen leaving Cristina Sagnier's hospital room on the night she disappeared, that you never returned to your hotel to collect your baggage, and that the head of the sanatorium told them you'd cut the straps that held down the patient. I then called an old friend of yours, Pedro Vidal, who was kind enough to come over to police headquarters. The poor man is devastated. He told me that the last time you two met you hit him. Is that true?"

I nodded.

"I must tell you that he doesn't hold it against you. In fact, he almost tried to persuade me to let you go. He says there must be an explanation for all this. That you've had a difficult life. That it was his fault you lost your father. That he feels responsible. All he wants is to recover his wife and he has no intention of retaliating against you in any way."

"You've told Vidal the whole thing?"

"I had no option."

I hid my face in my hands.

"What did he say?" I asked.

Grandes shrugged.

"He thinks you've lost your mind. He thinks you must be innocent and he doesn't want anything to happen to you, whether you're innocent or not. His family is another matter. I know for certain that Vidal's father has secretly offered Marcos and Castelo a bonus if they extract a confession from you in less than twelve hours. They've assured him that in one morning they'll get you to recite the entire *Canigó* epic."

"And what do you think?"

"The truth? The truth is that I'd like to believe Pedro Vidal is right and you've lost your mind."

I didn't tell him that at that very moment I was beginning to believe it too. Then I looked at Grandes and noticed something in his expression that didn't add up.

"There's something you haven't told me," I remarked.

"I'd say I've told you more than enough," he retorted.

"What haven't you told me?"

Grandes observed me attentively and then tried to hide his laughter.

"This morning you told me that the night Señor Sempere died he was overheard arguing with someone in the bookshop. You suspected that the person in question wanted to buy a book, a book of yours, and when Sempere refused to sell it, there was a fight and the bookseller suffered a heart attack. According to you, this item was almost unique, one of a handful of copies in existence. What was the book called?"

"*The Steps of Heaven.*"

"Exactly. That is the book which, according to you, was stolen the night Sempere died."

I nodded. The inspector pulled a cigarette out of the packet and lit it. He took a couple of long drags, then put it out.

"This is my dilemma, Martín. On the one hand you've told me a pile of cock and bull stories that either you've invented, thinking I'm an idiot or—and I'm not sure if this is worse—you've started to believe yourself from repeating them so often. Everything points to you, and the easiest thing for me would be to wash my hands of all this and pass you over to Marcos and Castelo."

"But—"

"But, and it's a tiny, insignificant but, a but that my colleagues would have no problem at all dismissing altogether. And yet it bothers me like a speck of dust in my eye and makes me wonder whether, per-haps—and what I'm about to say contradicts everything I've learned in twenty years doing this job—what you've told me is not the truth but is not false either."

"All I can say is that I've told you what I remember, Inspector. You may or may not believe me. The truth is that at times I don't even be-lieve myself. But it's what I remember."

Grandes stood up and began to walk around the table.

"This afternoon, when I was talking to María Antonia Sanahuja, or Irene Sabino, in her pension, I asked her if she knew who you were. She said she didn't. I explained that you lived in the tower house where she and Marlasca spent a few months. I asked her again if she remembered you. She said she didn't. A while later I told her that you'd visited the Marlasca family tomb and that you were sure you'd seen her there. For the third time that woman denied ever having seen you. And I believed her. I believed her until, as I was leaving, she told me she was feeling a bit cold and she opened her wardrobe to take out a wool shawl and put it around her shoulders. I noticed that there was a book on the table. It caught my eye because it was the only book in the room. While she had her back to me, I opened it and I read a handwritten inscription on the first page."

" 'To Señor Sempere, the best friend a book could ever have: you opened the doors to the world for me and showed me how to go through them,' " I quoted from memory.

"Signed by David Martín," Grandes completed.

The inspector stopped in front of the window.

"In half an hour they'll come for you and I'll be taken off the case," he said. "You'll be handed over to Sergeant Marcos, and I'll no longer be able to help you. Have you anything else to tell me that might allow me to save your neck?"

"No."

"Then grab that ridiculous revolver you've been hiding for hours in your coat and, taking great care not to shoot yourself in the foot, threaten that if I don't hand you the key that opens this door, you'll blow my head off."

I turned toward the door.

"In exchange I ask only that you tell me where Cristina Sagnier is, if she's still alive, that is."

I looked down. I couldn't find my voice.

"Did you kill her?"

I let a long silence go by.

"I don't know."

Grandes came over and handed me the key to the door.

"Get the hell out of here, Martín."

I hesitated for a second before taking it.

"Don't use the main staircase. At the end of the corridor, to your left, there's a blue door that opens only from the inside and will take you to the fire escape. The exit is on the back alley."

"How can I thank you?"

"You can start by not wasting time. You have around thirty minutes before the whole department will be hot on your heels. Don't waste them."

I took the key and walked to the door. Before leaving I turned round briefly. Grandes had sat down at the table and was looking at me, his expression blank.

"That brooch with the angel," he said, touching his lapel.

"Yes?"

"I've seen you wearing it on your lapel ever since I met you," he said.

20

The streets of the Raval quarter were tunnels of shadows dotted with flickering streetlamps that barely grazed the darkness. It took me a little over the thirty minutes granted to me by Inspector Grandes to discover that there were two laundries in Calle Cadena. The first, scarcely a cave behind a flight of stairs that glistened with steam, employed only children with violet-stained hands and yellow eyes. The second was an emporium of filth that stank of bleach, and it was hard to believe that anything clean could ever emerge from there. It was run by a large woman who, at the sight of a few coins, wasted no time in admitting that María Antonia Sanahuja worked there six afternoons a week.

"What has she done now?" the matron asked.

"It's an inheritance. Tell me where I can find her and perhaps some of it will come your way."

The matron laughed, but her eyes shone with greed.

"As far as I know she lives in Pension Santa Lucía, in Calle Marqués de Barberá. How much has she inherited?"

I dropped the coins on the counter and got out of that grimy hole without bothering to reply.

. . .

The pension where Irene Sabino lived languished in a somber building that looked as if it had been assembled with disinterred bones and stolen headstones. The metal plates on the letter boxes inside the entrance hall were covered in rust. There were no names on the ones for the first two floors. The third floor housed a dressmaking workshop pompously entitled the Mediterranean Textile Company. The fourth floor was occupied by Pension Santa Lucía. A narrow staircase rose in the gloom, and the dampness from the sewers filtered through the walls, eating away at the paint like acid. After walking up four floors I reached a sloping landing with just one door. I banged on it with my fist. A few moments went by until the door was opened by a tall, thin man, seemingly escaped from an El Greco nightmare.

"I'm looking for María Antonia Sanahuja," I said.

"Are you the doctor?" he asked.

I pushed him to one side and went in. The apartment was a jumble of dark, narrow rooms clustered either side of a corridor that ended in a large window overlooking the inner courtyard. The air was rank with the stench rising from the drains. The man who had opened the door was still standing on the threshold, looking at me in confusion. I assumed he must be one of the residents.

"Which is her room?" I asked.

He gave me an impenetrable look. I pulled out the revolver and showed it to him. Without losing his calm, the man pointed to the last door in the passage. When I got there I realized that it was locked and began to struggle with the handle. The other residents had stepped out into the corridor, a chorus of forgotten souls who looked as if they hadn't seen the sun for years. I recalled my miserable days in Doña Carmen's pension and it occurred to me that my old home looked like the new Ritz Hotel compared with this purgatory, which was only one of many in the maze of the Raval quarter.

"Go back to your rooms," I said.

No one seemed to have heard me. I raised my hand, showing my weapon. They all darted back into their rooms like frightened rodents, except for the tall Knight of the Doleful Countenance. I concentrated on the door once again.

"She's locked the door from the inside," the resident explained. "She's been there all afternoon."

A smell that reminded me of bitter almonds seeped under the door. I knocked a few times but got no reply.

"The landlady has a master key," suggested the resident. "If you can wait . . . I don't think she'll be long."

My only reply was to take a step back and hurl myself with all my might against the door. The lock gave way after the second charge. As soon as I found myself in the room, I was overwhelmed by that bitter, nauseating smell.

"My God," mumbled the resident behind my back.

The ex-star of the Paralelo lay on a rickety, disheveled bed, pale and covered in sweat. Her lips were black and when she saw me she smiled. Her hands clutched the bottle of poison; she had swallowed it down to the last drop. The stench from her breath filled the room. The resident covered his nose and mouth with his hand and went outside. I gazed at Irene Sabino writhing in pain while the poison ate away at her insides. Death was taking its time.

"Where's Marlasca?"

She looked at me through tears of agony.

"He no longer needed me," she said. "He's never loved me."

Her voice was harsh and broken. A dry cough seized her, a piercing sound ripping from her chest, and a second later a dark liquid trickled through her teeth. Irene Sabino observed me as she clung to the last of her life. She took my hand and pressed it hard.

"You're damned, like him."

"What can I do?"

She shook her head. A new coughing fit seized her. The capillaries in her eyes were breaking and a web of bleeding lines spread toward her pupils.

"Where is Ricardo Salvador? Is he in Marlasca's grave, in the mausoleum?"

Irene Sabino shook her head. Her lips formed a soundless word: *Jaco.*

"Where is Salvador, then?"

"He knows where you are. He can see you. He'll come for you."

I thought she was becoming delirious. Her grip weakened.

"I loved him," she said. "He was a good man. A good man. He changed him. He was a good man . . ."

The terrible sound of disintegrating flesh emerged from her lips, and her body was racked by spasms. Irene Sabino died with her eyes fixed on mine, taking the secret of Diego Marlasca with her.

I covered her face with a sheet. In the doorway, the resident made the sign of the cross. I looked around me, trying to find something that might help, some clue to indicate what my next step should be. Irene Sabino had spent her last days in a four-by-two-meter cell. There were no windows. The metal bed on which her corpse lay, a wardrobe on the other side, and a small table against the wall were the only furniture. A suitcase sat under the bed, next to a chamber pot and a hatbox. On the table lay a plate with a few bread crumbs, a jug of water, and a pile of what looked like postcards but turned out to be images of saints and memorial cards given out at funerals. Folded in a white cloth was something shaped like a book. I unwrapped it and found the copy of *The Steps of Heaven* that I had dedicated to Señor Sempere. The compassion awoken in me by the woman's suffering evaporated in an instant. This wretched woman had killed my good friend, and all because she wanted to take this lousy book from him. And yet, as Sempere told me, every book has a soul, the soul of the person who wrote it and the soul of those who read it and dream about it. Sempere had died believing in those words and I could see that, in her own way, Irene Sabino had also believed in them.

I turned the pages and reread the dedication. I found the first mark on the seventh page. A brownish line, in the shape of a six-pointed star, identical to the one she had engraved on my chest with the razor edge some weeks earlier. I realized that the line had been drawn with blood. I went on turning the pages and finding new motifs. Lips. A hand. Eyes. Sempere had given his life for some paltry fortune-teller's mumbo jumbo.

I put the book in the inside pocket of my coat and knelt down by the bed. I pulled out the suitcase and emptied its contents on the floor: nothing but old clothes and shoes. In the hatbox I found a leather case containing the razor with which Irene Sabino had made the marks on my chest. Suddenly I noticed a shadow crossing the floor and I spun round, aiming the revolver. The tall, thin resident looked at me in surprise.

"I think you have company," he said.

I went out of the room and headed for the front door. As I stepped onto the landing I heard footsteps climbing the stairs. A face appeared in the stairwell, squinting up, and I found myself looking straight into the eyes of Sergeant Marcos two floors down. He moved out of sight and his steps quickened. He was not alone. I closed the door and leaned against it, trying to think. My accomplice observed me expectantly.

"Is there any other way out of here?" I asked.

He shook his head.

"What about the roof terrace?"

He pointed to the door I had just shut. Three seconds later I felt the impact of Marcos and Castelo's bodies as they tried to knock it down. I moved away, backing along the corridor with my gun pointed toward the door.

"I think I'll go to my room," the resident said. "It's been a pleasure."

"Same here."

I fixed my eyes on the door, which was shuddering with every blow. The old wood around the hinges and the lock began to crack. By now I was at the end of the corridor and I opened the window overlooking the inner courtyard. A vertical shaft approximately one meter square plunged into the shadows below. The edge of the flat roof was just visible some three meters above the window. On the other side of the shaft a drainpipe was secured to the wall by means of round metal bands, all corroded by rust, with black tears of damp oozing down the spattered surface of the pipe. Behind me, Marcos and Castelo continued to thunder at the door. I turned round and saw that it was almost off its hinges. I reckoned I had only a few seconds left: there was no alternative but to climb onto the windowsill and jump.

I managed to grab hold of the drainpipe and rest a foot on one of the bands that supported it. I stretched up, reaching for the upper section of the pipe, but as soon as I seized it, it came away in my hand and a whole meter of the pipe tumbled down the shaft. I almost fell with it, too, but managed to hold on to a piece of metal that attached one of the bands to the wall. The drainpipe on which I had hoped to climb up to the flat roof was now impassable. There were only two ways out of my current situation: to return to the corridor that Marcos and Castelo were about to enter at any moment or to descend into the black gorge. I heard the door being flung against the inside wall of the apartment and let myself begin to slide, holding on to the drainpipe as best I could, tearing off quite a bit of skin in the process. I had managed to descend about a meter and a half when I saw the shape of the two policemen in the beam of light cast by the window onto the darkness of the shaft. Marcos's face was the first to appear as he leaned out. He smiled. I asked myself whether he was going shoot me right there and then. Castelo popped up next to him.

"Stay here. I'll go down to the apartment below," Marcos ordered.

Castelo nodded. They wanted me alive, at least for a few hours. I heard Marcos running away. It wouldn't be long before I saw him looking out the window scarcely a meter below. I glanced down and saw that there was light at the windows of the second and first floors, but the third floor was in darkness. Carefully I lowered myself until I felt my foot touching the next band. The third-floor window was now in front of me, with an empty corridor leading from it toward the door at the far end. I could hear Marcos knocking. By that time of day the dressmakers had already closed and nobody was there. The knocking stopped and I realized that Marcos had gone down to the second floor to try his luck there. I looked up and saw that Castelo was still watching me, licking his lips like a cat.

"Don't fall—we're going to have some fun when we catch you," he said.

I heard voices on the second floor and knew that Marcos had succeeded in getting into the apartment. Without thinking twice, I threw myself with all the strength I could muster against the window of the third floor. I smashed through the windowpane, keeping my face and neck covered with my coat, and landed in a pool of broken glass. I hauled myself up and, as I did so, noticed a dark stain spreading across my left arm. A shard of glass, sharp as a dagger, protruded just above my elbow. I caught hold of it and pulled. The cold sensation gave way to a blaze of pain that made me fall to my knees. From the floor I saw that Castelo had started to climb down the drainpipe. Before I was able to pull out the gun, he leaped toward the window. I saw his hands grabbing hold of the outer frame. Instinctively, I jumped up and started hammering at the frame with all my might, putting the whole weight of my body behind every blow. I heard the bones in his fingers break with a dry, snapping sound, and Castelo howled in pain. I pulled out the gun and pointed it at his face, but his hands had already begun to slip. A second of terror in his eyes, and then he fell down the shaft, his body ricocheting against the walls, leaving a trail of blood in the patches of light that filtered through from the lower windows.

I dragged myself toward the front door. The wound on my arm was throbbing and I could feel a few cuts on my legs, but I kept moving. On either side of the passageway there were rooms in semidarkness full of sewing machines, bobbins of thread, and tables topped with large rolls of material. I reached the main door and took hold of the handle. A tenth of a second later I felt it turn. Marcos was on the other side, attempting to force the lock. I retreated a few steps. A huge roar suddenly shook the door and part of the lock shot out in a cloud of sparks and blue smoke. Marcos was going to blast the lock away. I took shelter in the nearest room, which was filled with motionless figures, some with arms or legs missing: shop-window mannequins all piled up together. I slipped in between the torsos just as I heard a second shot. The front door opened with a bang. A halo of gunpowder floated in the hazy yellow light that seeped in from the landing. I heard Marcos fumbling with the door, then the sound of his heavy footsteps in the hallway. Glued to the wall, hiding behind the dummies, I clutched the revolver in trembling hands.

"Martín, come out," Marcos said calmly as he advanced. "I'm not going to hurt you. I have orders from Grandes to take you to the police station. We've found that man Marlasca. He's confessed to everything.

You're clean. Don't go and do something stupid now. Come on, let's talk about this at police headquarters."

I saw him walk past the doorway of the room where I was hiding.

"Martín, listen to me. Grandes is on his way. We can clear this up without any need to complicate matters further."

I cocked the hammer. Marcos's footsteps came to a halt. There was a slight scraping sound on the tiles. He was on the other side of the wall. He knew perfectly well that I was in that room and that I couldn't get out without going past him. I saw his profile slink through the doorway and melt into the liquid darkness of the room; the gleam of his eyes was the only trace of his presence. He was barely four meters from me. I began to slide down against the wall until I reached the floor. I could see Marcos's shoes behind the legs of the dummies.

"I know you're here, Martín. Stop being childish."

He stopped and didn't move. Then I saw him kneel and touch the trail of blood I had left. He brought a finger to his mouth. I imagined he was smiling.

"You're bleeding a lot, Martín. You need a doctor. Come out and I'll take you to a doctor."

I kept quiet. Marcos stopped in front of a table and picked up a shining object that was lying among scraps of material. Large textile scissors.

"It's up to you, Martín."

I heard the shearing sound made by the edge of the scissor blades as he opened and closed them. A stab of pain gripped my arm and I bit my lip to stifle the groan. Marcos turned his face in my direction.

"Speaking of blood, you'll be pleased to hear that we have your little whore, that Isabella girl. Before we start with you we'll have some fun with her . . ."

I raised the weapon and pointed it at his face. The sheen of the metal gave me away. Marcos jumped at me, knocking down the dummies and dodging the shot. I felt his weight on my body and his breath on my face. The scissor blades closed only a centimeter from my left eye. I butted my forehead against his face with all my remaining strength and he fell to one side. Then I lifted my gun and pointed it at him. Marcos, his lip split, sat up and fixed his eyes on mine.

"You don't have the guts," he whispered.

He placed his hand on the barrel and smiled at me. I pulled the trigger. The bullet blew off his hand, flinging his arm back. Marcos fell to the floor, holding his mutilated, smoking wrist, while his face, spattered with gunpowder burns, dissolved into a grimace of pain, a silent howl. I got up and left him there, bleeding to death in a pool of his own urine.

21

Somehow I managed to crawl through the narrow streets of the Raval as far as the Paralelo, where a line of taxis had formed outside the Apolo theater. I slipped into the first one I could. When he heard the door, the driver turned round; he took one look at me and pulled a face. I fell onto the backseat, ignoring his protests.

"Listen, you're not going to die on me back there, are you?"

"The sooner you take me where I want to go, the sooner you'll get shot of me."

The driver cursed under his breath and started the engine.

"Where do you want to go?"

I don't know, I thought.

"Just drive and I'll let you know."

"Drive where?"

"Pedralbes."

. . .

Twenty minutes later I glimpsed the lights of Villa Helius. I pointed them out to the driver, who couldn't get rid of me fast enough. He left me at the entrance to the mansion and almost forgot to charge me the fare. I staggered up to the large front door and rang the bell, then collapsed on the steps and leaned my head against the wall. I heard foot-steps approaching and at some point thought I saw the door open and heard someone saying my name. I felt a hand on my forehead and I seemed to recognize Vidal's eyes.

"I'm sorry, Don Pedro," I begged. "I had nowhere else to go . . ."

I heard him call out and after a while I felt various hands taking my legs and arms and lifting me. When I opened my eyes again I was in Don Pedro's bedroom, lying on the same bed he had shared with Cristina during the few short months of their marriage. I sighed. Vidal was watching me from the end of the bed.

"Don't speak now," he said. "The doctor is on his way."

"Don't believe them, Don Pedro," I moaned. "Don't believe them."

"Of course not."

Vidal picked up a blanket and covered me with it.

"I'll go downstairs to wait for the doctor," he said. "Get some rest."

After a while I heard footsteps and voices in the bedroom. I could feel my clothes being removed and glimpsed the dozens of cuts covering my body like bloodstained ivy. I felt tweezers poking into my wounds, pulling out needles of glass as well as bits of flesh. I felt the sting of antiseptic and the pricks of the needle as the doctor sewed up my wounds. There was no longer any pain, only tiredness. Once I had been bandaged, sewn up, and mended like a broken puppet, the doctor and Vidal covered me with a sheet and placed my head on the sweetest, softest pillow I had ever come across. I opened my eyes to see the face of the doctor, an aristocratic-looking gentleman with a reassuring smile. He was holding a hypodermic syringe.

"You've been lucky, young man," he said as he plunged the needle into my arm.

"What's that?" I mumbled.

Vidal's face appeared next to the doctor's.

"It will help you rest."

A cold mist spread up my arm and across my chest. I felt myself falling into a chasm of black velvet while Vidal and the doctor watched me from on high. Gradually, the world closed until it was reduced to a single drop of light that evaporated in my hands. I sank into that warm chemical peace from which I would have preferred never to escape.

. . .

I remember a world of black water under the ice. Moonlight touched the frozen vault, breaking into thousands of dusty beams that swayed in the current as it pulled me away. The white mantle draped around her body undulated, the silhouette of her body just visible in the translucent waters. Cristina stretched out a hand to me and I fought against that cold, heavy current. When our fingers were only a hair's breadth apart, a somber mass unfolded its wings behind her, enveloping her like an explosion of ink. Tentacles of black light surrounded her arms, her throat, and her face, dragging her inexorably toward a dark void.

22

I awoke to hear Víctor Grandes saying my name. I sat bolt upright, not recognizing where I was—if anything, the place looked like a suite in a luxury hotel. The shooting pain from the dozens of cuts that streaked my torso brought me back to reality. I was in Vidal's bedroom in Villa Helius. Through the closed shutters, a hint of midafternoon light. A fire was blazing in the grate and the room was warm. The voices came from the floor below. Pedro Vidal and Víctor Grandes.

Ignoring the stinging of my skin, I got out of bed. My dirty, bloodstained clothes had been thrown onto an armchair. I looked for the coat. The gun was still in the pocket. I drew back the hammer and left the room, following the trail of voices as far as the stairs. I went down a few steps, keeping close to the wall.

"I'm very sorry about your men, Inspector," I heard Vidal saying. "Rest assured that if David gets in touch with me or if I hear of his whereabouts, I'll let you know immediately."

"I'm grateful for your help, Señor Vidal. I'm sorry to bother you in the circumstances, but the situation is extremely serious."

"I understand. Thank you for your visit."

The sound of the front door closing. Vidal's labored breathing at the foot of the staircase. I went down a few more steps and found him leaning his forehead against the door. When he heard me he opened his eyes and turned round.

He didn't say anything, just looked at the gun I held in my hands. I put it down on the small table at the bottom of the stairs.

"Come on, let's see if we can find you some clean clothes," he said.

I followed him to a huge dressing room that looked more like a costume museum. All the exquisite suits I remembered from Vidal's years of glory were there. Dozens of ties, shoes, and cuff links in red velvet boxes.

"This is all from when I was young. It should fit you."

Vidal chose for me. He handed me a shirt that was probably worth as much as a small plot of land, a three-piece suit made to measure in London, and a pair of Italian shoes that would not have disgraced the boss's wardrobe. I dressed in silence while Vidal observed me with a pensive look.

"A bit wide in the shoulders, but you'll have to make do," he said, handing me a pair of sapphire cuff links.

"What did the inspector tell you?"

"Everything."

"And you believed him?"

"What does it matter?"

"It matters to me."

Vidal sat on a stool by a wall that was covered in mirrors from ceiling to floor.

"He says you know where Cristina is," he said.

I did not deny it.

"Is she alive?"

I looked him in the eye and, very slowly, nodded my head. Vidal gave a weak smile, eluding my eyes. Then he burst into tears, emitting a deep groan that came from his very soul. I sat down next to him and hugged him.

"Forgive me, Don Pedro, forgive me . . ."

. . .

Later, as the sun began to drop over the horizon, Vidal gathered my old clothes and threw them into the fire. Before he abandoned my coat to the flames he pulled out the copy of *The Steps of Heaven* and handed it to me.

"Of the two books you wrote last year, this was the good one," he said.

I watched him poking my clothes about in the fire.

"When did you realize?"

Vidal shrugged.

"Even a conceited idiot can't be fooled forever, David."

I couldn't make out whether there was resentment in his tone or just sadness.

"I did it because I thought I was helping you, Don Pedro."

"I know."

He smiled.

"Forgive me," I murmured.

"You must leave the city. There's a cargo ship moored in the San Sebastián dock that sets sail tonight. It's all arranged. Ask for Captain Olmo. He's expecting you. Take one of the cars from the garage. You can leave it at the port. Pep will fetch it tomorrow. Don't speak to anyone. Don't go back to your house. You'll need money."

"I have enough money," I lied.

"There's never enough. When you disembark in Marseilles, Olmo will go with you to a bank and will give you fifty thousand francs."

"Don Pedro—"

"Listen to me. Those two men that Grandes says you've killed . . ."

"Marcos and Castelo. I think they worked for your father, Don Pedro."

Vidal shook his head.

"My father and his lawyers only ever deal with the top people, David. How do you think those two knew where to find you thirty minutes after you left the police station?"

A cold feeling of certainty washed over me.

"Through my friend Inspector Víctor Grandes."

Vidal agreed.

"Grandes let you go because he didn't want to dirty his hands in the police station. As soon as he got you out of there, his two men were on your trail. Your death was to read like a telegram: Escaping murder suspect dies while resisting arrest."

"Just like the old days on the news," I said.

"Some things never change, David. You should know better than anyone."

He opened his wardrobe and handed me a brand new coat. I accepted it and put the book in the inside pocket. Vidal smiled at me.

"For once in your life you're well dressed."

"It suited you better, Don Pedro."

"That goes without saying."

"Don Pedro, there are a lot of things . . ."

"They don't matter anymore, David. You don't owe me an explanation."

"I owe you much more than an explanation."

"Then tell me about her."

Vidal looked at me with desperate eyes that begged me to lie to him. We sat in the sitting room, facing the French windows with their view over the whole of Barcelona, and I lied to him with all my heart. I told him that Cristina had rented a small attic in Paris, in Rue de Souf-flot, under the name of Madame Vidal, and had said that she'd wait for me every day, in the middle of the afternoon, by the fountain in the Luxembourg Gardens. I told him that she spoke about him constantly, that she would never forget him, and that I knew that however many years I spent by her side I'd never be able to fill the void he had left. Don Pedro's gaze was lost in the distance.

"You must promise me you'll look after her, David. That you'll never leave her. Whatever happens, you'll stay by her side."

"I promise, Don Pedro."

In the pale light of evening all I could see was a defeated old man, sick with memories and guilt, a man who had never believed and whose only balm now was to believe.

"I wish I'd been a better friend to you, David."

"You've been the best of friends, Don Pedro. You've been much more than that."

Vidal stretched out his arm and took my hand. He was trembling.

"Grandes spoke to me about that man, the one you call the boss.

He says you are in debt to him and you think the only way of paying him back is by giving him a pure soul . . ."

"That's nonsense, Don Pedro. Don't pay any attention."

"Would a dirty, tired soul like mine be of any use to you?"

"I know of no purer soul than yours, Don Pedro."

Vidal smiled.

"If I could have changed places with your father, I would have, David."

"I know."

He stood up and gazed at the evening swooping over the city.

"You should be on your way," he said. "Go to the garage and take a car. Whichever you like. I'll see if I have some cash."

I picked up the coat and went out into the garden and over to the coach house. The Villa Helius garage was home to two automobiles that gleamed like royal carriages. I chose the smaller, more discreet car, a black Hispano-Suiza that looked as if it had not been used more than two or three times and still smelled new. I sat at the steering wheel and started the engine, then drove the car out of the garage and waited in the yard. A minute went by, and still Vidal hadn't come out. I got out of the car, leaving the engine running. I went back into the house to say good-bye to him and tell him not to worry about the money, I would manage. As I walked across the entrance hall I remembered I'd left the gun on the table. When I went to pick it up it wasn't there.

"Don Pedro?"

The door to the sitting room was ajar. I looked in and could see him standing in the middle of the room. He raised my father's revolver to his chest, placing the barrel at his heart. I rushed toward him but the roar of the shot drowned my shouts. The weapon fell from his hands. His body slumped over and he fell to the floor, leaving a scarlet trail on the marble tiles. I dropped to my knees beside him and supported him in my arms. Dark, thick blood gushed from the hole where the bullet had pierced his clothes. Don Pedro's eyes locked on mine while his smile filled with blood, and his body stopped trembling, and he collapsed. The room was filled with the scent of gunpowder and misery.

23

I returned to the car and sat in it, my bloodstained hands on the steering wheel. I could hardly breathe. I waited a minute before releasing the hand brake. The lights of the city throbbed under the shroud of the evening sky. I set off down the street, leaving the silhouette of Villa Helius behind me. When I reached Avenida Pearson I stopped and looked through the rearview mirror. A car had just turned into the street from a hidden alleyway and positioned itself some fifty meters behind me. Its lights were not on. Víctor Grandes.

I continued down Avenida de Pedralbes until I passed the large wrought-iron dragon guarding the entrance to Finca Güell. Inspector Grandes's car was still tailing about a hundred meters behind. When I reached Avenida Diagonal I turned left toward the center of town. There were barely any cars around so Grandes had no difficulty following me until I decided to turn right, hoping to lose him through the narrow streets of Las Corts. By then the inspector was aware that his presence was no secret and had turned on his headlights. For about twenty minutes we dodged through a knot of streets and trams. I slipped between omnibuses and carts, with Grandes's headlights relentlessly at my back. After a while the hill of Montjuïc rose before me. The large palace of the International Exhibition and the remains of the other pavilions had been closed for just two weeks, but in the twilight mist they looked like the ruins of some great, forgotten civilization. I took the large avenue to the cascade of ghostly lights that illuminated the exhibition fountains, accelerating as quickly as the engine would allow. As we ascended the road that snaked its way up the mountain toward the Great Stadium, Grandes was gaining ground until I could clearly distinguish his face in the rearview mirror. For a moment I.was tempted to take the road leading to the military fortress on the summit, but I knew that if there was one place with no way out, it was there. My only hope was to make it to the other side of the mountain, the side that looked down onto the sea, and disappear into one of the docks at the port. To do that I needed to put some time between us, but the inspector was now about fifteen meters behind me. The large balustrades of Miramar opened up before us, with the city spread out below. I pulled at the hand brake with all my strength and let Grandes smash into the Hispano-Suiza. The impact pushed us both along almost twenty meters, raising a spray of sparks across the road. I let go of the brake and went forward a short distance while Grandes was still struggling to regain control, then I put my car into reverse and accelerated hard.

By the time Grandes realized what I was doing it was too late. Thanks to one of the most select makes of car in town, I charged at him with a chassis and an engine that were far more robust than those protecting him. The force of the crash hurled Grandes from his seat and his head struck the windshield, shattering it. Steam surged from the hood of his car and the headlights went out. I put my car into gear and accelerated away, heading for the Miramar viewing post. After a few seconds I realized that in the collision the back fender had been crushed against one tire, which now scraped on the metal as it turned. The smell of burning rubber filled the car. Twenty meters farther on the tire blew and the car began to zigzag until it came to a halt, wreathed in a cloud of black smoke. I abandoned the Hispano-Suiza and glanced back at where Grandes's car still sat—the inspector was dragging himself out of the driver's seat. I looked around me. The stop for the cable cars that crossed over the port and the town from Montjuïc to the tower of San Sebastián was about fifty meters away. I could make out the shape of the cars dangling from their wires as they slid through the dusk, and I ran toward them.

One of the staff was getting ready to close the doors to the building when he saw me hurrying up the road. He held the door open and pointed inside.

"Last trip of the evening," he warned. "You'd better hurry."

The ticket office was about to close but I scurried in, bought the last ticket on sale, and rushed over to join a group of four people waiting by the cabin. I didn't notice their clothes until the employee opened the door. Priests.

"The cable railway was built for the International Exhibition and is equipped with the latest technology. Its safety is guaranteed at all times. From the start of the journey this security door, which can be opened only from the outside, will remain locked to avoid accidents or, heaven forbid, a suicide attempt. Of course, with Your Eminences on board, there is no danger of—"

"Young man," I interrupted. "Can you speed up the ceremony? It's getting late."

The employee threw me a hostile glance. One of the priests noticed my bloodstained hands and crossed himself. The young man continued with his long-winded speech.

"You'll be traveling through the Barcelona sky at a height of some seventy meters above the waters of the port, enjoying spectacular views of the city until now available only to swallows, seagulls, and other creatures endowed with feathers by the Almighty. The trip lasts ten minutes and makes two stops, the first at the central tower in the port, or, as I like to call it, Barcelona's Eiffel Tower, the tower of San Jaime, and the second and last at the tower of San Sebastián. Without further delay, I wish Your Eminences a happy journey, and on behalf of the company I hope we will see you again on board the Port of Barcelona Cable Railway in the not-too-distant future."

I was the first person to enter the cable car. The employee held out his hand as the four priests went by, hoping for a tip that never graced his fingertips. Visibly disappointed, he slammed the door shut and turned round, ready to operate the lever. Inspector Víctor Grandes was waiting there for him, in a sorry state but smiling and holding out his badge. The employee opened the door and Grandes strode into the cable car, greeting the priests with a nod and winking at me. Seconds later we were floating out into the void.

. . .

The cabin lifted off from the terminal toward the mountain edge. The priests had all clustered on one side, ready to enjoy the evening views over Barcelona and ignore whatever murky business had brought Grandes and me together in that place. The inspector sidled over and showed me the gun he had in his hand. Large reddish clouds hung over the water of the port. The cable car sank into one of them and for a moment it felt as if we had plunged into a lake of fire.

"Have you ever been on this before?" Grandes asked.

I nodded.

"My daughter loves it. Once a month she asks me to take her on a return trip. A bit expensive, but it's worth it."

"With the amount of money old Señor Vidal is paying you for my head, I'm sure you'll be able to bring your daughter here every day, if you feel like it. Simple curiosity: what price did he put on me?"

Grandes smiled. The cable car emerged from the crimson cloud and we found ourselves suspended over the port, with the lights of the city spilling over its dark waters.

"Fifteen thousand pesetas," he replied, patting a white envelope that peeped out of his coat pocket.

"I suppose I should feel flattered. Some people would kill for two duros. Does that include the price of betraying your two men?"

"Let me remind you that the only person who has killed anyone here is you."

By now the four priests were watching us with expressions of shock and concern, oblivious to the delights of the vertiginous flight over the city. Grandes gave them a cursory glance.

"When we reach the first stop, if it's not too much to ask, I'd be grateful if Your Eminences would get off and allow us to discuss a few mundane matters."

The tower on the docks of Barcelona port rose before us like a cupola of steel with great metal threads wrenched from a mechanical cathedral. The cable car entered the dome and stopped at the platform. When the door opened, the four priests hastened out. Grandes, gun in hand, told me to go to the far end of the cabin. One of the priests looked at me anxiously as he got off.

"Don't worry, young man, we'll call the police," he said, just before the door closed.

"Yes, please do!" replied Grandes.

Once the door was locked, the cable car resumed its course. We emerged from the tower and started on the last stage of the crossing. Grandes went over to the window and gazed at the view of the city, a fantasy of lights and mist, cathedrals and palaces, alleyways and wide avenues woven into a labyrinth of shadows.

"The city of the damned," said Grandes. "The farther away you are, the prettier it looks."

"Is that my epitaph?"

"I'm not going to kill you, Martín. I don't kill people. You're going to do that for me. As a favor. For me and for yourself. You know I'm right."

Saying no more, the inspector fired three shots at the locking mechanism of the door and kicked it open. The door was left hanging in the air and a blast of damp wind filled the cabin.

"You won't feel anything, Martín. Believe me. The impact will take only a tenth of a second. It's instant. And then, peace."

I gazed at the door. A fall of over seventy meters into the void opened up before me. I looked at the tower of San Sebastián and reckoned there were still a few minutes to go before we would arrive. Grandes read my thoughts.

"Soon it will all be over, Martín. You should be grateful to me."

"Do you really think I killed all those people, Inspector?"

Grandes raised his revolver and pointed it at my heart.

"I don't know, and I don't care."

"I thought we were friends."

He muttered in disagreement.

"You don't have any friends, Martín."

I heard the roar of the shot and felt a blow to my chest, as if I'd been hit in the ribs with a jackhammer. I fell on my back, unable to breathe, a spasm of pain spreading through my body like petrol on fire. Grandes had grabbed my feet and was pulling me toward the door. The top of the tower of San Sebastián appeared between veils of cloud. Grandes stepped over my body and knelt behind me, then started pushing me by my shoulders. I felt the cold air on my legs. Grandes gave another push and my legs slid over the edge. The pull of gravity was instant. I was beginning to fall.

I stretched out my arms toward the policeman and dug my fingers into his neck. Anchored by the weight of my body, the inspector was trapped and couldn't move from the doorway. I pressed with all my might, pushing on his windpipe, squeezing the arteries in his neck. He struggled to free himself from my grip with one hand while the other groped about for his gun. Finally his fingers found the trigger. The shot grazed my temple and hit the doorframe, but the bullet bounced back into the cabin and went clean through his hand. I sunk my nails deeper into his neck, feeling his skin yield. Grandes groaned. Using all the strength I had left, I managed to get more than half my body back inside the car. Once I was able to grab hold of the metal walls, I let go of Grandes and threw myself away from him.

I touched my chest and found the hole left by the inspector's shot. I opened my coat and pulled out the copy of *The Steps of Heaven*. The bullet had pierced the front cover and the four hundred pages of the book, so that it peeped out, like the tip of a silver finger, through the back cover. Next to me, Grandes was writhing on the ground, grabbing at his neck with despair. His face was purple and the veins on his forehead and temples stood out like tensed cables. He looked at me, pleading. A cobweb of broken blood vessels spread across his eyes and I realized I had squashed his windpipe and that he was suffocating. I watched him as he lay shaking on the floor in agony. I pulled the white envelope from his pocket, opened it, and counted fifteen thousand pesetas. The price of my life. I put the envelope in my pocket. Grandes was dragging himself across the floor toward the gun. I stood up and kicked it out of reach. He grabbed my ankle, begging for mercy.

"Where's Marlasca?" I asked.

His throat emitted a dull moan. I fixed my eyes on his and saw that he was laughing. The cable car had already entered the tower of San Sebastián when I pushed him through the doorway and saw his body plunge eighty meters through a maze of rails, cables, cogwheels, and steel bars that tore him to pieces as he fell.

24

The tower house was buried in darkness. I groped my way up the stone staircase until I reached the landing and found the front door ajar. I pushed it open and waited on the threshold, scanning the shadows that filled the long corridor. I took a few steps, then stopped, not moving a muscle. I felt the wall until I found the light switch. I tried it four times but without success. The first door to the right, three meters away, led into the kitchen. I remembered that I kept an oil lamp in the larder and there I found it, among unopened coffee tins from the Can Gispert emporium. I put the lamp on the kitchen table and lit it. A faint amber light suffused the kitchen walls. I picked it up and stepped out into the corridor.

As I advanced, the flickering light held high, I expected to see something or someone emerge at any moment from one of the doors on either side. I knew I was not alone; I could smell it. A sour stench, of anger and hatred, floated in the air. I reached the end of the corridor and stopped in front of the last room. The lamp cast its soft glow over the wardrobe that had been pulled away from the wall and the clothes thrown on the floor—exactly as I had left them when Grandes had come to arrest me two nights before. I continued toward the foot of the spiral staircase and warily mounted the stairs, peering behind my shoulder every two or three steps, until I reached the study. The ruby aura of twilight flooded in through the windows. I hurried across the room to the wall where the trunk stood and opened it. The folder with the boss's manuscript had disappeared.

I crossed the room again, heading back to the stairs. As I walked past my desk I noticed that the keyboard of my old typewriter had been destroyed—as if someone had been punching it. Gingerly, I went down the steps, entered the corridor, and put my head round the entrance to the gallery. Even in the half-light I could see that all my books had been hurled onto the floor and the leather of the armchairs was in tatters. I turned round to examine the twenty meters of corridor that separated me from the front door. The light from the lamp reached only half that distance, beyond which the shadows rolled on like black water.

I remembered I'd left the door to the apartment open when I came in. Now it was closed. I walked on a couple of meters, but something stopped me as I passed the last room in the corridor. When I'd walked past it the first time I hadn't noticed, because the door to that room opened to the left and I hadn't looked in far enough to see. But now, as I drew closer, I saw it clearly. A white dove, its wings spread out like a cross, was nailed to the door. Drops of blood dripped down the wood. Fresh blood.

I entered the room. I looked behind the door, but there wasn't anyone there. The wardrobe was still pulled to one side. The cold, damp air that emanated from the hole in the wall permeated the room. I left the lamp on the floor and placed my hands on the softened filler around the hole. I started to scratch with my nails and felt it crumble beneath my fingers. I looked around and found an old paper knife in a drawer of one of the small tables piled up in a corner. I dug the knife edge into the filler. The plaster came away easily; it was only about three centimeters thick. On the other side I discovered wood.

A door.

I searched for the edges using the knife, and the shape of the door began to emerge. By then I'd already forgotten the close presence that was poisoning the house, lurking in the shadows. The door had no handle, just a lock that had rusted away from being covered by damp plaster for years. I plunged the paper knife into it and struggled in vain, then began to kick the lock until the filler that held it in place was slowly dislodged. I finished freeing it with the paper knife and, once it was loose, the door opened with a simple push.

A gust of putrid air burst from within, impregnating my clothes and my skin. I picked up the lamp and entered. The room was a rectangle about five or six meters deep. The walls were covered with pictures and inscriptions that looked as if they had been made with someone's fingers. The lines were brownish and dark. Dried blood. The floor was covered with what at first I thought was dust but, when I lowered the lamp, turned out to be the remains of small bones. Animal bones broken up into a layer of ash. Numerous objects hung from a piece of black string suspended from the ceiling. I recognized religious figures, images of saints, Madonnas with their faces burned and their eyes pulled out, crucifixes knotted with barbed wire, and the remains of tin toys and dolls with glass eyes. The silhouette was at the far end, almost invisible.

A chair facing the corner. On the chair I saw a figure. It was dressed in black. A man. His hands were cuffed behind his back. Thick wire bound his arms and legs to the frame. An icy coldness took hold of me.

"Salvador?"

I advanced slowly toward him. The figure did not move. I paused a step away and stretched out my hand. My fingers skimmed over the man's hair and rested on his shoulder. I wanted to turn his body round but felt something give way under my fingers. A second later I thought I heard a whisper and the corpse crumbled into dust that spilled through his clothes and the wire bonds, then rose in a dark cloud that remained suspended between the walls of the prison where for years this man's body had remained hidden. I looked at the film of ash on my hands and brought them to my face, spreading the remains of Ricardo Salvador's soul on my skin. When I opened my eyes I saw that Diego Marlasca, his jailer, was waiting in the doorway, with the boss's manuscript in his hand and fire in his eyes.

"I've been reading it while I waited for you, Martín," said Marlasca. "A masterpiece. The boss will know how to reward me when I give it to him on your behalf. I admit that I was never able to solve the puzzle. I fell by the wayside. I'm glad to see the boss found a more talented successor."

He put the manuscript on the floor.

"Get out of my way."

"I'm sorry, Martín. Believe me. I'm sorry. I was starting to like you," he said, pulling out what looked like an ivory handle from his pocket. "But I can't let you out of this room. It's time for you to take the place of poor Salvador."

He pressed a button on the handle and a double-edged blade shone in the gloom.

He threw himself at me, shouting angrily. The blade sliced my cheek open and would have gouged out my left eye if I hadn't jumped to one side. I fell backwards onto the bones and dust covering the floor. Marlasca grabbed the knife with both hands and crashed down on top of me, putting all his weight on the blade. The knifepoint stopped only centimeters from my chest, while my right hand held Marlasca's throat.

He twisted to bite me on the wrist and I punched him hard in the face with my free hand. He seemed barely to flinch, driven by an anger that went beyond reason and pain, and I knew he wouldn't let me out of that cell alive. He charged at me with incredible strength. I felt the tip of the knife cut through my skin. I hit him again as hard as I could. My fist collided with his face and I heard the bones of his nose crack. Marlasca gave another shout, ignoring the pain, and plunged the knife into my flesh. A sharp pain seared through my chest. I hit him once more, searching out his eye sockets with my fingertips, but Marlasca raised his chin and I could only dig my nails into his cheek. This time I felt his teeth on my fingers.

I shoved my fist into his mouth, splitting his lips and knocking out a few teeth. I heard him howl and then he hesitated for a second before coming at me again. I pushed him to one side and he fell to the floor, dropping the knife, his face a mask of blood. I stepped away from him, praying that he wouldn't get up again. A moment later he had crawled over to the knife and was getting to his feet.

He grasped the blade and threw himself on me again with a deafening shriek, but this time he didn't catch me by surprise. I reached for the handle of the lamp and swung it at him with all my might. The lamp smashed against his face, spreading oil over his eyes, his lips, his throat, and his chest. It caught fire immediately. In just a few seconds a blanket of flames covered his entire body. His hair shriveled. I saw a look of hatred through the tongues of fire that were devouring his eyelids. I picked up the manuscript and fled.

Marlasca still held the knife in his hands as he tried to follow me out of that accursed room and fell facedown on the pile of old clothes, which burst into flames. The fire leaped at the wood of the wardrobe and the furniture that was piled up against the wall. I rushed toward the corridor but still he pursued me, arms outstretched, trying to catch me. As I reached the door I twisted round and saw Diego Marlasca being consumed by the blaze, furiously punching the walls, which caught alight at his touch. The fire spread to the books scattered in the gallery and then the curtains. It writhed across the ceiling like bright orange snakes, licking the frames of doors and windows, creeping up the steps to the study. The last image I recall is of a doomed man falling to his knees at the end of the corridor, the vain hopes of his madness lost and his body reduced to a human torch by a storm of flames that spread relentlessly through the tower house. I opened the front door and ran down the stairs.

Some of the neighbors had assembled in the street when they saw the first flames in the windows of the tower. Nobody noticed me as I slipped away. Shortly afterwards, I heard the windowpanes in the study shatter. I turned to see the fire embracing the dragon-shaped weather vane. Soon I was making my way toward Paseo del Borne, walking against a tide of local residents who were all staring upwards, their eyes captivated by the brightness of the pyre that rose into the black sky.

25

That night I returned, for the last time, to the Sempere & Sons book-shop. The CLOSED sign was hanging on the door, but as I drew closer I noticed that there was still a light on inside and that Isabella was stand-ing behind the counter, alone, engrossed in a thick accounts ledger. Judging from the expression on her face, it predicted the end of the old bookshop's days. But as I watched her nibbling the end of her pencil and scratching the tip of her nose with her forefinger, I was certain that as long as she was there the place would never disappear. Her presence would save it, as it had saved me. I didn't dare disturb that moment so I stayed where I was, smiling to myself, watching her unawares. Suddenly, as if she'd sensed my presence, she looked up and saw me. I waved at her and saw that despite herself her eyes were filled with tears. She closed the book and came running out from behind the counter to open the door. She was staring at me as if she couldn't quite believe I was there.

"That man said you'd run away. He said we'd never see you again."

I assumed Grandes had paid her a visit before he died.

"I want you to know that I didn't believe a word of what he told me," said Isabella. "Let me call—"

"I don't have much time, Isabella."

She looked at me, crestfallen.

"You're leaving, aren't you?"

I nodded. Isabella gulped nervously.

"I told you I don't like farewells."

"I like them even less. That's why I haven't come to say good-bye. I've come to return a couple of things that don't belong to me."

I pulled out the copy of *The Steps of Heaven* and handed it to her.

"This should never have left the glass case containing Señor Sempere's personal collection."

Isabella took it and when she saw the bullet still trapped in its pages she looked at me in silence. I pulled out the white envelope that held the fifteen thousand pesetas with which old Vidal had tried to buy my death and left it on the counter.

"And this goes toward all the books that Sempere gave me over the years."

Isabella opened it and counted the money in astonishment.

"I don't know whether I can accept it . . ."

"Consider it my wedding present, in advance."

"And there was I, still hoping you'd lead me to the altar one day, even if only to give me away."

"Nothing would have pleased me more."

"But you have to go."

"Yes."

"Forever."

"For a while."

"What if I come with you?"

I kissed her on the forehead, then hugged her.

"Wherever I go, you'll always be with me, Isabella. Always."

"I have no intention of missing you."

"I know."

"Can I at least come with you to the train or whatever?"

I hesitated too long to refuse those last few minutes of her company.

"To make sure you're really going and I've finally got rid of you," she added.

"It's a deal."

We strolled down the Ramblas, Isabella's arm in mine. When we reached Calle Arco del Teatro, we crossed over toward the dark alleyway that ran deep into the Raval quarter.

"Isabella, you mustn't tell anyone what you're about to see tonight."

"Not even Sempere junior?"

I sighed.

"Of course you can tell him. You can tell him everything. We can hardly keep any secrets from him."

. . .

When the doors opened, Isaac, the keeper, smiled at us and stepped aside.

"It's about time we had an important visit," he said, bowing to Isabella. "Am I right in supposing you'd rather be the guide, Martín?"

"If you don't mind . . ."

Isaac stretched out his hand and I shook it.

"Good luck," he said.

The keeper withdrew into the shadows, leaving me alone with Isabella. My ex-assistant—now the new manager of Sempere & Sons—observed everything with a mixture of astonishment and apprehension.

"What sort of a place is this?" she asked.

I took her hand and led her the remaining distance to the large hall that housed the entrance.

"Welcome to the Cemetery of Forgotten Books, Isabella."

Isabella looked up toward the glass dome and became lost in that impossible vision of white rays of light that crisscrossed a babel of tunnels, footbridges, and bridges, all leading into a cathedral made of books.

"This place is a mystery. A sanctuary. Every book, every volume you see, has a soul. The soul of the person who wrote it and the soul of those who read it and lived and dreamed with it. Every time a book changes hands, every time someone runs his eyes down its pages, its spirit grows and strengthens. In this place, books no longer remembered by anyone, books that are lost in time, live forever, waiting for the day when they will reach a new reader's hands, a new spirit . . ."

. . .

Later I left Isabella waiting by the entrance to the labyrinth and set off alone through the tunnels, clutching that accursed manuscript I had not had the courage to destroy. I hoped my feet would guide me to the place where I was to bury it forever. I turned a thousand corners until I thought I was lost. Then, when I was convinced I'd followed the same path a dozen times, I discovered I was standing at the entrance to the small chamber where I'd seen my reflection in the mirror in which the eyes of the man in black were ever-present. I found a gap between two spines of black leather and there, without thinking twice, I buried the boss's folder. I was about to leave the chamber when I turned and went back to the shelf. I picked up the volume next to the slot in which I had confined the manuscript and opened it. I'd only read a couple of sentences when I heard that dark laughter again behind me. I returned the book to its place and picked another at random, flicking through the pages. I took another, then another, and went on in this way until I had examined dozens of the volumes that populated the room. They all contained different arrangements of the same words, the same images darkened their pages, the same fable was repeated in them like a pas de deux in an infinite hall of mirrors. *Lux Aeterna.*

. . .

When I emerged from the labyrinth Isabella was waiting for me, sitting on some steps, holding the book she had chosen. I sat down next to her and she leaned her head on my shoulder.

"Thank you for bringing me here," she said.

I suddenly understood that I would never see that place again, that I was condemned to dream about it and to sculpt what I remembered of it into my memory, considering myself lucky to have been able to walk through its passages and touch its secrets. I closed my eyes for a moment so that the image might become engraved in my mind. Then, without daring to look back, I took Isabella's hand and made my way toward the exit, leaving the Cemetery of Forgotten Books behind me forever.

. . .

Isabella came with me to the dock, where the ship was waiting to take me far away from that city, from everything I knew.

"What did you say the captain was called?"

"Charon."

"I don't think that's funny."

I hugged her for the last time and looked into her eyes. On the way we had agreed there would be no farewells, no solemn words, no promises to fulfill. When the midnight bells rang in Santa María del Mar, I went on board. Captain Olmo greeted me and offered to take me to my cabin. I said I would rather wait. The crew cast off and gradually the hull moved away from the dock. I positioned myself at the stern, watching the city fade in a tide of lights. Isabella remained there, motionless, her eyes fixed on mine, until the dock was lost in the night and the great mirage of Barcelona sank into the black waters. One by one the lights of the city went out, and I realized that I had already begun to remember.

Epilogue

1945

Fifteen long years have passed since the night I fled the city of the damned. For a long time mine has been an existence filled with absences, with no other name or presence than that of a traveling stranger. I've had a hundred names and a hundred trades, none of them my own.

I have disappeared into huge cities and villages so small that nobody had a past or a future. In no place did I linger more than was necessary. Sooner rather than later I would flee again, without warning, leaving behind me only a couple of old books and secondhand clothes in somber rooms where time showed no pity and memory burned. Uncertainty has been my only recollection. The years have taught me to live in the body of a stranger who does not know whether he committed those crimes he can still smell on his hands or whether he has indeed lost his mind and is condemned to roam a world in flames that he dreamed up in exchange for a few coins and the promise of evading a death that now seems to him like the sweetest of rewards. I have often asked myself whether the bullet that Inspector Grandes fired at my heart went right through the pages of the book, whether I was the one who died in the cabin suspended in the sky.

During my years of pilgrimage I've seen how the inferno promised in the pages I wrote for the boss has taken on a life of its own. I have fled from my own shadow a thousand times, always looking over my shoulder, always expecting to find it round a corner, on the other side of the street or at the foot of my bed in the endless hours before dawn. I've never allowed anyone to know me long enough to ask why I never grow old, why no lines appear on my face, why my reflection is the same as the night I left Isabella in the port of Barcelona, and not a minute older.

There came a time when I believed I had exhausted all the hiding places of the world. I was so tired of being afraid, of living and dying from my memories, that I stopped where the land ended and an ocean began—an ocean that, like me, looks the same every morning—and, worn out, I collapsed.

It is a year to the day since I came to this place and recovered my name and my trade. I bought this old hut on the beach, just a shed that I share with the books left behind by the previous owner and a typewriter that I like to think might be the same one on which I wrote hundreds of pages that perhaps nobody remembers—I will never know. From my window I see a small wooden jetty that stretches out into the sea and, moored at the end, the boat that came with the house, a simple rowboat in which I sometimes go out as far as the reef, at which point the coast almost disappears from view.

I had not written again until I got here. The first time I slipped a page into the typewriter and placed my hands on the keyboard, I was afraid I'd be unable to write a single line. I began writing this story during my first night in the hut. I wrote until dawn, just as I did years ago, without yet knowing whom I was writing it for. During the day I walked along the beach or sat on the jetty opposite the hut—a gangway between sky and sea—reading through the piles of old newspapers I found in one of the cupboards. Their pages brought me stories of the war, of the world in flames that I had dreamed up for the boss.

It was while I was reading those chronicles about the war in Spain, and then in Europe and the rest of the world, that I decided I no longer had anything to lose; all I wanted to know was whether Isabella was all right and if perhaps she still remembered me. Or maybe I only wanted to know whether she was still alive. I wrote a letter, addressed to the old Sempere & Sons bookshop in Calle Santa Ana in Barcelona, that would take weeks or months to arrive at its destination, if it ever did arrive. For the sender's name I wrote *Mr. Rochester,* knowing that if the letter did reach her hands, Isabella would know whom it was from. If she wished, she could leave it unopened and forget me forever.

For months I continued writing this story. I saw my father's face again, and I walked through the offices of *The Voice of Industry,* dreaming that I might be able, one day, to emulate the great Pedro Vidal. Once more I saw Cristina Sagnier for the first time, and I went into the tower house to dive into the madness that had consumed Diego Marlasca. I wrote from midnight until dawn without resting, feeling alive for the first time since I had fled from the city.

The reply arrived one day in June. The postman had slipped the envelope under my door while I slept. It was addressed to *Mr. Rochester* and the return address read simply: *Sempere & Sons Bookshop, Barcelona.* For a few minutes I walked in circles round the hut, not daring to open it. Finally I went out and sat by the edge of the sea. In the letter I found a single page and a second, smaller, envelope. The second envelope, which looked worn, just had my name on it, *David,* in a handwriting I had not forgotten despite all the years that had flowed by since I last saw it.

In the letter, Sempere's son told me that after a few years of tempestuous and intermittent courting, he and Isabella had married on 18 January 1935 in the church of Santa Ana. The ceremony, against all odds, had been conducted by the ninety-year-old priest who had delivered the eulogy at Señor Sempere's funeral and who, in defiance of the bishop's eagerness to see the back of him, refused to die and went on doing things his own way. A year later, only days before the civil war broke out, Isabella had given birth to a boy whose name would be Daniel Sempere. The terrible years of the war brought with them all manner of hardships, and shortly after the end of the conflict Isabella contracted cholera and died in her husband's arms, in the apartment they shared above the bookshop. She was buried in Montjuïc on Daniel's fourth birthday, during rain that lasted two days and two nights, and when the little boy had asked him if heaven was crying, his father couldn't bring himself to reply.

The envelope with my name on it contained a letter that Isabella had written to me during her final days and that she'd made her husband swear he would send to me if he ever discovered my whereabouts:

> *Dear David,*
>
> *Sometimes I think I began to write this letter to you years ago and still haven't been capable of finishing it. A lot of time has passed since I last saw you and a lot of terrible, miserable things have happened, and yet not a day goes by when I don't think of you and wonder where you are, whether you have found peace, whether you are writing, whether you've become a grumpy old man, whether you're in love, or whether you still remember us, the small bookshop of Sempere & Sons and the worst assistant you ever had.*
>
> *I'm afraid you left without teaching me how to write, and I don't even know where to begin to put into words all the things I would like to say to you. I would like you to know that I have been happy, that thanks to you I found a man whom I've loved and who has loved me. Together we've had a child, Daniel. I always talk to him about you, and he has given my life a meaning that all the books in the world wouldn't be able to explain.*
>
> *Nobody knows this, but sometimes I still go back to that dock where I saw you leave and I sit there awhile, alone, waiting, as if I believe that some day you'll return. If you do, you will see that despite all the things that have happened the bookshop is still there, the plot of land on which the tower house once stood is still empty, and all the lies that were said about you have been forgotten. So many people in these streets have blood on their souls that they no longer dare to remember, and when they do they lie to themselves because they cannot look at their own reflection in the mirror. In the bookshop we still sell your books, but under the counter, because they have been declared immoral. This country is filled with more people who are intent on destroying and burning books than with those who want to read them. These are bad times and I often think that there are worse times to come.*
>
> *My husband and the doctors think they are fooling me, but I know that I have little time left. I know I will die soon and that by the time you receive this letter I will no longer be here. That is why I wanted to write*

to you, because I wanted you to know that I'm not afraid, that my only sorrow is that I'll leave behind a good man who has given me his life, and my Daniel, alone in a world that every day seems to me more as you said it was and not as I wanted to believe it could be.

I wanted to write to you so that you know that, despite everything I have experienced, I'm grateful for the time I have spent here, grateful for having met you and for having been your friend. I wanted to write to you because I'd like you to remember me and, one day, if you have someone as I have my little Daniel, I'd like you to talk to that someone about me and, through your words, make me live forever.

From one who loves you,
Isabella

Two days after I received that letter I realized I was not alone on the beach. I felt his presence in the first breath of dawn but I would not, and could not, flee again. It happened one afternoon after I sat down to write by the window, while I waited for the sun to sink into the horizon. I heard the footsteps on the wooden planks of the jetty and I saw him.

The boss, dressed in white, was walking down the jetty holding the hand of a girl of about seven or eight. I recognized the image instantly, the old photograph Cristina had always treasured without knowing where it came from. The boss reached the end of the jetty and knelt down beside the girl. Together they watched the sun spill over the ocean in an endless sheet of molten gold. I stepped out of the hut and walked along the wooden gangway. When I reached the end, the boss turned and smiled at me. There was no threat or resentment on his face, only a hint of melancholy.

"I've missed you, dear friend," he said. "I've missed our conversations, even our small arguments . . ."

"Have you come to settle a score?"

The boss smiled again and shook his head.

"We all make mistakes, Martín. I was the first. I stole what you loved the most. I didn't do it to hurt you. I did it out of fear. Out of fear that she might drive you away from me, from our work. I was wrong.

I've taken a long time to admit it, but if there is anything I do have, it is time."

I observed him carefully. The boss, like me, had not grown a day older.

"Why have you come here, then?"

The boss shrugged his shoulders.

"I came to say good-bye."

His eyes concentrated on the girl whose hand he was holding and who was looking at me curiously.

"What's your name?" I asked.

"Her name's Cristina," said the boss.

I looked into her eyes and she nodded. I could only guess at the features, but the look was unmistakable.

"Cristina, say hello to my friend David. From now on you're going to live with him."

I exchanged glances with the boss but didn't say a word. The girl stretched out her hand to me, as if she had practiced that movement a thousand times, and then laughed in embarrassment. I leaned down toward her and shook it.

"Hello," she said in a quiet voice.

"Very good, Cristina," said the boss approvingly. "And what else?"

The girl looked as if she'd suddenly remembered something.

"I was told you're a maker of stories and fairy tales."

"One of the best," the boss added.

"Will you make one for me?"

I hesitated a few seconds. The girl looked anxiously at the boss.

"Martín?" the boss whispered.

"Of course," I said at last. "I'll make you as many stories as you want."

The girl smiled and, drawing closer to me, kissed me on the cheek.

"Cristina, why don't you go down to the beach and wait there while I say good-bye to my friend?" the boss asked.

Cristina nodded and walked away, looking back and smiling with every step. Next to me, the boss's voice sweetly whispered his eternal curse.

"I've decided to give you back what you loved the most, what I stole from you. I've decided that for once you will walk in my shoes and will feel what I feel. You won't age a single day and you will see Cristina grow; you will fall in love with her again and one day you will see her die in your arms. That is my blessing, and my revenge."

I closed my eyes, saying no to myself.

"That is impossible. She will never be the same person."

"That will depend on you, Martín. I'm giving you a blank sheet. This story no longer belongs to me."

I heard his steps fade away, and when I opened my eyes the boss was no longer there. At the foot of the jetty, Cristina was looking at me intently. I smiled at her and she hesitated, then came over.

"Where's the gentleman?" she asked.

"He's gone."

Cristina looked around her, at the endless, deserted beach.

"Forever?"

"Forever."

She smiled and sat down beside me.

"I dreamed that we were friends," she said.

I looked at her and nodded.

"And we are friends. We always have been."

She laughed and took my hand. I pointed in front of us, at the sun dipping into the sea, and Cristina watched it with tears in her eyes.

"Will I remember one day?"

"One day."

I knew then that I would devote every minute we had left together to making her happy, to repairing the pain I had caused her and returning to her what I had never known how to give her. These pages will be our memory until she draws her last breath in my arms and I take her with me to the open sea, where the deep currents flow, to sink with her forever and escape at last to a place where neither heaven nor hell will ever be able to find us.

Meet with Interesting People
Enjoy Stimulating Conversation
Discover Wonderful Books

VINTAGE BOOKS / ANCHOR BOOKS

Reading Group Center
THE READING GROUP SOURCE FOR BOOK LOVERS

Visit ReadingGroupCenter.com where you'll find great reading choices—award winners, bestsellers, beloved classics, and many more—and extensive resources for reading groups such as:

Author Chats
Exciting contests offer reading groups the chance to win one-on-one phone conversations with Vintage and Anchor Books authors.

Extensive Discussion Guides
Guides for over 450 titles as well as non–title specific discussion questions by category for fiction, nonfiction, memoir, poetry, and mystery.

Personal Advice and Ideas
Reading groups nationwide share ideas, suggestions, helpful tips, and anecdotal information. Participate in the discussion and share your group's experiences.

Behind the Book Features
Specially designed pages which can include photographs, videos, original essays, notes from the author and editor, and book-related information.

Reading Planner
Plan ahead by browsing upcoming titles, finding author event schedules, and more.

Special for Spanish-language reading groups
www.grupodelectura.com
A dedicated Spanish-language content area complete with recommended titles from Vintage Español.

A selection of some favorite reading group titles from our list

Atonement by Ian McEwan
Balzac and the Little Chinese Seamstress by Dai Sijie
The Blind Assassin by Margaret Atwood
The Devil in the White City by Erik Larson
Empire Falls by Richard Russo
The English Patient by Michael Ondaatje
A Heartbreaking Work of Staggering Genius by Dave Eggers
The House of Sand and Fog by Andre Dubus III
A Lesson Before Dying by Ernest J. Gaines

Lolita by Vladimir Nabokov
Memoirs of a Geisha by Arthur Golden
Midnight in the Garden of Good and Evil by John Berendt
Midwives by Chris Bohjalian
Push by Sapphire
The Reader by Bernhard Schlink
Snow by Orhan Pamuk
An Unquiet Mind by Kay Redfield Jamison
Waiting by Ha Jin
A Year in Provence by Peter Mayle